ONCE A MAN INDULGES

TONY KELSEY

WobblyShop Publishing
U.S.A

ISBN: 978-0-578-85698-8
WGA #2035688

Cover design: Gannon S. Fitz-Nye
Cover art: Ibrandify, Renata.s/Freepik
Cover photo: Yanalya/Freepik
Cover font: Junkohanhero
Author photo: Adam Pawlikiewicz

Printed in the United States of America

For Julie –

Without your love and encouragement this
would never have been possible.

Once A Man Indulges

"If once a man indulges himself in murder, very soon he comes to think little of robbing; and from robbing he next comes to drinking and Sabbath-breaking, and from that to incivility and procrastination."

Thomas De Quincey

JULY 1949

She was wearing the same dress I'd seen her in the night before, her shoes on the floor next to the bed where they had been kicked off. There was a hole in the hose on her right foot. The big toe and the one next to it poked out, both with chipped red polish and needing a trim. I didn't really want to stare at her feet but it was better than looking at the angry hole in the side of her head, and the splatter all over the wall.

They say the first person you kill is always the hardest, that it will weigh on your conscience. I wouldn't know about that. Those first ones didn't seem so hard to me. It was later, when they started to add up. There's probably something easy about it when it's nice and neat. This wasn't so neat. Someone was going to have to clean up Sonja Hoff's brains, replace the mattress and maybe even the curtains, dotted not only with her blood but a lariat, wagon wheel, and rather prophetically, an old-west six shooter. But it wasn't like the place didn't need a good cleaning anyway.

I told Greenberg what he wanted to hear. He'd never actually seen Sonja Hoff before so I confirmed it was her. He clapped me on the shoulder before practically skipping out to the sitting room to call his captain with the big news. I did my best to appear nonchalant by pretending to take notes on a pad while staying out of the way of both the fingerprint man and his black dust, and the photographer and his flash bulbs. Eventually my eyes went back to that big toe. For a second the intimacy of seeing it so naked and neglected sent a wave of shame and revulsion through me.

The photographer turned to everything on top of the vanity across from the bed. There was her purse. In it, I was sure, would be the matchbook I'd given her the night before. He shot a photo of things as they lay, the flashbulb popped out onto the floor. He dug in his coat pocket for a new one, snapped it into place, and took another photo from a different angle. That flashbulb clattered off somewhere under the bed. Then he snapped the latch and dumped the contents of her purse. Lipstick. Some keys on a ring. Handkerchief. Whatever. A whole bunch of shit. And sure enough, the Rail Yard matchbook. He pushed it all around with the eraser end of a pencil until he was satisfied with the layout. When he bent over his bag to load up his pockets with more flashbulbs, pulling them one by one off a cardboard holder, I excused myself to pass in the tight space between the bed and vanity. In one quick motion the matchbook was in my hand.

As I went out through the sitting room and kitchenette I heard Greenberg saying into the phone it was a suicide. A logical conclusion. There was no sign of a struggle, and the gun was on the bed by her right hand. That would explain the small entrance wound and burn marks at her right temple and the large, gaping hole the size of a golf ball on the left. And of course, all the brains on the wall.

Even outside the air was filled with a faint hint of gunpowder, which seemed to dance fondly with the musty, pinched stink of rotting wood and the sweaty poignancy of human desperation. I imagined this wasn't the first dead body they'd had at the Howdy Partner Mo-tel.

When Greenberg came out I was smoking a cigarette lit with a stick pulled from the Rail Yard matchbook. An ambulance was trying to jockey in between all the marked and unmarked police cars in the small parking lot.

"Suicide, huh?" I said, offering him a cigarette and the matches. "That's convenient."

He lit his and dropped the matches into a pocket. I snapped my fingers twice. He dug them out and dropped them into my open palm.

"Let me guess, you think she was murdered."

"Did you see her watch? And the shorter nails on her left hand? She was a southpaw."

"Hardly conclusive," he said, spitting a piece of tobacco off his tongue.

"Plus, I saw her at Marquand's. She wrote with her left hand. Don't believe me. Ask him."

"So she couldn't use her right hand?"

"Would you use your left hand to shoot yourself?" I said.

The ambulance men in their white suits and black bow ties began unloading the stretcher from the back. They moved as if they had already done the drill a dozen times that day. The fat one was chewing a cigar stub.

"Right here, boys," Greenberg called to them. Then to me he said, "Why do you want to fuck this up?"

I wanted to tell him I knew for a fact she didn't do it. Instead I said, "I'm not trying to fuck anything up. But, you can't possibly believe she'd really blow her own brains out."

"Maybe she's ambidextrous. Can anyone prove she wasn't? And there's nothing here suggesting anything other than a suicide." He took off his hat and dug his fingers through a tangle of thick hair. "It wouldn't be the first time I'd seen someone kill themself because they were guilty about something. Hell, people off themselves because they've got nothing else to do that day." He put the hat back on and said, "Anyway, this wraps everything up. And God knows, there's nothing I want more than to be finished with this goddamned mess."

We moved aside for the ambulance men. "Lieutenant, I gotta be honest," said the one with the cigar. "I'm beginning to really dislike you."

"Yeah? Why's that, Charlie?"

"Every time I see your ugly Jew face we've got a fucking mess on our hands."

"Does my being Jewish really have anything to do with it?"

"I'm beginning to wonder," Charlie said.

"Nice," I said after they went inside.

"He's okay. We fuck with each other." He flicked a nonexistent ash with his thumb on the butt and faced me. "Okay. For the record, here's what I'm thinking. Loitzel and Hoff kidnap the baby. Somehow it winds up dead. They end up fighting about something and she kills him. In the end, the guilt over the baby and the fact she killed lover boy gets to her. So, she takes the easy way out."

I took a step off the covered walkway and turned towards the rising mountains dotted with scrubby brush, staggered pines and aspen with their bright green leaves. The sun was slipping away, painting everything with the sepia tones of early evening, when shadows turn distorted and washed out like dried coffee spills on white linen. I smoked the cigarette down to my fingertips and tossed it away just as the neon sign started buzzing to life. The green tubing flickered a few times before lighting. With crooked letters that were supposed to go with the friendly, western motif it said Howdy Partner Mo-tel. Only they didn't look so friendly anymore, they looked like they were about to fall off. Howdy and Partner started to flash, one after the other. A couple seconds later the red neon below started buzzing. It said Vacancy.

"She didn't kill herself," I said, turning back to him. "And I'll give you this one too. She was pregnant."

CHAPTER 1

FOUR MONTHS EARLER
LATE FEBRUARY 1949

The first time I spoke to Sonja Hoff was on the phone. The conversation lasted barely a minute and I didn't even get her name. I wonder now what I would have done if I'd known it would be the catalyst for everything that would happen over the next four months: Her death, the death of all the others and my own decline into hell. But, there it was, two simple sentences: "I would like to make an appointment for Colonel Marquand. Today if possible," she said. That was all it took for me to be reeled in, as if I were a fat, dumb sucker fish and a juicy piece of rotting flesh suddenly appeared in the muck where I wallowed. Christian *fucking* Marquand! Who would have thought? The goddamned *Hero of the Skies*. The baby-faced kid with the shit-eating grin and a chest full of medals who sent seventy men plummeting to their fiery deaths in the first world war, and who would become a newsreel heartthrob when he beat insane odds by flying solo across the Atlantic. Then across America. Then around the world. Eventually the ballsy fucker would break every altitude and speed record, personally design a dozen airframes and become a millionaire several times over.

Sure, he had it all. Fame. Fortune. And presence. A big presence. Conversations stopped and dogs stood up when he entered a room. He could whither the toughest men with barely a glance while making women weak in the knees from a hint of a smile. I'd seen it firsthand. Many times. There's no doubt his self-confidence filled a room to the point that everyone else was left gasping for air. Most people would be over the moon with the idea that Christian Marquand wanted to meet with them. But I knew the man personally. And while the entire country treated him like a god and worshipped his vanity, I always knew him to be supremely controlling and on most occasions a complete asshole.

I made a point of straightening up; stuffing newspapers in the trash, dumping ashtrays, and wiping out the little sink that always seemed a little out of place on one wall. I knew it was all stupid shit he would notice, and that meant he could use it against me, without his even uttering a word. When that was done I aligned the two straight back chairs in front of the desk and spent a few minutes in front of the mirror. I retied my tie, smoothed my hair and brushed my teeth with a finger. Then I drank down a shot from the bottle in the desk and waited on the couch with a cigarette.

One hour later, the outer office door buzzer sounded. I took a deep breath and opened the inner door. Marquand was standing in the middle of the room, tall, not broad, but imposing nevertheless in a long grey cashmere overcoat and wide-brimmed hat.

"Colonel. What a surprise."

"Captain Thorpe," he said pulling off a glove and offering me his hand. "You look like you've been hitting the chow line for seconds."

"Not so hard to put on some weight once you get away from C-Rats."

"You're not wrong there." He jerked a thumb at the empty desk and chair in the outer office. "Where's your secretary?"

"I'm between girls." I lied, parrying what I was sure was the first in a series of Marquand-style jabs.

"You need a German girl, Thorpe, like me. They're so damn efficient. Germans in general."

"Yeah, too bad we just killed so many of them," I said.

"That was just unfortunate. So much wasted talent," he said, putting his hat and gloves on my desk and handing me the overcoat to hang up. "On both sides," he added.

"Yeah, maybe unfortunate. But *that* fight was brought to us."

"Was it though? I think you know how I feel about that."

"Everyone knows how you feel about it, Colonel. If I were a betting man, I'd say it looks like you're getting ready to run for office."

"Is that right?" he said, taking a seat in one of the straight-backed chairs and crossing his legs.

"You're not?"

He shot me his trademark smirk and it was a true beauty. Cocky and confident and all about fuck you and the shitty horse you rode in on. "It's crossed my mind," he said.

"Well, if it's about sheer popularity, I'd say you have it in the bag."

"That's what they say."

"But, if it's about issues, you're going to have a hard time on the left."

The smirk dissolved and he emitted a little snort. "Advice from the east coast, liberal elite?" His cool blue eyes moved to my suit, then around the room. They finally settled on the little sink. I could hear the running critique in my head. Slowly Marquand's eyes returned to my face. "This is a long way from Central Park West and Princeton," he said.

"It used to be a dentist's office," I said.

"Oh. Very good then."

"You have to admit, the left is a bit put-off by the whole America First and hyper-nationalism stuff."

"More advice?"

"I'm just being conversational. We can get to the point if that's better for you. After all, you're a busy man. With a German secretary."

Marquand laughed. "You always were a difficult man, Thorpe. I'm glad to see you still have your fighting spirit."

"I owe it all to you, sir."

"Is that what you think?"

"I'm not saying we're alike in any way. But, there's no question I owe everything I was as a pilot to you."

"You're wrong there, Thorpe. We're more alike than you realize. Maybe we came from completely different worlds, but what unites us is our ability to survive. And, the fact that you listened when you were told something. That's what a survivor does. They listen to instructions and put them into practice. I did the same thing when I was a young man. It's why we're sitting here today and all those other sad bastards went down in flames." Marquand uncrossed his legs and leaned forward. "So, how did you end up here? And I don't mean here," he said, indicating the office. "I mean in Denver. And as a detective."

"A series of things, I suppose. Did you hear about the accident at Samar? It was maybe three months after you left." He furrowed his brow and tilted his head, so I went on. "Ken Ochs had a blowout on takeoff, lost control and crashed into the supply area. Things got really ugly, really fast. Everything went up. Ammo. Oxygen tanks. Fuel. It was worse than any bombing we'd had from the Japs. Ended up with over fifty wounded and fourteen killed. Ochs one of them, obviously." I took a cigarette from the box on the desk and used a stick match, struck on the edge of the desk.

"Ochs was the big man?"

"Yeah, the big cowboy with the bad jokes," I said. "He was from up around Sterling."

"Sterling, Colorado?"

"Right. Up I-80S towards Nebraska. Ochs and I had become pretty good friends. So, after the war I was passing through Denver and thought I'd go see his folks. I guess I liked the wide-open spaces and didn't have a good reason to continue on. And you? How did you end up in Colorado?"

"Louise fell in love with Colorado when I was going through training at Buckley Field. I like it too, but...," he gestured towards the saucer sized snowflakes that were falling outside the window. "I don't really care for the winter. Not exactly flying weather, right? But, spring is beautiful. And summer. So, we got a place in town and last year, a vacation home up in Morrison, past the amphitheater."

"Sounds nice," I said.

"I'm really surprised you gave up flying. As a matter of fact, I could use a good pilot. If you want to get back to that. We're wrapping up tests on a high altitude reconnaissance plane. The Air Force wants it in service by Q4 '50. When that's finished we'll start testing a new airframe that's not all that different from the Corsair. You could be a good fit."

"The reconnaissance plane, the XA-13? I read about it in the papers. Wasn't your wife the navigator on the cross-country tests?"

"She was. Louise is an extremely talented pilot in her own right. Not many people know, but she was pregnant during those endurance tests. She's quite the woman," he said, scooting his chair back a little.

"Oh, I forgot," I said, holding up the cigarette.

"If you don't mind."

I stubbed it out in the ashtray and fanned the air.

"I guess I'm a bit late, but congrats on Christian Junior," I said.

"Nearly two now."

"Another Mighty Marquand, I'm sure."

"Wouldn't that be nice," he said, eyes on his hands.

"So that's the reason for the visit? You want me to fly your new fighter?"

"We can talk about that, at some point. I'm actually here to hire you to look into some threats I've been getting."

"Okay," I said, a bit surprised by that turn. "What kind of threats?" I took a pad from the center drawer and unscrewed the cap on my pen.

"They're letters. I'd like you to find out who is sending them and make them stop."

"Do you have any with you?"

"I burn them. I don't want Louise coming across them. Don't worry, there will be more. There's always more," he said, noting my expression.

"Is it blackmail?"

"No. Of course not."

"What do they say?"

A flash of exasperation darted across his face. "They're just threats. To me. To my family. Crazy nonsense from some lunatic. I don't know."

"You don't know? You read the letters."

"I can't remember exactly what they say. It's just threatening language. Stuff like I should watch my back."

"Okay," I said, drawing the word out to show my own exasperation.

"You're the detective. Detect who's doing it. Make them stop."

Marquand reached in his coat and took out a lovely calfskin wallet. From it he pulled a $1,000 bill and put it on the desk.

"What's that?" I asked.

"A retainer. I'll give you another thousand in two weeks."

"That's crazy. My rates are $25 a day plus expenses."

"Money is not an object, Thorpe. I can't have Louise coming across one of these things. She's pregnant again and can't be exposed to any undue stress. We had a difficult time with the first pregnancy and…" He paused and took a deep breath.

"And what are you thinking I can do about them?"

"Haven't you ever had to rough someone up in your line of work?"

"Not really."

"Fine. Do whatever you want so long as the letters stop," he said, pushing the bill across the desk.

"Colonel, that's way too much…"

"Don't be an idiot. It's a retainer. I'm retaining your services and your undivided attention when the time is appropriate." He stood up and took the cashmere overcoat from the hook. "I'll call you when the next letter comes. Hell! There's probably one at the house right now."

I shook his hand and he was gone, out through the front office and into the hall. Even after the outer door finished it's slow, dying-like effort at closing, I could hear his footsteps going away.

I sat for a while looking at Grover Cleveland and his walrus mustache. Across the back and below United States of America in Old English script were the words *One Thousand Dollars* in neat, block letters. It was pretty. A work of art if you stop to admire the little details. But, it also evoked this feeling of danger. I laid it down, framing it in the center of the desk blotter, and poured myself   a   drink.

CHAPTER 2

Cyril's in Five Points was a landmark. Not because it was big or fancy. It wasn't. But, it was known for being the home of bluesy, doleful jazz and people who nursed stiff drinks and never intended to use the floorboards for anything other than getting from one place to another. Considering it was in the heart of the neighborhood known as the Harlem of the West, I was lucky to play there at all. And I'd have to get a whole lot luckier if I ever wanted to play any other night than a Monday. Guys spent decades working themselves into bands that headlined Fridays or Saturdays, and, while I could hold my own, I could never live long enough to be that good, that moody or that black.

If anything, the snow was only coming down harder since I left the office, so I parked as close as possible to the back door and struggled through the tiny, one-man kitchen with my bass fiddle. Even a small club like Cyril's had to serve food if they were going to pour drinks. It was the law. But the law didn't say it had to be anything more than bagged chips and flat, ham and cheese sandwiches.

Out front Lew and Ronnie were solemnly laying down a gentle rendition of *Stormy Monday* with Lew on the electric guitar and Ronnie playing the piano. I returned their nods, unzipped my fiddle cover and joined them. There was barely a smattering of people in the whole club, mostly dotted into small groups or couples. After a few minutes, Carlotta came from the bar and made her rounds. When she passed by the stage I motioned her up. The three of us

11

went on playing for a little while, swaying and drifting along through two solos each until she returned with glasses and a bottle of bourbon.

"What's up with all this, Fuzzy? Are we getting drunk?" Lew asked.

"I had a windfall, boys. Drinks on me." Nodding to the drum kit, I said, "No Roscoe tonight?"

"You know that negro don't go out in snow, man!" Lew exclaimed.

"That's why he's buying tonight, 'cuz Roscoe ain't here," Ronnie said.

"That's goddamned smart," Lew said to Ronnie. "There ain't enough windfall on earth to satisfy Roscoe's taste for liquor."

"Well, he's gonna miss out then," I said pouring the drinks. "I'm also sending out for steak-fucking-sandwiches. With French fries! None of my friends are eating those sad excuses for ham and cheese tonight."

"What the hell, Fuzzy! Did you rob a bank or somethin'?" Lew asked.

"You guys wouldn't even believe it if I *could* tell you." I raised my glass and we toasted.

"'Bout time some motherfucker had somethin' good happen to 'em." Ronnie said.

"You really sending out for steak sandwiches? I'm mighty hungry and I don't like a man playing tricks on my stomach," Lew asked.

"Goddamned right I am." I said, waving at Carlotta.

We played a full set before the food arrived, and with only a dozen or two people in the main room, we decided to break and eat. We took one of the tables off to the side of the stage and unwrapped the sandwiches from the stiff white paper. They were steaming hot and just as delicious as I'd imagined with plenty of sautéed onions and peppers. Lew opened his up and piled it high with fries then splattered the whole thing with ketchup. It was like watching a kid as he made a satisfying mess of his hands and face. Carlotta brought beer in ice cold mugs so we could wash everything down in style. Lew went to wash up and returned with his coat on. He needn't say a word. Ronnie and I got our coats and followed him out through the kitchen. Huddled by the trash cans Lew took out a stick of tea and fired it up with a lighter. As always, when it was my turn, I coughed my head off.

"Damn, Fuzzy. You can't hold your smoke," Lew said, slapping me on the back.

"I know, I know," I wheezed, passing it to Ronnie who expertly sucked the rolled joint between his fat fingertips. He held the smoke forever before blowing out a giant cloud.

"Holy shit! That would have killed me," I said, already feeling my cheeks getting hot.

"You just need more practice," Ronnie said.

I let them pass what was left back and forth and watched the fluffy snowflakes drift in the streetlight. I was thinking it was like being inside a snow globe and it made me wonder who was looking in on us.

We started off the second set with *Blues After Hours* and let that pull us into some deep, wallowing New Orleans funk. After a while the place got lively with swaying bodies and tapping toes and a hep cat called Gravy Davey, who played with another band, hopped on the drums. We ramped up the tempo and rolled into *Chicken Shack Boogie* and followed that with the other boogie woogies. I slapped and plucked the bass until my fingers were sore and my shoulder was screaming with pain. I was about as content as a guy could get.

CHAPTER 3

Most of what I was doing when Marquand showed up with that crisp thousand dollar bill was infidelity work. Cheating husbands. Cheating wives. Cheating mistresses. It wasn't anything I would call exciting. If anything, it was depressing; all those tears, all that anger. And betrayal. Lots of betrayal. I often wondered why people would even care to know. The outcome was rarely good. Maybe never good. It was messy work but I'd gotten really good at it. And it paid. I'd done plenty of other stuff. Exciting stuff. But with excitement there's always the chance a guy could get hurt. Infidelity was easy. Set up somewhere. Snap some pics. Take some notes. Then help people ruin their lives. Push, pull, click, click.

Once I'd deposited all that money from Marquand and caught up on some bills it was hard to keep regular hours at the office. Some days I would lay around the house reading the paper and drinking coffee until well after noon. Other days, when I wasn't in the mood to wait on the percolator or irritate my shoulder by shoveling coal, I'd walk the two blocks to Dina's Diner on Tennyson. I especially liked the short walk on cold mornings when I could see my breath and my footsteps made squeaking sounds in the fresh snow. It seemed like an adventure. Like Jack London trudging through the Yukon. Then there was Dina's smile, a nice smile. Warm and friendly, like her diner. And there was always a spot for me at her busy counter.

"What's on the docket today, Detective?" she asked, pouring me a cup of coffee. "Murder, mayhem and thievery?"

"Always mayhem, sister," I said, playing along with her conspiratorial tone.

The fellow to my right turned to look. I gave Dina a wink and nod and she laughed.

I liked watching her. She worked the counter with easy chit-chat and a familiar manner. Her long, slender fingers almost intimate, maybe even sensual in the way they touched a cup or plate, sometimes an arm or shoulder. And, I liked the mystery of her hair, always tightly braided into a thick rope that hung over a shoulder. Most of all I liked when I caught her looking at me, the big smile replaced with a coy little grin.

After my food had come and my empty plate was whisked away, she returned with a donut in a box and the pot of coffee. "You've been in a lot lately," she said. "Not that I'm complaining."

"Where else would I go? You take such good care of me."

"Always for my special customers."

"Oh! I'm a *special* customer."

There was the coy little grin before she scooted off to the other end of the counter.

The guy next to me said, "You need to move on that."

"Yeah?"

"Are you blind? She's all over you. Ask her out."

I did just that when she came back. She wrote down her address on a slip from her pad. When I got up to leave, I shook the man's hand. He wished me luck. I went next door for a shave and haircut. That afternoon I sprawled on the couch and listened to the radio while flipping through *Life* Magazine. Oscar the goldfish, apparently picking up on my mood, swam enthusiastically around the quartz rock in his bowl so I gave him an extra shake of food so he'd know we were on the same page. He gobbled happily and I enjoyed watching him with his own little windfall. After a while I got up to take a bath and press a shirt.

Dina wore her hair down, the mystery solved. It showered her shoulders with dark, heavy curls, somehow making her cheekbones even more pronounced. She leaned close to me during the movie and I could smell a hint of her perfume. A couple of times our hands touched in the popcorn box. She held my arm on the street after.

"Humphrey Bogart was awful!" she said.

"You didn't like him?"

"I love him as an actor," she said, "but I hated that character! He was so greedy. And crazy!"

"Yeah. And, greed got him in the end." I pointed to a bar across the street. "Can I buy you a drink?"

Once we were inside and settled into a booth, a waitress came by to put down paper napkins printed with Dempsey's in green script. Dina ordered a Hot Toddy. "You must see a lot of crazy things as a detective," she said.

"Sometimes. It's mostly infidelity work though. That's what pays the bills, anyway."

"So, of all you've seen, who cheats more? Men or women?"

"From what I've seen, it's pretty even."

"Has it changed your opinion of marriage?"

I chuckled, "Oh no. Marriage changed my opinion of marriage." She didn't look like she liked that statement so I said, "You've never been married."

"No."

"Sorry. I don't mean to blast all marriage. Mine just wasn't all it was cracked up to be."

"How long were you married?"

"Three years. We met when I was in flight school, and like idiots, we got married a month after meeting, before I shipped out. Three years later, I get home and we both realize it was a huge mistake. I sort of knew it all along, but it was nice to imagine coming home to someone." I shook two cigarettes from my pack and offered one to her. She shook her head so I put hers back and lit mine with the candle on the table. "I knew in the back of my head she wasn't exactly *waiting* for me."

She was toying with the corner of a napkin, her fingernails freshly painted an incandescent ruby red. After a minute she said, "I'm sorry."

"It's all good."

Changing the subject she said, "I liked the younger guy best. In the movie."

"Curtin? Yeah, he was a good character. Tim Holt, the actor, he was a B-29 bombardier in the Pacific."

"Did you know him?"

"No, he was Air Corps. But I did run across Tyrone Power. He was a Marine pilot."

"What was he like?"

"Seemed like a nice guy. And a good pilot from what I heard." I exhaled smoke above her head. "I *did* fly with Christian Marquand."

"*The* Christian Marquand! Really?"

"Yeah, he joined up with my squadron in the spring of '44 and flew combat missions with us for a couple months."

"I didn't know he flew military planes."

"Oh sure. Back before he got famous he was a fighter pilot in the first world war."

"What was he like?"

"Well...obviously he's an incredible pilot. He came over as a civilian contractor for Vought, the company that built the plane I flew. He showed us how to increase bomb loads and flying distances without increasing fuel loads. He made it all seem so easy even though it was all advanced techniques. He ended up flying missions with us. I can't even tell you how much I learned from him. But as a human being..." I flicked an ash. "Well, to put it nicely...he's in a class all his own."

The waitress returned with the drinks and placed them on the napkins.

Dina drank from her mug and licked her lips. "What do you mean by that?"

"I don't want to be rude but, he's kind of an arrogant asshole," I said.

"Wow. I'd never guess that. He always looked so humble in the newsreels."

"Anything but humble." I toyed with the cigarette for a moment and said, "But I get it. He was a gangly kid who was all elbows. Then all of a sudden he's an ace with the Medal of Honor and promoted to colonel. All before he was even twenty-three years old. So, yeah, I can see how that would go to your head."

She took the long plastic swizzle stick out of her drink and ran it through her lips before setting it on the table. "Was he bossy?" she asked.

"Not really. He was just imperial in his manner. Had to have his own tent and his own cook and stuff like that." I fished the maraschino cherry out of my drink and ate it. "And he wasn't all that friendly. He didn't drink. Didn't smoke. Didn't joke around. He wasn't likable, and everyone was always intimidated by him."

"Well...he was the first person to fly around the world by

himself or whatever. He probably figured he earned the right to have certain things."

"He wasn't the first, he set the record for the fastest solo flight around the world," I said.

"For me, he was always a hero. When we were just coming to America, Christian Marquand was the example of everything good and possible in this country. He made us believe. We really thought it was the land where anything could happen if you worked hard enough."

I had to look away from her to keep from laughing out loud at the idea of Christian Marquand representing anything good. At another table a young couple sat on the same side of the booth. They were smiling about something. Then the girl kissed the man's cheek leaving a big lipstick mark.

"He's pretty ruthless," I said, finally turning back to Dina.

"Did you stay in touch?"

"No."

I knew from her expression that she got the drift and should let it go. She turned and watched something out in the dining room. Her lips were full and moist and her eyes bright jade in the soft light. I was thinking about what she would be like to kiss and how her breasts might feel in my hands. She looked down at the swizzle stick she'd bent into a triangle, one end stuffed inside the other. When she raised her eyes to me I smiled and she smiled back.

"Sorry about all that at the house," she said. "My brother can be rather over-protective sometimes."

"No. He was nice. Your sister-in-law too."

"He just looks scary," she said.

"Yeah! He's as big as a house."

She laughed. "That he is. But he's the nicest guy you could ever meet. He'd give a stranger the shirt off his back."

"What's he do?"

"He owns a butcher shop."

"Oh, yeah!" I said. "I don't think I want to imagine that guy with a meat cleaver in his hand. I probably shouldn't even be out with you!"

"Probably not!" she crinkled her eyes and I laughed. "It actually works out great. I get a big cut on all the meat I buy from him."

"That must help."

"It does. But, thank the Lord, business has been great. I never actually thought it would be this good."

"That's swell. I'm happy for you." I held up my glass. She tapped mine with her mug and we both took a drink.

"Were you always a detective? Like before the war too?" she asked.

"No. I went to law school for a while. But it was horrible. Truly the most pedantic shit I've ever experienced in my whole life. It made the boring days in the military seem exciting. To tell the truth it was even more boring than being a detective," I said.

"I always thought being a lawyer or a detective would be so exciting."

"No. Ninety percent of the time it's completely mind-numbing."

"Not like the movies then."

"Not like the movies."

The waitress came by. Dina said she was fine so I asked for the check.

"And, what about your family? Are they here?"

"They're back east," I said.

"Do you miss them?"

"No."

She watched me in a way that I knew was just a pause while thoughts rolled around in her head. I felt like I should say more, if anything, to be polite. But there wasn't much I could say that I wanted to hear with my own ears so I finished my drink and tossed the cherry stem in the glass. "We don't have anything in common," I finally said.

She reached across the table and laid her fingertips on my hand. They were warm, as if those incandescent nails really were on fire. "I'm sorry. I didn't mean to make everything weird."

"Not at all," I said. "I'm just thinking about your brother and that meat cleaver. I should probably get you home or he'll turn me into chops!"

She took my arm as we walked back under the bright lights of the Oriental Theatre. In the car on the way home we exchanged small talk about the neighborhood. She told a story about a lonely guy who came into her restaurant. She was still talking about how she thought it was so funny he liked a scoop of ice cream with his pancakes when we pulled up in front of her brother's house. I could tell she was looking at me but it was hard to see her almond shaped eyes in the darkness. She didn't finish the story, instead she slid across the seat and put her lips to mine. They were soft and full.

CHAPTER 4

When the call came it was Marquand himself. Another letter had arrived and he wanted me to come to the house. Before I could ask a single question he rattled off the address and clicked off.

Country Club was the city's premier old money neighborhood, at least as old as money got in Denver. It had actually sprouted up during the first part of the current century but was dotted with elaborate mansions perched on painstakingly manicured grounds all designed to look like they'd been there for several generations. It got its unofficial name from the proximity to the all-white, all-protestant Denver Country Club; a walled-in sporting retreat for the upper tier and their jaunty offspring. Marquand was on Circle Drive, which was just that, a big circle that cut its way through the standard grid layout. The circle made it possible for the lots to be carved even bigger, allowing ample space for private tennis courts, swimming pools and putting greens, all so they'd never have to actually rub elbows with the everyday folks at the Country Club.

A polished brass placard read 467. It was mounted next to an open wood gate that when closed would have repelled the Mongol horde. I followed the drive up a slight curve and parked off to the side under a trio of giant leafless elms. As I suspected, the house was enormous, with an abundance of brick and Corinthian columns and hand-cut laurels. The stairs leading up from the drive were wide enough for a Marine brigade and shouldered on either side was a staggered wall of pedestals and ornamental stone pineapples. Dotting the grounds were little shrubs that someone had spent a great deal of time making into the same pineapple shape. Or maybe, I thought, they were supposed to be bombs. Across the property were groupings of tiered gardens and another building, a miniature of the big house, that must have been a guest or pool house.

I tossed my cigarette and crossed the drive, my feet crunch crunching on the pea gravel. The doorbell launched what may have been an entire orchestra sitting at the ready for just this sort of call, and soon a grey-haired negro in a tuxedo opened the door. I told him who I was and that Marquand was expecting me. His footsteps drifted off for about a mile and I occupied myself in a mirror, patting my hair and straightening my tie.

In from the foyer a wide decorative staircase swept to a second floor. Peach colored light rained down in shadowy streams from a cathedral ceiling topped with a stained-glass dome. Off to the right was a long narrow dining room with mahogany walls, furnished with a table for thirty. On the far wall, between two rows of vertical stained-glass windows, hung a tapestry on a rod as big as my wrist. The woven scene depicted knights appearing before angels who seemed to be guarding a little stone building. In the building was a raised table and golden chalice. One of the knights was kneeling at the doorway, his hands held together in prayer.

"Mr. Thorpe?" It was a blue-eyed blonde, dressed in a stylish wool suit and not entirely modest heels. "I'm Sonja Hoff, Colonel Marquand's secretary."

"We spoke before on the phone," I said, taking her hand.

"I see you were enjoying the tapestry."

"Sir Galahad, right?"

"It's called *The Vision of the Holy Grail*. A one-of-a-kind at that size by the rug-maker William Morris from artwork of Edward Burne-Jones. It is quite valuable. Are you familiar with tapestries and their history?"

"Not really."

"It's quite an intriguing study actually. Sometimes this one is also called *The Attainment*."

"Do you think the Colonel imagines himself as Sir Galahad?"

She shot me a look. "Maybe he does. You should ask him, no?"

"I'm guessing he does, no?" I said.

The coldness in her eyes dropped a few degrees. "Is this making fun of my accent?"

"Not at all. German, right? How long have you been in the country?"

"Not so long now, Mr. Thorpe." She turned. "Come. The Colonel, he is waiting."

We went down a short corridor and then turned into a long hallway with floor-to-ceiling windows on one side. A few feathery flakes of snow had begun to fall, making it postcard perfect. The yard at the back of the house was impressive. Marquand obviously had an army of gardeners on the payroll.

Sonja Hoff, sensing my slowing, stopped. "The gardens are quite exquisite in the spring and summer."

"I'm sure they are."

The hall ended with a predictably spacious clearing decorated with a desk, leather chairs and a stone fireplace lit with single gas log. Sonja Hoff motioned to a chair saying she would see if the Colonel was ready for me. I started to occupy myself by surveying the walls peppered with all sorts of things devoted to Marquand's ego, but it was a broken wood propeller leaning against the corner that got my attention. The plaque near it read:

Stabsfeldwebel K. R. Boelcke
K.u.K. Luftfahrtruppen, Austria-Hungary
Shot Down
15 October 1918, Murvaux, France
By
Captain C. A. Marquand
27th Aero Squadron, 1st Pursuit Group, U.S.A.
71st Kill

I put my hand on Boelcke's propeller. Another month and he would have made it to the armistice. Poor bastard's luck had ran out. But in the end, luck runs out for all of us. It brought to mind all the aircraft I shot down and the men in them who went to their deaths. Even if I knew who they were I was pretty damn sure I wouldn't want their names engraved on a brass plaque for my wall.

"Mr. Thorpe…" Sonja Hoff motioned me inside.

Marquand greeted me at the door with his arms outstretched as if he were going to hug. "Thorpe! I'd like you to meet Mrs. Marquand. Louise, this is Captain Thorpe."

She and I shook hands as Marquand jumped into a rapid-fire

conversation with himself about how we knew each other. He was talking so fast I couldn't follow a single word and instead found myself thinking how Louise Marquand looked like a woman who enjoyed the company of other women. It wasn't so much the short brown hair and boyish slacks as the smear of red lipstick. It was as if she just learned how to apply it and didn't actually like how it felt on her lips.

"Forgive me for barging in here before your meeting. Christian will never admit it, but he hates I do this sort of thing when he's working."

"No harm done," I said. "It's a pleasure to meet you."

"Pleasure to meet you too," she said as Marquand yammered on about how he always kept him in line and was his fucking rock or something.

"Are you still flying, Captain?" Louise Marquand said.

"Please, call me Harry. And no," I said. "I was shot down in '44. That was the end for me."

"You don't miss flying?"

"Oh sure. Of course I do."

"I don't think I could give it up. Not if I lived to be a hundred," she said.

"I get it," I said. "But, I had an injury, and they grounded me."

"I didn't know you were shot down," Marquand said.

"Zero got me. Over Bougainville," I said directly to him.

"Oh, I'm so sorry. That must have been horrible," Louise said. "And what line of business are you in now?"

"Thorpe's a Princeton man," Marquand blurted. "Did I mention that? What year Thorpe?"

"Class of '38."

"Christian! Why don't you get off the man."

Marquand took his arm off my shoulder. "Mrs. Marquand's father was a benefactor at Princeton. Class of aught five, right dear?"

"Yes, 1905," she said as if it were the ten thousandth time in her life she'd had to mention the fact.

"And Mrs. Marquand's sister went to Bryn Mawr," he said, obviously evoking the sister-school connection. "Louise went to Smith."

"All very good schools," I said.

"All around the same time you graduated, Thorpe. Louise was

1937 and Loren was…1940?"

"Christian. It's not polite to mention years when discussing a lady's past."

"What do I know?" Marquand said grinning at me. "I'm just a hick from Iowa who didn't get past the 11th grade."

"So you're from here, Mr. Thorpe? Or the east coast?" she asked.

"My family is in New York. And Rhode Island."

"Thorpe. We might know some Thorpes. My sister and I grew up on the Upper East Side."

"My family has a home on the Upper West Side."

"Oh! Maybe we do know each other then. Where did you go to school?"

"Allen-Stevenson. Then Andover."

"Oh!" she said, her eyebrows rising. "We're just public schoolers."

"I think I would have preferred public school, actually."

"What does your father do?"

"Banker."

"Hmmm…Thorpe," she said, thinking.

"Thorpe's a lawyer," Marquand bleated, squeezing my shoulder.

"Well, not exactly," I said. "I went to law school for two years."

"And where was that?" Louise said.

"NYU."

"How do I not know you?" she said, looking hard at me.

"Louise's father was Senator Chambers," Marquand said.

"I didn't realize," I replied.

"Yes, we try to keep that a secret," she said.

"I understand. I'm the same about my family."

"Well, Mr. Thorpe. It was a pleasure to meet you. But I will leave you to your business. I can tell Christian is nearing the point where he will actively throw me out." She pinched Marquand playfully on the arm and he smiled at her, then me, then her.

"It was nice meeting you as well," I said, taking her hand.

She smiled. It was a nice smile. I could see how a man would find her attractive. Then she started out the door. "Do you get back to the city often, Mr. Thorpe?" she asked, turning back.

"No. Not so much anymore."

"I think I miss the city more than I'd miss flying."

"I agree," I said.

She went out and closed the door behind her.

"Obviously I don't want her knowing about any of this letter stuff," Marquand said, his tone returning to the one I was much more familiar with. "We can't have the women getting worked up."

"She looks to me like she could handle it."

I could see the muscles around his eyes tightening. "Thank you for noticing, but I'm sure I know my wife better than you. There's the sister too, the Bryn Mawr one, she's quite frail and can't be exposed to things like this. You get the picture?"

"What would she have to do with it?"

"She lives here. In the house. So you can see why I'm being cautious. And, as I said, she's frail. Bad heart. This sort of thing, you know, could have an effect on her." Marquand crossed the room and sat down behind his aircraft carrier sized desk. I followed along and sat twenty feet away in one of three chairs facing him.

"Alright, then," he said. "Down to business. A letter arrived this morning. Just like the others. It was addressed to me personally which means Victor brings it here and Miss Hoff doesn't open it. She's not to open any personal mail."

"Victor. The butler?"

"Yes."

"Okay. Can I see it?"

"I burned it," he said, pointing to the fireplace behind me.

"You burned it?"

"I told you, Thorpe, I can't run the risk of anyone seeing something like that. You see how Louise comes and goes whenever she wants."

"I thought we agreed you would save the next letter for me to see."

He stared at me for several seconds, tap tapping his fingernail on the desk blotter. "Well, I burned it," he said.

"Did you save the envelope?"

"No. I did not."

"Okay," I said, starting to get up. "Call me when the next one comes."

"Sit down! And don't use that tone with me."

"You couldn't slip it into your pocket until I arrived?"

"That's neither here nor there. What could you do if you actually saw it?" We sat staring at each other for a long tick. Then Marquand started again: "The fact is, I'm getting threatening letters. They say something bad might happen to me or my family. They don't have a return address and they are not signed. I suggest, detective, that you backtrack. Go to the post office and work backwards from there."

"Do you think the post office just lets anyone poke around with the mail?"

"You're a licensed private detective."

"It would really help if I could actually see one of the letters myself."

"Are we back to that," he said, raising his voice.

"Okay. Let's try this again. What's the usual routine? For example, do you have a typical schedule? Are you going to the club? Or, you mentioned a Morrison house. How often are you going there?"

"Usually every weekend," he said.

"And who normally goes?"

"We all do. Louise. And Christian and myself."

"Anyone else come and go with you?"

"Loren. The sister. And a few staff. What's this got to do with anything?"

"If you're getting threats, don't you think it makes sense to step up security? You know as much as I do, a typical routine presents the greatest opportunity. You're going to need to start varying your schedule. Nothing can be the same. Different times, different routes, different days. You have a chauffeur, right? He needs to change how you get to the same old places like work, bank, lunch, or whatever. Everything must be unpredictable, and he needs to stay on the lookout for possible threats or tails. And that's just the start. I'll also need to look around the grounds, at both the houses. There can't be any vantage or take down points. We may need to install lighting or secure windows, doors or other points of ingress. Even the driveways. I drove right up onto the property. That gate should be secured at all times. There's a lot to do, but I can oversee all of it for you, Colonel."

"Jesus, Thorpe! That stuff is only going to make everyone panicky."

"I can understand your concern, but until we isolate the threat we need a heightened level of security. It's the only real option we have."

"I don't disagree with that."

"So I have your permission…"

"No! You're not listening to me. I can't have the lives of these women disrupted like that."

We glared at each other for almost a minute before Marquand stood up and walked over to glassed, French doors looking out onto the garden. He crammed his hands in his pockets and didn't move as snow swirled gently onto the covered porch, almost to his feet.

I let myself sink in the chair and burn holes into his back with my eyes. Eventually I tired from thinking bad thoughts about him and let my gaze wander the room, littered with all his glory. Along with the dozens of photos were two glass cases with medals and citations. One held his Medal of Honor, the highest military decoration for bravery, with its little white stars dotting a sky blue ribbon. Another held a cross, with a swastika in the center and hanging from a red, black and white ribbon. I recognized the framed photo next to that one. Herman Göring was presenting the Nazi Iron Cross to a grinning Marquand. It made me think of all the controversy surrounding the incident. The story and photo had made every paper in America. Eventually I gave a little cough and said, "What do you think we should do then, sir?"

Marquand came back over, leaned against the front of his desk and looked down on me. "Work with me, Thorpe. We need to find this person and make them stop. I know what kind of man you are. I've seen you in combat. You're someone who isn't afraid to do what is right…even when that means the right thing is the difficult choice. That's why I came to you first. But we cannot disrupt the lives of these women in this household. We can't having them thinking they're living in some sort of hostile environment. Can you understand that?"

I'd be lying if I said the thousand dollars wasn't on my mind. It was a lot of money. Months of infidelity work, maybe even years, and all the boring headaches that came with that. So instead of arguing with the man, I said, "I assure you, Colonel, I'll make the letters stop. And we won't get anyone riled up over this."

He just stared at me, so I said it again.

"Good. Start with the post office. See what they can tell you. I'll make arrangements for Richard, that's the chauffeur, to visit your office so you can speak to him. But I can't have you poking about the houses. Understood?"

"Yes, sir."

"Good." He reached in his coat and took out that damn gorgeous calfskin wallet and handed me another thousand dollar bill. I tried telling him it wasn't necessary but he insisted. We shook hands, and he said, "If you need more, for expenses or getting someone at the post office to cooperate, just let me know."

"Yes, sir. I will."

Sonja Hoff hopped to her feet when he opened the office door. I followed her down the long glass hallway and back through the foyer.

"So, did you ask the Colonel if he thinks he's Sir Galahad?" she asked, as I pulled on my coat.

"I didn't need to," I said.

CHAPTER 5

On the porch I lit a cigarette, then I crossed the drive. I was about to get into the Dodge when I saw a woman with a broad hat and long scarf in the garden. Her eyes were down and she was walking as if deep in thought. I leaned against the door and watched while she made her way back and forth. It was sad and lonely and beautiful with the snow dancing around her.

On one of her turns she saw me and stopped. When she continued to stand motionless I hung my cigarette on my lip and walked over to the edge of the path. Up close I could see it was one long route that led into and out of the center without crossing itself.

"Sorry. I didn't mean to stare. But you looked so peaceful," I called to her from the edge.

"That's the whole point," she called back.

"Is it a labyrinth?"

"Yes."

"I've never seen one before."

"Aren't you the Princeton man?"

"I am."

"And you've never seen a labyrinth?"

"As far as I know, they don't have a labyrinth at Princeton."

She started walking again. "Can I have one of those?"

"A cigarette? Sure."

I started towards her but she held a hand up for me to wait. Following the path around and around at her slow pace she eventually exited on the side where I was waiting. She took the cigarette with a gloved hand and put it to her lips.

"Do you do this often? In the snow?" I asked.

"It's especially affecting when it's snowing."

"How'd you know I went to Princeton?"

"My sister told me. Princeton's a very big deal in my family. My father bled orange and black."

"So I heard. You must be the Bryn Mawr girl."

"I am," she said, tilting her head back and looking up at me under the brim of her hat.

"Why not Princeton?"

"My father went to Princeton and my brothers went to Princeton. It would never be appropriate for a woman to walk the same hallowed halls as a Chambers man. Are you sure you went to Princeton?"

"I did. But I like to think I am anything but a typical Princeton man," I said.

"Isn't that already obvious," she stated.

I laughed. "You're judging me by my '36 Dodge?"

"No. Your coat."

I looked down at my coat. "I like this coat."

"Is it the only one you own?"

"Is there something wrong with that?"

"Not if you like it."

"You must be...Loren? I'm Harry."

"Yes, the crazy sister-in-law," she said, her gloved hand slipping into mine.

"I think you were described to me as frail, not necessarily crazy."

"Frailty is a form of insanity. Or vice versa. I forget," she said.

"I wouldn't know."

"There's not a lot you know."

I looked her in the eye and said, "I'm beginning to think I could use a drink. And I bet one wouldn't hurt your demeanor any. Care to join me?"

"Where do you intend to get this drink?"

"I'm pretty sure I have a pint in the glove box," I said.

"I don't drink, or anything else, in a man's car. At least not anymore. Offer to *buy* me a drink and I might accept."

"Okay. How about I buy you a drink?"

"Thank you."

"Do you need to tell someone where you're going?"

"I'm thirty. Not thirteen," she said. "Besides, I love doing things that will send Christian into a tizzy."

"I don't know if I like how that sounds," I said holding the car door for her.

"Be daring. The reward is always worthwhile."

"That's something I could live by."

She started to get in and stopped. "Is that a double bass in your backseat."

"It prefers to be called a bass fiddle."

"Oh, a blues man," she said, getting in.

"Sounds like you know your music," I said.

As we drove to a bar five blocks away I went ahead and told her the abbreviated story how I had started with the cello and rebelled against everything to be a bull fiddle man. Once in the bar we took a booth near the back. Loren ordered an Old Fashioned and I told the waitress I'd have one too.

"So, you either drive around with a bass fiddle to impress women or you're in a band," she said.

"I play with the Lew Pettigrew quartet on Monday nights at a place called Cyril's. It's in Five Points."

"I know Cyril's," she said. "I was classically trained, too. Piano. But I gave up Bach for jazz. So, I get the whole rebellion thing."

"And you still play?"

"I do."

"And what else is it that you do, Miss Chambers?"

"Really? Miss Chambers? I thought we were beyond that."

"I stand corrected. Loren," I said with mock formality.

"What do you mean what do I do? I'm a Bryn Mawr girl. Am I supposed to be doing something?"

"Well, since I'm assuming you aren't married, I thought you might be heading a charitable organization or volunteering at the hospital."

"I'm too frail," she said.

"You don't look so frail to me."

She was anything but frail. No, on the contrary. She actually looked dangerous. Like a little firecracker that would take your fingers off if you were too stupid and slow to react. The lids around her eyes were blackened with so much makeup it was as if she hadn't slept in a year, but the contrasting light inside those deep brown orbs made me think she could quite possibly never need to sleep. The color of her lips was a dark ruby, the sort of dark red that led you to suspect she might have just finished a bite at someone's neck. I imagined kissing her. It was the looming sadness in those eyes that drew me in, it was unlike anyone else I've ever met, as if she might be able to understand my own pain. And those menacing canines, lurking behind those blood red lips. Frail? No. That was not a word I would ever use to describe Loren Chambers.

"Maybe a tad unpredictable," I added.

The waitress brought our drinks and I ordered two Rueben sandwiches and a basket of French fried potatoes.

"I just love it when a man assumes I want a Rueben sandwich," she teased.

"You won't be disappointed," I said.

"No?"

"I'll stake my reputation on it."

"That's a bold statement."

"I'm a bold guy."

"Are you? Really?" she asked.

I smiled my very best smile at her, she shook her head and laughed. "To the lost souls of the Ivy League," she said raising her glass.

After we touched glasses and drank she asked, "And what do you do, Princeton man?"

"I flew with the Colonel during the war."

"Present tense, please."

"I'm doing security work for the Colonel."

"Oh, another one of those hush-hush things."

"Are there a lot of those?"

"Everything about Christian is hush-hush and overly mysterious."

I shook two cigarettes from the pack. She took one and put it to her lips. I used a thumbnail on a match to light hers and then mine.

She blew smoke and said, "That looks painful."

"Nah."

She picked up her glass and finished it off. I followed suit and waved two fingers at the waitress.

"Security work. What exactly does that mean?" she asked.

"You know I can't talk about it."

"Can't or won't?"

"Shouldn't."

"Because I'm the frail sister-in-law who will drop dead if something exciting happens?"

"He did say something to that effect."

"Sounds like something he'd say."

The waitress came up with the sandwiches. They were piled high and dripping sauce. Loren picked up her pickle and took a bite.

"Why all the contempt?" I asked.

She finished chewing and said, "Tell me your secret and maybe I'll tell you mine."

The way she said it made me smile. It was as if she knew that detective work is all about compromises. And as horrible as it sounds, many times they come at a sacrifice to ethics. But it's really just another way to get at an elusive truth. Break a few rules and suddenly everything opens up. It wasn't as if I would eagerly breach a client's privilege, but there were times when it became necessary. In this case, Marquand was hardly helpful, *and* he was burning the letters. So, it seemed like a good idea to have someone on the inside. Someone who could be my eyes and ears in both households. Plus, I'll admit it, I liked Loren's breezy familiarity.

"Deal," I said, "but you can't tell anyone."

She held two fingers in the air and she said, "Scout's honor."

Someone put money in the jukebox and Evelyn Knight came on singing *A Little Bird Told Me*. After the *Dooo ooo ooo* intro Loren sang along rocking her head back and forth:

A little bird told me that you love me
And I believe that you do
This little bird told me I was fallin'
Fallin' for no one but you

I couldn't help but laugh and she stopped singing to join me.

"So? What's your big secret?" she said.

"I'm a private detective. The Colonel hired me to look into some letters he's been receiving."

Loren had just taken a huge bite from her sandwich and looked about to choke. "What?" she said with her mouth full. "A Princeton man is a private detective!"

CHAPTER 6

I woke up screaming to the same nightmare I'd had a hundred times. The cockpit is filling with smoke and I need to get out of the aircraft. In reality, even with my bloodied shoulder and immobile left arm I was able to go through all the steps for bailing out, slide open the canopy and leave the airplane. But in the nightmare, both arms are covered in blood and no matter how hard I try, I cannot move a single muscle. I squirm and fight. I try desperately to inch a hand towards the release for the harness but my arms seem to weigh a thousand pounds. And even if I could get to the harness, how would I ever be able to disconnect the radio cord and oxygen tube, let alone reach the canopy release lever? It's then, through the thickening smoke, that I clearly see the hands on the altimeter spinning wildly. I am plunging to earth. I wrestle harder against whatever is holding me. I kick frantically at the rudder pedals. The aircraft tosses then rolls over. I can see the ground approaching fast. At first I can only make out rooftops and trees, then I begin to discern other things; a long white fence, cows in a field and finally a person. As the figure comes into focus and I see it's a woman. A young woman with dark hair. She is smiling as she looks up at me but her expression changes to confusion and then there's terror in her eyes. She realizes I am about to crash on top of her. It's always that moment when I begin screaming.

I pulled myself up into a sitting position, the movement sending a shock of piercing pain through my shoulder and up the side of my neck. I breathed into the pain a minute, letting it subside before throwing off the blanket and swinging my feet to the floor. My watch said it was a little after four a.m. My undershirt was drenched in sweat so I pulled it off and wandered into the kitchen to have a glass of water. Then I went ahead and started a pot of coffee. When it was ready I poured a cup and went to fill the tub. I put Oscar on the closed toilet lid and climbed in. He looked sleepy in his bowl, barely moving, but I liked to imagine he was happy to keep me company.

For some time I soaked while massaging the ache in my shoulder. After a while my mind began to drift. Soon it made its way to Loren and the *Little Bird Told Me* song, her head rocking back and forth as she sang. What an iniquitous little smile and such brooding eyes. I thought about what it would be like if she suddenly bit me with those menacing little canines. I let my hand wander to my arousal and imagined it was Loren taking me, light and gentle and then firm—her skin against mine, building a wave of pleasure. After a few minutes I was satisfied and relaxed, and Oscar didn't look like he'd seen anything too shocking.

At the office I devoted the morning to catching up with paperwork and paying bills. Then I walked a block to a bookstore and browsed the aisles for two hours before selecting a Michener about the navy in the South Pacific. I was reading it on the office couch when the outer door buzzed.

I opened the inner door to find a bulgy-eyed fellow sitting in the chair behind the receptionist's desk.

"Can I help you?" I asked.

He stood as if powered by a battery on its final pulse of energy. "Sorry. I didn't think anyone was here. So, I was going to wait."

"That's fine. I was just surprised to see you there instead of in one of those," I said, pointing to the three chairs for waiting.

"I hope you don't mind. I wanted to see what it was like. Here. Behind the desk. It didn't seem like it was anyone's in particular."

"Do you need a detective?"

"I think I do." His hand came away from his side, powered by the same dying battery. The joints on his thin fingers were swollen; the tips curved and lifeless as if they belonged to the hand of a corpse. I took it in mine and found it surprisingly warm.

"Steven Vincent," he said.

"Harry Thorpe."

"Is there something I can help you with, Mr. Vincent?"

He blinked at me. "I hope so."

"Why don't you come in and tell me about it."

"That would be great!"

He followed me into the inner office.

"Can I take your coat and hat?"

"No," he said, examining the hat in his hand.

I gave one of the chairs in front of the desk a little pat and asked him to take a seat. He took a full three seconds to lower himself. Once he did he turned his head and looked at the little sink. "This is really nice!"

I took a cigarette from the engraved box on the desk and lit it. "What is it that I can help you with?"

He blinked at me. "Can I get one of those?"

"Sure." I pushed the box at him and tossed the box of matches across the desk.

He put a cigarette to his lips and used the corpse fingers to light it. Exhaling he held the cigarette in front of his blinking bug eyes. "Those are good! What kind are they?"

"Lucky Strike."

"Really good!"

"What can I do for you Mr. Vincent?"

He took another couple drags and flicked the tip in the plastic ashtray I'd pushed toward him. "It's the newspaper. Someone takes my newspaper."

"Yes…?"

"I come home and it's gone."

"Please try to be specific."

"Yes, you probably want specifics. Don't you. Let me think…" He put the cigarette to his mouth and closed his eyes. He sat for a full minute, taking slow drags on the cigarette and exhaling through his nose as the ash grew.

Finally I said, "Maybe you should just give me an overview. I'm plenty quick on my feet, so I'll just ask for details if I need them along the way."

He opened his eyes and took the cigarette from his mouth. "That's a good idea!" he said.

"Just an overview, okay? Keep it short and simple."

He knocked the ash off in the ashtray with a finger; the nail a crusty bone tip. "Well…I work in the early mornings. And when I get home I like to read the paper. And it's not there. I know it should be because I pay the boy. When he comes around. He says he brings it. And...my neighbor says he gets his. His paper, I mean. But I don't."

I was dying to know what the hell he did for a living but I wasn't going to distract him now that we were on a roll. "You get the Rocky Mountain News then. Not the Post?"

"The Denver Post gets delivered in the afternoon," he said, exhaling smoke.

"Yes. I know that. I was just saying that you get the News." I grabbed the ashtray, crushed out my cigarette and pushed it back at him. "So you want me to figure out what happens to your paper. Right?"

"That's right!" he said, blinking at me.

"Do you get the paper every day?"

"Only on weekends."

"Oh. So the paper is missing on weekend mornings?"

"No. I get it on weekends."

"Hold on. I think we're getting confused. What days do you pay to have the paper delivered?"

"Every day," he said, inspecting the cigarette again.

"And it's missing on weekday mornings but not on weekends."

"That's right!"

"Is it missing every weekday morning?"

He looked at me and blinked three times. "Not Saturday and Sunday."

"Yeah, I thought we'd figured that part out. But it's missing every morning that isn't Saturday and Sunday?"

"Last Monday it was there. But then not again the other days. Except Saturday and Sunday. It was there then."

"How long has this been going on?"

"So far...since Monday again."

I used all the power in my body to keep from screaming.

"I got a deal for you. I'll take the case. I'll figure out who's taking your paper and make sure they stop." I pushed a pad of paper and pencil at him. "Just write down your address for me. Okay, Mr. Vincent?"

He stubbed out the cigarette. "How much will it cost? You getting them to stop taking it."

"No charge. I'll do it for free. Just write down your address, okay?"

His bug eyes widened to the point I thought they'd pop out. "That's cheap!"

"Yeah, well, we run a special here sometimes and people get things for free. You came in at just the right moment. But don't think it can happen again, okay? You can't get another freebie. Ever again. The next time I've got to charge you a hundred bucks just for the consultation. So I'd suggest you write down your address and count your lucky stars that you came in today, Mr. Vincent."

"That's great! Can I have another one of those," he said, pointing a finger at the cigarette box.

"Take a couple. Take three. And keep the matches."

He dug three out and put them and the matches in his shirt pocket.

"Now write down your address," I said.

He took the pencil in hand and wrote for an eternity. When he finished I jumped to my feet, ran around the desk and thrust my hand at him. "Great! We're all set then! Before the week is out you should be getting your paper."

He took my hand and I pulled him up out of the chair.

"No more worries, Mr. Vincent. Your lucky day."

"I've never been lucky at anything."

"You are today, my friend!" I spun him around and propelled him towards the door. "But don't tell anyone. Especially your friends! I mean, you can tell them you won this free service, but please, don't mention my name. It really pisses off the other detectives that I do this sort of thing. So I don't need it getting around. You understand. Right, Mr. Vincent?"

He blinked at me.

I opened the outer door. "Well, thanks for coming by. But remember, it's a hundred bucks, just to stop in to chat next time. So keep that in mind. And don't worry about the paper. I'll have that problem taken care of before the week is out. Have a great day, Mr. Vincent."

The phone started ringing just as I was giving him a smile and wave and closing the door. He waved back weakly still muttering, "Never. I've never been lucky with anything."

I dashed back into the office and snatched the receiver. "Thorpe. Private Detective."

"So abrupt! That can't possibly be good for business," the

female voice on the other end said.

"I'm sorry. Can I help you?"

"Maybe. Or maybe I can help you."

I sighed audibly. "Oh no! Not interested."

"Manners, boy!" she admonished.

"Loren?"

"You really need to work on your telephone etiquette."

"You wouldn't believe what just happened here," I said.

"The detective business got you all worn out?"

"Please! Don't start with me. You haven't worked a day in your life."

"So who's smarter? Me or you?"

"You, obviously," I said. "Did you call just to harass me? Or is there something more to this?"

"I'd like to talk to you," she said.

"Isn't that what we're doing?"

"No silly, in person. I have an idea."

"Did you want to come here? I could give you the nickel tour, then you can really make fun of me."

"No. I want you to meet me at the library?" she said.

"The library?"

"Richard, the chauffeur dropped me off. I come here all the time, so it's a safe place for us to meet on the sly." The last part she said with an exaggerated conspiratorial tone. "He's coming back to get me at five."

I looked at my watch. It was almost four. "The main library in Civic Center Park?"

"Yes. I'll be in mysteries on the second floor," she whispered.

"Mysteries…that sounds about right. I'll be right there."

"Toodles!" she said and clicked off.

I threw on my coat and hat and locked up. I skipped the elevator and took the stairs then headed off up 16th Street. Loren was in mysteries just as she said. She was wearing a long sleeve black blouse and high-waisted brown skirt with a leopard print pillbox perched on the back of her head. When she saw me she motioned that I follow. I brought along the matching leopard coat she'd draped over a chair. Even in heels she was tiny. We found two easy chairs against some windows overlooking the park.

"So, you come here a lot?"

"What else does a Bryn Mawr girl have to do? Actually, I do like mysteries. Agatha Christie is a wonderful way to spend an afternoon."

"Hercule Poirot or Miss Marple?" I asked.

"Definitely Hercule Poirot."

"Ditto."

She crossed her legs and let her shoe slide off a heel, dangling from her toes. For a minute I took her in, from her stockinged leg upward. She was everything I like to look at, slim and confident and put together like she'd been poured from a martini shaker and dotted with a red pimentoed olive. She was sex the way you like it to be, in the afternoon with a cigarette and ceiling fan turning the air just enough to cool the sweat on your body.

"What do you think? Cute outfit?" she said, looking down at her skirt and touching the fabric with her fingertips.

"Oh, it's cute alright," I said.

"You're looking at me like you don't like it."

"I like it. Very much," I said. A coquettish smile returned to her face and she bobbed her foot making the shoe swing. I looked at her again and then finally mustered: "Maybe you should just tell me about these ideas you have."

"I was thinking—we're going to the Morrison house this weekend. I could look around for anything suspicious and report back to you. I could be your eyes and ears on the inside."

"Mmmm, I don't know, Mata Hari" I said. "Maybe it's not such a good idea for you to get *that* involved."

"I could keep an eye on the staff and see if anyone acts suspiciously. You said yourself it could be an inside job."

"Who all is going?"

"Louise, the baby and myself go up Friday and stay through Sunday. Christian usually comes up in the evenings."

"Why's he only up there in the evenings?" I asked, taking out my cigarettes.

She held out her hand for one. "The Morrison house is much smaller and the baby can be quite fussy. Christian says he needs the quiet to work," she said with exaggerated annoyance.

I lit hers, then mine and put the pack in my pocket. "More contempt, I see."

"Gosh, did I really sound like that?"

I shook my head and chuckled. "You're something. And…you never did tell me why you have such a beef with him."

She spent a minute examining her cigarette. Eventually she said, "We clash. We're completely different personalities. It's all fine so long as you don't upset the emperor and his ways. But I'm not the kind of girl who gives a damn about his ways. And I sure as hell will not kowtow to his whims." She took a long drag from the cigarette and exhaled through her nose. "That's my *beef*," she said.

"Okay. I can relate to that. Now, what's with the whole frail thing? What's that about?"

She took a piece of tobacco off her lip and flicked it away. Her eyes came up to mine.

They were dark and cold and so sexy at the same time. "I have a heart condition," she said.

"I'm sorry..."

"Don't be. It's what it is. If there's one thing I hate, it's everyone—quote, unquote—protecting me from everything that's be bad for me. I won't tolerate it. Okay?"

"Of course," I said.

Her foot stopped bouncing and she stared at me. She swung her hand out over the arm of the chair and tapped her cigarette one, two times with a slender finger, the nail short and shaped with polish so red it was almost black. Her eyes moved down off my face, across my suit, to my shoes. When her eyes again met mine she tilted her head slightly and put the cigarette to her lips. "So..." she said.

I waited for her to continue.

"What should I look for in Morrison?"

"Just keep your eyes open to anything out of the ordinary."

"Do you need to deputize me?"

"You know I should."

"I'll report back everything I see," she said, dropping her cigarette to the floor, uncrossing her legs and stepping on it.

"You should have told your driver to pick you up over at the Congress bar," I said.

"Are you needing a drink?"

"I think so," I said.

"What if I need you after hours," she asked. "What if something happens or I find out Bertie has a hand grenade stashed in with the potatoes?"

I took out a business card and wrote my home number on the back. "Call me," I said. She unsnapped her purse and dropped it in.

We sat motionless for a few moments.

"Richard's very punctual and he gets nasty if he has to circle the block."

We stood and I helped her on with the leopard coat. She offered her hand, this time without a glove. It was the first time I'd touched her flesh.

"Talk to you soon, chief," she said. I watched her walk to the elevators. At the window I could see her on the sidewalk. A few moments later a spotless Cadillac pulled to the curb and she got in.

I walked over to Bendemann and Sons on 17th and bought three new suits. Then I got that drink.

CHAPTER 7

After casing the neighborhood with a couple passes I parked two doors down from Steven Vincent's house. At that location I could keep an eye on his yard through the windshield and watch for someone coming up the block in the mirror. The circulation desk at the *News* told me delivery times for the area should be between five and five-thirty. My watch said it was 4:45. However unlikely it was that someone was stealing the paper that early, I still wanted to be there before it was dropped. Just in case.

For being such a strange fellow Vincent's house looked perfectly normal. It was a red brick bungalow with clean white trim, lace curtains and a milk box on the porch. Most of the other houses had a low-lying wall right at sidewalk level but the slope disappeared when it got to Vincent's property. His lot was on a flat, wide corner and would be an easy target for a lazy thief. All they had to do was cut across the lawn to shave the corner and scoop up the paper in the process. A block away and they'd be on the streetcar.

I left the car running so I'd have some heat but the fan didn't work like it used to. It was a good thing I wore wool socks and brought a Thermos of coffee. I spun off the top and poured into the little cup that also served as the cap.

At around ten after five the delivery boy showed up on his bike, loaded down with two full canvas slings. I could see his breath puffing in the cold, and when he got closer I saw there was steam rising from his winter cap. Standing on the pedals he weaved his way down the street flinging papers. After he'd tossed one onto Vincent's snow-patched grass he crossed over to the next block, doing the same and then disappearing around a corner.

I waited another ten minutes before shutting off the engine. It wasn't long before it felt as if I'd opened a window instead. I tried kicking my feet together and slapping my gloved hands to keep blood moving but it didn't help much. I wanted more coffee but I knew that would only make me need to piss, so I put the Thermos away.

After a while a car came down the street and slowed. I never imagined the thief being someone who'd make their move on Vincent's paper from a car, but I'd learn to give up on assumptions long ago. I pulled a sap out of the glove box and slid down in the seat. The driver swung in to the curb and gave the horn two quick honks. A minute later a little guy with a blue windbreaker over a long white apron came out to get into the car.

Similar scenes played out over the next hour with people passing by on their way to the streetcar stop, some carrying papers they'd picked up, presumably from their own yards. But no one went near Vincent's house. As I figured, the urge to piss was coming on strong and my toes were nearly frozen solid. I gave them a wiggle, but it was useless. They were numb. I was just about to call it a day when I saw a man in the mirror on the other block. My watch said it was 7:11. Maybe it was my lucky day after all.

I slumped low when he crossed the intersection to Vincent's block and waited for him to pass while peering over the back of the seat. He was wearing a long camel overcoat, a matching narrow brimmed hat and carried a briefcase. As he reached Vincent's yard his head shot back and forth and he quickened his pace. Two more times he looked up and down the street, then without breaking stride he cut across the grass, snagged the paper and disappeared around the corner.

I pulled off my gloves and hit the starter. As soon as the engine roared to life I let the clutch fly. The Dodge bolted from the curb. I cranked the wheel and slid around the corner. The man was quickly approaching the alleyway with the paper tucked under his arm. I stomped the gas and raced to a point just in front of him, bounced the curb and slammed on the brakes directly in his path, almost sliding into a chain link fence. Jumping from the driver's side I ran around the back of the Dodge and trapped him between the car and the fence. His first reaction was wide-eyed surprise—then quick-as-a-wink he lowered his head and shoulders, preparing to run.

"Hold it," I yelled, readying myself for a tackle. "Where are you going with my goddamned newspaper?"

His eyes shot to where it had dropped on the sidewalk.

I held out the sap so he would clearly see it. "*I said*–Where are you going with my goddamned newspaper?"

He let go of the briefcase and put his hands in the air as if I were a stickup.

"Do you pay for that paper?" I continued. "No! I pay for the fucking thing. And you think you can come along and take it…"

"It won't…happen…," he said, straightening up, his hands moving even higher. He appeared to be in his forties, with a flabby face and chin tucked right into his shirt collar.

"You're lucky I don't crack your goddamned head with this thing."

"I can pay…for the others…"

"I don't need your money! I just want my paper left alone. Do you get that, asshole? Or do I need to tap out some Morse code on your fucking cranium?" I said, swinging the sap in his direction.

"I get it," he said.

"Do you?"

"I get it!"

"I better not even see you walking down my block ever again. Got it?"

"Yes, I get it, please!" he said. "It won't happen again."

"Okay. Put your arms down," I told him, seeing a car coming down the street.

He lowered them cautiously, his eyes making roundtrips between my face and the sap.

I took the paper, got in the Dodge and backed off the grass, leaving him standing there. I circled around to the front of Vincent's house and dropped the paper on his porch. As I drove off towards the office I laughed so hard I almost pissed myself.

CHAPTER 8

We were halfway through the second set at Cyril's when I saw Loren at a table towards the back of the house. She was alone, sipping a drink and lightly swaying with the music. It was a couple minutes before our eyes met. I flashed her a worried expression but she shook her head and waved. When we took our break I went right over.

"You guys are really good!" she said. "I like your sound a lot."

"Is everything okay?"

She smiled and blinked her eyes. "Great. Why?"

"I thought something might have happened."

She waved her gloved hand, "No. This is strictly a social call."

"So nothing was out of the ordinary in Morrison?"

"No. I wanted to hear you play." She leaned closer and whispered, "For a white boy, you have some *blues* in you."

I laughed. "I'll take that as a compliment," I said.

Carlotta came by and I ordered another Old Fashion for Loren and a bourbon for myself. Loren asked me about the guys in the band, so I told her what I knew about each and how we came together. Just as I was finishing, Ronnie approached, wearing his coat and hat.

"Hey Fuzzy, are you..." he tilted his head towards the alley.

"I'm good," I said. "Ronnie, meet Loren."

"Hello, Miss Loren," he said, taking her hand and bowing slightly.

"I enjoyed your set very much," she said. "You play very well."

"Thank you, ma'am."

"Loren plays the piano," I said.

"Nothing like you," she said to Ronnie.

"Aww, you're way too kind, Miss Loren. And mighty pretty too." Then to me he said, "You better not let that one get away."

"Go on!" I said. "I'll catch up with you onstage."

Ronnie winked at Loren and went away laughing.

"He seems like a character," she said.

"He is."

"Did he call you Fuzzy?" Loren asked.

"Yeah. Because my name is Harry."

"Oh. That's funny. Maybe I should start calling you Fuzzy."

"Please don't."

"Where's he going? Aren't you playing another set?"

I told her we step outside between sets for a smoke.

"Everyone in here is smoking," she said.

"I don't know. It's a silly thing we do. Fresh air and a smoke."

"Reefer?" she said, giving me a sideways look.

"They're musicians."

"And you too?"

"It's not a big deal," I said.

Her expression made me feel otherwise, but I let it go.

When we finished the third set, and after I had the bass zipped into its case, I offered to give her a ride home.

"I'm in no hurry," she said, following me out to the Dodge. "How about you give me the Fuzzy Thorpe tour of Denver's seedy underbelly? Surely, you've worked some exciting cases around here."

"Wow," I laughed. "You really have no idea what it's like being a detective." I drove up Larimer pointing out a few places where I'd done some casework. "On the right is the world-renowned Griffin Hotel. One of the city's finest flop houses," I said, affecting the tone of a sophisticated tour guide. "A fine establishment for those who prefer the companionship of a lady with plenty of experience. The famous detective Harold Thorpe III solved the case of the missing toilet paper after staying two nights in room 429 by assiduously surveilling the premises and, as they say, the *goings-on*."

"No! You're a Harold the Third?" Loren shrieked.

"With regret, I admit I am. And on the left is…"

"Wait! I want to hear more about the case of the missing toilet paper."

I told her about the guy in 214 who would sneak around in the middle of the night, gathering all the supplies from the hall baths so he could sell them to another flop house down the street at a discounted rate.

"What did he say when you caught him?" she asked.

"I didn't confront him. I was just there to figure out what was happening to all the supplies. The hotel called the cops. When they went in his room everything was there. Dumb bastard's probably doing 3 years now for stealing shit paper."

"I don't know if that was dumb or kind of clever," she said.

"It's always dumb if you get caught," I said pulling up in front of my house. "No pressure, but would you like come in for a drink?"

"Is this where you live?"

"Chez Thorpe," I said, pointing to one side of a duplex. "Final stop of the Fuzzy Thorpe tour."

"Then, of course. How could I skip seeing where the famous detective lives?"

Inside, she immediately gravitated to Oscar in his bowl. "You have a fish. What's his name?"

I told her and she bent down and tapped the bowl with a finger calling out his name in a high-pitched voice. Oscar was nonplussed, as usual.

"I don't think he likes me," she said.

"Are you kidding? Look at him smile."

She looked again, then laughed at herself for doing so.

I poured drinks and cleaned up a little while she went in to powder her nose as she put it. When she came out she tossed her purse with her coat. Then surveying the room she said, "Cozy."

"Oh yes, very cozy. And so much easier than all the maintenance that went into the pool and stables at my old place."

She gave me a look that suggested I wasn't all that funny. Then she turned to my bookcase and ran a hand across the bindings, her ruffled black dress making a swishing sound as she moved. On one shoulder was a row of tiny silver buttons and around her waist a thin silver belt. Her hair was swept back and her ears bare, the only jewelry a silver bracelet on one wrist as wide as a piece of wire. "I thought I was a voracious reader," she said. "...oh, you have

Murder on the Orient Express. That's my favorite Agatha Christie."

"That's probably my favorite, as well. Although the Ackroyd book is really good too."

"Which?" she sniffled, her hand going to her nose.

"*The Murder of Roger Ackroyd*."

"I don't think I've read that one," she said, looking at me.

She moved to the other bookcase and began scanning titles. She pulled down a leather-bound anthology and begun flipping through it. "You're Thoreau is all dog eared."

"I mark the things I like."

She sniffled again so I took out my handkerchief and offered it to her.

"No, it's okay," she said. "It must be the trees."

"The trees that don't have any leaves." I stated, putting the handkerchief away.

She returned the book to the shelf and took a seat on the couch next to me. "Maybe I'm allergic to cigarette smoke." She made a face I knew was supposed to be Marquand, with her chin elongated and her lips pursed, then faked a coughing spasm and waved the air.

I laughed.

She sniffled and touched her nose again with her finger and thumb. "I don't know what got me. Maybe I'm allergic to detectives."

"Most people are."

"How long have you lived here?"

"A couple years."

"It's a twin home?"

"Yes. But, here they call them duplexes," I said.

"Isn't a duplex a two-story apartment?"

"That's New York talk. For some reason they call them duplexes here," I said, crushing out my cigarette.

"Either way, it's cute," she said.

"Cute! Is that better or worse than cozy?"

She took a cigarette from my pack on the table and suddenly jumped to her feet. "Oh! I forgot! I have something for you." From her purse she took a small box. Inside was a silver Zippo lighter, my name engraved on the back in block letters.

"What's this?" I said.

"That thing you do with the matches made *my* thumb hurt," she

51

said. "Of course, I didn't know you were a Harold the Third."

"I would have refused it if you'd put that on it." I snapped it open and lit her cigarette. She blew smoke through lips shaped for a kiss. "Thanks!"

As I was admiring the lighter she said, "I hope that isn't going to upset your little act."

"What act?"

"Your whole down-and-out thing."

"Where did that come from? Because I made a joke about stables?"

"The whole act you have going; stick matches, ratty old coat, scuffed shoes. It really doesn't suit you."

"I don't even know what that means," I said, thinking her eyes were made up so heavy it was almost as if she'd been punched.

"Don't be so smug. I know your background. You're no different than me."

"Is that right?"

"Andover? Please! And look at your book collection. Who are you trying to fool?"

"Drink your drink," I said uncrossing my legs and sitting forward to finish my bourbon. She raised her glass to her mouth, took a long drink and returned it to the table, her tongue darting out to lick her lips. I took the cigarette from her hand and flicked it into the fireplace across the room. Then I pulled her close. She slid into my arms and our lips met. Hers were warm and wet and so timid at first. She was so small in my arms and yet almost dangerous, like a wild creature I could trust to be only temporarily tamed. After a minute I took her hand and she followed me into the bedroom. The light from the streetlamp lit it with shadows from the curtains and trees. I sat on the bed and she moved between my legs, putting both hands on the side of my neck. She kissed me for a long time before pulling away to unfasten the row of buttons at her shoulder. Her hair had come loose, partially hiding her face and eyes. When her dress and slip both fell away I saw she wasn't wearing a bra and her figure was long and subtle like a girl of youth. I placed my hands on her firm waist, then moved them up to her small perfect breasts. She pushed me back on the bed and climbed on top of me.

Afterward I lay on my side for a long time watching her. She seemed to be following the shadows of the trees moving on the ceiling, the makeup around her eyes smeared in a sad way. Rhythmically she blinked with the rising and falling of her chest as she took short, steady breaths. A thin line of sweat shone on her forehead and upper lip. Finally, I reached over and took some hair off her face.

"I guess that clears up the rumor that Bryn Mawr girls are all lesbians," I said.

"Some are eventually converted. Others just fake it." She lay still for a few minutes again before saying, "Do you like it here?"

"Are we starting the down-and-out thing again?"

"No," she said. "It seems like it would be nice. I'm serious."

"In the summer I like to sit on the porch and read. You can hear the music and the roller coaster at Elitch's," I said, referring to the amusement park three blocks away.

"I haven't ridden the rides since I was a girl."

We laid in silence for some time and then I said, "You're very beautiful."

"Stop," she said, turning away.

"You are." I pulled her back.

"I'm skinny and crazy and have these ridiculous canines," she said touching her teeth with two fingers. "And you know I have a bird heart. I'm frail."

"I don't care."

"And, I have to be honest, I hate Thoreau," she said. "And I snore. Especially when I've been smoking too much. And I can't drive worth a damn."

I laughed.

"Do you think we should be worried about those letters?" she asked.

"No," I said. "It's probably some nut. Famous people always get hate mail at some point. Politicians too. Your father probably got crackpot letters from time to time."

"Yeah, I guess so."

We lay quiet again until she said, "I was just kidding about some of those things I said a minute ago."

"What? That you snore and hate Thoreau?"

"Yes."

"Don't tell me which. I'd rather keep guessing."

"You're going to have to call me a cab pretty soon."

"Where do they think you are right now?" I asked.

"Having sex with you, of course!"

"Of course."

"Who cares. They think I am running naked through the neighborhood talking to myself."

"Hmmm, I might like to see that."

"I really do need to get going."

"If you lay here a few more minutes with me I'll personally take you in a down-and-out '36 Dodge."

She rolled to her side away from me. "Come close," she said. I curled in with her, my arms around her. She tucked her knees up and reached back pulling me to her.

CHAPTER 9

Over the next week I thought a lot about Loren Chambers. Mostly I replayed the images of her in my bed and no matter how hard I tried, I couldn't shake the idea that I wanted to see her again. Not just see her but hold her and touch her and know what she kept behind her steely protective layer. I was slumped on the couch in the office bouncing these sorts of thoughts around in my head when the outer door buzzed. When I went out the room was empty except for a paper bag on the receptionist desk. Inside were two cartons of Lucky Strikes. No note.

I opened the hall door and standing there was Steven Vincent.

"Hi, Mr. Thorpe."

"Mr. Vincent! What are you doing?"

"I wanted to thank you." He held out his skeleton hand and seeing no alternative I shook it.

"You've been getting your paper okay?"

"That's right!" he said blinking at me.

"Well, why are you out here in the hallway? Come in."

"No! I remember what you said. About the hundred dollars if I came back."

I looked into his bug eyes and felt sorry I'd said that. "Thanks for the cigarettes," I said.

"They're really good. I never tried that brand before." He dug in his coat pocket and pulled out a Lucky Strike pack. "See, I got my own now."

"L.S.M.F.T." I said.

"What?"

"It's on the bottom of the pack. Lucky Strike Makes Fine Tobacco."

He turned his pack upside down to look and two cigarettes fell out onto the floor. "Whoops," he said beginning to bend over in his dying battery way. I reached down and got them for him. "You can keep those if you want. I owe you," he said straightening up.

"I've two cartons," I said. "Thanks to you."

He tried again looking at the bottom of the pack and this time did so without losing any. "L.S.M.F.T. Sure enough." He brought his bug eyes back to my face, "They're right!"

"Thanks for the cigarettes, Mr. Vincent," I said, holding up the two singles from the floor. "All of them."

"Thank you, Mr. Thorpe. And don't worry. I didn't tell any of my friends about you. Just as you said." He held out his hand and I shook it again. He turned and started down the hall, one foot in front of the other like a crank-up robot trying to make its way across heavy carpet. When he reached the elevator, I gave him a little wave.

I laid around the office for another hour or two. The rain was drumming against the windows in a pleasant sort of meditative way and it was nice to doze to the sound. When I got up to leave my shoulder was aching from all the inactivity so I thought I'd go for a drink. I drove on over to Billy's Inn, a little white stucco bar modeled after a Mexican hacienda only without the courtyard and minus the Mexican décor. Billy and his wife Judy opened the place sometime after the repeal of prohibition and it became a regular hangout for northsiders, partly because it was stumbling distance for many, but mostly for Billy's breezy personality and fair pours.

"There he is! Mr. Harry Thorpe. Old Grand-dad and rocks?"

"You know it, Billy."

He tossed a couple cubes in a glass, placed it before me on a paper napkin and free-poured from the bottle. We talked about the rain and the coming spring and with every sip the Old Grand-dad warmed my throat and stomach and slowly numbed the throb in my shoulder. When Billy went in the kitchen to order my food I took out a paperback copy of Paton's *Cry, the Beloved Country*. I continued from my last dog-ear, right at the point when Jarvis learns of his son's death.

After a while someone put money into the jukebox. An older couple I'd seen several times before got up to dance in the tight space between the bar and the pool table. The woman's hair whirled as they executed perfect turns and twirls.

"What you reading this time?" Billy asked as he set down my hamburger and fried potatoes.

I held it up for him to see.

Shrugging he said, "Never heard of it. Any good?" I told him it was and he buzzed off to tap beers for a couple mailmen in uniform we all knew by name.

I ate my food and watched the older couple dance. When they stopped everyone clapped. They took little bows. A man sitting near them paid for their next round. The jukebox kept playing and another couple got up but they didn't quite make it through an entire song. They kept bumping into the pool table. *A Little Bird Told Me* came on just as I was finishing my next drink. I imagined Loren singing it, her head rocking back and forth. I caught Billy's eye for another. A little later a man sat next to me and talked about his in-laws visiting from out of town. Then a wave of people came and went buying one, two three cocktails, some stayed even longer. I was a bit wobbly on my feet going out to the car. When I got home I hauled the bass in with me and put jazz on the radio, poured another drink and jumped in with Sidney Bechet & His Feetwarmers. They were playing *Baby Won't You Please Come Home.*

CHAPTER 10

Eventually I couldn't take the ringing any longer and pulled myself off the couch to stumble into the kitchen to answer the wall phone. Victor was on the line. I made him repeat himself a couple times. His words slammed into my skull, like hammer blows. Marquand's kid had been *taken*.

"What do you mean?" I said.

"Someone used a ladder and took him from his room. He's gone, Mr. Thorpe! The Colonel, he says you gotta come quick!"

I scribbled directions to Morrison on a scrap of paper and rushed to pull on my shoes and coat. It took nearly an hour to get to the curvy climb that started after I passed the entrance to Red Rocks Amphitheater. I was beginning to think I'd missed the turn when I spotted the Grapevine Road sign. I followed the right forks and soon the road turned to dirt. Finally I edged over a rise and there was the house, lit up with lights and spinning red strobes. I don't know why I expected it to be a little mountain cabin. No, it was much more like a full-blown English country home with decorative half-timbering and peaked roofing.

I had to show my P.I. license to a uniform in a car with door-mounted spotlights to get onto the property. He let me pass after radioing someone and verifying that I worked for Marquand.

The yard was ablaze with headlights, cars on and off the grass. I parked on a slope and found Marquand standing with a group of cops in both suits and uniforms. They were discussing what looked to be a crudely constructed ladder lying in three pieces in the wet grass.

"And you moved the ladder up from the tree line?" a short cop in civilian clothes was asking Marquand.

"I didn't personally move it."

"Who moved it?"

"Victor, he's the butler," Marquand said, pointing at the negro, who was tuxedoed just as I had seen him before. "And one of the Morrison policemen. I don't know which one he was. Victor, do you know which one helped you with the ladder?"

"Yes, Colonel." Victor said. "He's over there." He pointed at two uniforms standing on the porch. Just as he did so the two cops turned and began to go into the house.

Marquand yelled, "You there! Stop! Stay out of the house!" Marquand spun on the short man: "I told you I don't want anyone in the house until the man who checks for fingerprints arrives."

The short cop waved his arms and called for them to stay out of the house. To Marquand he said, "Eventually though, we're going to need to take photographs and conduct interviews. But we'll wait until the print man gets here."

"Interviews! Who are you planning to interview?"

"We need to speak to everyone who was at the house tonight."

"You're not going to interrogate my wife. Her son is *missing*, Detective! Do you think putting her through that is going to yield something? And for God's sake, my wife has known Victor since she was a girl! Do you honestly think I'm going to let you interrogate that man?"

"It's all normal procedure, Colonel," a fat man with a neck of jelly said. "We aren't going to *interrogate* anyone. We just need to ask questions."

"We need to do whatever we can to reconstruct exactly what happened, what people heard and saw," the short cop said.

"Absolutely not!" Marquand barked. "If you have questions, ask me. I was here tonight. But I won't allow you to treat my wife and staff as if they're somehow complicit in this. I'm not pleased with how this is being handled at all. My son is missing and all we're doing is standing around wasting time. Who's in charge here?"

"That would be me, sir," the short cop said.

"And you are?"

"Lieutenant Greenberg. State Patrol."

"Greenberg, huh. I'm going to want to speak to your superior,"

Marquand said. Seeing me, he pushed through the group and took my arm. We walked off across the grass and out of the glow of the headlights. He reached in his pocket and handed me a white envelope.

"Take it and don't let anyone have it," he said.

"What is it?"

"The ransom note."

"You haven't shown it to them?"

He pushed my arm holding the note down and glanced back at the cops. "Put it away."

"Jesus, Colonel, I can't take that! It's evidence." I tried to give it back but he nudged my arm down again.

"Put it in your pocket! If we give them the note it'll become a Federal case. Do you see how inept these men are, Thorpe? Can you imagine if we let the feds take over?"

"Why did you call the cops if you don't want them to investigate this?"

Marquand stared at me for a moment and finally said, "I wasn't thinking clearly. How *could* I be? But now I realize we need to make sure this stays a missing person investigation so we can pay the ransom and get Christian back."

He might have been making sense, but I was flying on adrenaline and all those drinks at Billy's. I looked down at the note in my hand.

"Come on, Thorpe. Don't go stupid on me," he said, leaning into me. "The only chance we have is paying the ransom. Do you think I give a shit about their procedures? I want my son back. And these idiots will only put that in jeopardy. We can worry about who did it after, but right now we need to keep this to ourselves and get my boy back."

I slipped the envelope in my pocket. Marquand squeezed my shoulder before going back to the group.

A photographer had started taking pictures of the ladder on the ground, the flash popping and lighting the yard. I watched him for a while as he moved from the ladder to the flower beds around the base of the house. Eventually I was able to catch Victor's attention and motioned him aside. He looked cold without an overcoat and his eyes were bugged out with all the commotion.

"I don't really know, Mr. Thorpe. All of a sudden everyone was running around looking for the child and the Colonel got his rifle and we ran outside. I didn't know what was going on. I thought maybe Christian got out of the house. I was thinking everyone was scared because a mountain lion might be out there or something. But the Colonel said someone took him and told me to call the police. And after that I ran outside and the Colonel was coming up from the tree line down over there saying he'd found a ladder." He'd stopped to breathe before continuing with, "Oh, Lordy! Then I don't know what happened. I think the Colonel told me to get the flashlight. But when I did the batteries were dead. So the Colonel told me to take the jeep into town to buy some—but I don't drive at night, Mr. Thorpe. And where was I gonna get batteries at this time of night? Thank Jesus the Morrison police came before I had to do that. They went down with the Colonel to the trees and saw the ladder. That's when me and one of the police carried it up here. And the Colonel showed them the nursery and the open window."

"Who discovered that Christian was missing?" I asked.

"I think it was Joanna."

"Who's Joanna?" I asked, just as two more police cars with flashing lights arrived. Both pulled on to the grass and maneuvered over to where the other cars had their headlights trained at the side of the house.

"The nursemaid. Joanna is the baby's nursemaid," Victor said. "She normally stays in Denver when we come up here, but the child's been sick and fussy so Mrs. Marquand sent for her."

"And you're here on a Wednesday? Don't you usually go back to Denver on Sunday night?"

"Yes sir. But like I was saying, the child was sick and Mrs. Marquand didn't want to travel with him like that."

I thanked him and he started off to bring coffee out for the cops. He was halfway to the house when I called after him and went over. "You said you were going to have to drive to Morrison yourself. Where's the chauffeur?"

"He took Miss Chambers down yesterday and the Colonel told him to take the day off."

"Mrs. Marquand's sister?"

"Yes sir."

"Do you know why she went back to Denver?"

"No sir."

I had a hundred more questions bumping into each other in my head but I let him go and waited in the shadows thinking about

Loren returning to town. Reaching in my pocket for a cigarette I felt the ransom note. It was like touching a hot piece of coal.

I walked back over to the group. A new man I recognized named Dmytryk, the State Patrol Chief, was talking to Marquand. He sported a sliver of a grey mustache and wore one of those rain coats I hated, tied at the waist and collar flipped up.

"Don't worry, Colonel," he was saying. "I will oversee the entire investigation. I already have men preparing to search a two mile radius and we have bloodhounds on the way. When daylight comes we'll be able to search out five miles or further."

"I don't want any bloodhounds, Major," Marquand said, referring to Dmytryk's former military rank. "They'll only destroy whatever evidence is still out there."

The short cop who had identified himself earlier as Greenberg said, "It's standard procedure for something like this. It allows us to track the exact route the child may have taken."

"No bloodhounds," Marquand said facing Greenberg and speaking down on him. Then turning back to Dmytryk he said, "I won't allow it!"

"Very well, sir," Dmytryk said.

"I'm ready to do everything in the world to get my son back safely, but I'm not willing to compromise evidence that may be out there with bloodhounds or hundreds of men stomping willy-nilly through everything."

"Yes sir, I understand completely," Dmytryk said.

"Very well, Major. I'm glad that someone who actually *does* understand will be heading this up. Until you got here it seems as if I'd been running the investigation all by myself. Hell, I'm the one that discovered most of the evidence! Don't get me wrong, I'm not saying I don't want to be involved. I most certainly do. I *deserve* to be involved. It's my son! But if I see any more incompetence I'll find someone else who can do the job."

"I understand, Colonel. Completely. I guarantee, we will include you all the way," Dmytryk said.

"And I don't want anyone harassing my family or my staff. Look what they've been through tonight. Do you think it serves any purpose to harass them further right now. This man was insisting on *interrogating* my wife," Marquand said pointing to the man with the jelly neck.

"I never said anything about interrogating..."

Dmytryk held up his hand. "We won't question anyone without your knowing about it first, Colonel. I can promise you that. The next thing we'll do is get photographs taken. Out here and in the house, if that's okay with you."

"We've taken photos out here already," Greenberg said.

"Of?" Dmytryk said.

"Of the ladder, the grounds..." Greenberg said, turning to point at the ladder pieces.

Two plainclothes cops had one of the sections against the house. It looked like they were trying to get the base to line up with muddy indentions between some shrubs.

"What the fuck are you doing?" Greenberg shouted.

The two cops stopped and looked at him.

"Get away from the house!" Greenberg ordered.

"We were seeing if the ladder matched the holes," one of them said.

"Get the fuck away from the house!"

"Lieutenant!" Dmytryk said.

"How're we going to make a plaster cast of the shoe prints when those morons are standing in them?" Greenberg said to Dmytryk.

The cops stepped out of the mud and laid the ladder piece on the grass. Both looked back at the muddy spot between the shrubs.

"Jesus Fucking Christ! Are you a couple boots?" Greenberg said to them.

"Lieutenant!" Dmytryk said again more sternly.

"What?" Greenberg asked, turning back.

"It's neither here nor there," Dmytryk said. "You got photographs. Right?"

"Yes, sir. But we were going to make plaster casts of the shoe prints and indentations."

"Well, we got the photographs. That's good enough." Then Dmytryk said to Marquand, "We don't need the plaster if we got the photographs. Is this where you found the ladder, Colonel?"

"No. Down by the tree line." Marquand pointed.

"Did you get photographs of the ladder down there?" Dmytryk asked Greenberg.

"It was already up here."

"I thought you said the photographs were all taken, Lieutenant. Get the ladder back down there where it was found and take some there."

Greenberg stared at him. We all stared at him.

"I'm speaking to you," Dmytryk said to Greenberg.

I couldn't help but blurt out, "Does that make any sense?"

Everyone looked at me.

"Who is this man?" Dmytryk asked.

"He works for me," Marquand said. "He's going to be assisting with the investigation."

I took out the P.I. license and showed it to Dmytryk, then Greenberg. Neither seemed impressed.

"Thorpe, you know Major Dmytryk, don't you? He'll be heading the investigation. I want you to work with him as you see fit," Marquand said, starting one of those conversations where he volleys all by himself. "And Major, I'd like for you to include Captain Thorpe in everything you do. I think it will be extremely beneficial for us to attack this from two angles. We need your expertise and we need Thorpe's ability to pursue side leads. The kind that might not be, well, proper for the State Patrol to pursue. I have a pretty good idea of the kind of people who'd want to do this to me. And I want Thorpe to follow up on those without hindering your investigation. And vice versa, of course. It'll work best that way. Don't you agree?"

"I agree completely, Colonel," Dmytryk said, eyeing me.

I nodded when Marquand looked at me.

"Good," Marquand said as another police car with flashing lights crested the hill.

"That'll be the print man," Greenberg said.

Dmytryk turned back to him and said, "Get the ladder down to where it was found and have photographs taken there. I'm going to supervise inside. Now!"

Greenberg leaned his head in the direction of the man with the jelly neck and said, "You heard the Chief. Get the photographer and find the butler so we can figure out where the hell it was when they found it."

"Alright, L.T.," jelly neck sighed, before lumbering off. Greenberg told the two moron cops to pick up all three ladder pieces and they started off towards the trees.

"Colonel, would you like to watch the fingerprint man?" Dmytryk asked.

"I'll be right there."

Dmytryk marched off in the direction of the house. Marquand and I watched in silence. Finally he said, "See what I mean, Thorpe? There's no way these people can get my son back. It's up to   us."

CHAPTER 11

The fingerprint man had unloaded two cases and was in the process of dusting the window ledge when we entered the nursery. I was surprised at how modestly furnished it was with just a crib, dresser and rocking chair. In the corner an electric heater was buzzing, giving the room a slightly burned smell. There were windows without curtains on two walls and three doors leading out to the hall, a bathroom and a small closet. The bathroom also had its own hall door and another that connected it to the nursemaid's room.

As the print man started dusting the window frame and glass, Marquand began going through the events of the evening with Dmytryk. He said he'd been in the study directly below the nursery when Joanna came to see if he had the baby. When he said he didn't, they searched the entire house.

"I told Victor to call the police and I got my rifle and went outside." Marquand's voice sounded steady, but he actually took out a handkerchief and dabbed his eyes. "That's when I found the ladder down by the tree line," he added.

"And you moved it then?" Dmytryk said, stepping out of the way of the print man who was moving on to the furniture.

"After the first policeman arrived. I asked Victor to help him. I wanted to get it up in the light near the house. When we got it up by the house that's when the other policeman, the one with the flashlight, saw the footprint and marks in the mud by the house."

Greenberg, who'd come in when Marquand was wiping his eyes, stared at his notepad through reading glasses. He said, "Footprint. There was just the one?"

"That was all I saw," Marquand replied. "There were more by the driveway, but only one under the window."

Greenberg raised his eyes and removed his glasses. "There were more by the driveway?"

"Yes. The policeman with the flashlight saw them."

"You didn't mention any footprints near the driveway before."

"I'm *mentioning* them now. The policeman knew they were there." Marquand said without looking at Greenberg.

"Okay. Not much good that'll do now that fifty people have trampled that whole area into a bog."

"Is that necessary, Lieutenant?" Dmytryk said.

"What?" Greenberg said to Dmytryk. "We could've preserved them if we'd known they existed. We haven't been able to cast a single print tonight."

"Well go and see that they're preserved now," Dmytryk said.

"What's to preserve? Cars have driven through there…"

"Lieutenant, I'm not telling you again. Go preserve what's left of the footprints. And you and I are going to have a talk later."

Greenberg made a big show of putting his glasses and notepad away and literally skulked from the room.

"He's disrespectful and he doesn't know his place." Marquand said. "It's men like that who shirk their military obligations and end up going through life without any bearing whatsoever. They have no concept of proper respect and order."

Dmytryk began to respond but the print man got to his feet and said, "I think that's about it here, fellas."

"What did you get?" Dmytryk asked.

"A couple smudges near the window. That's it. This room is clean."

"Clean?"

"Yep. Not a print to be found. Someone wiped it all down, and wiped it down good."

"Maybe they were wearing gloves," Dmytryk said.

"I'm sure they were. But there weren't even prints for the child or anyone else. Not anything worth cataloguing anyway. It's been wiped."

"Are there any pry or tool marks on the window," I asked.

"I didn't see any," the print man said. "Makes sense, though. The window doesn't lock."

"It warped over the winter and doesn't latch anymore. I planned on getting it replaced," Marquand said.

"What's next on the agenda, Chief?" the print man asked, closing his cases.

Dmytryk told him about the ladder and we all went downstairs. I stood on the porch and lit a cigarette while they went to look at the ladder which had been brought back up from the tree line. Reporters scurried after Marquand and Dmytryk, their flash bulbs popping in tempo with their bombardment of questions. Greenberg was rallying a group of uniforms that he unleashed on them like herd dogs.

After a few minutes Greenberg came around the side of the house and joined me on the porch. "Can I bum one of those?" he asked. I shook a smoke out and let him fire it up himself with Loren's Zippo. "These goddamned reporters are going to piss me off," he said exhaling. "Pascetti!" he yelled at a uniform, "put up some rope or something. Keep them away from the house."

The uniform dashed off, apparently to find rope.

"Fuck!" Greenberg groaned. "They're like roaches."

"It's big news," I said.

"I get it. But, goddamn! Do they have to act like fucking pariahs?"

We smoked in silence. I was thinking about his word choice when he said, "What's your name again?"

"Thorpe."

"How did you get involved?"

I almost mentioned the letters but I thought of the one in my pocket. So, instead I said, "Marquand had me on retainer in case he needed a private detective. Business stuff."

"Private dicks," he snorted. "Always with the secrets."

"Client privilege," I said, field stripping my butt and dropping the paper into my pocket. "I'll share one tidbit with you, though."

"Indulge me."

"One of those windows in the nursery can't lock. The wood's all warped."

I could see him thinking. Then he said, "Now, who do you suppose would know something like that?"

"Good luck with that," I said, walking off the porch.

A uniform found me later, curled into a frozen ball on the seat of the Dodge. He said Marquand wanted to see me in his study. I gave him a nod and a wave and spent a few minutes shaking a massive headache. Eventually I made my way up to the house where Victor and Bertie the cook were serving coffee and an assortment of cookies from a linen draped table on the porch. Victor showed me where the study was located. I knocked with a finger and slid open one of the pocket doors. The walls were lined with leather-bound books and serene paintings of mountains and trees. There was a patterned sofa against one wall and two cloth chairs in front of a river rock fireplace. Marquand was sitting behind a little desk in the corner with the reading lamp on.

"Drink?" He asked, taking a quart of vodka from a drawer. I had never seen this man drinking before, so it was even more surprising when he poured us both a couple of inches. I drank mine down and he offered me another by motioning with the bottle. Then he replaced the cork and put it away in the desk.

"Let's see the note," he said.

I took it from my pocket. As I handed it over, I realized it was still sealed.

"You haven't opened it yet?"

"There wasn't time. The police were just arriving when I found it." He looked in the desk for an opener but finally tore one end off and shook out the note.

"How did you know it was a ransom note?"

He shot me a look and said, "What else would it be?" He unfolded a single sheet and lay it out before us. I got up and stood behind him. Scrawled in pencil it said:

Dear Sir!
Have 50000$ ready - 25000$ in
20$ bills 20000$ in 10$ bills and
5000$ in 5$ bills
In 3-4 days
we will inform you were to deliver
the Mony.
We warn you not to notify the Police
The child is in good care.

Under the writing there were two interconnected triangles. The area where they overlapped was filled in with red ink. I read it through three or four times then sat back down. "Is that how the other letters were signed? With those triangles?"

"Yes," he said. "That's not near the money I thought they'd ask for. I can get that in the morning."

"We have three or four days. I think you should wait. If you're not around tomorrow it might look strange."

I watched him read through it another couple times.

"You don't think all this police activity is going to put Christian at risk, do you?" he asked finally.

"Obviously they want the money so I think it would be pretty foolish to do something that would give you a reason not to pay. They're probably not happy the cops are here, but..." I let my words trail off. I finished what was in my glass and set it on the desk. My stomach wasn't happy but I knew the vodka would ease the throbbing in my head.

"I'd pay no matter what," he said. "If I thought it meant there was a chance of getting him back."

"Of course." I put my hand out and he gave me the note. I held it up to the light and said, "When you get the money you need to make sure the bank marks it. They'll need to record all the serial numbers too. It's best if the bills are in sequential order."

"I don't care about any of that."

"But, that's how we'll be able to track them down later."

"I can't care about any of that right now. I just want my son back. And I'm not going to do anything to jeopardize that."

"The note doesn't say anything about marked or sequential bills. If it specifically said not to use them then I'd agree with you. But I think it's worth the risk."

"Of course it's worth the risk to you. It's not your son."

I put the note on the desk. "I'm sorry. That's not what I meant."

He closed his eyes and put his fingertips to his temples. There were red splotches at his neckline and his shoulders were slack. In that moment of complete silence I could hear a dog barking below us. Then without moving, Marquand said, "I'll think about it."

We sat for a long time in more silence. Or sort of silence, considering there was the barking. I wasn't sure if he wanted me to stay or leave.

"Where did you find the note?" I asked softly.

He opened his eyes and sat back. "On the window sill."

"Was the window opened or closed?"

"I don't remember. Closed, I think."

"And you were in this room, with the nursery right above you?"

"Yes."

"You didn't hear anything? The ladder against the house?"

He cocked his head. "Do you hear anything now? There's a hundred cops roaming around."

"I'm just saying," I said. "Has it occurred to you that this might be an inside job? Think about it. Someone climbs up the side of the house, in the window, and back out again with Christian and no one hears anything? Not a single sound? And the dog? Does it have full rein of the house?"

"Normally, yes. We put him in the crawlspace considering..."

"Okay. So the dog was up here? And it didn't bark?"

"I don't think so. No. Not that I recall."

"All of that seems a little strange to me," I said. "Not to mention, there isn't a single fingerprint in the nursery. And who would know the window can't be locked? What if they put the note on the windowsill so you'd think they went out that way when they probably went right out the front door."

"Or the back stairs," Marquand said.

"Or the back stairs. And don't you normally go home on Sunday? Have you ever stayed past Sunday?"

"Rarely."

"This is Wednesday. If this was an outsider, they'd expect you to be back in the city, right? When did you decide to stay past Sunday?"

"That night."

"And when did you decide to stay on after that?"

"We were planning to go home each day. But Christian wasn't getting better. Louise took him to the doctor in Morrison yesterday. We decided to stay one more night since Christian was still fussy, even on his medicine."

"Who would know those things?"

Marquand looked at me without saying a word.

"Whoever knew those details, and can get in and out of the house without making any noise, or having the dog bark at them, is the person who took your son."

He sat forward and picked up the note. I could see his mind was racing. He flipped it over and examined the back again. Then he looked up and said, "Could it be Loren?"

CHAPTER 12

Just before sunrise it began to rain. The print man, who had been waiting for daylight to dust the ladder, got everyone scrambling to move the pieces first onto the front porch and then into the house. I helped push furniture aside in the sitting room. Two sawhorses were brought in and all three sections were then laid out across them. Marquand didn't say anything during the commotion but the hubbub roused Mrs. Marquand. Briefly she stood at the doorway and watched, her eyes puffy from crying. With her was a young woman who I guessed to be Joanna, the nursemaid.

Two uniforms assisted the print man, flipping and turning the pieces as he dusted and taped prints onto index cards. The rest of us watched and drank coffee. Bertie brought in a tray of fresh-baked muffins and all progress stopped as everyone ate. Greenberg returned from organizing a Marquand-approved search of the grounds. Apparently I had become his source for cigarettes since he came right over and asked for one.

"Do I look like a cigarette girl," I said, handing him the pack.

"You'd be the ugliest cigarette girl in the state," he said, putting a butt to his lips.

"I'm going to start charging a nickel apiece."

He held out his hand for the lighter. "Thanks, pal," he said slapping the lighter back into my hand. Then he crossed the room to talk to Dmytryk and Marquand who were standing in the dining room. Marquand waved his hands at Greenberg and yelled for him to get away.

"There is no smoking in this house," Marquand announced. "If you want to smoke, go outside. Off the porch. And police your butts!"

Greenberg carefully knocked the tip into an unattended coffee cup and put the butt in his pocket. Marquand violently fanned the air around him when Greenberg approached them again. I couldn't hear what they were saying, but after a couple minutes Marquand waved me over.

"I'm going to allow them to interview some select members of the staff," he said to me. "They're especially interested in the ones who weren't here tonight, Richard, Sonja and the others at the house in Denver. I also said they can talk to Loren since she was here until yesterday. I want you to accompany them. I was going to sit in, but Major Dmytryk thinks this might keep some of them from opening up."

"Yes, sir," I said.

"When are you planning on doing this?" Dmytryk asked Greenberg.

"This morning," Greenberg replied. "As soon as we have daylight I'll get the search outside started. We can go then." To Marquand he said, "Can you have someone call down there, Colonel? I want to make sure everyone stays put until we get there."

Marquand called Victor over and relayed the instructions.

"Is there anyone else we should know about? Anyone that might have known you were going to be up here the last couple nights?" Greenberg asked Marquand.

"No one I can think of."

"I think we should talk to the nursemaid too since she normally doesn't come up here weekends. She was aware of the unusual routine. And I'm sure she knew about the window not being able to latch," Greenberg said.

"I'm okay with that, but..." Marquand said, as if thinking it through. "I want you to wait until later or tomorrow. She's taking care of Louise and I don't want to upset my wife any more than she already is."

"Absolutely, Colonel," Dmytryk said.

A sergeant in uniform came in and told Greenberg they were ready to start the search of the grounds. Greenberg followed him out.

"He might be a bit…unrefined. But he's very thorough," Dmytryk said to Marquand.

"I want you in charge of the investigation, Major. I don't trust his kind."

"Yes, sir. You can be sure of that."

Marquand patted the shorter Dmytryk on the shoulder and said, "Just make sure you keep me or Thorpe involved. I want to know what's going on with the investigation at all times."

"You have my word, Colonel." Dmytryk offered his hand to Marquand who didn't notice at first. When he did, he gave him a little shake. I went out on the porch to smoke the last cigarette I had in my pack.

The rain was light but steady and the cadre of uniforms going off towards the tree line were decked out in black slickers and plastic hat covers. A group of reporters huddled under a tree and puffed away on their own cigarettes while trying to keep their notepads and cameras dry. When Greenberg came back up the hill a few minutes later they tossed their butts and ran to the rope line he'd ordered set up, calling out questions. He ignored them, came up on the porch and slapped his soaking wet hat against the rail.

"Okay, babysitter. Are you ready to go to town?" he asked.

"What's up with your man Dmytryk? I mean, I get it. I know Marquand, and he's a domineering asshole. But your guy is a fucking, ball-less wonder."

"That suck ass? He'd do anything to get elected to something."

"Sounds like you're not exactly pals."

"You were a G.I., right? Where'd you serve?" Greenberg asked.

"Pacific. Marines."

"Okay. I'm sure you saw some shit. I was merchant navy in the Atlantic. That is, until I got burns all up and down my legs from a torpedo hit." He took the butt he'd snubbed out earlier from his pocket. I handed him the Zippo. When he had it fired up he said, "But that fuck got himself a medal for some bullshit in North Africa and ever since he's been parlaying that into one opportunity after another. So, that's all he cares about. Getting ahead in life. He's never going to ruffle feathers with someone like Marquand."

"Sounds like a real peach." I said, flicking my smoked down butt into the wet grass.

"That's a polite way of putting it."

I watched the reporters reconvening under the tree while

Greenberg smoked. When he'd puffed his down to his fingers, he shot it out into the yard near mine. "What do you know about these people at the Denver house?" he asked.

"Same as you. Nothing."

I followed in the Dodge down the hill and back through town. Greenberg rode with the jelly necked cop and Dmytryk rode in a marked car with a uniform. The gate at the Country Club house was closed so we parked on the street and waited for a transcriptionist to arrive. I clicked on the radio and caught the tail end of an update about the missing Marquand baby. The reporter said police weren't sure if the child had wandered away from the home or was abducted. Amos 'n' Andy came on after that. I switched them off and closed my eyes to the soothing drum of raindrops on the cloth top.

Greenberg woke me by slapping the roof. I followed them through the gate and up the drive. A man in a yellow slicker and hat had come out to let us in. He said his name was Arquila and that he was the groundskeeper. Inside, we were greeted by a nervous young woman with a thick Scottish brogue in a black and white maid uniform.

"Mr. Victor called and said you were coming. My name is Camille. I am at your service," she said, gathering our coats and hats.

"We're going to need a place where we can talk to each of you privately, Camille," Dmytryk said.

"Yes, sir. Please come with me," she said, leading us back to the long, windowed hallway. "And gentlemen, please refrain from smoking. The Colonel has asked for this to remain a smoke-free residence."

Turning opposite of where I knew Marquand's office was, she led us into a library where books covered two entire walls from floor to ceiling. A ladder on rails offered the opportunity to climb two stories for your favorite tome. At the far end was a fireplace I could have stood inside without ducking. Before it sat two leather chairs and a small table. At the other end of the room was a long table with lamps and hardback chairs, the kind you'd expect to find in a public library. Dmytryk selected a chair at the head of the table and we all settled in there. The transcriptionist opened his case and took out a little typewriter.

After a few minutes the maid and another identically dressed woman returned with trays of coffee, milk, biscuits and a pile of chocolate chip scones. Jelly neck, whose name turned out to be Tooley, and the rest of us dove into the food. Dmytryk wandered down towards the fireplace with his coffee cup to study a collection of photographs that showed Marquand posing with every famous person known to man.

"Chief, let's start with the secretary and then save the sister-in-law for last," Greenberg called to Dmytryk, while licking jam from his fingers.

"Fine," Dmytryk said from the other end of the room. "You can take the lead with the questioning."

When Camille returned a few minutes later with another pot of coffee, Greenberg told her we'd start with Sonja Hoff.

"Miss Hoff is not here, sir," she said.

"Where is she?"

"I don't know, sir. She's not in her room or at her desk. I haven't seen her all morning."

"Did you see her last night?" Greenberg asked, taking out his notepad and reading glasses.

"No. Not at all yesterday."

He asked her a dozen more questions about Sonja Hoff, but none that Camille could answer. Finally, Greenberg turned to Tooley, who was cramming a huge chunk of scone into his mouth, and said, "We didn't miss her up there in all the confusion, did we?"

Tooley mumbled something and shook his head.

Camille said, "She didn't go up with the family, sir."

"You're sure?"

"Yes, sir. She never goes to the Morrison house."

"Call up to Morrison," Greenberg said to Tooley, "and see if she's showed up there. If she hasn't, call downtown and see if they've heard anything."

Tooley mumbled something, put down what was left of his scone and began looking around for a telephone.

"Not in here. Go out in the hall or something," Greenberg ordered. Then to Camille he said, "How about the chauffeur?"

Two minutes later Richard was settled in across from us. His head bobbed up and down the whole time Dmytryk introduced us and went into far too much detail about what we were doing. Every so often Richard would steal a glance at each of us as if we were making faces at him when he wasn't looking. With Dmytryk's monotone voice and the captivating double row of buttons on Richard's grey chauffeur uniform, I nearly dozed off. Pretty soon I heard Greenberg say, "Okay. And why did you come back to town?"

"I had to bring Miss Chambers back."

"And...?"

"And..." Richard glanced at Dmytryk then me and the cop in uniform. "I drove her back here, to the house."

"I got that. What happened next?"

"Colonel Marquand said I could stay down here overnight. So I washed the car and put it away."

"You washed the car?" Greenberg said, looking up. "Wasn't it raining."

"Not when we got here. It started later. We arrived here at five, maybe five thirty, and I always wash the car after it's been to Morrison because of the dirt road."

"Okay," Greenberg said focusing on his notepad again. "After you washed the car...then what?"

"I put it away and went to my room."

Greenberg didn't say anything and stared at his notepad. Dmytryk looked up from his fingernails. After a minute Richard began to fiddle with one of the buttons on his coat, his eyes darting back and forth between Greenberg and Dmytryk.

"Lieutenant?" Dmytryk said.

"One second, Chief. I'm thinking."

Greenberg scribbled a few things, eventually sighed and said, "Did you go out again?"

"No, Richard said.

"You didn't?"

"No."

"What did you do?"

"I listened to the radio for a while. Then, I guess I went to bed."

"Can anyone confirm that?"

Richard glanced all around and finally said, "No. I don't think so."

The door opened and Tooley came back in. He shrugged and shook his head at Greenberg. Apparently he'd had no luck finding Sonja Hoff.

Greenberg nodded and went on with Richard. "Why did Miss Chambers come back to town?"

"I don't know. Maybe she was tired from the baby crying?" He twisted the button back and forth and stared at the top of Greenberg's head. He turned to Dmytryk and said, "The baby's been sick."

"What did she do after you got back here?"

"I don't know. Went to her room I guess. My room's above the garage. I don't see or hear much of what happens in the house."

"So you didn't see her again the rest of the evening?"

"No."

Greenberg went on asking questions for several minutes but the story stayed the same. When he finally told Richard he could go, he added, "Detective Tooley and Trooper Moritz are going with you to look at the car and examine your room."

Tooley, who was just starting on another scone, put it down and went out with Richard and the uniform.

The maid that helped Camille with the coffee came in next. She was plain and unafraid and spoke in sentences where the periods at the end were like stones dropped in a well. Across her nose and cheeks was a barrage of freckles, making her look younger and cuter than she actually was.

Arquila the groundskeeper followed her. He'd shed the yellow slicker and hat to reveal a plaid shirt under a corduroy coat. He was the exact opposite of the maid with answers that took the scenic route. He went into great detail about how he and his wife made preserves from raspberry bushes that ran the length of their property. Greenberg let him leave after an eternity and we all t turns going to the bathroom and grabbing a smoke outside.

When we were resettled Camille came in. She twis towel in her hands while perched with barely a chee of the chair. She wasn't pretty. But she had big that gave her store window sex appeal. As she became heavier and heavier taking on an a void of words.

"And what time did Mr. Smithson b date?" Greenberg asked.

"It was ten thirty, sir. You can as' tell you I was here."

"You saw Richard?"

79

"Aye, sir. He came in at eleven. I looked at the parlor clock. Mr. Smithson and I were having a cuppa before he took for home." She paused then added, "The missus, she said it's okay if we do that."

"What was Richard doing?"

She said something I couldn't make out. Greenberg must not have either as he asked her to repeat herself.

She went slower this time, "He came to ask Mr. Smithson to move his car since he was not able to get around it to put the Cadillac in the garage."

"And what time did you say that was?" Greenberg asked, his head coming up.

"Eleven," Dmytryk said.

Greenberg looked at Dmytryk then back to Camille.

"Aye. It was eleven, sir."

"Richard had been out with the car? Was he in his uniform?"

"No. He wasn't."

"Was he alone?" Greenberg asked.

"I don't know."

Greenberg scribbled. Dmytryk watched him and then shifted his gaze to one of the green glass lights on the table.

"Did Mr. Smithson go and move his car?"

"He decided he should leave," she said.

"Did you walk outside with Mr. Smithson, to say goodnight?"

"I did, but only for a moment. It was cold and I hadn't put me coat back on."

"Did Richard pull into the garage?"

Just as she was about to answer Tooley came back into the room. He started to say something but Greenberg held up his hand to silence him. "Go ahead," Greenberg said to Camille.

"Aye. I closed the gate after Mr. Smithson went out and I saw Richard drive into the garage."

"But you couldn't see if anyone was with him?"

"No, sir."

Greenberg waved Tooley over who whispered something in his Greenberg nodded and said, "Bring him in." Tooley went the room and out into the hall.

you see Richard again last night?" Greenberg asked

."

Tooley and the uniform came in with Richard, who looked as if he stepped in some shit.

"Thank you Camille, for all your help," Greenberg said. "You can go now."

She got up and paused. "Did you want some more scones or biscuits, sir?" she asked Dmytryk, who hadn't touched a single one.

He told her no. She took the empty tray with her on the way out, avoiding Richard who tried to make eye contact.

"Tell us what you found out," Greenberg said to Tooley.

"The car wasn't freshly washed as he'd said. There's rain spots all over it."

"I thought you said you hadn't gone out since you got back and washed the car," Greenberg said to Richard.

"I was going to tell you," Richard said, "but I didn't want the Colonel to find out…"

"Yeah…go on," Greenberg said.

"I took the car out last night."

"No fucking shit. And…?"

"And, well, I'm not supposed to take the car for personal reasons. Ever. That's why I didn't want to tell you."

"Do I look like I give a shit about house rules? We're here to get this baby back. Stop wasting our time."

"Okay, I understand. I'm sorry. It's just…I don't want to lose this job, Lieutenant."

Greenberg waved his hand, showing his impatience.

"I went downtown to listen to some music. I do it sometimes when the family's in Morrison. Otherwise I've got to ride the streetcar or take a cab. And no one's using the car, so I figure it's maybe okay if I just keep it clean and be careful…" He faded to a stop and waited for Greenberg to say something. When he didn't, Richard added, "I'm really sorry I didn't tell the truth, Lieutenant. I'm always careful with the car."

"Where did you go?"

"Casper's."

"Were you alone?"

"Yes. I never take anyone in the car. I swear to that. Never." Greenberg wrote something down and Richard, his eyebrows meeting together like jerky caterpillars, said, "You won't tell the Colonel will you? I really don't want to lose this job."

"We can't guarantee that we…" Dmytryk began, but Greenberg

cut him off: "Frankly, I don't give a flying fuck in hell what you do with the car. That's your business. Nail a hundred broads in the back seat for all I care. Just tell us the truth. We're looking for a missing baby. Not some dipshit that can't follow house rules."

Richard wiped his lip with the back of his hand and said, "Thanks, Lieutenant."

"Can anyone vouch for you? Can they say they saw you last night?"

"Mr. Smithson and Camille. They were here when I got home. I had to ask Smithson to move his car. He always blocks the path to the garage."

"What about before that? At Casper's? Can anyone confirm that you were there?" Greenberg asked.

"Yes. I know lots of people there. The bartender. The doorman. Both will say I was there."

"Did you unload anything into the garage?" Greenberg asked.

"What?"

"What did you do when you got back?"

"I just went up to my room and listened to the radio for a while. I had a couple drinks. Then I went to sleep."

"The garage and his room all looked clean, L.T.," Tooley said.

"Okay," Greenberg said. "You can go. But if your alibi doesn't fly, we're going to be back. And you're not going to like the questioning you get from Detective Tooley."

"I understand," Richard said, his head bobbing up and down. "Thank you, Lieutenant. Thanks."

It was a few minutes before Loren came in. In the meantime, Greenberg took off his glasses, rubbed his eyes and stretched. Dmytryk poured another cup of coffee. I went and stared out the window. It was raining just as it had been when we arrived. A big puddle had formed in a slight hollow in the grass and I watched the drops splash into it.

Greenberg yawned and said, "You want a bulletin put out on that Hoff dame, Chief?"

"Let's wait. I want to talk to Colonel Marquand first."

Greenberg yawned again, then Tooley yawned. "Now look what you've done," Tooley said.

Camille brought in Loren who wore a black dress with long sleeves and a sage scarf. Her hair was down, nearly hiding her face. She crossed her legs and folded her hands in her lap. A cuticle on her slender thumb had been chewed bloody. She never looked at me, even as Dmytryk pointed in my direction and said my name during the same stock introduction he'd given to all the others.

Greenberg asked a couple background questions about who Loren was and where she lived. Her voice was monochromatic, without details or emotion. But she did look gorgeous. I could almost feel the heat from her body.

Greenberg shifted in his chair, stared at the pad and asked, "Why did you come back to Denver yesterday?"

"Am I a suspect?" Loren asked.

"Not at all, Miss Chambers," Dmytryk said. "We're just establishing everyone's whereabouts so we can have a mental picture of what was happening at both residences."

"It seems that's the kind of question you'd ask someone suspected of the crime," she said, flipping her hair with her head. Her eyes were dark, darker than usual with purple circles under them. She looked as if she hadn't slept in days and for some reason it struck me as sexy. I couldn't help but think about what it would be like to kiss her again, to touch her and feel her against me.

"Of course it isn't," Dmytryk said. "We've asked everyone the same thing today. We don't feel anyone here is a suspect."

Greenberg raised his head and glared at Dmytryk who finally said, "Proceed, Lieutenant."

"It's best if you fully cooperate," Greenberg said.

"I'm happy to cooperate. But I don't see how my whereabouts has any impact on something that happened an hour away from here."

"It helps us establish the location and activity of each person. Basically, it allows us to continue our investigation in the right direction without being distracted by unknowns," Greenberg said. "You came back to town for some reason. What was it?"

"I don't think I have to answer that," she said.

"Did you come back to see someone?"

Loren said nothing. I began to wonder if maybe she did come back to see someone. Maybe it was me, and there I was, sitting at Billy's. Or, maybe it wasn't me. I scooted my chair on the floor to see if she'd look my direction but she stared straight ahead at Greenberg.

"Miss Chambers, did you go anywhere after you returned to Denver? Did you stop anywhere along the way?" Greenberg asked.

"Wouldn't that be my business?"

Greenberg took off his reading glasses and laid the pencil on the notepad. "Yesterday, yes. Today, no," he said. "Today your nephew is missing. That changes everything. And it seems like you'd want to do anything you could to help us get him back. Instead you're acting like you couldn't give a shit. You don't think that makes us think you have something to hide?"

Loren sat unmoved while Greenberg stared at her. After a minute he pushed the notepad and pencil away. The pencil rolled across the table and fell on the floor. "Frankly, Miss Chambers, I don't care why you came back to town or what you were doing...so long as it has nothing to do with this missing child. Do you understand? I don't care who you might be seeing. I don't care what it is that you do in your own time. None of that matters. We just want to return this child to its parents. Surely you can understand that. This is about your nephew and your sister."

Loren remained motionless.

I picked up the pencil and put it on the table next to the Greenberg's notepad.

"Why did you come back to Denver and what did you do last night?" Greenberg asked again.

She said nothing and we sat in silence for quite some time. Eventually, Greenberg made a big show of putting his glasses, notepad and pencil away. He stood up and said, "Get up, Miss Chambers. I'm putting you under arrest."

We all stared at him.

He turned to Tooley and said, "Go find the maid and get her a coat and hat." Then he faced Loren again. "You're under arrest, Miss Chambers."

"Lieutenant!" Dmytryk said getting to his feet.

Tooley didn't move.

"If she's not going to answer questions then she's going down," Greenberg said. Then to Tooley he ordered: "Go!"

Tooley jumped up and left the room.

"Lieutenant, I want to talk to you," Dmytryk said. Greenberg followed him to the other end of the room where they stood talking by the fireplace. I watched Loren, but she didn't move, her eyes steady on them. Her hands still folded in her lap.

When they returned Greenberg said, "I'm not saying it again. Get up. You're under arrest."

Loren slowly uncrossed her legs and stood. They were still facing each other when Camille and Tooley returned with a coat and hat. Tooley held the coat while Loren slipped into it.

"Turn around," Greenberg said. Then he cuffed her.

CHAPTER 13

Greenberg put Loren in the marked car and rode with her and the uniform. I was the fourth car trailing behind Dmytryk and Tooley and the transcriptionist. At the State Patrol building they all pulled into the guarded motor pool. I parked a block away at a meter. Loren was already checked in at the front desk and had been escorted up to the detective bureau when I got in the building. I went on up and watched from a distance as Greenberg was removing the cuffs and putting her into a holding cell. Then he, Tooley and Dmytryk went into an office with *C.S. Stanger, Captain* painted on the frosted glass portion of the door.

A uniform gave me directions to a cigarette machine at the end of the hall. When I got back Stanger's door was still closed so I sat on a long, pew-like bench and smoked. After I'd added my butt to the army of crushed ones in an overflowing ashtray I went ahead and lit another. Before I could finish that one Stanger's door opened and Dmytryk exited, without acknowledging me he went out into the hall. A minute later Greenberg and Tooley came out accompanied by a giant of a man who I guessed was Stanger. He was so big next to the tiny Greenberg I thought it looked as if he could slip the little man into a hip pocket. Stanger gave what appeared to be some final orders and went back in his office. Greenberg and Tooley meandered over to me.

"We're going to let her stew for a while. We thought we'd get a sandwich or something. You in?" Greenberg asked.

"I could eat," I said.

"How about Jerry's?" Tooley suggested.

"Fuck that!" Greenberg said. "I'll throw up if I have to watch you eat another pig ear sandwich."

"I promise, Lieu. I won't order that."

"That's what you said last time! No goddamned way. Let's go to that place in the Hotel George."

"That's good too," Tooley said. "I'll get the liver and egg salad."

"How about I bum one of them smokes you got," Greenberg said to me.

"Jesus! There's a machine down the hall!"

"I never buy 'em. They stunt your growth."

"Must have started when he was five years old then," I said to Tooley and handed Greenberg the pack.

The rain had pretty much stopped so we walked the two blocks. Tooley ordered liver and egg salad as promised. I got a roast beef and Greenberg a big bowl of chicken soup.

When Greenberg finished slurping his soup he said, "What's the deal with you and this broad?"

"How do you mean?" I said, chewing on my sandwich.

"Don't fuck with me, Thorpe. I see the way you look at her."

"Nothing! I told you, I'm working for Marquand." I put the sandwich down and wiped my hands.

"Bullshit!" he stated. When I failed to respond he said to Tooley, "Can you believe this guy? He thinks we're right off the turnip truck."

Tooley grunted, his mouth full.

"Don't play games. I need to know one way or the other before I go in there and start giving her the third degree."

I pushed my plate away.

"You gonna eat that?" Tooley said pointing to my pickle.

"It's yours."

He moved it to his plate.

"Well?" Greenberg asked.

I looked away and watched a man at the counter finish his coffee and drop a few coins next to the saucer. He slid off the stool, took his coat from the rack by the door and went outside. A second later he passed by the window going down the block. When I faced Greenberg he hadn't moved. His eyes were still on me and I knew he knew. So I told him about how we'd had a drink that day I saw her on the labyrinth and that she came to my house. I didn't go into any details. I just told him she'd come over and left it at that. When I finished he said *okay* and dropped the wadded napkin he was holding into the empty soup bowl. "Let me give you a little piece of advice. Don't ever hold out on me again. Got it? We can play your little client privilege game when we've got too, but if you ever hold back on anything pertaining to this case I'll fuck you. No joke. I'll make sure your ticket is pulled and maybe you'll even do some time. Are we good on that?"

"Yeah, we're good," I said.

"You seem like an okay Joe, Thorpe. And if someone seems okay, I like to make sure they know how I play. That way there's no surprises. Your job might be protecting Marquand's secrets, but right now we're trying to get this kid back. Don't forget that. Because I won't." He took his elbows off the table and clapped his hands together. "Okay! Let's go see what your girlfriend's got to say. Tooley, you're buying, right?"

Tooley protested around a mouthful of my pickle but ended up paying.

When we got back to the building Greenberg had me wait again on the pew. A uniform took Loren from the cell to one of the interrogation rooms. While I waited I smoked a half dozen cigarettes, flipped through several back issues of *Police Gazette* and paced a quarter inch of leather off the soles of my shoes. Two hours later Greenberg came back and said, "She's a dope head. She pays Richard to get it for her. That's what was going on. He went out to buy some shit for her and she got hopped up."

"Opium?"

"Heroin," he said. "We'll need to get Richard to cop to the story. And I might just let Tooley smack the fucker for good measure. But I'm satisfied. It took a while to break her, but, when it came out it looked the real deal. And, to be honest, she looks like a junkie anyway. I've got to go tell Stanger and Dmytryk. Take her home. They'll be processing her out downstairs in a few minutes."

"You're not going to charge her?"

"What do I care if your girlfriend wants the slow death? Besides, it's not like she's got the shit in her purse."

I wanted to tell him she wasn't my girlfriend. I wanted to punch a hole through his face. Instead I said thanks and went down to wait at the front desk. A few minutes later Loren was escorted out and once she'd signed a couple sheets of paper the sergeant said she could leave.

In the car she sat with her head down, hat and hair hiding her face, saying nothing. When we got within a couple blocks of the Country Club house she said she needed a drink. I turned around and drove back to Don's Club Tavern on 6th. We sat in a booth at the window and I ordered a bourbon for the both of us and lit her cigarette.

"I suppose he told you," she said finally.

"He did."

The drinks came and we sipped them. She worked the tip of her cigarette in the ashtray and stared out at the traffic. On the sidewalk a couple went by arm in arm. They were laughing about something. Loren crushed out her butt and gave a little cough, her hand at her mouth.

"I'd like another," she said.

I shook one out for her.

"No. Another drink."

I ordered another round and when it came she drank off the remainder of the first and gave the glass to the girl.

"It's just something I do," she said. "Once in a while."

"You don't need to say anything," I said.

"Maybe I want to."

"Okay."

A bus pulled to the curb outside and I watched her looking at the people as they each got off and went their separate ways. She turned back and looked at me, then lowered her eyes to her drink.

"They had me on morphine after my heart attack and I liked it."

"When was that?"

"I told you about my heart," she said, looking into my eyes.

"I didn't know it was a heart attack. I'm sorry."

"I don't want your pity."

I fingered the rim of my glass.

"And I don't need anyone judging me."

"I'm not. I just wish I'd known. I could have saved you from that shit today."

"Saved me? Do you think I need you to save me? I don't need you. Or anyone. And I don't need someone to *save* me."

I didn't know how to respond so I finished my drink and motioned the waitress to bring the check. I tossed a couple bills on the table and my empty glass on top of them.

"Let's go," I said.

She finished her drink and put her coat on. We walked the half block back to the Dodge in silence. I opened the passenger side door for her. She was just looking at me. Not saying anything. I was about to turn away and let her get in on her own when she said *please kiss me.* And I did.

CHAPTER 14

Over the next several days I spent a lot of time up at the Morrison house. I drank all the coffee Victor poured and ate my fill of the little powdered doughnuts Bertie made while watching the cops take endless pictures of the ladder; on the ground, as three segments, all together, stacked upon itself, with one man carrying it, with two and then three men carrying it, leaning against the house, in the back seat of a car, in the trunk, measured one way, measured another. Eventually they figured out the ladder could indeed fit inside a car and one man would be able to carry and put it together. However, the rung spacing, a full eighteen inches or more in some spots, meant the kidnapper had to be a tall man. At least as tall as me anyway.

After the day with all the photos, the cops showed up with two replicas of the original ladder. This time they leaned it against the house and climbed up and down on it. A canvas bag with thirty pounds of potatoes was used to simulate the baby. Three different cops of varying weights, heights and builds climbed up, into the window and then back out and down with the sack. Only the skinny cop was able to actually get in and out of the window. The other two got stuck at some point and had to be pulled in by their arms. The fat cop looked like he might be there for a while. When simulating the descent with the baby the medium-sized cop dropped the sack, theoretically killing the baby. The skinny cop had a hard time with the rung spacing and had to use both hands coming out the window while a cop inside held the sack for him.

At one point when the cops were climbing up and down Greenberg came over and asked for a cigarette.

"How's your girlfriend," he said puffing and handing the lighter back to me.

"Keep cracking wise, asshole, and see if you ever get another cigarette from me."

"Did I hit a funny bone?" Greenberg smirked.

"Yeah, and sometimes it makes me have these little uncontrollable reactions," I said, balling my fist and showing it to him.

"Smart move to hit a cop in front of two dozen other cops."

"Would they even notice?"

He smiled at that, then smoked in silence for a minute before asking, "Heard anything about that secretary?"

"Not a thing. I only talked to Marquand for a minute this morning. He has no idea where she could be," I said, skipping the fact that Marquand and I had agreed to meet the next day at my office to talk more about the ransom.

"This ladder thing throws me off," Greenberg said. "If it was her, why would this ladder even exist? And there's no way I can believe this broad would be able to build a ladder—even a shitty one like that. She must have had help."

"I'm thinking it's unfortunate the print man could only find twelve thousand cop prints on the ladder."

"Yeah, yeah, I know. Fucking Keystone Cops," he said.

"But, seriously–I don't think she would've been able to fit through the window. Or manage those rungs."

"Full figured broad?"

"I wouldn't say she passed through the factory line twice, but she had some curves. Enough to keep her from sliding in and out of that window without getting something hung up."

Greenberg laughed. "Either way," he said, dropping his butt on the grass and stepping on it, "she's going to be in the hot seat when we catch up to her. A blonde with a German accent and a curly headed baby can't hide for long."

He wandered off to join in on some of the ladder festivities and I got to thinking about Sonja Hoff. Greenberg was right. If she took the kid, she wouldn't be able to hide for long.

CHAPTER 15

Marquand showed up at my office the following day accompanied by a man I didn't recognize with a cold, gooey handshake. He was near Marquand's height but seemed half as tall with rolled shoulders and a tiny head topping a doughy torso. Adding to his other fine features were a yellowed walrus mustache that looked as if it smelled like rotten milk and rubber-soled shoes that squeaked on my floor. I hated him immediately.

"Dr. Loftesness is going to act as the intermediary," Marquand announced. "Between us and the kidnappers."

"We need an intermediary?" I asked, examining Loftesness again to see if I'd somehow misjudged him.

"Yes, that's what the kidnapper's want."

"How do you know that?"

"From the second note."

"You didn't tell me there was another note?" I said.

"I'm telling you now," Marquand sighed. "Dr. Loftesness put an ad in the Post. He said he'd pay $5000 of his own money to anyone who could guarantee the safe return of Christian. The kidnappers contacted him yesterday and said they want him to be the intermediary going forward. I think it's a good idea since it means we can trust them now." Marquand took an envelope out of his coat pocket and handed it to me. The postmark was Aurora, Colorado, dated for the previous day and addressed to Dr. Wm. Loftesness on Fairplay Street. The note was laced with misspellings and had the same scribbled handwriting and triangles at the bottom as the first ransom note.

It said:

Dr. Loftesnes — Present this letter to Mr. Ch. Marquand as proof we want you to be person we will acept the mony from. Next contact will be with man called Jim at Fairmont semetery. Quebec St. gate. Jim will give next instructions at semetry. Be ther at 5pm. No Mony now. No funny stuff. No cops.

I put it on the desk and looked at them. Marquand's eyebrows were up around his hairline and Loftesness looked like he might pee his pants.

"You got this letter yesterday?" I asked Loftesness.

"I did."

"When did you post the ad?"

"The day after the Colonel's son went missing. I read about it in the paper and knew I had to do something."

"Why?"

"Why what?"

"Why did you have to do something?"

Loftesness straightened in the chair as much as his saggy shoulders would allow and turned to look at Marquand. A glow of admiration came over him that almost seemed to whiten his mustache a little. He said, "Colonel Marquand is a national hero! I would do anything for this man."

"Including putting up your own five thousand dollars."

"Absolutely! Without hesitation. After all this man has done for our country?"

Marquand beamed, his chin up and eyes half-lidded.

"And what do you do, Dr. Loftesness?" I asked.

"I'm retired. Ophthalmology."

"Pretty good living, huh?"

"Yes," he said. "It was a very good practice."

"I would think so, throwing five grand out there like that."

"I believe in standing for causes."

"So do I. But most people don't get involved in strangers' causes unless they've got something personal to gain."

Loftesness clicked his tongue and suddenly Marquand wasn't happy anymore. "Is this really necessary?" he said. "You're treating the Doctor as if he's a criminal when he's here to help."

"No offense, Doctor," I offered to Loftesness. Then looking Marquand straight in the eye I said, "It's too coincidental, Colonel. Who is this guy and why the hell should we trust him? Do you *know* him?"

Loftesness clicked his tongue again and folded his arms across his chest.

"That's ridiculous," Marquand said. "You've got the note right there. The markings are exactly like the original."

He was right. The markings were like the original. But something about it still didn't jive with me. I ran the whole scene through my head and finally said, "It seems we're getting the run around, Colonel." Then, looking directly at Loftesness I added, "Someone's playing us."

"I'm actually glad you said that, Thorpe," Marquand said. "I've been thinking about how there weren't any fingerprints, and it seems like it might be more than just a random kind of thing. More like a professional job. Dr. Loftesness and I came to the conclusion that it would be a good idea to solicit more help. Outside help. Like the mob, for example. They always know what's going on, even if they're not directly involved. They hear things, they handle stolen goods, they supply guns. Basically, they're the eyes and ears of anything criminal that is happening all around the city. That means they'd be the perfect source of information on something like this."

Loftesness sat forward and said, "The Colonel and I thought it would be a good idea to have someone meet with them and see what they can find out for us. If they aren't involved, maybe they could listen for some word on the street. Or maybe they could tell us who's come to them for a hiding place or wants to launder some money. Any of those things. The mob's going to know. And if we talk to the right people, we're going to have a leg up in this."

"Seriously?" I asked Marquand. "You're taking advice from this guy? An optometrist?"

"Ophthalmologist!" Loftesness insisted.

I couldn't help but laugh out loud.

"Don't be so petulant, Thorpe," Marquand said.

I pointed at Loftesness. "I'll ask again, Colonel. Who *is* this guy?"

"He's the intermediary, Thorpe!" Marquand said, angrily slapping a hand on his knee. "The kidnappers are in control here. Can't you get that? We need to be moving fast now. And we need to keep our options open. Damn, man! Why do you have to be so difficult? I want my son back and I am not afraid to try anything and everything. Are you going to stand in the way of that?"

Marquand and I stared at each other for a long while. His eyes never blinked. I finally let out a sigh and said, "What is this plan? You want to meet with someone from the mob?"

"I want *you* to meet with them," Marquand said. "Dr. Loftesness has already made some calls and spoke with someone last night in the Capra family. They assured us that you'll be able to meet with Tony Capra himself."

"Oh you just called Tony Capra and said we want to meet with him. Really?"

"They were very enthusiastic when I said I was calling as a representative for Christian Marquand," Loftesness interjected.

I shot walrus face a nasty look before starting again, "But, Tony Capra? He's not the kind of guy we want to be playing around with."

"But he is the kind of guy who will know everything that's happening in Denver," Marquand said. "The meeting is set up for tonight. Either you're going to do this or I'm getting someone else."

I let out a moan that faded into, "I just don't see how this is going to help. As a matter of fact, it's going to complicate everything. What if Capra's involved? What if this gets in the news or the cops find out? They could slap us with withholding evidence. I could lose my license."

"I told you the other day, I don't care about any of that. I'm getting Christian back. That's my mission. And I'm willing to do whatever it takes to make that happen."

"Okay, then. Why can't *he* meet with Capra," I said, pointing at Loftesness.

"He's the intermediary! He can't be seen with Tony Capra! Use your head, Thorpe." We sat like that for a full minute before Marquand finally turned to Loftesness and asked him to wait in the outer office. Once he'd bounced up on his rubber soles and the door was closed, Marquand said, "Come on, Thorpe! I need you to do this. You saw him. He's nothing like us. We can't rely on him. That's why I need you. And right now, time is of the essence. They're expecting you at the Cavalcade Club no later than midnight tonight. Go and see what they know or can do for us to get

Christian back."

I nodded my head.

"And," he continued. "If it's about money, I can get you more money. Just say the word."

CHAPTER 16

At a glance the Cavalcade Club had all the appearances of a typical neighborhood bar, the kind of place where men gather to drown their worries in dime beer and watered down drinks before going home to a wife they can no longer stand. Over the door was the usual sign lit with a smattering of burned out bulbs. Flanking that were the predictable buzzing neon beer lights. But the Cavalcade wasn't typical in any way. It was the kind of place where a guy could get anything his heart desired and all it took was asking. Want a game? Fancy a nut? Need a fix? There were more than enough tables to gamble away a paycheck and plenty of broads who were once lookers that might or might not leave some scratching and burning. And for a few bucks here and a few more there it was possible to get a whole pharmacy of shit to sniff, smoke or put in a vein. On top of all that, there was the bartender who wouldn't hesitate to open a head with a bat. All courtesy of Tony Capra.

I ordered a Coke.

"Anything else?" the bartender grumbled, thumping the bottle down in front of me.

"I'm here to see Mr. Capra. I work for Christian Marquand."

He gave me the up and down, then went to speak to a couple slick-looking jobs sitting in a booth against the back wall. When he returned he picked up his cigarette without saying a word. One of the booth guys with a bald spot like Friar Tuck eventually got up and went out through a door labeled *Private*.

I sipped the Coke while keeping my eyes glued to the wall while listening to a fight that was playing on the radio. An Italian and a negro named Joey Sacks were working each other over in a spirited middleweight bout. It sounded to me like the negro was scoring all the points. Considering the setting, it was rather satisfying. Two rounds later Friar Tuck was at my shoulder. "Let's go," he said.

I followed him out the door and into a long, dark hallway. The other guy from the booth joined us and searched me, patting me up and down real good. Then Friar Tuck took me down some stairs and through another door that opened into a large carpeted room set up for gambling. On one side a raucous group was having a go on a crap table. Dotted around the rest of the room were red felt poker tables filled to capacity and tired looking girls wearing next to nothing. Or, just shoes in a few cases.

At the back of the space a jukebox with flashing lights next to a bar without stools emitted a happy little tune. I recognized Tony Capra from years of photos I'd seen in the papers. He was standing with several men with greased hair, dressed as if they owned the world and sporting grins to match. I was pretty sure from the bulges under their coats they were packing cannons.

"Good luck," Friar Tuck said.

As I made my way over one of the guys motioned me to the side of the bar. He gave me another quick pat down. When he'd finished, he turned me around and gave me a little shove towards Capra. It didn't feel like the time or place for handshakes, so skipping that I said, "Mr. Capra, Christian Marquand sent me."

He wasn't a big man. But he had a jaw like a bulldozer blade and the chest to back it up. His suit was perfectly tailored with thin lapels accented by a silk tie and pocket square the color of cranberries. "I have all the respect in the world for Christian Marquand," he said. "I don't meet with just anyone. But he's a hero to a generation. A *true* hero." When he offered me his hand I saw gold nugget cufflinks the size of almonds. His grip was a bit too firm as he sized me up but he really didn't need to as I was doing everything I could to look much shorter and as passive as a kitten.

"Yes he is," I said.

"What's your name?"

"Thorpe. Harry Thorpe."

He let go of my hand and instructed the bartender to pour two from *his* bottle.

"It's sad about his kid going missing. I've been reading about it in the paper. Not even two years old. Sad. Really sad. Whoever did that is not an American."

I nodded and told him I couldn't agree more.

The bartender set down two glasses. Capra handed one to me and waited while I tasted it before drinking his own. I smacked my lips and tried to look like I loved it even though I hate scotch. He drank from his glass and his chin softened, a little.

"Macallan is all I drink," he said, admiring his glass. "Thirty years old."

I raised mine to imply I was indebted to his impeccable taste, had another sip and made sure he thought I'd seen the promise land. He looked pleased.

"So why come to me?"

"Colonel Marquand thinks you can help."

"Colonel! I like that!" He turned to one of the others and said, "See the respect he gives his boss. Colonel!"

The other guy made a face like he thought Capra was crazy, but clearly in a way that implied he meant no harm.

"See how they treat me around here," Capra said to me. I nodded and grinned. Not too big of a grin. Just enough to keep everyone happy.

"And what does *Colonel* Marquand think I can do?"

"He thinks you can help us find his son," I said. "The Colonel knows you have more connections than anyone else in the city—and I mean that with the utmost respect, Mr. Capra—and he believes you could use your influence and connections to get to the bottom of who did this horrible thing."

Right then a cowboy at one of the poker tables hit it big and let out a piercing *yee-haw*. A blonde with Band-Aids on her heels rushed over and gave him a little dance that culminated with his head being mashed between her pendulous tits. Compliments of the winner, the bartender knocked out a round of drinks for the players. Capra watched intently as everything unfolded and when the game finally resumed he said, "If I didn't respect Marquand and all the things he's done for this country, I'd say no. But even for people I admire, I don't work for free. I'm a businessman. And with all business, there's overhead. I'm going to have to encourage others to provide information. So I'll need…compensation. You understand, right?"

"I do."

"Tell him I think my services are worth five thousand."

I nodded, thinking Marquand had just opened a whole new can of worms.

"He's getting a deal, you know," Capra said smiling at me.

"I'm sure he is."

He finished his drink and smacked his lips. "Good. Have it tomorrow night. Be in front of Sid King's at ten o'clock and don't be late."

Before I could respond Capra turned away as if I'd never been there and began speaking to one of the others. I scooted away, sipped my scotch for a respectable period of time and milled around the tables before getting the hell out of there.

In the Dodge I lit a cigarette and took a couple deep breaths. When I realized I was totally covered in sweat I rolled down the window and sucked at the cool air. *Tomorrow night all over again*, I said to myself. Then I pushed the starter and drove away. A few minutes later I was at the house and about to pull into the curb when I spotted a figure sitting on the darkened porch. I tapped the gas, continued down the street and parked around the corner. Unlocking the trunk, I got my .45 and made sure a round was in the chamber, then I started up the alley. I hopped the back fence and went down the side of the house making sure to stay on my toes. Just short of the porch I paused and listened a moment. The rocker squeaked as the person moved and I swung around, reached over the rail and placed the muzzle against the back of their head.

"Who are you and what do you want?" I demanded.

It was a woman's shriek and immediately I knew it was Loren.

Stuffing the gun in my pocket I ran around to the stairs and up onto the porch. Loren came into my arms.

"Oh my God you scared me to death! What were you doing? Didn't you just drive by?"

"Yes! But I saw someone sitting there and didn't know who it was."

"Do you always greet visitors like that?"

"It's just…I was at this place where…" I held her away from me so I could look at her face. "Are you crying?"

"No…"

"Oh! Did I make you cry? I'm sorry!"

She shook her head and I knew then that she had been crying

before I drove up.

I unlocked the door. Loren took my hand and pulled me directly to the bedroom. She pulled off her clothes and got under my blanket. I got in with her. She was warm against my body and soft against my lips and mouth. I tasted her. Then I entered her. She put her hands on the back of my neck and we kissed, her legs wrapped tightly around me, pulling me to her, in her.

When we finished, I got us each a cigarette and lit them with the Zippo. I could only really see her face when she drew on it and the tip lit her face. She looked happy and I liked her next to me on the small mattress. A car went down the street, the headlights throwing a beam that went from one end of the room to the other.

"I'm worried about Christian," she said. "Not the Colonel. I mean little Christian."

"It's all about money. He'll be okay."

"What if it isn't?"

"What else could it be?" I asked.

"You don't know the Colonel," she said.

CHAPTER 17

I'd just gotten under the bright lights of the Sid King's Crazy Horse Bar when a limousine as long as a battleship pulled up. Friar Tuck hopped out and held the door. Inside I ended up sandwiched between him and Tony Capra.

"I'm going to search you," Friar Tuck said, as we pulled from the curb. He patted me up and down, paying attention to my waistline, underarms and socks. A bulge he found in my coat pocket was the manila envelope with Marquand's five thousand dollars.

"That's all of it?" Capra asked.

"Yes."

He waved it off and Friar Tuck put the money into his own coat pocket.

"Are you a gambling man, Mr. Thorpe?"

"Not particularly," I said.

"I've got someone I want you to meet. He'll be doing legwork for you on this Marquand stuff. I hope he didn't think I'd be doing the heavy lifting myself."

"He's familiar with a chain of command."

"Good," he said, taking a pearl cigarette case out. Friar Tuck leaned across me with a lit match. Capra offered me one from the case. I declined, not wanting to be beholden to these guys for anything. He clicked it shut and put it back in his pocket.

"This guy I want you to meet, he has a little event going tonight. I thought we'd stop by. You sure you're not a gambler?

I've got five G's I could loan you. And I'll even give you a tip...*go brown.*"

I gave him a nice little chuckle but declined as the driver turned right onto Park Avenue and we started for downtown.

"Suit yourself, but you should never pass on a sure thing. They don't come around very often," he said, exhaling and inspecting a thumbnail. "This Marquand thing is big. I'm not sure five is going to be enough. Do you know how we get information off the street? We grease palms. And that can get pricey. Especially with something like this, where people are afraid to talk. I can't just start cracking heads. Is that what Marquand thought I'd do? Crack heads? I'm a businessman. And I've got to be sensitive to how my actions affect business. So, for now we grease the palms. Do you understand that?"

"Absolutely."

"Good," he said, putting the cigarette to his mouth. Tonight his cufflinks were pearls that must have come from oysters as big as hubcaps. I wondered if the cigarette case and cufflinks were a matched set and if the cigarette case the night before had been a hollowed gold bar.

I again told him I understood completely and he said 'good' three more times in a row, as if not only convincing me but himself.

We circled a block near Union Station and turned in at an abandoned warehouse. Two cops in uniform were directing traffic into adjacent lots. Cars were parking everywhere and people weaved through them to join a line that was forming at the rear loading dock. We slid into a spot next to the building that a kid in a dark hat and long coat was saving, then skipped past the others at the door and took a freight elevator down past two empty levels. At the bottom we shuddered to a stop on a vast room filled with people and what looked like a miniature arena with bleacher seats constructed of unpainted wood.

I followed Capra and Friar Tuck as we made our way through the crowd, Capra shaking hands and patting shoulders along the way. Another kid in a suit I couldn't afford was reserving seats in the front row. In the center of the bleachered space was a circular pit bordered by a three foot wall. Capra scooted in and motioned for me to slide in next to him. "My friend'll be here in a minute," he yelled over the racket. "I hope you don't need a drink because there's no alcohol. It's too hard to get in and out."

I shook my head.

"Last chance to get in on that action. There's money to be made," he yelled, pointing to a group of bet-takers that were working the crowd.

I smiled and shook my head.

Capra's presence seemed to set everything into motion. The crowd began to file onto the bleachers and the bet takers were swamped with last minute pledges. The noise off the concrete walls was deafening, making it difficult to speak, so I just watched men and women from nearly every corner of life climb onto the bleachers and push in for seats. A girl in a sable coat, accompanied by her greying sugar daddy, climbed in next to a pair of stiffs in overalls from the rail yard. A young couple that might have been newlyweds were sitting next to three sailors in cracker jack blues.

Because of the short walls surrounding the pit, I figured it was going to be a cock fight. I'd seen one in Miami and it had the same setup. I also promised myself I would never go again. Just as I was finishing that thought, several men in shirt sleeves made their way through the crowd with buckets and other supplies for ringside. I was watching them set up when a slight man with a pock-marked face and a nose like a toucan slid in next to me. He leaned across and tapped Capra's leg. Capra smiled and they shook hands. Speaking directly into my ear Capra told me his name was Johnny Two-Nose. I shook Johnny's hand and spoke my name into his ear. He nodded and smiled and said something back that I couldn't understand. Suddenly the crowd began to quiet and I saw a tuxedoed man waving his arms in the center of the ring.

Capra leaned into me so Johnny could also hear him speak. "Johnny knows lots of people. *Lots of people.* And Johnny knows how to get people to talk. He's the guy you'll work with from now on."

Get your bets in. Get your bets in–the tuxedoed man was yelling. *Last chance to place those bets!*

"Tony gave me the run-down," Johnny said. "We'll find out who took that baby. I already got some feelers out and I'm talking to more people tomorrow."

"That's great, Mr...ah...Two-Nose," I said.

"Johnny. Call me Johnny," he said, his breath smelling of anise, his teeth long and chalky. "And, if you ever need anything, ask for me at the Cavalcade. I'll make sure they know Harry Thorpe is a guy I'm working with. You won't get no trouble from no one."

"I appreciate that, Johnny."

"We all respect Christian Marquand and want to do the right thing."

"But," Capra said, patting my leg, "don't forget what I said about the greasing,"

"Tony's right," Johnny added. "Money talks."

"I understand," I said to Johnny, who offered me his hand again. We shook and he smiled broadly.

Bets are closed! Bets are closed!—the man in the tuxedo yelled, waving his arms. A minute later the crowd erupted as several men came to the edge of the pit from different sides. Little doors were opened in the low wall and they brought in two dogs. Johnny and Capra jumped to their feet, clapping wildly and I found myself on mine as well. But I could only clench my fists in my pockets as I knew what was about to happen.

The dogs were both bull terriers with large, egg-shaped heads and squat, stocky bodies. One was a mottled brown and the other pure white. I couldn't hear them over the crowd but they were barking and already struggling to get at each other, their teeth bared and saliva flying.

"Remember what I said," Capra yelled in my ear. "Brown! You'll see!"

The handlers in the pit passed the leashes to the other men and jumped out. Only the dogs remained inside. They strained to get at each other and after a hand-flashed countdown, were unclipped. Like a blur the dogs dove into each other and the crowd screamed. Immediately, the white dog sunk its teeth into the neck of its slower opponent and began shaking violently. The brown dog struggled to twist and free itself but was unable, even as they tumbled and fought around the ring. When finally pinned down near the wall, the brown dog was able to get hold of one of the white dog's legs and that got them rolling and spinning across the floor again. The plywood bleachers rocked and shook under the frenzied howls and stomping of feet. The whole ordeal seemed like it might go on forever and I wanted to look at anything but the bloody dogs. The three sailors were yelling through cupped hands. Another man was frantically waving his fist in the air. The girl across from me, in the sable coat, gleefully clapped her hands and jumped up and down. I found it hard not to be disturbed, yet mesmerized by her excitement. In the ring, the cement was streaked with blood as the dogs ripped at each other's flesh. It wasn't long before the white dog had the other, obviously exhausted and horribly maimed, pinned against the wall. There it began shredding the flesh of the brown dog's face before launching a savage attack on the neck and throat. Soon the only movement in the ring was the white dog's head, shaking, shaking, shaking as it deepened its grip. The brown dog's tongue hung pathetically, spittle and blood spraying as it coughed and struggled to breathe, its face a mess of chewed flesh and bare bone. The crowd erupted again when one of the men began to beat at the white dog over the short wall with what appeared to be a sawed off broom handle. When it finally released its grip, the man prodded it back as the brown dog desperately tried get to its feet. But before it was even capable of partially rising on one leg the white dog lunged again, latching onto its neck. The man jumped into the ring and beat at the white dog again until it let go. Prodded back to the opposite side, it wearily sat, chest heaving and tongue hanging nearly to the floor. It too had been disfigured in the fight. It looked as if an ear and eye were both missing.

The crowd screamed and applauded and stamped their feet and I realized Capra was pushing at me. I got out of his way. He was yelling something I couldn't hear, his face not four inches from Johnny's. Without waiting for a response, Capra turned and began crossing the open space. Johnny trailed behind, his arms out at his sides as if he was attempting an apology. Unsure what I was supposed to do, I followed and caught up to them in the empty hall. Capra had turned back on Johnny and was yelling, "What the fuck, Johnny? Do you know how much I lost on that?"

Johnny pulled the door open on a room where four other dogs were being held in cages against one wall and several men were having a lively discussion, apparently about the way things had unfolded in the ring. One of them, seeing Johnny and Capra, came right over. He shook his head and shrugged his shoulders, "I don't know…" he started.

"What the fuck was that, Dominic?" Capra asked him.

"I really don't know, Tony," Dominic said. "We filled the sonofabitch with so much dope I didn't think he'd be able to walk, let alone fight."

"Well I lost twenty bills on that shit!" Tony spat at him. "And you fuckers are gonna have to make that up! There's no goddamned way I'm losing on a fucking guarantee."

"I promise, Tony," Johnny said. "I'll make good."

"Sure, Tony, we'll make good on it. Bet against the black one in the next fight," Dominic said, pointing to one of the dogs in the cages that looked too doped to stand.

"Do I look like a chump to you?" Tony asked, rapping Dominic in the chest. "I wouldn't bet on your sure-fucking-thing if my life depended on it. You cocksuckers owe me."

"I'll make sure you get your money," Johnny said, moving as if he wanted to touch Capra's shoulder and thought better about it.

"And my winnings," Capra yelled.

"Of course, Tony. That too."

The door swung open and a blast of the crowd noise hit us like a shockwave. The men in shirtsleeves brought in the two dogs that had just fought. The white one was walking, but wheezing horribly. It looked so horrific up close with its missing eye that I didn't want to look. The brown dog was pulled in on a blanket. The dogs in the cages went crazy at the sight of the others. Dominic and another man kicked and yelled at them to shut up as the white dog was put back in its cage.

"Get this shit right," Capra screamed over the racket.

"Sure, Tony. We will," Johnny yelled.

Capra turned to go and I wasn't sure what to do, so I started to follow. He pushed me back. "He's with you," he yelled at Johnny.

"Sure, Tony. No problem."

When Capra had left, and the door closed, Johnny wheeled on Dominic. "What's the fucking matter with you?" he shouted so loud even the dogs stopped barking for a second. Spittle struck Dominic in the face. When he went to wipe it away Johnny hit him one, two, three times in the face. Dominic cowered and tried to duck as Johnny continued to strike him over and over. All the men scattered, knocking over a table as they moved to give them room. Johnny beat, then kicked Dominic as he fell to the floor and curled defensively into a ball. When Johnny stopped he turned on the others panting. "If you motherfuckers are going to tell me it's a fucking guarantee then it better be a fucking guarantee." Turning back to Dominic, Johnny kicked him in the stomach several times and followed that with a heel to the head, unleashing a torrent of blood across the tile floor. Someone near me let out a groan. When Johnny spun on him the man instinctively raised his arms to ward off the coming onslaught. Ripping a dog leash from the man's hands Johnny began swinging the metal clip at him. The man tried to shield himself from the blows with open hands above his head but the clip bit into his forehead and he soon fell to his knees, blood pouring into his eyes.

"Is that fucker still alive?" Johnny roared.

No one said a word and Johnny yelled again, pointing at the brown dog on the blanket. "Is that piece of shit still alive?"

"Yes Johnny," someone said.

"Get it up on the table," Johnny said, pointing to the overturned table.

Two men righted the table and the dog was lifted onto it. Johnny wrapped the leash around the neck and began pulling tight. Blood spurted from the dog's mouth and its legs kicked frantically. It seemed like two solid minutes before the body finally stopped moving. Johnny turned on the white dog from the fight and kicked at its cage, toppling it over. Even with its missing eye and ear the dog fought Johnny's attack, biting at his foot. Enraged further, Johnny began swinging the leash against the cage, then he started kicking more violently, almost stomping on the sides and bending some of the bars and mesh. All the while the dog was fighting back until all of a sudden the room exploded as Johnny began shooting. One two, three times he fired into the dog's head and body.

Everything was suddenly frozen. The dogs had stopped barking and the men stood rooted. Only the sound of the shots buzzed through   my   head.

CHAPTER 18

The cemetery had two entrances, the main one on Alameda Boulevard and a side gate on Quebec Street. Loftesness was supposed to meet the "Jim" mentioned in the ransom note near the Quebec gate. I entered the cemetery from Alameda, parked in the lot near the administration building and wandered through the headstones in the direction where he would be. The plan was for Loftesness to stay close to the gate and wait for Jim to make contact. Once the meeting was over, I would try following Jim to get an idea where little Christian might be held. Or, if that wasn't possible, I'd at least try to get something that might help us identify him. Since Loftesness was supposed to be alone, Marquand was going to stay hidden in his car outside on the street. Against my objections, he insisted on bringing his revolver.

I weaved my way over to a position near a large granite mausoleum that allowed a full view of Loftesness and the Quebec gate. He was already pacing back and forth in those God-awful, rubber-soled shoes, his head jerking at what I imagined was every little sound. I couldn't blame him for his nervousness, I was a bit antsy too and had to keep wiping my own sweaty palms on my pants. For the longest time he just went back and forth, and soon my mind began to drift to Johnny stomping Dominic and killing the dogs. The brutality seemed burned into my retinas, and there it was, replayed over and over every time I closed my eyes. More disturbing than the violence was the look on Johnny's face. And the soulless anger in his eyes as he strangled the brown dog to death. Not just anger, but total and complete pleasure in the act itself. I shook out a cigarette and tried to throw off the thoughts, and suddenly I noticed there was no Loftesness. He was gone. Not at the gate, not in with the tombstones. Nowhere. Before I really had a chance to react, something got me from behind. My knees went out and I went down like an empty suit.

When I came to, it was dark and cold. I was sure someone had poked a hole in the back of my head. I checked. It was just a nice lump about the size of a golf ball. No blood. I rolled on my side and threw up. There wasn't much to come, but I heaved until I couldn't possibly heave any more. My head was pounding so hard I was sure it could be heard from twenty feet away. After a while I wiped my eyes and mouth and pushed myself up to lean against a headstone. My watch said it was five after six. I'd been out maybe ten minutes. It seemed like a week. Then the shivers came.

When I was finally able to pull myself to my feet, I saw a flashlight approaching. I palmed my .45 and held it behind my back. Another whack on the head and they'd be lowering me into one of those graves. But it was just the security guard, looking for the owner of a Dodge. He informed me the cemetery was closed and followed me out. I'm sure he figured I was a drunk by the way I was weaving and stumbling. He would never know how lucky he was I didn't shoot him.

I took it slow and drove over to Country Club and parked in front of the house. Loftesness was with Marquand in his office. They were disappointed when I told them about my little nap and showed off the bump. They figured I had been out following Jim. Loftesness declined when I asked him to examine my head, reminding me that he was an ophthalmologist. Victor brought four aspirin, a glass of water and an ice pack.

Their disappointment in me turned to excitement when Loftesness retold the details of the encounter for my benefit. He said Jim finally appeared when it got dark, and the ransom was being increased to one hundred thousand dollars since the cops had been involved. Jim said we had one week to get the money. "And like we discussed," Loftesness continued, "I told him we wanted proof they had Christian. So he's going to send the sleeping suit in the mail."

"Did you get a good view of him?" I interjected.

"Not really. It was hard to see him, plus he was under a tree.

Anyway," he continued, "all of a sudden I had this idea-what if we continue communicating through the newspaper? So, I told him I'd put another ad saying the money is ready and that I'd sign it *Lofty* so he'd know for sure that it was us."

"Brilliant idea, Doctor," Marquand said.

"And? Did he agree to that," I asked.

"Yes. He said they would do the same thing. They will place an ad telling me where to be with the money."

"Okay. Good. And, did he mention little Christian?" I asked, checking the bump and my fingers to make sure I really wasn't bleeding.

"I was just telling the Colonel about that when you got here. He said Christian was fine and that a woman was taking care of him."

"He mentioned a woman?"

"Yeah, it was sort of like *the child is fine, we're staying at a hotel so there's nothing to worry about* and *there's a woman taking care of the baby.* That's pretty much his words exactly."

"Wow. That's interesting. Are you thinking what I'm thinking, Colonel?"

"Sonja," he said.

"But why would he be so stupid and tell us those things?" Then to Loftesness I said, "Did he have an accent?"

"It sounded kind of German to me."

"Maybe they figure we already know it's Sonja, so why pretend it isn't," Marquand said.

"Seems careless," I said, readjusting the ice pack and wincing as it touched the bump.

"Wait!" Loftesness said, jumping to his feet. "Shouldn't it be relatively easy to find two Germans and a child staying in a hotel?"

"I was just thinking the same thing," Marquand exclaimed.

CHAPTER 19

The next day we made a list of hotels and divided it up. After I'd coached Marquand and Loftesness on how to sound official and act like cops on the phone, I drove over to my office to call the ones on my list. Three hours later I was nearly finished and had nothing. My head was still throbbing from the clubbing so I took more aspirin and went to get something to eat at the restaurant in the lobby. I spent the extra nickel, opting for the brisket instead of the chicken, and followed that with a piece of cherry pie. When I finished, I walked a half block in the drizzle to a liquor store for a bottle of bourbon.

I had just returned to my building when a horn sounded and an unmarked police car splashed to the curb. Tooley reached behind the seat and popped open the back door. "Get in," he said.

"Hey," I said, slipping into the back seat. "What are you guys up to?"

"On our way back to Morrison. Again," Greenberg said, turning in the seat to face me. He had black circles under his eyes.

"You look like crap," I said.

"You don't look so good yourself."

"It's been a rough week."

"Where you coming from?" Greenberg asked.

"Picking up a little after dinner drink," I said, holding up the sacked bottle.

"So...what's been making your week so rough?" Greenberg asked.

"Nothing special. Just haven't been getting much sleep I guess."

"Nothing special. Really," he stated. "What about this guy Loftesness? We've been hearing his name floating around."

"Some eye doctor Marquand knows."

"And that's it?"

"That's all I know." I raised the bottle. "Anyone want a snort?"

Tooley passed, saying it would give him heartburn after just having chicken salad. Greenberg took the bottle, pulled the cork and took a long pull. When I was taking my turn he said, "So, you're not going to tell me about Loftesness."

"I know the same as you."

"And what about Tony Capra?"

I wasn't all that surprised he knew about Loftesness, but I'm sure I gave a little jerk when he mentioned Capra. I tried to look confused: "*The* Tony Capra?"

"Fuck you, Thorpe."

"Isn't that sweet."

Greenberg reached for the bottle. After drinking he wiped his mouth with the back of his hand.

"Okay," I said. "I'll tell you this—whatever Marquand has me pursuing—it's a dead end. So you needn't worry about it."

"And you know that for certain?" he asked.

"No, but I got a feeling."

"He's got a feeling," Greenberg said to Tooley.

"Yeah, I got a feeling," I said. "If it were anything worth a damn, you'd be the first to know."

"What a swell guy," Greenberg said, again speaking to Tooley.

I held my hand out and he gave me the bottle. "That's me. A real swell guy," I said toasting myself and taking a swig. "Did you guys put out a bulletin on Sonja Hoff?"

"Why should I tell you anything?" Greenberg asked.

"It seems to me like she's the one," I said, ignoring his peevishness.

"Is that right? Well, thank you, detective," Greenberg said. "Let me give you this little piece of advice. Watch yourself with Capra. You might just end up getting stung. And then we'll see who you come running to. Let's blow," he said to Tooley. "We're wasting our time."

Tooley shifted into gear. I opened my door and stepped out into the rain.

Greenberg rolled his window down. As they pulled out into traffic he called out, "He's not someone you play with, Thorpe. Be careful."

He was right. And I knew it. Involving Capra was only going to lead to trouble. I had to figure out a way to get Marquand to understand that. As soon as I got up to the office I called over to the Country Club house. Victor answered and a few minutes later Marquand came on the line, his voice filled with anticipation.

"What have you got, Thorpe?"

"I got nothing. Anything on your end?" I said.

"Nothing."

"What about Loftesness?"

"Don't you think I would have called you if he had anything?"

I ignored his tone and said, "Colonel, I'm a little concerned with this Capra thing. I'm afraid we'll never shake them now that you're paying them."

"You said all that earlier."

"I don't think you realize how dangerous these guys can be," I said, seeing Johnny's uncontrollable rage in my head.

"I'm sending Richard over with that money I owe you."

"Colonel! You don't need to do that!"

"Stop needling me, Thorpe. You're like an old woman. If I want to go with Capra, then I want to go with Capra. If I want to pay you, then I want to pay you. I don't need you questioning everything I do," he said and clicked off.

I poured myself a glass from the bottle and settled in on the couch. It would be easy to rationalize just about anything with money like that pouring in. And, in theory, if Johnny didn't stomp my brains out, and we got that baby back, things were looking pretty good. Better than they had in a long while. Plus, there was Loren; flawed and sexy and so incredibly intriguing. I'd never met a woman who could be so gorgeous and perilous at the same time. I laid back and let my mind meander all over her; the heaviness of her makeup and the dangerous looking teeth, the firmness of her stomach and those perky little breasts. And how her fingers felt on my flesh; soft and firm and completely aware of what they wanted. An hour or so later I was still laying there. The bourbon had warmed me through and the rain against the windows made for a pleasant little slumber. It was right about then the outer door buzzed. I figured it was Richard and yelled for him to come in. But it wasn't. It was Johnny Two-Nose and some other guy.

"Hey Johnny," I said, starting to get up.

Johnny held up a hand, "Don't get up on our account. God knows we don't want to disturb your little nap." Then to the half-ton beast with him he said, "Look at this, Ugo. I shoulda been a private detective. Drunk and passed out on the job. What a life!"

Again I started to get up but he told me to stay, and turning one of the straight back chairs, sat facing me. The beast with him gave the inner door a little push. It swung closed, the latch clicking loudly, leaving the room almost black without the light from the outer office. Snapping his fingers, Johnny told Ugo to turn on the desk lamp. When the light came on I got a good look at his cinder block face. It reminded me of Atlas shouldering the world in Rockefeller Center. I scooted my eyes back to Johnny.

"I thought I'd stop by and say hello. I'm sure you and your boss must be wondering what I've been able to dig up. And then, look at this, I've interrupted your siesta," Johnny said.

"I figured you'd contact me when you had something." I pointed to the bottle on the desk. "Can I pour you one?"

"No, no. Not me. Not when I'm working. Bad habit to get into. But, I appreciate what you said–about *me* contacting *you*. I hate when people pressure me. It makes me nervous and when I get nervous I'm not my usual friendly self," he said, the desk lamp casting shadows that hid half his face.

I nodded and tried to appear sympathetic or anything in general that wouldn't be construed as confrontational.

"Anyway," Johnny went on, "I came over here to tell you it looks like there's a guy who's looking to get some money washed. Supposedly a lot of money. The kick is, he don't have it yet. Has Marquand paid out anything?"

"Not yet."

"Well, this guy says it's going to be around a hundred G's. Sounds like it might be your man, right?"

"Totally. Do you have a name?"

"No name."

"Okay. Is he a German?"

"How the hell would I know. I'm not talking to him myself. Someone I know is dealing with him." He tilted his head back and said to Ugo, "Did they say anything about this guy being a Kraut?"

It took a few seconds and Ugo finally said, "Are you talking to me?"

"What? You think I'm asking this guy questions about the money guy? Yeah I'm talking to you."

"Sorry, Johnny," Ugo said. "I don't remember."

Even though the beast was three times the size of Johnny I was afraid what might happen next. So I said, "It's okay. I just wondered. Anyway, that's great stuff, Johnny."

"Yeah. I thought you might like it. But you need to get some more grease. Okay? What you gave Tony before, that just isn't going to hack it."

"Sure. I'll talk to Marquand," I said.

"Good. You do that. I already promised some people a little taste to keep things moving out there. I don't want to look stupid when I can't come through. Got it?"

"Absolutely. How much do you need?"

"Ten more should be good."

I whistled and said, "Damn, Johnny. That's a lot of dough."

Johnny screwed up his face as if I'd just said I was wearing panties. "What? If someone took one of my kids, I'd pay a hundred G's to get them back. And if I didn't have it, I'd sure as shit figure out a way to get it. You got kids, right? You know what I'm saying."

"It's just that a lot of money, and I need to talk to Marquand. I'm sure he'll pay."

"I hope so." As he was saying that, the outer door buzzed. Johnny gave a slight jump, then raised his chin at me.

"A delivery," I said. "Some papers and such from Marquand."

"Okay, we'll go. I just wanted you to know that we're onto something. You make sure to tell Marquand. All right?"

"Of course. Do you think you might know more about this guy before the ransom is paid?"

"Not if we don't get more grease. Do you see why I'm saying that's so important?"

"Sure, Johnny. I totally get it."

"Good," Johnny said, standing and straightening the chair before the desk. Then he opened the door. There stood Richard in his chauffeur uniform. He started to come in but stopped dead in his tracks as soon as he saw Johnny. I told Richard we were just finishing up and he slid over by the three empty chairs in the waiting area.

"I'll be in touch," I said to Johnny.

"Good. Good." He offered his hand and I shook it. I didn't bother shaking Ugo's hand as he went by. He was too busy chomping his gapped teeth at me, as if he wanted to take a bite out of my neck. Then he belched a laugh at his cleverness, a blast of onions and rotten teeth in my face.

Johnny paused and turned toward Richard, who was concentrating on the rain spattered chauffeur hat in his hands.

"I know you. Don't I?" Johnny said.

Richard barely raised his eyes.

"What's your name?"

"Richard Carmasino."

"You look familiar to me. You come around the Cavalcade?"

"I been there."

"You a player?"

"No," Richard said.

"Oh…" Johnny grinned, "you got a girl there."

"No," Richard said straight faced. "I just get a drink sometimes."

"Nobody just gets a drink at the Cavalcade," Johnny said, his grin fading. Then after a long moment he turned to me and gave a one finger salute.

When they were gone and the outer door closed, I followed Richard into the inner office. "For you," he said, holding out an envelope.

I put it on the desk. "You know him?"

"I seen him around."

"The Cavalcade. Is that where you get the dope for Loren?"

He shot me a look. But it faded. I was sure by that point he'd been through the wringer with Greenberg and Tooley and had to figure I'd know the whole story. He pointed to the bottle on the desk and said, "Mind if I?"

I got another glass from the metal shelf above the sink and poured us both a couple fingers. He swirled the contents around a few times before drinking it down.

"I didn't want all that to come out, you know," he said. "I like her."

"Yeah? How long you been getting stuff for her?"

"Couple years, I guess. It's just once in a while. I think other times she gets reefer or shit for herself."

"Why you?"

"You think she wants to deal with people like that?" he said, thumbing towards the door.

"And she pays you?"

"What do you think?"

"So she was at the house the entire night the kid disappeared?" I asked, sitting down behind the desk.

"As far as I know. She was there when I left and there when I got back."

"Then there's no way either of you could have gotten all the way up to Morrison and back in time?"

"In time for what? To take that kid?" He scoffed, settling into one of the chairs and leaning back, the front legs coming off the floor.

I didn't say anything.

Richard made a sound and shook his head. "I already told the cops everything. Ask them about it."

I took a cigarette from the engraved box and turned it to him. He took one and used matches pulled from a pocket.

"I'm asking about Loren Chambers. Not you," I said. He watched as I lit my cigarette with the Zippo. "Could she have made it up to Morrison and back while you were out buying her junk?"

"That's over two hours travel time."

"Why the hesitancy in your voice?"

"There isn't any. There's just no way she could've got up there and back."

I motioned toward the bottle and he poured himself another inch.

"But…" I prodded.

"But nothing."

"I see it in your eyes," I said. "What are you hiding?"

"I'm not hiding nothing." He drank off the contents of his glass and leaned forward to set it on the desk. The chair legs thumping the floor. "There was just this time, with the baby, I'm thinking about. With Loren."

"Go on."

He took a long drag on the cigarette and let it out as an exaggerated sigh. "Shit! Okay, there was this time, when he was just born, and he disappeared from his crib or whatever. Everyone was going apeshit looking for him. Upstairs. Downstairs. They were running all over the goddamned place. And for some reason Victor told me to check the garage. I'm thinking, what the hell would a baby be doing in the garage? Like he was, what? A month old? But whatever. Victor's the head-nigger-in-charge, so I go out to the garage and as I'm passing the trash I hear this noise. And there he was. In the trash."

"Little Christian was in the trash?"

"Yeah. That's what I'm saying."

"And?"

"And come to find out, it was Loren that threw him out."

"How do you know it was her."

"Because she and her sister got into this humongous fight over the whole thing. I mean, like giant fucking fight. Screaming, hollering, the whole nine yards. And in the middle of it all, Loren yells that she *threw the goddamned baby out.* Those were her words."

"You heard her say that?"

"Everyone did," Richard said, pouring himself another drink.

CHAPTER 20

Loftesness received the sleeping suit the next day in the mail. Marquand had the nursemaid look at it. She confirmed it was the one the child was wearing the night he went missing, having sewn it herself from an old flannel nightgown. Since Marquand was going to the bank that afternoon to get the money, Loftesness went ahead and called the *News* to place the ad. He told the woman on the other end of the phone it only needed to say, *Money is ready. Lofty.* She confirmed that it would run the following day.

The three of us took coffee on a portico outside Marquand's office that was surrounded by an explosion of tulips. Camille brought muffins, still warm from the oven. Marquand didn't touch his but Loftesness and I didn't leave a crumb.

"We'll probably hear from them in the next couple days. Then we'll make the exchange and you'll have your son back, Colonel. I've got my five thousand to add to the money when you're ready for it," Loftesness said, wiping his mouth and refolding the napkin. "Is that a putting green you have there?" he said, pointing off into the garden.

Marquand turned his head and looked at Loftesness as if surprised by the question. "Yes," he said.

"It's a beautiful garden." Loftesness said, scooting his chair back. I thought he was leaving, but instead he slumped down, closed his eyes and settled in for a sunbath.

I didn't really want to talk about Johnny Two-Nose with Loftesness present, but it didn't look like he was going anywhere. I finally gave in and said, "Colonel, I met again with one of Capra's men and they want another ten thousand."

Marquand turned to look at me. Loftesness opened his eyes.

"On the surface it might seem like a swell idea to involve them," I said. "But how are we going to shut them down?"

"They can't ask for more money once Christian's been found," Marquand said.

Loftesness sat forward and poured himself more coffee.

I toyed with the fringe on my napkin and eventually put it on the table. "But until then they're in full extortion mode," I said.

"How is it extortion if they're the ones that are digging up everything we know so far?" Marquand returned his cup to its saucer. "The police don't know anything about someone wanting to launder money."

"I completely agree with the Colonel," Loftesness said to me.

I wanted to slap the gross walrus mustache off his face. Instead I said, "The police don't even know we're paying a ransom."

"Because they would only bungle the whole thing," Marquand said. "And get my son killed. We continue dealing with Capra until I say we stop. I don't want to discuss it further."

I said *okay* and after a while excused myself to leave. Without looking at me, Marquand said they'd call when they heard something. Outside on the porch I lit a cigarette and wandered over the edge of the labyrinth. The grass between the stones was bright green with new growth.

Two days later Marquand called me at the office and said he and Loftesness were on their way over. When they arrived, Marquand handed me the morning paper, and while I had just finished flipping through the want ads, I'd obviously missed the one he had circled with red ink. It said, *Lofty: Northwest corner Lincoln & Colfax. 4pm today.* I wasn't sure what to say and I guess they felt the same as we all three just sat there and looked at each other with nervous grins. I handed the paper back to Marquand and finally ventured, "Are you ready, Colonel?"

"I bought a new suitcase yesterday."

"And the bank has the serial numbers?"

"Yes. Dr. Loftesness convinced me that was a good idea."

I gave Loftesness a look. If he didn't actually appear terrified under his nervous grin, I would have been convinced he was involved somehow.

"Then we're all set," I said. "That's a good intersection for us with all the one-way streets. I should be able to follow no matter what direction they approach from."

"I'm not so sure I want you following them, Thorpe." Marquand said. "We're so close now, I don't see the need to put Christian at further risk. Let's just let Dr. Loftesness give them the money."

The expression on his face was so foreign to me that I wasn't sure what to say. Was it concern? Or dread? Maybe it was a glimmer of hope. "Are you sure, Colonel? This might be…"

"No! I don't want you following them," he said.

"Okay," I said. Then to Loftesness, "Just see if you can get the plate number as they drive away. And anything else that may be helpful later. Voices, complexions, rings, anything. Try to have your senses on full alert. But don't worry if you don't pick up on everything. In a stressful situation you may be pinpointed. Just try to focus on…"

"Does any of that matter?" Marquand interrupted.

"What do you mean? Of course it does," I said.

Marquand stared out the window a minute. "We'll have Christian back," he finally said. "So, none of that matters."

"Don't you want to know who did this?"

"I guess I was thinking it was Sonja all along."

"Even if it is. Do you want to just pay her?"

"Of course not!" Marquand snapped.

CHAPTER 21

The three of us waited for Loftesness' taxi at the Country Club house without saying a word. Marquand stared off into the distance. Loftesness chewed on his fingers and I mostly smoked on the edge of the putting green. When the time came, we all shook hands and Loftesness climbed into the back of the taxi with the new suitcase filled with one hundred and five thousand dollars. As he drove off, the doctor gave a diffident little salute. Marquand returned it smartly as if Loftesness was a man headed into battle. Then we went to wait in the office.

Marquand stayed behind his desk, absently fiddling with a crystal paperweight and staring out the French doors. I slumped in one of the leather chairs by the fireplace. For a while I tried thinking about anything but Loftesness and what might be happening. Four o'clock came and went. Then four thirty. Soon I was checking my watch every five minutes, each time giving it an absentminded winding until Marquand told me to stop. Mrs. Marquand came in before five o'clock. Her eyes were red and ringed with dark circles, as if she hadn't slept a wink since little Christian disappeared. I excused myself and stood outside with the door closed until she finished crying into Marquand's shoulder.

Five o'clock came and still nothing. A fire started in my stomach, filling my mouth with that metallic acid taste. I tried sitting up straight in hopes it would lessen the intensity. It didn't. At five-fifteen Victor came to offer tea. Marquand waved him off. I asked for a bromo. It didn't help.

At five-thirty I was beginning to wonder where Loftesness' body would turn up. Most likely he'd be dumped in the Platte River. It might take a few days, but eventually a hobo would find him. Of course he'd first dig through Loftesness' pockets, then look for a cop. I was playing that scene in my head when the phone started ringing. Marquand snatched the receiver from the cradle and jumped to his feet. After a couple hurried questions we were running down the hall and out of the house. As we jumped into the Dodge he yelled at Victor on the porch to tell Mrs. Marquand that we were on our way to get Christian. Before Victor could even respond I let the clutch fly, tires churning pea gravel. We bounced out of the drive and into the street.

"Where am I going?" I shouted.

"Union Station."

"Did he say what happened?"

"He said something about a goose chase. But he has a key for a room at the Baxter Hotel," Marquand hollered as we skidded almost sideways onto Speer Boulevard.

I zigged in and out of traffic, stomping the gas and brake alternatively.

"What else did he say?"

"Someone asked his name and they took the suitcase."

Within minutes we screeched to a stop in front of Loftesness standing on the curb. Once the three of us were mashed together on the bench seat I had the Dodge moving again even before Loftesness was able to close the door.

"Baxter Hotel," I said. "Is that Sherman or Grant?"

"Sherman and 9th," Loftesness yelled back, handing an envelope to Marquand.

"Was it the same guy from the cemetery?" I asked.

"I don't know. It was hard to tell."

I could see the piece of paper Marquand took from the envelope was stationary from the Baxter Hotel with a key taped to it. Below the key was 310 written in pencil. "It's 890 Sherman Street," Marquand read off the paper.

"Did you get a look at his face?" I asked Loftesness.

"No. It was so fast. He came from behind. He had a gray overcoat though," Loftesness said.

"What took so long?" I asked.

"He made me take a bus and a streetcar and a couple cabs to

about five or six different stops."

"How did you know where to go?"

"They told me to go to specific telephones and wait for a call. A couple times people had instructions for me."

"Hurry up, Thorpe!" Marquand yelled.

I stomped the gas pedal to the floor and steered into the oncoming lane around two cars waiting while someone parallel parked.

"What people?" I shouted over the engine.

"Just people. Like a ticket taker at a movie house. He told me where to go next."

"Okay, okay! Just drive," Marquand ordered.

"Turn here! Sherman is one way southbound," Loftesness hollered.

The tires screamed as we slid around the corner, the Baxter within view.

"Use the stairs," I ordered. "It'll be faster."

I slammed on the brakes as we slid to a stop in a parking space for cabs. All three of us bolted from the car, the doorman yelling after us. I flashed him my P.I. license saying it was official business. Inside we took the stairs, hurtling them two at a time. On the third floor I motioned for them to slow down and we stopped to breathe. I took the .45 from my shoulder holster and we started down the hall. Loftesness was trailing behind, puffing like a train. When I turned to press a finger to my lips I saw Marquand had his .38 out.

"Colonel, put your weapon away," I whispered. When he hesitated I said, "We don't need to be shooting each other. Put it away. You're going to want to carry your son anyway." He put it back into his coat pocket.

Outside 310 we stopped. I listened but couldn't hear anything. Marquand slowly ripped the key off the paper while Loftesness flattened himself against the wall and tried to breathe quietly through his mouth. I motioned to Marquand that maybe we should knock, so I did. Still I didn't hear anything so I knocked again a little louder. Nothing. Marquand inserted the key and turned the lock. The bolt clicked back with the effect of a thunderclap. None of us moved. I turned the knob and pushed the door wide.

It was a standard pay-by-the-week hotel room, a bed, small desk and a couple chairs. I motioned for them to wait and went first. I swept through quickly, looking behind the door, checking the bathroom and closet. I called for them and they came in. We looked everywhere; under the bed, in drawers, the tub, even out on the fire escape. There was no sign of a note or a child or that there ever had been one in that room.

After those first few frantic minutes Marquand ripped the paper out of his pocket and stared at both sides. "Did the man say anything to you?" he demanded.

"No. He just asked me my name and handed me the envelope," Loftesness said, his voice wavering.

"He didn't mention Christian?"

"No! I thought instructions would all be in the note."

"What are we missing?" Marquand asked me.

"Maybe there's something here somewhere."

We looked again. We looked everywhere. We started slowly and methodically and soon we had the bed torn apart, and the drawers out of the dresser and desk. We searched the folded towels, under the carpet, the transom, the lamp shades and behind the furniture. We touched every single inch of that room and found nothing.

After a while I went downstairs and spoke with the front desk. The room had been booked for one night under the name John Jones. The desk clerk couldn't remember anything more than it was an average looking man who arrived by cab earlier that morning, paid cash and left without actually going up to the room. He didn't think he had an accent.

For a long time we just sat amid the piles of bedding and drawers and stared at each other in silence. Once in a while Loftesness would blurt out snippets of his encounters, but it was just mind-churning babble without a beginning or end. Pretty soon we got up and silently rode the elevator down and climbed into the Dodge. I pulled the parking ticket from under the wiper and threw it in the gutter.

CHAPTER 22

At the Cavalcade I told the same bartender from the first visit that I was there to see Johnny. He gave no indication of remembering me and went to speak to a couple thugs in the back booth who I'd never seen before. Ten minutes and two cigarettes later Johnny appeared at my side. It was like we were old pals. He gave me a big smile and an equally big handshake and I almost expected an arm wrapped around my waist as he guided me to an empty booth. The bartender promptly followed us over and Johnny ordered two glasses of the *good* scotch with water backs.

"I know I said a man should never drink when he's working. But I've got some big news and I got a feeling you'll want to celebrate," he beamed. Then turning serious he said, "Did you bring the money?" I gave him the envelope and he put it in his coat without looking in it. "Good. I like to get all that out of the way. Alright, now for the big news. Oh wait! We should have our drinks first."

I played along.

"Good." He grinned at me again. Then his face dropped. "I didn't even think to ask. Are you a scotch man?"

"Bourbon. But scotch is fine."

"Tony's got us all drinking scotch. It's one of his passions. Did you know they even spell it differently in Scotland where scotch comes from. It's whisky, w-h-i-s-k-y. And over here, whiskey is spelled w-h-i-s-k-E-y. That's bourbon whiskey. Scotch is made from malt which is some sort of cereal, but not the breakfast kind.

Bourbon is made from corn, which actually seems weird to me. Anyway, I'm sure you probably knew all that. But I bet you didn't know that both whisky or whiskey with the E-y mean *water of life* in Latin. Pretty interesting, huh?"

"Very," I said, just as the bartender put down a bowl of nuts and our glasses.

"Tony told me all that. He knows everything about scotch. He's even been to Scotland, to where it's made, and drank some right out of the barrels." Johnny made a motion to toast my glass and we both took a drink. It tasted like the Macallan from the other night. Johnny licked his lips and said, "I still think it tastes a little like iodine. But it's good, isn't it?"

I told him it was. He tasted again, put the glass on the napkin and took a drink from his water. If I hadn't seen him stomping Dominic with my own eyes I'd almost think he was a regular guy having a regular drink with an old friend. But the images were still in my head and no matter how big the grin or how silly the conversation, I knew what lurked inside him and that I'd always need to be on guard.

"Okay. Now for the big news. You know how I told you a guy was asking about getting some money washed? Well, there's a woman involved too. Some ginch with a German accent."

"Wow!" I said, making sure I appeared even more impressed than I was, and I was actually pretty damn impressed. "That's great. Was there any mention of a baby?"

"No, my man didn't say anything about a baby."

"Still," I said, "that *is* some big news, Johnny."

"See! We'll come through for you."

"Totally. Does your man know where they're staying?"

"No. He just said there was the German dame. And…" he said, taking a slip of paper from his pocket and holding it up like a prize. "The guy drives a black '39 Ford. Here's the license plate number."

I took the paper. Genuine surprise, I'm sure was written all over my face.

"See what you can get with a little grease," he said, a toothy smile expanding under his giant nose. Holding up his scotch we toasted again. After we drank I put the paper in my pocket and let him talk about things I didn't hear while my mind spun around the fact that we might be really close to getting that kid back. I weighed out all the various scenarios and imagined Sonja Hoff in cuffs and little Christian back in his mother's arms. Johnny ordered another round and I watched his lips moving until I was finally able to wheel the conversation towards a point where I could get out of there.

Driving up 38th Avenue I debated on calling Greenberg and almost stopped twice when I saw pay phones. He could have someone looking up the license plate in a matter of minutes and before midnight they'd be kicking in a door somewhere. But the more I thought about it the more I felt I owed it to Marquand to make good on this myself. After all it was his fifteen grand that got us the plate number. Plus, I had my own connection at Motor Vehicles, so we didn't really need Greenberg to track down the owner. But more than anything else, it didn't sit right with me that all the glory and fanfare would go to Greenberg and that asshole Dmytryk when they hadn't turned up anything worth a shit the entire time.

When I pulled up in front of the house I saw someone waiting again on the porch in the rocker. This time Loren waved at me so I parked the car and got out. When I went up on the porch she stepped into my arms. I kissed her and held her tight against me. She tasted of cigarette and spearmint and smelled like honeysuckle and right then I wished I'd never asked Richard questions about her.

"How's your sister," I whispered in her ear.

"The same."

"I'm sorry," I said, holding her and feeling a sad, heaviness weighing her down. I wanted to blurt out the stuff Johnny told me but I was afraid to give any false hopes. Instead, and hoping to cheer her up, I said we should go out.

"I don't have any stockings on."

"You don't? No, I guess you don't," I said, my hands finding no sign of a garter. "You're a naughty girl, Miss Chambers."

"Do you like naughty?"

"I think I do. C'mon, let's go out. It'll take our minds off everything. Plus, I want to be seen with you."

"You aren't worried about being seen with a barelegged woman late at night?"

"It's bohemian," I said kissing her again. "Let's go dancing."

She sat close to me in the Dodge and I drove aimlessly for a while, enjoying her hand on my thigh and head resting against my shoulder. After a bit we ended up in front of Casper's. The red and green neon lit us as if we'd found ourselves at the end of a gaudy rainbow. A poster out front said the Seth Crane Quartet was playing. It looked like it had been there a decade, the sun having bleached the color and the corners curled.

"Well?" I asked her.

"Sure," she said, slowly uncurling her legs from the seat.

"We can go somewhere else if you want. I just thought if you want to dance, this is the place."

"No. It's fine. I used to come here a lot during the war. I don't want you to think anything if someone recognizes me."

"We've all got history," I said.

She put her hand in mine and let me guide her out of the car. Inside, I held her as we wheedled our way through the mixed crowd and burrowed into a corner near the bar. Everyone was bouncing to an electrified beat of *Lady Be Good*, the notes from Seth Crane's saxophone ricocheting off the bare brick walls like sunlight through a honey pot. Loren smiled at me and sashayed in time with the others, her eyes gorgeous in the emerald light. I put my hand where I would normally feel the garter. She was smooth and sexy and shifted her feet, inviting my hand around her hip. Raising herself on tiptoe, she moved so I could kiss her. When I did, her tongue came into my mouth and she pressed against me.

"If you're looking for bohemians you don't need to look much further," she said into my ear. "This place is packed with them."

"I like it," I said as we moved together to the music.

The bartender had worked his way down to our end. I yelled for two double bourbons and ginger ale.

"You surprise me," Loren said.

"Why's that?"

"You're a reefer-smoking musician and you dress like a, well, like a detective. I never expected you to be such a hipster. You should lose the tie sometimes, and maybe grow some scruff?" she said, touching my chin.

"Sure. A *hipster* detective. That would go over well with the clients."

"You never know."

I laughed, imagining that scene in my head.

"What's so funny?" she asked.

"I'm too old for that stuff. Anyway, I don't necessarily relate to labels. Bohemian. Nihilist. Anarchist. None of it really matters to me. I couldn't care less what the next person calls themself."

"Communist?"

"Sure. Whatever floats your boat."

"You're pretty noncommittal."

"So long as there's not another war about it."

"Maybe you're a pacifist."

"Maybe. I've probably just had my fill of dropping bombs on people in honor of some label." I said.

The bartender returned with our drinks and the glasses were passed over to us by a negro couple at the bar. "No more bombs," Loren said raising hers. I toasted her back and we drank to it.

We listened to the music and watched the crowd. Loren flattened against me in our little space, her hand finding mine and holding tightly.

"I need to make a call," I said into her ear. She gave me a puzzled look, so I explained it was something to do with work. She asked if it was about little Christian but I gave her a guarded shrug. We switched places and she gave me a quick departing kiss.

There were two pay phones hanging on the wall outside the bathrooms. I tried to shelter the receiver from all the noise and dialed zero so I could get the operator to help with a home number for the guy I knew at the DMV. When the line started ringing I fed in another nickel.

"Glenn Barnes?" I shouted into the receiver.

"Yes."

"It's Thorpe. Harry Thorpe."

"Thorpe? I can barely hear you."

"I'm at Casper's. Hey, I need a favor."

"It's after eleven. And you're calling me at home."

"I know. I'm sorry," I shouted, cupping my hand around the mouthpiece. "I'll pay you double on this. Okay? But I need you to look up a plate first thing in the morning."

"Hold on," he said

A cigarette girl in a daring outfit came down the narrow hall, so I bought a pack from her tray. The drummer shifted into what I recognized as the long intro to Seth Crane's version of *After Hours*. I'd seen them perform it before and it was a remarkable rendition. All the musicians would be exiting the stage now, leaving just the drummer. Then, one at a time they would return and join in. The effect added to the dramatic progression that would result in a huge ending.

Barnes came back on the line and said, "This better be important. The kid's cryin' and everything here."

"Like I said, it's worth thirty to you."

"What? Can't hear you."

"Forty. It's forty to you," I shouted.

"Okay. Give me the number."

I read the plate number off Johnny's slip of paper and he read it back.

"I'll call you around eight," he said.

"Thanks, Barnes. I owe you."

Pushing my way back through the crowd I saw the bassist, a guy everyone called Lazy Pete, climbing back on the stage. A second later he started thump bumping in with the drums and the crowd gave a big round of applause for the drummer's solo.

As I came up on Loren I saw she was talking to a man, her back to the wall, his back to me. When Loren saw me, she said something and he turned. It was Seth Crane.

"Fuzzy, how are you?" Seth said, leaning into me and offering his hand.

"Good, Seth. You're knockin' em dead as usual."

"Yeah," he said surveying the crowd. "We get things hopping. Are you still with Lew?"

"I am."

"Lew can sure make that guitar talk," he said moving a little to make room for me, but I stayed where I was and lit a cigarette. He turned back to Loren. I couldn't hear their words, and with the familiarity in how they were speaking, I wasn't sure I wanted to know what was being said. She was touching his arm as she spoke, and he, listening intently, nodded and smiled with teeth as white as sugar in his dark face. Soon the crowd erupted again as the bass player gave a really technical finish to his solo. Then the piano man dove in. Crane straightened to glance at the stage then began speaking directly into Loren's ear.

I occupied myself watching the mix of people until the bartender caught my eye. He had a beer for Crane. I touched his shoulder and he took it from me, his eyes yellowy in that jaundiced sort of way that is so much more pronounced in negroes. He turned back to Loren to say something and she wrapped her arms around his neck. He kissed her cheek and then moving to go, gave me a salute with the beer bottle.

Knowing what was coming next the crowd went crazy when he climbed back on stage. And, just as I remembered, he launched into a beautiful solo before they swept into a monster finish. When the crowd finally quieted down and the band had slipped into *All the Things You Are*, Loren said to me, "We met during the war."

"I figured."

"Are you jealous?" she asked.

"Sister, I'm the least jealous guy in the world."

"You looked it."

I noticed the band had transposed the chords in the second half of the song by a tritone, giving it a moody feel. I bent toward her to say, "I couldn't hear anything and wasn't going to poke my face into your conversation."

"What if I told you I fucked him," she said.

I looked at her. Her expression hardened when I shrugged and said, "I'm sure he's fucked a lot of women." I leaned close to her and said, "What do you want me to say? You obviously want to get some sort of reaction out of me. I just don't know what it is."

She looked away, her lips firmly together.

Then I said, "Is he the one that got you on heroin?"

Her head spun back, eyes cold as a razor blade.

"Because if I were you…I wouldn't share a needle or anything else with him anymore. He's got sick junky eyes."

She pushed at me to get out. I put my arm around her and pulled her tight. She struggled against my chest and pushed at the side of my face. I could feel the entire length of her slim body against me and my desire for her heightened as she fought to get away. After a moment of us trapped in our little dance she began to bend with my grip and soften. Her lips came to mine and we kissed. When I pulled away and looked into her eyes I was surprised to see how dark they were, like deep, cool pools. I imagined myself on a precipice poised to leap just as she slapped me. I think the force of the blow surprised her more than it did me. For me it was like an exclamation point.

She kissed me again, her hand on the back of my neck.

CHAPTER 23

I rolled over and looked at my watch when the phone started ringing. It was twenty after eight. I ran to the kitchen naked to pick it up.

"I got what you want," Barnes said, skipping the pleasantries. "Ready?"

I let the receiver dangle almost to the floor while I grabbed a pencil and scrap of newspaper. When I came back on the line, Barnes said, "It's a black '39 Ford registered to an Andreas Loitzel, L-o-i-t-z-e-l, at 1121 Mariposa Street."

"Thanks, Barnes," I said tossing the pencil on the table. "I'll come by tomorrow with your lettuce."

"Tomorrow's Saturday, Sherlock. Just come by next week."

I told him I would and we hung up. I dropped the piece of paper in my hat on my way through the dining room.

"What time is it?" Loren asked, once I'd climbed back in bed.

"Just about 8:30."

"Shit. I've got to go," she said without moving. "Can you drop me off or am I taking a cab?"

"Cab. Sorry, but I got somewhere I need to be." I put my hands on her shoulders and began to give her a massage. She rolled flat on her stomach and started purring.

"Can you at least do that for a couple minutes?"

I started at her shoulders and worked my way down and forty minutes later we finally got out of bed. I called for a cab and made a pot of coffee. When Loren came out of the bathroom I poured her a cup and we sat at the kitchen table. She watched Oscar in his bowl who appeared to ignore her.

"See." she said. "He doesn't like me."

"I wouldn't worry about it. He's not a very good judge of character."

She tapped Oscar's glass and made a sad face when he did nothing. "So today, is it about Sonja Hoff?" she asked, touching her nose and sniffling.

"Just some things I need to check out."

"Is that what the phone calls are about?"

I told her they were without shedding any details.

"Do you really think she took him?" she asked, again rubbing her nose and sniffling. "Wow, something got me," she said.

I looked into her eyes and said, "Maybe I don't want you sniffing dope in my bathroom."

Loren lurched as if I'd slapped her. The anger I'd seen the night before flushed her face and I really did want to give her a whack.

She jumped to her feet, banging the table, causing her coffee to spill and Oscar's water to nearly slosh over. "You don't know what you're talking about!"

"No?"

"You don't know anything about me."

"I know when you're all doped up."

"Oh! Like you're some goddamned angel. When is the last time you drew a sober breath?"

"In case you don't recall, prohibition was overturned. I'm not doing anything illegal."

"Fuck you!" She pushed past me.

I turned to watch while she gathered her things in the living room.

"Loren, wait…"

"No! Fuck you! Who are you to judge me?" she said, angrily buttoning her coat.

"I'm not judging you. I just…"

"Like you're some moral authority all of a sudden? What the hell do you know? What do you know about anything, let alone me or my life? Hell, you couldn't even do anything to protect little Christian. That's how pathetic you are. That little boy is missing all because of you. *And* Christian. You're nothing but a worthless drunk, and he's too goddamned obtuse to see he hired a useless piece of shit. And then you want to judge me?" she said, facing back to the kitchen.

I said nothing.

"You can't even do your job," she said, stepping out onto the porch and slamming the door hard enough to make the cups and saucers bounce in my cabinet. Through the living room window I could see her go down off the porch and into the light rain that had started. A minute later a cab pulled up.

I finished my coffee and washed our cups in the sink. Then I used a towel to wipe up her spill, and moved Oscar to the living room where I sat and smoked a cigarette. Her words hurt. She wasn't entirely wrong. I had fucked up. But at that moment, the thing I regretted most was saying anything about the dope. Or, I thought, not stopping her and telling her that I might be falling in love   with   her.

CHAPTER 24

Loitzel's house was white stucco with these ridiculous swirls and peaks that made it look as if it were coated in dirty meringue. It was built in so close to the next house that Loitzel could loan his neighbor a cup of sugar by opening a window and handing it straight across into their kitchen. All the houses on the block were like that.

I didn't see a '39 Ford out front so I drove around and up the alley. Nothing there either, not even a cement pad for a car. I went back up the street and parked a few doors down from the house. In the glove box I found an old business card that said my name was James Hale and I was a real estate broker.

Making sure it looked as if I were somehow interested in the property and the neglected yard, I stepped slowly onto the porch. After knocking three times I scooted sideways between the houses. When no one answered my banging on the back door I used my burglar tools to let myself in.

The kitchen was plain and actually looked more unused than clean. It was a tiny space without room for a table or chairs. I dried my feet on a tiny patch of rug inside the door and began to have a look around. Off to the side was a back bedroom, vacant except for two suitcases. I gave each a shake. One was empty. The other was filled with a woman's shoes and dresses, all rolled and stuffed as if packed on a moment's notice. I looked at the labels, and in the shoes, but didn't see any stitched names identifying the owner. The suitcase itself didn't have a tag or initials either. I figured a third suitcase would have this woman's underthings and makeup. And that would be with her, wherever she was.

I went back through the kitchen and stopped to look in the Frigidaire. It was mostly empty except for a carton of eggs, something smelly wrapped in brown paper and five bottles of milk. The dining room was furnished with a cheap table and three chairs with plastic cushions. A small living room was decorated with a ratty couch faced off with a plaid chair. In between them was a coffee table strewn with newspapers. I continued on to the front bedroom where the sheets and blanket were all pulled up and tucked neatly. A few dust balls cowered under the bed with a lone black sock. On the dresser a large dish was filled with coins, several matchbooks and some specs of pocket linen. It was pretty clear by the lack of ashtrays in the house that Loitzel wasn't a smoker. But a man who's with a woman who smokes will pick up matchbooks here and there to give her a light. I opened the flap on one, a single match was missing. On the cover it said *Howdy Partner Mo-tel*. The other matchbooks were from bars. I dropped the mo-tel one into my pocket.

In the top drawer I found three photographs inside a folded sheet of paper. One was actually a postcard. The photo on the front showed skiers on a mountain slope, the back described the setting as *Winter Park Ski Area, Colorado, 1948*. The next photograph was a man and woman sitting shoulder-to-shoulder in a restaurant booth. The man, I'd never seen before, had a long tanned face, topped with fair wispy hair. The woman with him was Sonja Hoff. The last one was a photo booth strip of the same couple mugging for the camera with clownish expressions. In the fourth picture in the strip they were weren't clowning, they were kissing. I folded the paper as I'd found it and pushed it back under the shirts in the drawer.

I was just about to return to the living room when something caught my eye on the floor next to the baseboard. It was a bobby pin, the kind a woman uses to keep her hair pulled back. With it was a single strand of blonde hair. I set both on the coffee table in the living room as I crossed to the kitchen. In the trash under the sink I found two soggy cigarette butts, both with lipstick on the end. I was just about to dig a little further when a car door slammed out front. I sprinted to the window and peeked out through the blind. A black Ford was parked and the man from the photos was coming up the walk. Flopping down in the plaid chair I faced the door with the .45 in my hand.

He froze when he saw me.

After I had him close the door I told him to take off his coat and spin in place so I could see his waistline all around. "No quick moves," I said. "You don't want this thing barking at you, and I don't particularly feel like shooting someone today."

He sat on the couch where I pointed and kept his hands in the air. His hat, like the coat, was soaked through from the rain and his boots muddy. The expression on his face told me this wasn't the first time he'd had someone put a gun on him.

"Take your hat off," I ordered.

He did as told and again raised his hands.

"What do you want?" he asked, a heavy German accent decorating his words.

"I'm asking the questions here. Why are you so wet and dirty?"

"I work outside."

"What work?"

He told me he was a groundskeeper for a man named Foster in Morrison. On Grapevine Road. I asked him if he knew the Marquand house and he nodded saying the Foster's lived a kilometer away from there.

"Where's Sonja Hoff? And where's the kid?"

"I don't know what you are saying."

I raised the gun and made sure his eyes went to it.

"Don't fuck with me. What's with all the milk in your icebox?"

"You think the milk is for child?" He laughed. "I have a, ah, ah, stomach pain I drink this milk for."

"Where's the kid?" I asked again.

"What kid?"

"Stop with the bullshit lies. I'm not in the mood to play games. Where's Sonja Hoff?"

His eyes remained on my face but he didn't say a word. It seemed like a long time went by. Eventually I raised the gun and said, "This thing isn't going to feel so good when I start banging it against your skull." I pointed with the muzzle at the bobby pin on the table. "Who's that belong to? And how about the suitcase back there full of women's clothes?"

He glanced at the bobby pin and then back to me.

"You know what it's for, don't you?"

"*Ja.* I know what it's for."

"Whose is it?"

"Who do you work for?"

I took out one of my P.I. business cards and tossed it to him. He looked it over and seemed none too impressed.

"I saw the pictures in your dresser," I said. "I know you know who I'm talking about. I'm not asking again, where is she, and where's the kid?"

"I didn't believe Sonja when she said this would happen."

"Go on."

"She told me someone like you would come and accuse us of this crime. She said Marquand would make sure we take all this blame. That's why she ran away. Yes, I know Sonja. I love Sonja. And she loves me. But we didn't take the child. And you, Mr. Private Detective for Christian Marquand, you might as well shoot me now, because I will never tell you where Sonja is."

"I just might do that," I said.

"Please. Go ahead. And try torturing me while you're at it. But I warn you, the Russians already tortured everything out of me. It will just waste your time. Go on. I am prepared for this murder."

"Don't be so melodramatic. I'm here to find the kid, dipshit. Not murder anyone."

"I told you, we don't have that child."

"Okay. Let's say I believe you. Where's Sonja and why's she hiding if she doesn't have the kid?"

"I need to explain this to you?"

"What if I'm not working for Marquand?"

"This is a good joke," he said, grinning at me.

I fired a round into the wall next to his head. He flinched, but it wasn't like he'd shit his pants.

When the ringing in my ears came down some, I said, "Stop fucking around. If she doesn't have the kid, why is she hiding."

He stared at me hardly breathing, eventually he said, "You need to ask her that."

"Great. I'd love to talk to her."

"*Ja*, I am sure you would. Shall we ring her now?" he said, without moving a muscle.

"Seriously, smartass. If she doesn't have the kid, she's got nothing to worry about. I wasn't hired to find her. I was hired to find the kid. Why don't you tell her that. Give her my card. Have her call me."

"*Ja*, okay."

I didn't like his attitude at all. If I thought it would help I'd have given him a few lumps. But this guy wasn't going to say anything else, no matter what I did. He'd obviously do anything for Sonja Hoff, and it seemed like that meant protecting her from Marquand. When I'd finished tossing that about in my head, I said, "Why should I believe you?"

"What do I have to lose? Don't believe me, if this is your preference. I can only tell you that we do not have that child. We try only to get away from this and Marquand without getting blamed for it all."

It sounds silly, but detective work is about gut feelings most of the time. And my gut was telling me this guy wasn't pulling my chain. You can tell, after a while, in their eyes. In the way they hold their head or phrase their words. "If you don't have the kid, who does?" I asked.

"Maybe you should look closer."

"What's that mean?"

"Maybe it's someone close to Marquand. How about that crazy woman that killed the dog."

"What woman? And what dog?"

"That sister-in-law. The crazy one."

CHAPTER 25

The Howdy Partner was out towards Morrison at the foot of the mountains in an idle little town called Golden, known mostly for the Coors Brewery. The mo-tel was one of those typical dumps leftover from the motor tourist and traveling salesman days in the 1930's. A room, accessed directly from the parking lot, could be rented by the day, week or longer for those desperate enough. I parked under the carport attached to the office and went inside. A woman with a slender cigarette dangling from a skinny lip was perched behind glass, the same kind that was used for ticket windows at movie houses with a hole and a slot to pass things back and forth. She was scratching an emery board on an inch long fingernail and had a transistor radio tuned to Peggy Lee. She raised her eyes for all of one second and continued filing. "It's $2.50 a night or fifteen bucks for a seven-day week," she said.

"I'm actually looking for someone."

"Call the cops. We're not missing persons."

I tapped the P.I. license against the glass to get her to look at it. "Do you have a woman named Sonja Hoff staying here."

"Even if I'd heard that name before, I'd never tell you."

"She's got blonde hair, about five foot eight inches tall with a German accent. She might have a boy with her who has curly hair and is not quite two years old."

"Even if I cared about all that, we don't give out that kind of information here. This ain't no fleabag mo-tel like you might be used to," she said, shifting her attention to a thumbnail the size of an oyster shell.

"I just need to ask her some questions. It's part of an ongoing investigation."

She looked up at me. "Are you hard of hearing?"

"No."

"I'm surprised you can speak so clearly. Ain't most deaf people mutes as well? You seem dumb, but you're speaking just fine."

"Look lady, there's no need to give me the business. I'm investigating a crime and this woman might be a witness."

"I'm going to say it again. We don't give out people's information. Call a cop if you got problems. Now hit the bricks before I call one myself."

I thought about poking my .45 at her through the hole in the glass, but instead I took a $5 bill out of my wallet and said, "How about you sell me one of them packs of gum there."

"Ten cents," she said tossing one through the window without waiting for me to say which flavor.

I poked the five dollar bill through to her.

"I don't have change for that! Give the gum back."

"Keep the change," I said, wagging the bill at her.

After a moment's hesitation she snagged it and stuffed it into a sweater pocket.

"Blonde with a German accent. About so tall," I said holding my hand out.

She picked up another pack of gum and said, "Maybe you want a Juicy Fruit too?"

I poked another five through the hole and she stuffed it away with the first one.

"She ain't using that name you said, but there's a *heinie* in Number eleven with blonde hair."

"Does she have a kid with her?"

"I never seen any kid."

"What name is she using?"

She let out a three second sigh and flipped open the register.

"Mrs. S. Andreas."

"Thanks," I said. "What about my Juicy Fruit?"

She grabbed a pack from the display and tossed it to me. I went out through an adjacent space where a console radio was poised before a couple mixed and matched kitchen chairs and pedestal ashtrays. A handwritten sign on the wall said *Lounge Hours 6 – 9*

144

PM. FREE! No Alcohol!

Number 11 was at the far end of the row and there was no answer. I was just about to jimmy the door with the stiff plastic card I carried in my wallet, but I could see the woman watching me from the full-length window in the lounge. So I cut across the parking lot and returned to the office.

"I could have told you she wasn't there," the woman said, going back behind the glass.

"Thanks for saving me the trouble. Do you know where she went?"

"Maybe you need some mints."

I took two bucks out of my wallet and showed it to her. "It's all I got."

She wiggled her fingernails so I poked the bills through the hole.

"I have no idea," she said.

"What good does that do me?"

"But I saw who she went with. Some scarecrow with a Ford."

"Tall, skinny guy?"

"Ain't that what I said?"

"But no kid?"

"Like I said before, I never seen a kid."

"Okay. Was it a black '39 Ford?"

"Ford. It was a Ford."

"And it was black?"

"Black. Maybe blue. What do I know?"

I went out to the Dodge and stood thinking for a minute. I could see her looking at me over her counter. I unclipped the top and pulled it down. It was a beautiful day and it would be nice to drive up to Morrison with the sun on my face. I climbed in and unwrapped the Juicy Fruit. The woman looked away when I gave her a little wave as I drove off.

It had only been a few weeks since I'd been up at the Morrison house but the spring rain made it an entirely different experience. I wandered among pine trees tipped with baby needles, ringed by a carpet of wild flowers a week or so from their first bloom. A breeze frolicked in the treetops intimating memories of an ocean surf, frivolous and free. I watched a bee the size of my thumb zip by on his little mission. It was so different without two dozen cops and twice as many reporters trampling everything. Even the ground near the house where the ladder had been placed was tilled and smoothed and planted with several new shrubs all in a row. The aluminum edging, crushed that night between the dirt and the grass, was replaced, along with a fresh strip of sod. I lit a cigarette and turned to admire the view of the hills rolling off into the distance, spotted with colors and textures. It was almost as if nothing had happened there. As if nothing could happen there.

Victor came out on the porch. "Afternoon, Mr. Thorpe," he called out.

I waved to him and crossed the yard. "It sure is beautiful up here," I said.

"Yes sir, it is."

"Seems sad that the Colonel is selling. But I totally understand."

"Miss Louise says she never wants to see this house again. There's too many bad memories now."

"I know you have the whole house to pack up, but I was wondering if I could ask you a few questions."

"Of course, sir. Can I get you a cup of coffee?"

I told him that would be great and followed him into the kitchen. Once I'd persuaded him to join me we sat at the butcher block table with our cups. To warm him up, I asked a bunch of questions which led us to talking about his childhood. He told me about growing up in Louisiana and a twin brother who was actually eleven months older.

"A twin eleven months older?"

"That's right," he chuckled. "It all started because my momma dressed us alike. You know how you get things at a discount when you buy them in pairs? That's what she did. She'd buy two blue shirts and two brown pants. Two of everything. So we were always dressed just alike. The kids would always say, 'Here come the Petit Twins.' And we was always the Petit Twins after that. I suppose they meant it as teasing, but it never bothered us."

"That's a great story. It sounds like you and your brother were really close growing up."

"Oh yes, sir. We was always close. I don't think we fought a day in our lives. We're still close, even with him in Louisiana and all. There's not a week we don't write each other."

"That must be nice, to have a relationship like that," I said. "I never talk to my brother, and we used to fight all the time when we were kids." I put a spoonful of sugar in my coffee and gave it a stir.

"He was two years older and I think his favorite pastime was torturing me. It was one thing when we were little. But when I got older, it led to some real knock-down, drag-out fights. I suppose in some ways that's pretty normal, though. For siblings to fight. You've been around this family a long time. I bet you saw some doozies with Louise and Loren. I heard they fought a lot." I said, trying to be nonchalant with the direction I was guiding the conversation.

He shook his head and rolled his eyes to show disbelief, "Oh Lordy, Mr. Thorpe. Those girls fought like cats and dogs. They still do. But when they were little, it couldn't have been worse if they'd been boys. Punching, kicking and everything."

"Didn't Loren throw little Christian out in the garbage during one of their fights?"

Victor got up to refill my cup. "Yes, sir. She sure did. That was a bad fight that day."

"And Loren killed a dog another time?" I asked.

"That was Miss Louise's dog, last summer," he said, looking at me as if wondering how I knew those things. Then he put the coffee pot back on the stove. When he turned back, he said, "Oh, I see where you're going. You think Miss Loren has something to do with little Christian's disappearance. Is that what you're getting at?"

"And? What do you think?"

"No, sir. I don't believe that for a minute. These girls might fight a lot, but it's nothing like that." He arranged some cookies on a plate and put them on the table. "They're just completely different personalities and there's some jealously there between them. But Miss Loren would never harm that child."

Picking up a cookie, I asked, "Jealousy? Like what?"

"Oh, just the usual stuff. One of them had something and the other wanted it. They been like that ever since I met them when they were five and eight years old. It was a doll or a dress, or whatever the other had. When they got older it was all about boys." He pulled a linen napkin out of a box that had been packed and laid it on the table for me. "It just got worse over time and especially after the Colonel and Miss Louise were married. That was a big blow for Miss Loren. She got really sick, and it took a long while for her to get better. I think when little Christian came along it was another blow. But, Miss Loren is not the kind of person that would harm a child. She really does love her sister.

That time with the baby in the garbage was just her acting out, not about hurting him. That sort of thing is expected when two sisters love the same man."

I put the cookie back on the plate. "You're saying they both love Marquand?"

He lowered back into his chair. "More like *loved*. Miss Loren was in love with the Colonel once too," he said matter-of-factly, as if he figured I knew all about that too. "That's what was behind all the acting out. It's just like when they were girls."

"Right," I said. But my mind was already somewhere else, and even though his lips kept moving I wasn't hearing a word he was saying. After a couple minutes I said, "Let's go back. Did Loren kill a dog or not?"

"That's what the Colonel said. But if you ask me, there's no way she poisoned that dog.

No, sir. That old boy just snuck himself one last meal, and it just so happened the meal he snuck was the poison for the rats. But, see now, I got you thinking that Miss Loren could do things like that, and that's not what I'm saying at all, Mr. Thorpe."

CHAPTER 27

I drove over to Billy's Inn and ordered a bourbon and ginger ale. Ginger ale always seemed to settle my stomach. And it wasn't feeling all that great lately. After two it was getting better, so I ordered a pastrami sandwich.

Retard, I kept saying to myself. Why would the maid say that? Was little Christian retarded? Could that be why Marquand never showed me the letters? Did they say something about the kid not being normal? And, did that play into the kidnapping? If it did, it would seem likely they would try to extort more money against the threat of exposing that the Mighty Marquand had fathered a retard.

I finished the last of the sandwich and was munching the remaining chips when a man came in and climbed on the stool next to me.

"Hear about that kid?" he asked me.

"What kid?" I said, almost choking.

"That little girl, stuck in the well. Hey Billy," he called out, "did you hear about that girl stuck in the well out in California."

"Yeah," Billy said, coming over. "Did they get her out?"

"No. Not yet. They're trying to dig down parallel to the well to get at her."

Billy set a beer in front of the man and said, "How long's it been now?"

"Almost 48 hours. There's no way they'll get her out alive."

"Sure they will," another man said.

"No way," the first replied.

"Care to put some money on that? Billy can hold for us."

I watched while the two men agreed on the amount and handed their money over to Billy. Soon another man who had come in joined the action. I finished my drink and got up to leave.

"Calling it a night, Harry?" Billy asked.

I gave him a little salute.

When I got in the house I flicked on the radio and went out to the kitchen to get the bottle and a glass. A special report came on. They'd reached the girl, but she was dead. She'd suffocated as a result of the tight space, her knees pinned against her chest.

I listened to the report for a long time, and was still on the couch with the radio playing when the phone started ringing. I saw the bottle on the table was empty. It was all I could do to pull myself up and get into the kitchen to pick up the receiver.

"Mr. Thorpe? They've found a body," a voice said.

"Yeah, yeah. I heard."

"Sir?"

"On the radio," I said, my tongue moving in my mouth as if I'd gargled with glue.

"On the radio? Already?"

"The little girl in the well. I heard about it."

"No, Mr. Thorpe! It's Victor. Colonel Marquand's butler."

"What?" I said.

"The police called. They found a body up near Kittredge. On the side of the road. The Colonel wants you to meet him up there…"

CHAPTER 28

I was afraid I'd gone too far. But soon enough, I came upon a motorcycle cop making everyone turn around. Even after showing him my P.I. license he wouldn't let me pass. He did agree to radio ahead to see if a Lieutenant Greenberg could vouch for me. It was obvious by the way he walked back to my car that he still wasn't going to let me go on.

"There's no one named Greenberg up there," he said, around dark glasses under an 8-point cap. "Pull over there and wait. If he shows, you can go up with him."

I parked on the side of the road and leaned against the car smoking a cigarette that almost made me puke. My head was a throbbing mass of poison and seemed to have the balance of a half-filled bucket of slop. I tossed the cigarette after it brought on some retching and watched the Kittredge cop turn people around. Most of them were families on nice little Sunday drives. Only they'd found themselves on a road leading to a dead baby. It all brought to mind a case I'd worked about a year earlier, the trees and rocky hills eerily similar to the spot where the boy in the box had been found. I was able to momentarily shake the haunting images by concentrating on the cop, who was now busy making reporters pull to the side of the road. But the pitiable feeling, I knew that wouldn't shake so easy.

Eventually Greenberg showed. Once the cop checked his identification and cleared him to go I climbed in. We swung into the oncoming lane around the motorcycle.

"I guess Marquand gave you the rundown," he said.

"I only talked to the butler," I replied. "He said they found a body."

"Goddamn! You smell like a distillery."

I took out the Juicy Fruit and put a stick in my mouth. He held out his hand so I gave him a piece.

"What do you know?"

"Same as you," he said. "A dead baby in the brush."

"Where's Tooley?"

"Working a stabbing at a truck stop."

"Lucky him."

Just beyond a long, treelined bend we could see several police cars, an ambulance and Mountain States telephone truck about fifty yards off the road in a turnoff. We bounced the shoulder, went down the dirt cutout and slid in next to the truck. Greenberg yanked the hand brake and said, "Supposedly the Ma Bell guy found the body."

The area beyond the turnoff had been roped off. In the middle of the underbrush, just short of the river, was a white sheet covering what I assumed was the body. On this side of the rope everyone stood in a group smoking cigarettes—their eyes on us as we approached. A few of the uniforms I recognized from the night of the kidnapping.

Greenberg introduced himself as the lead investigator for the State Patrol and explained I was a private cop working for Marquand. A man in a cowboy hat and tan uniform with brown pocket flaps and epaulets said he was the Kittredge Sheriff. "You fellers can look all you want," he said. "But let's keep the scene good and clean. Okay?"

"We know how to work a crime scene, Sheriff," Greenberg said.

"I'm sure you do," the sheriff snorted, pushing his cowboy hat back on his wide forehead. "I heard all about the fine work you fellers did at the Marquand house."

Greenberg showed his teeth and made a noise like a chuckle.

We ducked under the rope and made our way down the slight embankment to the sheet.

"Fuck him," Greenberg mumbled.

"Your reputation precedes you," I said.

"Yeah? Fuck you, too."

Greenberg kneeled at the edge of the sheet and took hold of a corner. "Close your eyes," he said.

It was nothing like the boy in the box who had been dumped a week or so before being found and minus the head injuries was in relatively good shape. This body looked more like trash than human remains. It was dirty and decaying in that deflated way the dead look after they've gotten past the bloating and been exposed to the elements. It reminded me of some of the dead Japs I'd seen on Green Island. The ones we found out past the perimeter. The jungle eats you up quick though. The weather had definitely slowed things down with this one. But something had found it long before the Ma Bell guy and pulled it up out of its shallow grave. An arm and leg had both been ripped away and the stomach and genitals eaten. There was no doubt it was a child though. It had a head full of bright blonde curls.

Greenberg let the sheet fall back, got to his feet and brushed off a knee. "Something's been making a meal of it. Another week or so and there wouldn't be much left. Let's go see what the Ma Bell man's got to say before Dmytryk gets here with Marquand and starts fucking everything up. No offense to your employer, of course," he added, sarcastically.

"Oh. So Marquand's coming with Dmytryk?"

"You think Dmytryk would miss all this?"

The telephone man wore boots laced to his knees and a cap similar to the one Richard the chauffeur wore, only with a Bell Telephone patch. He hardly slowed his attack on a bloodied fingernail while answering Greenberg's questions.

"I seen plenty of dead people in the war," he said, "but I never seen a dead baby."

"Yeah, it's not the same," Greenberg said, looking at him over his glasses and pad. "What were you doing when you found it?"

"I was getting ready to run some line between those poles on either side of the body. For a new party line from Kittredge to Morrison. I'd just hooked up on that pole and was walking the line over to the other one when I damn near stepped on it."

"Did you move anything?"

"I moved some leaves to see what it was. I thought maybe it was an old doll. But I knew when I saw the eye sockets."

"What did you do then?"

"I climbed the pole and tapped in. I had the operator connect me with the Kittredge police. Is this the Marquand baby?"

Greenberg told him we wouldn't know for certain until an examination was completed. "And," he added, "there's bound to be a bunch of boys from the press up here before long. Don't you go telling them it's the Marquand kid. Okay? We don't know that for certain."

The man assured us he wouldn't say a word and Greenberg went through a few more questions before letting him continue the destruction of his fingernails in the cab of his truck. The sheriff, who had wandered over just as we were finishing, said, "The Jefferson County Coroner's man is on his way. Should be here in half an hour."

"Just to let you know," Greenberg said to him, "I've got some people coming too. There'll be a bunch of *fellers* from the lab and my chief is coming with Christian Marquand, which means all the boys from the press will be tagging along. You might as well turn the scene over to us."

"I don't think so. Up here we go by the rule book. This is my scene until I get told otherwise."

"I can't wait to see you say that to my chief."

"I'll be more than happy to say it to Harry Truman hisself," the sheriff said. Then he cleared his sinuses and swallowed hard.

Greenberg didn't say a word, and the sheriff, a satisfied look on his face, went back to join the others. Not a minute later three State Patrol cruisers came around the bend. As they pulled into the turnoff I could see Dmytryk and Marquand in the first car.

"I've talked to the Governor," Dmytryk was already saying to the sheriff as we came up. "He's assured me you will be duly notified that we are taking over this crime scene."

"Well until then, I ask that you proceed accordingly and don't touch anything," the sheriff said.

Dmytryk brushed past him and started calling out unnecessary orders for the lab techs.

The sheriff grabbed his sleeve, "Whoa there fellers. This isn't your scene yet."

Dmytryk pulled his arm away. "Excuse me! This is going to be my crime scene in about two minutes. Let's not be petty here. My men need to get started."

"I'd like to see if it's my son," Marquand said.

The sheriff, speaking to Marquand, said he didn't have a problem with that. Then facing Dmytryk, said, "But, I don't want any of your men stomping around down there."

A baby-faced Kittredge deputy accompanied the group of us down to the body.

Greenberg began to kneel so he could pull back the sheet but Dmytryk waved him away and took hold of the corner. Once Marquand nodded that he was ready Dmytryk drew it back. At first Marquand stood motionless, then he crouched down and put his hand to his mouth. For a moment I thought he might begin sobbing but he reached out and touched the remaining foot. Marquand turned it slightly between two fingers and I could see that the toes were overlapping, one stacked on the other.

"Sir, you mustn't…" the deputy started.

Marquand raised his eyes and I saw they were rimmed with tears, the color blanched from his face. He lay the tiny shriveled foot back down and slowly got to his feet. Taking a handkerchief from his coat pocket he dabbed his eyes and said to Dmytryk, "It's him."

"You're sure, Colonel?" Dmytryk asked.

Marquand didn't say anything and Dmytryk had enough sense not to ask again. After a long pause with all of us trying not to look at Marquand, the Colonel said, "Can I have a moment alone with him? I won't touch anything."

We all climbed out of the gully and stood by the cars while Marquand kneeled again. Greenberg and I occupied ourselves with cigarettes while Dmytryk gave detailed instructions to the photographer how he wanted photos taken. Most would be staged so he would be at the center of the action. The sheriff went to take a radio call that had come for him in one of the Kittredge cars. That, I was sure, would be the order to turn over the scene.

When Marquand came up from the gully his eyes looked clear and the color returned to his face. Ducking under the rope he called out for Dmytryk. "Major, I want the body examined by Dr. Foulks. He's the doctor in Morrison that saw Christian the day he went missing."

Dmytryk scanned the group with an authoritative look and said, "I think that's a splendid idea, Colonel."

"Chief," Greenberg said. "Normal procedure is for the coroner to examine the body first. That ensures evidence is properly preserved for trial."

"I know policy, *Lieutenant!*" Dmytryk retorted. "But this is not a normal situation. Colonel Marquand makes an excellent suggestion. The most important thing right now is identifying the body. Who could be better suited for that then the child's very own pediatrician?"

"I'm just saying that we might have trouble in court if something doesn't go right."

"That's absurd. We'll be strengthening the case. It will be a positive identification from a medical professional who is uniquely familiar with the decedent. The Colonel is right on track with this."

Marquand turned to me for the first time since arriving and said, "Captain Thorpe, go into Morrison and tell Dr. Foulks we'll be bringing the child for him to examine."

I stood rooted, unsure if I should move on those orders. Considering the situation, it seemed ridiculous I would be included in anything that was transpiring.

Dmytryk looked at me a moment. "Yes, go. We'll be right behind you," he said. Then he turned and called for the ambulance drivers to get a stretcher.

Greenberg started in again with Dmytryk, even though I'm sure he must have known it was a pointless undertaking. I could still hear them going at it when I realized the Dodge was down around the bend. As I turned back I saw the sheriff sitting in the front seat of one of the Kittredge cruisers. His cowboy hat was back on his head, and he looked anything but defeated.

"You fellers are bound and determined to ruin this whole thing, ain't you?" he said.

"Can one of your men take me down the road to my car?" I asked.

"Get in," he said, pulling his leg into the car and slamming the door.

As we started down the road, he said, "I'm no genius, but I can recognize morons when I see them. I heard what went on at that Marquand house. There's no way they'll get a conviction with the way they're handling this."

"You're wrong," I said. "They'll get whatever conviction they want. All they have to do is walk the *Mighty Marquand* as a grieving father into a courtroom. "

"Maybe so. But they got to catch someone first."

I didn't have anything to say against that.

As we pulled up to my car he turned to me and said, "I hope God sees a way to bring some justice on behalf of that child."

I watched him turn around and go back up the road and imagined him driving past that turnout and right on to Kittredge. It would be the smart thing to do.

CHAPTER 29

It took about ten minutes for me to get to Morrison, where I asked a gas station attendant directions to Foulks' office. As it turned out, the office was in the doctor's house and he answered the door himself; a crooked man, bent over a tiny cane and wearing a Western style bow tie. At some point in time his examination room had been a small living room in an equally small house. But that was a long ago as it was still outfitted with the same equipment the doctor probably purchased when setting up practice a century before. A wooden examination table sat in the middle of the space and several cabinets lined one wall containing a wide variety of glass bottles, most with yellowed labels and cork stoppers. A tiny desk with a hinged writing space was centered on an opposite wall below certificates and diplomas so old the ink was not much more than faded memories.

"When will they be here?" Foulks asked.

"I'm not really sure. Maybe an hour. Maybe less."

"Good, good. That will give me time to get all prepared," he said, pulling on a head mirror. "I'll need for you to go over to Red Rocks Vista Lane and look for Dr. Lundford. My eyes aren't as good as they used to be and I'll need him to assist. I'd say we could ring him up, but if you utter the tiniest thing on the party line Maud Crawford will have it all over the county in a matter of minutes."

As I watched him dig ancient-looking instruments out of a worn leather bag I tried to imagine why Marquand wanted this old man examining his son's body.

"Go on, son," he said, shooing me with wrinkled hand. "Red Rocks Vista Lane. Head south and then left. Blue house. Red barn."

I left him to his preparations and drove as he said to Lundford's. The sign out front proclaimed he was a veterinarian. *Oh, brother* I said out loud as I pulled into the drive.

Wooden arrows planted every few yards in the grass directed me to an addition on the side of the house that served as an office. A young woman with short red hair and denim pants over pointy cowboy boots came out. She said Lundford was in the barn and led me over. Inside we found the doctor wrapping the leg of a Palomino mare. He kept working while I gave him the rundown on the situation and agreed to come with me as soon as he'd finished and cleaned up.

I waited by the Dodge and had a cigarette. Pretty soon Lundford and the girl came out of the barn and crossed the yard. He went on into the house but the girl ambled around until finally leaning against a fender with one leg bent, the heel of her boot hung on a tire rim.

"You always been a detective?" she asked, taking the cigarette I offered and letting me light it for her.

"Since the war."

"My father was killed at Anzio."

"Oh, so Lundford isn't…"

"My father? Oh no!" she said, looking over her head at the house.

"Well, sorry to hear about your dad."

"It's okay. I'm used to it now," she said in a way that made me believe she was. "What did you do before the war?"

"I was in school."

"In Denver?"

"New York," I said, doing my best to pretend I wasn't noticing those tight denim pants and wondering about her and Lundford.

"That must have been exciting."

"Not what I was studying."

"No, I meant living in the city. I'd love to live in a big city one day. All the restaurants and nightclubs and people dressing fancy."

"Yeah, I guess, but everything's dirty and the air stinks most of the time. At least it's pretty up here."

"But boring. Everything here is always the same. And everybody knows your business," she said, shifting her weight and almost laying across the fender. "Do you think it's the Marquand baby?"

"I can't say."

"I've been reading all about it. It's really sad. So, you know Christian Marquand?"

"Yeah," I said.

"I'd give anything to meet him. He's such an amazing man."

Thankfully Lundford came out of the house. He'd changed into a suit but still wore a cowboy hat and boots. He told the girl to reschedule his afternoon appointments. She stood hands on hips and watched as we drove off. Not more than five minutes after we arrived at Foulks' the other cars started pulling up. Once the rear of the ambulance was lined up with the side steps to the porch, the driver set the brake and he and the other attendant began to take the stretcher from the back. There was hardly a bump under the white sheet, belted down as if it might actually make an unsettling move. Marquand stood next to me and watched while they carried it into the house.

As it turned out, there wasn't a spare inch in Foulks' examination room. Crammed in around the table was a handful of cops from different departments including the Morrison chief and Dmytryk and Greenberg representing the State Patrol. There was also a photographer and the two ambulance guys. It was a good thing the remains were not much more than two feet long since it would have been impossible for Foulks and Lundford to move around the table. I decided to wait on the porch where I could faintly make out the words inside. "…trauma to the head," Lundford said at one point.

After a couple minutes Marquand came out. He stared off down the street and finally took a seat on the bench next to me.

"I thought I could watch," he said.

"I'm so sorry, Colonel."

He patted my leg and we sat without speaking before Marquand uttered, "I sure didn't expect it to end up like this. I had such hopes and dreams for that boy."

The sadness in his voice and sheer heaviness of him next to me made me wish there was something to say. But all I could think to do was mention how they were being blessed with another child. It must have sounded as hollow out loud as it did in my head since Marquand didn't respond and we sat again in silence.

A breeze picked up carrying Lundford's voice another direction. The only sound was the rustle of leaves in the trees. Eventually I said, "I guess we should back away and leave it to them now. I'll get you a final invoice. And a refund too."

He turned and looked at me.

"The police and the DA are going to take over everything now," I said. "Since it's a homicide. You should probably tell them you paid a ransom. That's going to play a huge part in finding who did this."

"Yes, I suppose..." He faced forward again and let out a sigh.

"I'll make sure to fill them in on everything I dug up."

"Did you find Sonja?" he asked.

"We don't have to go into it that now, Colonel?"

"No. I'd like to hear what you found out."

I looked off across the yard and said, "Capra's people gave me a license plate for a man who supposedly asked about getting some money laundered. It's a caretaker for a neighbor of yours in Morrison named Foster. The caretaker's a German national. Supposedly he and Sonja Hoff are a couple."

His head came around quick. "How did you find that out?"

"The caretaker told me himself. I dropped in on him yesterday and he said he and Sonja Hoff are looking to run away together. But he also said they're being set up and was pretty adamant they had nothing to do with the kidnapping. I even acted like I was going to shoot him and he didn't budge."

"Was Sonja there?" he asked in a near whisper.

Something in his voice gave me an uneasy feeling. It made me think of Loitzel–saying how Marquand would be looking for them. And, right then I decided it might be smart to hold back on the whole Howdy Partner thing. At least for a while. "No. I didn't see her." I said. "I'm not sure where she is."

He faced away and said nothing then leaned forward and put his elbows on his thighs staring at his hands. After a minute he looked at me and said, "You really don't know where Sonja is?"

"I have a lead. But nothing solid."

"What kind of lead?"

"Just a lead I was working, Colonel. Do you really want to get into this now?"

"What lead?"

"Like I said, nothing solid. But, I might have something in a day or two if you really want me to keep looking."

"Have you said anything about this to them?" he asked, lowering his voice even further and jerking his head towards everyone inside. "Did you tell them about the German?"

"What's going on, Colonel?"

"Have you?"

"No! I haven't said anything to anyone."

"Okay. Good. I don't think we should tell them. Let them run around and turn up whatever they can. But I think you're on the right track, Thorpe. If you turn any of this over to them, they'll just muck it up. Keep working on it. I want to know who did this."

"Okay, but I'm not totally convinced they're involved."

"You've got to trust me on this one. We both know Sonja is behind this," Marquand whispered.

CHAPTER 30

Dr. Foulks determined the cause of death to be blunt force trauma to the head. He made his ruling based on the softened bone at the top of the skull. He could not, however, determine the gender based on what remained of the child. Foulks did say that because of the deformity on the right foot, and the fact that he had examined the child for flu-like symptoms the day before the abduction, he was able to positively identify the body as Christian A. Marquand Junior.

Greenberg said it was Dr. Lundford who had actually done most of the examination. Lundford described to Foulks what he was seeing and Foulks made his discoveries and final determination based on the veterinarian's observations. None of that was mentioned in Foulks' official report. As a matter of fact, the report never even mentioned Lundford's presence in the room at the time of the examination.

Later, William Mercer, the Jefferson County Coroner and Harvard Medical School graduate class of 1941 said the cause of death could not be determined. He described the softness at the top of the skull as the fontanelle, the soft spots on a baby's head which allow the bones of the skull to flex as it passes through the birth canal. Dr. Mercer's report also said that in most children the frontal fontanelle would not close completely until a child reached the age of two. For some people the fontanelle may never close or closes at a much later point in growth and development. In those rare occasions the result could be attributed to a genetic disorder, which may also cause an underdevelopment or deformity in bones called cleidocranial dysostosis. Greenberg said he asked Mercer if there was any connection to the deformed toes on the remaining foot and the softness of the fontanelle. Mercer had said he believed it to be quite likely. Unofficially, Mercer said he believed the child was smothered to death using a *burking* method.

"Burking method. I've never heard of that before," I said to Greenberg, who had stopped by the office with Tooley on their way from the examination with Mercer.

"Burking is when the murderer simultaneously compresses the chest of the victim while smothering him. Mercer said it was named after a guy named Burke who lived in Scotland in the early 1800's. He and a buddy would kill bums and sell their bodies to medical schools. One of them would sit on the victim's chest while the other held their mouth and nose. It leaves no visible injuries and makes it appear like the death is the result of natural causes."

Tooley shook his head in disgust and put his shoe back on having finished a very thorough massage of his arch and toes.

"Mercer said it would be extremely easy for an adult male to do this to a child. You would just use a pillow or blanket and get the same result."

"So Mercer thinks he might have been suffocated. Does means he was dead before he went out the window?" I said.

"*If* he went out the window," Tooley corrected.

"Yeah, *if*. What's next?"

"Well," Greenberg said, "the report gets filed with the coroner records. The official cause of death will be Foulks' version, at least for the death certificate and the investigation. It all comes down to some technicality about who declared the cause and time of death first."

"What are they saying is the time of death?"

"They agreed on that one," Tooley said, grimacing as he moved his feet in his new shoes. "Sometime around March first."

"Okay, so basically the day he went missing," I said.

Greenberg finished off what was in his glass and said, "Mercer told us Marquand is having the funeral home pick up the body tonight."

"That seems fast."

"Yeah, it does. But we can't keep Marquand from laying the poor little bastard to rest. I'm sure he wants some sort of closure."

"Marquand's wife is pregnant," I said.

"No kidding?" Tooley said.

"How do you know?" Greenberg asked.

"Marquand told me. When he first came to see me."

"Maybe we should drink a toast," Tooley said, picking up his empty glass and holding it out to me.

"No more drinks," Greenberg said to him. "We've got to go see Dmytryk "

"Fuck it," I said, "I'm drinking a toast." I poured and drank it down while they watched. "To Marquand's kid!" I said, raising the empty glass.

"Let's hope kismet looks favorably on this one."

"What's kismet, L.T.?" Tooley asked.

"Fate," Greenberg said, getting up to leave.

I lay on the couch for a long time after they left. The new bourbon had reconciled an agreement with the bourbon from the previous night and I was enjoying the numbing effect of the truce. I reread the afternoon paper about little Christian being found on the side of the road and studied the pictures, most of them featured Dmytryk in his usual poses. The front page article said Sonja Hoff was the primary suspect and a search for her was underway across the country. After a while I let the papers slide to the floor and roll away from my aching shoulder to stare at the shadows as they grew darker across the walls.

I hadn't told Greenberg anything about the retard stuff. It might have been relevant at that point, but I also didn't want to be responsible for getting little Christian officially stamped with that label. As it was, they figured he had some sort of deformity. I could still hear Marquand's voice in my head saying how he had so many hopes and dreams for the boy. I'm sure some of that sadness was for the lost dreams that plague any parent of a child with a deformity or disability.

When the phone began ringing it was completely dark in the office except for the flash of the red neon parking sign that had been added to the side of the building a couple days earlier. I'd moved on from feeling sorry for Marquand to torturing myself with the thoughts of him and Loren together. The more I let those develop the more I realized she might still be on the hook for him. That only made me feel worse. In a way it was a suffocating feeling. As if someone were burking me. And when that thought came to mind I attacked myself for letting little Christian get killed, in his crib, with the air pushed from his lungs. *That poor fucking kid*...no one protecting or saving him from the cruelty of the world. I was just as responsible, maybe even more responsible for allowing such a shitty end to come to his brief, little life. When the phone began to ring again I jumped up, thankful for the chance to escape my own persecution.

It was Sonja Hoff on the other end. I recognized her voice and the accent immediately.

"Can you help me?" she said.

"Where are you?"

"The newspapers say I am suspect. They say I kill that child." Her voice became a sobbing, tearful plea, "Please, Mr. Thorpe. I did not do this thing. Will you help me."

"Tell me where you are. I'll come there."

She paused a moment and said, "No. You will tell police where I am? Can you not just tell them I am innocent?"

"What evidence or alibi do you have?"

"What do you mean?"

"How can you prove you're innocent?" I said, taking out a cigarette and lighting it with Loren's Zippo.

"I did not do this. I did not do this child murder."

"C'mon, where are you? Let's talk."

"Why do you not believe me?" she begged.

I was going to tell her that I knew she was at the Howdy Partner but I figured that would spook her and she'd hit the road. I wanted her to stay exactly where she was.

"Look, you're obviously holed up good or they would've found you by now. Think of something that will convince me you're innocent and then call me. But right now, if I were you I'd stay in hiding. If they catch you now you'll be taking a one way trip to Old Sparky."

"What is this Old Sparky?"

"The electric chair. So think hard."

She hung up.

I sat in the dark and thought about the fear in her voice while clicking the lid open and closed on the Zippo. I'm sure mentioning the electric chair didn't help, but I figured she wouldn't be going anywhere soon. I just needed a little time to try and rope her and Loitzel together, then it would make sense to make a drop on them.

I poured myself another drink and sprawled out on the couch. I tried not to think about that dead baby but I couldn't keep my mind from the horrible little vision and how deflated and rotten it looked. That again led me to think about the boy in the box, two years earlier, how nearly pristine he appeared with his fresh haircut. I tortured myself with the thought that someone took him to get a haircut then beat him to death and dumped his body like trash in a box on the side of the road. And then I was flooded with the relentless vision of all those dead Japs. There had been so many of them in their various degrees of decomposition. Some were bloated in the heat, others were black and decaying. The older ones had already become partially skeletal. But the burned ones were the worst. They never decayed or changed. They were frozen in a moment of horror with mouths agape, lips burned away to reveal toothy eternal screams with arms and hands clawing frantically at the air. After a while I got the bottle and did my best to finish it off. When the phone rang again I rapped my knee against the desk getting to it.

"What?" I slurred into the receiver.

"Mr. Thorpe?"

"Who is this?"

"Can you see me? Tomorrow? Please. I will try to think of something to help you prove I did not do this crime."

"Sonja Hoff. You call again," I sang. "What a surprise the spider says to the fly."

"What?"

"Sure, doll. I'll help you. I knew you'd eventually decide to confess your sins. Father Thorpe will give absolution, dear child. Two Hail Mary's and a beer chaser..."

CHAPTER 31

I was laying on the floor, the empty bourbon bottle on its side with me. It took about five minutes for me to conclude that I hadn't been hit with it. Not literally anyway. There was just the one leftover bump from the cemetery, no longer so tender to the touch. I tried rolling onto my side but screamed out as my weight compressed my shoulder. This led to a coughing fit that nearly killed me. Once I finished I lay panting with tears running from my eyes into my ears. When the phone started ringing I scrambled to my feet, mostly to quiet the bell and save my head from the piercing sound. It was Greenberg and he was pissed. "What the fuck is this shit about a kidnapping," he was yelling. "You idiots paid a ransom and you didn't tell us? Are you out of your goddamned minds?"

I kept six inches between the receiver and my ear.

"You compromised this investigation, Thorpe!"

"I don't know..." I said without much conviction.

"*And*, you leave me swinging. I had to find this shit out from Dmytryk. We're six weeks into this and I fucking find this out now?"

"Marquand wanted to pay..."

"Fuck you and fuck Marquand! If you keep anything else from me, I'm going to charge you. You got me?"

"I guess this means I'll need another date for the prom," I said.

"Make jokes, asshole," he said. "Who did you pay and when was this?"

I gave him the condensed run-down. But by the time he slammed the phone down he was even more infuriated.

I placed the receiver back in the cradle and sat at the desk with my head on my good arm for a long time. Then I splashed water on my face, brushed my teeth with a finger and combed my hair. The face in the mirror looked like it belonged to a dead man.

Downstairs I hit the restaurant for the early bird special of eggs, toast and coffee. I felt no better, only worse, and expected things to go downhill from there. After sitting on the couch with my head in my hands for the remainder of the morning I got up and called over to the Marquand house. Instead of asking for the Colonel I used my handkerchief over the receiver and asked for Mrs. Marquand. I told Victor I was Sergeant Jonsen with the State Patrol.

I didn't actually expect her to come on the line but she did. Again I gave the fake name and after expressing my condolences asked what pediatrician they saw in town. I explained it was routine investigatory stuff. She told me it was Dr. Gannon S. Fitz-Nye on Eighth Avenue, her voice surprisingly steady in that upper-class-resolve sort of way.

I thanked her and was about to hang up but decided to ask about the funeral.

"There won't be a funeral, Sergeant. My husband prefers a private service and my son's body is being cremated."

"I don't think we were aware there was going to be a cremation."

"Yes. Today," she said.

Again I expressed my condolences and we clicked off. I lit a cigarette that tasted like it had been soaked in horse piss and stood looking out the window. The sky was clear, almost as clear as a perfect afternoon up in Morrison. The wind of the last few days had taken all the smog off towards Kansas somewhere. I could see a work crew from the city down on Broadway. They were busy with long pry bars, shovels and picks, ripping up the streetcar rails so there would be more room for cars and trucks. Streetcars, I guessed, were no longer part the American dream. Not when every new house had a garage and a car to go with it.

I flicked my ash into the ashtray and poked at it with the tip, breaking it down to dust. *Cremation* I thought. Interesting choice. It was certainly final.

CHAPTER 32

Gannon S. Fitz-Nye was obviously doing a bang up business. His office was situated just north of Country Club in a newer building along 8th Avenue that also catered to dentists and shrinks and specialists of every kind. The waiting room was furnished with not only expensive leather and chrome reproductions but some snazzy modern art and a smiley young receptionist with dimples as deep as coin slots. The dimples flattened right out when I flashed her my fake DA investigator card and said I was there about the Marquand murder.

Twenty minutes later she led me past a couple examination rooms that made Foulks' setup look like something from Whitehall and Jack-the-Ripper days. Fitz-Nye's personal office was large and clean in that modern minimal way. Everything was white or gray with the exception of another large art piece that I recognized as a Braque but had always thought resembled cat barf. He was a slight man with a mass of black hair gelled over the top of a bald scalp. I couldn't help noticing a pearl pinkie ring and perfect manicure when he extended his hand.

"How can I help you...Mr. Casy," he said examining the fake business card.

"As you see, doctor, I'm here from the District Attorney's office. I just need to ask a few questions with regards to Christian Marquand Junior. I understand you were his pediatrician?"

"Yes, that is correct," he said, gingerly laying the card on his all-but-spotless desk.

"We're working with Dr. Mercer, with the Jefferson County Coroner's office, and the purpose of my visit is to establish some baseline knowledge that can be used comparatively to ensure positive identification of the remains. As you may or may not have heard, there was a significant decomposition due to exposure to the elements. Dr. Mercer was able to determine a great deal as he is quite knowledgeable in the area of postmortem medicine. But we need to double-check certain findings. It's all routine and ensures we're not overlooking any details. I'm sure you understand. By the way, do you think I could get a glass of water? It has been a long day already. I just came from a meeting with the family's dentist and have several more appointments today as well." I barely gave Fitz-Nye pause to buzz for the girl before taking out my notepad and continuing. "Now, let's see, I have here that the child had a mild deformity of the right foot and an unclosed frontal fontanelle, both of which may have been caused by the genetic disorder cleidocranial dysostosis. It also appears that the child may have been at least mildly retarded. Was the left foot deformed as well? We don't have any information pertaining to that since we were not able to locate the left foot. It seems scavengers may have taken it as well as portions of the arms and hands. As a matter of fact the genitals and a large amount of the abdomen were eaten away too. So, was the deformity in the one foot only?"

"Yes, it was just the right foot," he said, his hands folded on the desk.

"And did you know about the cleidocranial dysostosis?"

"No. I did not. The last I saw of the child the fontanelle seemed to be closing accordingly. But I was aware of the developmental disability as there were some concerns with the delays in adaptive behaviors."

The girl came in with my water and flashed us some dimple. Fitz-Nye gave her a visual pat on the ass and she skipped out of the room. I took a tiny sip from the glass and placed it on the corner of the desk eliciting a disapproving meeting of his eyebrows.

"I believe," I said, "Dr. Mercer was thinking that the cleidocranial dysostosis may have contributed to not only physical deformities in the bones and joints but may also become present in the child's cognitive functioning."

"The child was…I don't recall exactly," Fitz-Nye said, making a half-hearted move towards the only file on his desk, "eighteen months…"

"Twenty months."

"Twenty months is still early for the fontanelle to be fully closed. Obviously Dr. Mercer is not an expert in pediatrics. I have always believed that the limitations in cognitive functioning were due to the stresses that were placed on the fetus during the third trimester and, as a result, I believe there were signs indicating the existence of mental retardation. As you can imagine, I see this sort of thing on a fairly regular basis. And in most cases the cause of limited cognitive or adaptive functioning is either genetic preconditions, such as a genetic disorder, or from outside conditions that affect the fetus' ability to properly develop. However, I will need to disagree with Dr. Mercer. I don't think cleidocranial dysostosis was present in the Marquand child. I say that mainly because I am unaware of cleidocranial dysostosis leading to developmental disabilities. It's purely a disorder affecting the bones or joints."

Fitz-Nye leaned back in his chair and examined the fingernails on his right hand, the way a woman would, palm down. "You see," he went on, "the Marquand child displayed a very classic condition that one might call *slow*. He possessed the delayed language skills, deficits in memory and delays in adaptive behavior skills. In my experience these conditions are quite common with children who experienced a loss of or significant decrease of oxygen during labor. Of course they can also present themselves if the mother were exposed to diseases or toxins during the pregnancy, like polio for example. But, with the Marquand child, I have always felt the deformity and reduced cognitive ability was a result of stress and deprivation of oxygen in utero."

"Had you discussed this with the parents?" I asked.

"With the mother, I did. Dr. Mercer is probably unaware, but Mrs. Marquand participated with her husband in an airplane test flight when she was in her third trimester. It was at an extreme altitude and over a very long distance. It is my belief that this is what led to the conditions evident in the child. Mrs. Marquand experienced vaginal bleeding towards the end of the flight and was afraid she may be having a miscarriage. The remainder of her pregnancy was anything but routine and I know there was an occurrence of dystocia during delivery. I am not sure exactly what happened, but Mrs. Marquand expressed it was a very difficult delivery and she thought it may not be possible for her to become pregnant again."

"Dystocia?"

"An abnormally positioned fetus. A breech birth."

"Did Mr. Marquand know about any of this?"

"Mrs. Marquand specifically told me she did not want any of that discussed in front of her husband. I believe it is her intention to protect Mr. Marquand from the true cause of the developmental delays and deformities. Which, I will admit, is not uncommon in many families, especially with diagnoses of abnormalities." Fitz-Nye sat forward, made a production out of examining his jeweled wristwatch, and put his hands on the desk. "Is there anything else, Mr. Casy? I really should get on to my next patient."

"What does the Colonel...Mr. Marquand think was the cause?"

"I have no idea, Mr. Casy. But as far as I know, he thinks it is purely the result of a genetic precondition." Fitz-Nye stood and offered his hand. I let him walk me out and watched his eyes climb all over the girl who giggled and gave him some more dimple.

CHAPTER 33

Apparently the Juicy Fruit wasn't doing much for my boozy breath. The librarian scrunched her tiny nose before leading me back to Periodicals. I waited with a cigarette as she gathered and spread out several newspapers from all across the country with articles pertaining to Marquand's test flight. The *Denver Post* had a detailed front page story, mainly due to the fact that Marquand had taken up residence in the city. It was dated Friday, May 2, 1947, and carried a large headline proclaiming *Marquand Test Success*. The story said the flight originated at Muroc Army Air Field near San Bernardino, California and was concluded at the Topeka Army Air Field, just south of Topeka, Kansas. The entire trip was 1,250 miles at a service ceiling of 47,000 feet. It took two hours and forty nine minutes to complete in Marquand's self-designed XA-13, twin-engine, two seater. It wasn't a record setter but it clearly demonstrated the potential for his high altitude reconnaissance aircraft. Toward the end of the article there was even a mention of Louise Marquand being seven months pregnant at the time. All the large newspapers carried similar stories, most including a map of the route with identical newswire photographs of the Marquands and the gleaming silver plane before takeoff. None carried photographs at the completion of the flight.

I made a point of stopping by the main desk to thank the librarian. She smiled back. "I've had a rough few days," I said, running a hand through my hair.

"I see that," she said.

In the lobby I stopped in a telephone booth and rang up the Marquand house. Again I used my handkerchief on the receiver and told Victor I was Sergeant Jonsen. This time I asked to speak to Loren. When she came on the line I said, "It's me. Harry. I'm at the library. Want to meet me in mysteries?"

"Why?" she said, ice in her voice.

"Because I want to see you."

"We just got back from the memorial service."

"Oh shit. I'm sorry. I forgot about that."

"Anyway, I don't think I want to see you," she said.

"Loren, I'm sorry."

I could hear her breath, soft on the other end.

"Tonight," I said. "Come by the house."

Without a word she hung up.

I placed the receiver back in the cradle, slid the door open and lit a cigarette. I smoked it down sitting there on the little seat thinking about Loren and Marquand. I had to know, needed to know, if she still loved him. Eventually I put my toe on the butt and pulled myself up to drift back to the office.

I no sooner stepped into the outer office when the inner door swung open and I was grabbed by the sleeve. The next thing I knew I was laying half on, half off the couch with Ugo looking down on me and Johnny grinning from behind my desk.

"Just let yourself in and take over the place, Johnny," I said scooting the lower half of my body up onto the couch.

"If you had a secretary to keep us company, maybe we'd stay out there. But it gets so lonely," Johnny said.

"Yeah, yeah. I know. Get a secretary."

"Anyway, you won't be so sore when you hear what I got for you."

I started to get up but Ugo pushed me back down.

"Take it easy! I pay the rent around here. I'm just taking my coat off for fuck's sake."

I tried again to get up and again Ugo pushed me down.

"What am I? Your playtoy?" I asked.

"Let him be," Johnny said. "Mick's getting pissy."

When I moved to stand up Ugo pushed me down another time, the big gapped grin spread across his entire block head. Johnny burst out laughing.

"I guess I am your goddamned playtoy," I said to Ugo who

continued grinning at me.

"Okay, enough of that," Johnny said, waving a hand at Ugo.

I cautiously got to my feet and hung up my coat and hat while keeping one eye on the monster.

"You know the guy trying to wash the money? There's a meeting scheduled with him in a few days," Johnny said without moving from the desk chair. "We're just waiting to get the location. But it might cost a bit more," he added.

"More? Like what?"

"Two. Maybe three."

"Damn, Johnny. That's a lot of money?" I said, taking a seat in one of the straight-back chairs.

"Do we have to have that talk again?" he said.

"Alright. Fine. Who's the guy?"

"The guy with the license plates! *Che cazzo!*" Johnny said, putting a hand to his forehead. "Ugo, doesn't it say *detective* on the door out there?"

Ugo got a blank look on his face and opened the door to look at the glass in the outer door. "Yeah, Johnny, it says detective."

I had to laugh at the seriousness of Ugo's moronic expression.

"*Mio Dio!* I'm surrounded by numbskulls. Close the door before I make you go stand out there!"

Ugo closed the door, confusion washing over his face.

"The guy with the license plate I gave you…" Johnny started again, "He's the one laundering the money. Right? Do you need me to spell it out further for you?"

"I get it," I said. "But why do we even need to go through with the exchange. I have his address. I'll call the cops and give them an anonymous tip. They'll go bust in his place right now."

"You think the guy has the money sitting around his house? Maybe tucked under his mattress?"

"Probably not," I said.

"Exactly."

"Okay then! What's the plan, General."

Johnny put a foot up on my desk and leaned over to rub the toe of a gleaming wingtip with a licked thumb. "Who said we're doing an exchange? All you need to know is where it's happening. He shows up and boom! The cops grab him with Marquand's dough. You idiots wrote down the serial numbers didn't you?"

"Are we even sure it's that guy?" I asked.

"What have I been saying?"

"What's he look like?"

"Hell if I know. I ain't been dating him," he said.

"Get your man to tell you what he looks like."

"You're getting mighty bossy. Anyway, what difference does that make?"

"I'm just not convinced it's the right guy."

His tone shifted to the one I'd heard in that room at the dogfight. "Are you really questioning what I'm telling you, Mick?" He put his foot on the floor and sat forward. Ugo took a step towards me as if he might grab me by the neck.

"Alright. Wait!" I said, holding up a hand. "It's just that I talked to that guy and he didn't seem like the real deal."

"Whoa! What do you mean you talked to him?" Johnny said.

For a moment my life flashed before my eyes and right then Ugo did grab me by the necktie. "Hold...hold on!" I stammered, balancing on tiptoes as Ugo held me in the air like a doll. "It was just a..."

"Shut the fuck up!" Johnny said. "What do you mean you talked to him?"

I wasn't sure if I was supposed to say anything or not until Ugo gave me a shake. "You gave me his plate number," I said. "I figured you knew I'd look into him."

"Looking into him ain't talking to him."

"Okay. Right! I see that now."

"Don't bullshit me."

"I'm not, Johnny. I totally see I fucked up," I said.

"What did he say to you?"

"He said he didn't have anything to do with it. But I'm sure he was talking out his ass. Why would he admit anything. Right?"

"And that was it?"

"Yeah. That was it."

"And you didn't think you were going to send this guy running? What the fuck's the matter with you?"

"What can I say, Johnny? I fucked up," I said, continuing to placate him.

Johnny got to his feet and came over to stand in front of me. "Yeah. You did, *citrul*," he said. "You better hope this fucker hasn't taken a powder." Then to Ugo he said, "Put him down. Let's go."

Ugo tossed me onto the couch. I nearly bounced off to the

floor.

"Try not to do anything else stupid," Johnny said.

They went out into the hallway with Ugo flashing me his signature teeth chomping bit. I sat on the couch for quite some time thinking about everything that had transpired, and how lucky I was to get through that without getting stomped. When it began to rain, drops peppering the south windows, I got up and looked down on Broadway. The workers tearing up the streetcar rails were gone. They had apparently progressed further into downtown. The strips where the rails used to be were covered over with dirt and readied for asphalt. It looked like a long scar.

I waited around the office for a while mostly because I had nowhere else to be. The phone rang twice. Infidelity cases both times. I told them I was unable to take new clients. They sounded sad. People losing hope. It seemed contagious and made me realize I wasn't staying in the office for any specific purpose so I went home. It was still raining with the same cautious tempo two hours later when I noticed the lights of a cab in front of the house. I opened the door and watched Loren come up the walk in her long stride, a large black hat hiding her face. At the bottom of the porch stairs she saw me standing in the doorway and paused. I stepped out and she came into my arms. She leaned back for me to kiss her. Her eyes were dark, not just in the evening light and the shadow of her hat, but with her typical heavy makeup. I was sure there was something there I could never see or understand.

"I'm glad you came," I said.

Loren put a finger to my mouth to hush me so I held her close, her breath warm on the side of my face.

CHAPTER 34

I woke early and watched Loren's breathing. She lay with her bare back towards me and I smoothed her hair thinking about the night before. After a while I got up and tried to quietly shovel coal into the furnace. Once I had the fire going I went back up to the kitchen and shook some food into Oscar's bowl. He eagerly gulped it up in his excited little way while I started a pot of coffee. As it bubbled and groaned I massaged my shoulder and neck to ease a bit of the pain from shoveling. When the coffee was finished, I took two cups into the bedroom. Loren was awake, laying on her other side, facing the doorway.

"Did I wake you?"

"No," she said. "I was just listening to you move around."

"I wanted to get the heat going."

"Do you have sugar?"

When I'd returned with the bowl she asked, "Do you ever hear the people next door?"

"I've heard them moving furniture or something. I think these walls are pretty thick. Why? Are you worried about last night?"

"Maybe," she smiled, sitting up and pulling the sheet over her breasts.

I watched her put spoonfuls in her cup and when she was satisfied I put sugar bowl on the bedside table and lay down next to her.

"I could get used to being served in bed every morning."

"You look wonderful," I said.

179

"I'm sure my makeup is smeared all over my face."

"A little, but I like it."

"My smeared makeup?" she asked, pulling back her hair.

"Yeah. It makes your eyes so mysterious."

"You're a strange man, Harry Thorpe."

I sipped my coffee. "Maybe that's why you like me. We're both a bit strange. This is what? Three times now? And you haven't worn a bra. Is that your usual thing?"

"Why in hell would I need a bra?" she said pulling the sheet down briefly to reveal her breasts. "Yes, I wear a bra sometimes. Does it offend your puritan nature if I don't?"

"Not at all. I think I might like it that you don't."

Looking down into her coffee she said, "I wore one yesterday. For the memorial."

"Is your sister okay?"

"She's heartbroken, of course. But she's very put together. It was me that couldn't stop crying." She toyed with the edge of the cup with a slender thumb, the nail short like a man's, and finally said, "He was a very innocent child."

"They said he might have had some disabilities."

"He was a special little boy, with special challenges. This will sound horrible, and I don't mean it that way, but he's probably better off where he is now. He could never live up to being a Marquand. It would have been a very difficult life for him."

She blinked her eyes tightly and I took one of her hands in mine. When she opened them she asked, "When does Elitch's open?"

"Next month. Would you like to go?"

"I would. Can you really hear it from here?"

"Oh sure. Especially people screaming on the roller coaster. And the noises from the shooting gallery. But I like when I can hear the music coming from the Trocadero. Sometimes I sit on the porch and listen. It depends which way the breeze is blowing, so it sort of comes and goes."

"You could leave the window open and hear it while laying in bed."

"We can try it sometime."

"We could lay here naked," she teased.

"We can do that anytime you want," I said giving her a wink.

She put both of our cups on the bedside table and curled up

against me, my arm wrapped around her, my hand on the bare skin of her belly.

"I'm sorry about the other day," she said.

"Don't worry."

"You can't get too attached to me."

"Because of that?"

"Well, that, and I'm crazy you know."

"You keep telling me."

"I might not be ready to stop," she said after a minute. "Using, I mean."

"I understand."

We stayed curled up like that. I thought she'd fallen asleep but after some time she said, "Those scars…were you shot?"

"Something like that."

"You were a bomber pilot?"

"I flew Hellcats at first and then Corsairs." She gave a little shrug. "They're fighter planes. But we did bombing missions too. Off carriers sometimes. And the various islands."

"Did you like it? The flying, I mean."

"Very much."

She uncurled herself, arched her back and stretched her arms and legs. Then she threw back the sheet and kicked at the blanket. "You either need to make love to me or make me something to eat, mister."

When we had finished I went into the kitchen and made some toast. I put out butter and jam. Loren came from the bedroom barefoot wearing one of my shirts and we ate the toast and drank fresh cups of coffee. She brushed crumbs from my cheek and giggled at the stupid faces I made. I wanted to spend the day with her but she needed to go to Louise. After a while she got dressed and I called her a cab. On the porch she kissed me until it arrived. I thought about how I should ask her the questions that had been eating at me—the ones about her and Marquand together. About the dog she poisoned. But I couldn't bring myself.

181

CHAPTER 35

I was staring out the office window and wondering if Johnny was actually going to come through with the meeting location for the money exchange when the door buzzer sounded. It was Sonja Hoff and she was actually quite beautiful in her disguise. Nearly all of her hair was tucked up under a large floppy hat, her blue eyes hidden behind dark glasses. It left her a china doll of smooth pale cheeks and ruby red lips.

"I wait one hour for you the other night," she said pushing by me.

"What? What night?"

"The night I talked to you! You said you were coming to meet me but you never showed up."

"I did?"

"I should have known better," she said.

I struggled to recall what she was talking about and then like a clearing fog the phone conversation came back to me. "Oh shit! That's right. I'm sorry."

"How perfect is this?" she said. "The person I ask to help me is nothing but a drunk."

"It's not like that," I said. "Something came up and I…" She could have been crying or shooting daggers at me behind her glasses and I'd never know. "Okay. You're right. I *was* drunk. It was a really bad day. But it won't happen again, Miss Hoff. I want you to trust me. I want to help."

"You want to help? Then how can you say such mean things to

me? This Old Sparky! You must know I did not murder that child!" she said.

I motioned her to one of the chairs. She slowly turned and took a seat as if weighed down with a hundred pounds of reluctance.

"I really do want to believe you." I said.

"The papers and everyone say I did this. But it's not true."

"Marquand's convinced it was you too."

"He is such a liar!"

"But you did take the baby?"

"No! I did not take him. And I did not do anything to him."

I opened the cigarette box and turned it towards her. She took one with gloved fingers and I reached across to light it. The flame from the Zippo illuminated her eyes for a split second. They were on me, not the tip of her cigarette, and she wasn't crying.

"You're not nearly as distressed as you were the other night," I said.

Her head tilted and even without being able to see her eyes I knew she didn't understand.

"Nervous. Worried. Upset," I said to clarify.

She blew her smoke sideways. "And you're not so drunk either. I have the time to think. I presume I cannot trust anyone anymore. I wanted to trust you. *So ein Misthaufen!*" she said curling a disgusted lip at me.

"I *can* help."

She pulled off a glove and pinched a piece of tobacco from her lip with pointed fingers. "What does Colonel Marquand say?"

"He says it's you. And Loitzel. He says you're blackmailing him because of the baby's deformity," I added for good measure.

"That is not true."

"And, speaking of Loitzel. Where is he?" I occupied myself with my own cigarette while waiting, rolling the tip around in the ashtray and puffing on it. She didn't move a muscle. "Miss Hoff, I know about you and Andreas Loitzel. You must know I talked to him."

"He says it is too dangerous for us to be seen together." she said finally. "He protects me. And I love him. But I also do not want him to hear such things as you ask. You probably cannot understand. But I cannot hurt him. Not like that."

"Yeah?"

"Christian and I, we had become lovers. But I stopped it. This is why he…he hates me so."

"Not a lot of new information there," I said, studying the glowing tip of my cigarette as a way to convey only moderate interest.

"Why do you say this? Like that?"

"I'm just saying I'm not surprised. I figured you two had something going from way back. I'm not sure what that has to do with anything though."

"It was not from *way back*."

"How was it then?"

"It started here. In America. After he sent for me and I began working for him."

"Marquand sent for you?"

"Yes." She dropped the butt on the floor and I heard her shoe grinding it out.

I made sure she saw the ashtray for her next cigarette, if there was going to be one and said, "Why was he sending for you if you weren't sleeping together in Germany?"

"I met Christian as a Kindermädchen for a German family he knew. After the war he send for me. So I could work for him here."

"My German's a bit rusty. Kindermädchen? A nanny?"

"Yes. A nanny."

"Marquand sent for a nanny? Whose nanny were you? Göring's?"

"No. Another man."

"Who?"

"Klaus Kesseling," she said, slipping her glove back on.

"And who was he?"

"A scientist."

I let out a sigh and said, "C'mon, Miss Hoff. We could spend all day going back and forth like this but it's only going to be fun for another minute. Spill with the whole story already. Was Kesseling some kind of aircraft engineer? And what were you really doing? Because God knows you weren't really a Kindermädchen."

"I do not know these things. Yes, he must have been an aircraft engineer. Christian come to the house many times for dinner. He and *Herr* Kesseling become very good acquaintances. But then the whole family was killed. In Dresden. I stay behind in Berlin to attend to the piano of *Frau* Kesseling. It was very expensive and had been in her family for many, many years and I was to arrange for safekeeping. I was to join them later in Dresden. But then the bombs came and," she shrugged. "So I stay in Berlin."

"And you weren't sleeping with Marquand in Germany?"

"No."

"I know Marquand pretty good. He isn't going to give a shit about some nanny unless of course you..." I said, raising my eyebrows and wagging my head.

"It's not like that."

"You're telling me he just sent for you out of the blue?"

"He was looking for *Herr* Kesseling I am sure. And he found me. I tell him I am the only one to survive. So he send passage and I come. Why is this so, how do you say?"

"Peculiar?"

"Yes. Why is this so peculiar?"

I pushed a paperclip around the blotter with a finger and said, "Because that isn't like Marquand. It must be the Kesseling connection. Or," I said, looking directly into her dark glasses, "you're not telling me everything. I don't see what's the big deal if you were sleeping together in Germany."

"Stop saying that! I have told you the whole story."

"Yeah, maybe," I said, dropping the paperclip into a drawer. "How about you start telling me who took the kid. Was it Loitzel? Or someone else that worked in the house?"

"I tell you already. I do not know who took that child. Andreas and I, we just want to be away from all this. And away from Christian. We want to have our lives. We would never bring harm to a child."

"Does Marquand know about Loitzel?"

"No. That is why...that is why I am hiding. Andreas and I make plans to go away now. And so now that I have left he is saying I did this kidnapping so that you will find me."

"Well, you definitely picked a bad time to run off," I said, crushing out my cigarette.

CHAPTER 36

I drove over to the Marquand Country Club house to get the additional two thousand Johnny said he needed. Marquand told me he wasn't going to be there but Victor would have an envelope. The gate was open so I pulled into the drive and parked on the gravel. The yard was pretty. The peonies were getting ready to bloom by the labyrinth and the bomb or pineapple-shaped boxwoods were lit with bright new leaves. A brown bunny scampered between the safety of two bushes. It made me think of Sonja Hoff. Trying to get away. There wasn't any logical reason for me to help her. Her story didn't ring entirely true. But she would have to be stupid and careless to trust me if she'd been involved in that child's murder. Maybe it started as some sort of extortion over the deformity and retardation. God knows, Marquand would pay a ton of money if he thought it meant he could keep control of a situation. Or maybe it was an accident. Hell, even the cops reenacting the crime dropped the simulated baby. I tossed my cigarette and started across the drive thinking I was an idiot for not just going to Greenberg. But what was I going to tell him? I didn't know anything for certain. The logical thing would be to wait for the money exchange and see who would turn up with all that dough. Until then, Sonja Hoff had better do as I told her and stay low at the Howdy Partner.

Victor and the dog I'd heard the night of the kidnapping answered the bell at almost the exact same moment. Not surprisingly, it was a Bichon Frise, the de rigueur dog of choice for the rich. And typical of dogs that size, it acted like it would take my leg off if it could get at me. Victor told me to wait by holding up a finger and pulled it away by the collar. Before he could return, Loren came to the door.

"Detective," she said.

"Miss Chambers," I said, mimicking her formal tone.

"What an unexpected surprise."

"The Colonel asked me to stop by for something."

"I don't believe *the Colonel* is here," she said glancing over her shoulder and then stepping out onto the porch.

"He said Victor would have what I need. But I'm not so sure," I teased, letting my eyes roam over her. She wore a pair of high-waisted pants and silk blouse with large square cuffs. Her hair was up and back and her makeup was almost understated.

"Shhh!" she said, pulling me off the porch and down a stone path through the shaved grass. Once we'd rounded a large shrub she threw her arms around my neck and kissed me.

"Make love to me in the garden," she breathed.

"In broad daylight?"

"Yes. I'm feeling so bohemian."

I kissed her and let my hands explore her body until Victor showed up. He scratched a toe on the stones, then coughed.

"Yes?" Loren said, pushing away from me.

"Mr. Thorpe..." Victor said, holding out an envelope without really facing us.

As I went over to take it Loren said, "Thank you, Victor. I'll summon you if we need anything else."

Victor, looking as if he'd been clipped, turned and disappeared around the hedge.

"Oh!" I said. "The Bryn Mawr girl can be curt."

"That wasn't curt. Besides, the man should know better than to interrupt a girl's bohemian adventures in the garden. Come back," she said, holding her hand out to me.

"Seriously. That wasn't necessary."

She dropped her arm, her expression softening. "Darling, are you really going there?"

I didn't say anything, and I didn't move.

"Victor is a servant," she said. "He *serves* us. I didn't treat him indifferently. I treat him as I would any servant."

"You acted like an asshole with the man. Now he'll tell

Marquand what he saw?"

"Do I care if he does?"

If she had been a man I would have smacked her one. Instead I said, "You know, I heard something about you that I never wanted to believe. But now I can see it. I heard you had a tantrum one time and threw little Christian out with the garbage."

Loren's eyes narrowed and her spine stiffened as if she were about to hiss. "Did Christian tell you that?"

"I think I heard it from that state cop, actually."

She pushed past me and started up the stone path.

"Where are you going?" I asked. "I thought we were going all bohemian in the garden."

She spun around and said, "You have no right to talk to me like that."

"Oh? Really? Tell me about the time you poisoned Louise's dog. Or how about the heart attack you had when Marquand dumped you and married Louise?"

She turned to walk away but I grabbed her arm, just above the elbow. She swung hard with her other hand. Much harder than the time she slapped me at Casper's. I made sure to grab her hand so she couldn't do it again and pulled her close. "Hold on," I said.

"Let go!" she shrieked.

I held her as tight as I could while she fought and said, "Loren, I need to know. At some point. You know I love you."

Her resistance ebbed for a moment and I wasn't sure if she was going to kiss me, bite me or spit in my face. Then she wrestled to get free with even more abandon, the point of a shoe stabbing into my left shin. I hugged her so tightly she squeaked. When she finally gave in I spun her back off the path and onto the grass. She looked woozy and unsteady. Tears filled her eyes and she snatched her arm from my grip in defiance.

"What do you want from me?" she said.

"Do you love him?"

Avoiding my stare, she said, "I loved him. Once." When her eyes did come up to my face they were red with anger and she spat, "But I'm sure you know all about it!"

I didn't say anything.

Tears rolled over her cheeks and at first she swiped at them angrily. "I was young. And stupid. And he was the goddamned Mighty Marquand! I got suckered by his charm and looks and I really thought we could have a life…" she said, working really hard to keep from breaking down completely. I moved towards her but she faced away and stepped further onto the grass, a shoulder raised against me. When she finally continued she said, "All my life I've only wanted to be happy. I've wanted someone to take notice of me. To love me. And when it was Christian it was like a dream come true. Finally I was as good as Louise. Better than Louise! And she took that away."

"So you were…engaged to Marquand," I said numbly.

Her shoulder moved higher and I knew the answer.

"Why did he break it off?"

"He never broke it off!" she said, turning to face me. "He came back from Germany and married Louise. Just like that. I didn't have any idea until she called me at school to say they were in love and planning to elope. Do you know what that did to me? Do you have any idea what it was like to lose out to her again!"

"But, why…?"

"Because I was sick! I saw it in his eyes when I told him. It was like a switch was thrown. But I wanted to think he would understand, that he cared. But, I remember it so vividly. We were at Delmonico's and I said, *you know, they say I'll be lucky to live to forty.* It was stupid and flippant and I guess I thought it would make him want to love me more." She paused a moment, looking at the ground. "But his eyes went cold. And I knew. I didn't want to admit it, but I knew that's when he stopped loving me."

I held a hand out to her. When she took it, I moved close, taking her in my arms.

"Little Christian. He was damaged too," she whispered into my shoulder. "Just like me. And when I saw the way Christian looked at his own child, it was the same thing. I could see he didn't want him anymore either," she sobbed. "Oh God! Do you know how that breaks my heart?"

I held her for a long time and soon she deflated in my arms. I swooped her up and carried her around the hedge, up onto the porch. I pushed the door open. *Which room is yours?* I asked. *The third door on the left,* she breathed, and I carried her upstairs and into her room. She hardly moved as I laid her on the bed. I slid her shoes off and pulled up the quilt. As I started to leave she called my name, her hand coming out from under the covers. I held it. Then I kissed her eyelids and let myself out.

In the Dodge I lit a cigarette. Then I cried.

CHAPTER 37

I ended up at Mary Zimmerman's bar not far from Country Club. It was nothing more than a converted living room in her house along First Avenue. I worked hard at keeping my glass empty while Mary went on and on about a plan she had for a new bar on one of the empty lots behind the house.

"With that new shopping complex coming you should make a fortune," a guy with a tan face and wearing a golf shirt said. "Maybe you need an investor, Mary."

"What I need is a new name," she said.

"I read they're going to call it the Cherry Creek Shopping Complex," another fellow said. "You could name the bar something that goes with that."

"Maybe *The Creek*," golf shirt said.

"Or *The Cherry*," a third man added, holding up the maraschino cherry from his drink.

"Maybe you should just call it *Crickets*," I said, not really agreeing with the whole grand idea. "Since there won't be any left once they get done bulldozing everything and pouring blacktop all over the place."

"*Crickets*. I like that," Mary said. "For all you late nighters that come in here and chirp at me."

"Chirp, chirp," I said, shaking my glass at her so she'd pour me another. The others fell into suit and held their glasses up while chirping.

Eventually I had to get away from all the chattering and the jukebox playing an endless stream of every Peggy Lee songs I hated. I don't recall actually getting into the Dodge but I do remember bouncing the curb somewhere along Speer Boulevard and driving through shrubbery in the median. By some miracle I didn't head right off into the Platte River or mow over some hobo sleeping off a binge under a bush.

The next morning I woke up on my dining room floor, half in and out of my pants. The side of my face tender and bruised from the impact with the floor. I gingerly rolled onto my back making sure not to roll on my bad shoulder and lay for a good long time. I couldn't have felt worse if two guys had worked on me with baseball bats.

Summoning all my energy, I finally tottered into the bathroom to shave and wash up. After that I made a pot of coffee and swallowed some aspirin. It wasn't long before everything came up. After a third trip to the bathroom my head was throbbing so hard it seemed to shake the whole house.

I drove past Dina's to a place where I knew no one would recognize me. I had a big breakfast of eggs, sausage, bacon, potatoes and toast. Instead of coffee I had some tomato juice. It was a horrible mix but it seemed to actually settle my stomach. When I finished I went next door to a liquor store and bought two cans of beer, thinking the hair of a dog might help. I drank them down with the car door open, just in case it was all going to come up. It didn't. When it finally seemed like I might survive, I pulled the door shut and drove to the library.

The same librarian who helped me before was working the counter. It was pretty obvious from her rolled eyes that she couldn't believe I'd lived long enough to return. I mopped the sweat from my face with a shaky hand and did my best not to breathe on her while explaining I was looking for whatever she had on a German scientist name Klaus Kesseling.

She asked me to wait in a chair in Periodicals. A half hour later she came to get me. Spread across the long table was a number of newspapers.

"If you need more," she said, "I can submit a request to the Library of Congress. Whatever they had could be sent by microfilm in about a month."

I thanked her and apologized for how I bad I knew looked with my bruised face and watery eyes. Her mouth turned up politely at the corners and I watched her go, heels clicking on the marble floor.

As it turned out, Dr. Klaus Kesseling had been tried at Nuremberg with twenty-two other medical professionals and was hanged in August 1947. He was convicted on charges that he performed medical experiments on prisoners of war and civilians of occupied countries. At the trial it was also revealed he had routinely performed abortions on women who suffered from physical or mental handicaps. This had gone back as far as 1937, when he was officially appointed head of the Nazi Euthanasia Program, a series of racial hygienist policies designed to strengthen the Reich and build a master race. Prior to his appointment, Kesseling had been one of Hitler's personal physicians in Berlin.

I folded the papers into a stack and returned to the counter to tell the librarian there was no need to order the microfilm. I got all the way outside before going back to ask if she could direct me to an area where I could research genetics and eugenics on my own. She flipped through the card file and gave me a slip of paper that included numbers corresponding to three rows on the third floor.

For the next few hours I wandered the aisles, puffing on one cigarette after another and leafing through books pulled from the shelves. I started with Plato, remembering old Professor Warren's political theory lectures. He'd told us that even in ancient Greece, eugenics had been practiced as an idea for maintaining racial superiority. After flipping through *The Republic* and rereading the part where Plato advocated government control of marriage and reproduction I moved along until I found Darwin's *Origin of Species*. But it wasn't Darwin that was all that interesting. It was his cousin, Francis Galton, who said natural selection as Darwin defined it was hindered by society's organization around the social idea that we need to protect the weakest. Galton thought societies that supported the weak and underprivileged were in direct opposition to the true idea of the survival of the fittest.

As I went through other books I kept coming back to Galton. His stance seemed to serve as the catalyst in the modern way of thinking about eugenics. And while I didn't actually see anything in his writings demonstrating a specific advocacy of euthanasia and abortion, he did stress the importance of selective breeding. "Mandated breeding practices," he had written, "ensured inferior and superior mixing would be prevented, strengthening society as a whole." This way of thinking was championed by all sorts of people, including Alexander Graham Bell and Woodrow Wilson, who was a proponent of compulsory sterilization for certain *defective people*. It was his support that led to a whole host of states enacting laws that prohibited the feeble-minded or epileptic from marrying, and requiring the sterilization of people who were similarly identified as unfit. I even found a journal of medicine report predicting that over 60,000 Americans would be sterilized against their will for some sort of state deemed physical or mental defect before 1950.

I looked carefully but wasn't able to find much pertaining to the Nazi eugenics policy. Most of that I figured would still be classified information and not even available through the Library of Congress for several years. But there was a newly published book about the Nuremberg trials, and sure enough Kesseling was mentioned. But what was even more compelling was the fact that an American eugenicist named Paul Popenoe had been cited by the defense during Kesseling's portion of the trial.

I located Popenoe's book, *Sterilization for Human Betterment*, back in the first row on a shelf near the floor. It was filled with statistics and arguments claiming that a sterilization policy in California was so successful that he felt it should be used as a model for establishing similar programs all across the country. California, it seemed, had been sterilizing the mentally ill and mentally retarded in state psychiatric hospitals. Popenoe thought the program not only benefited society as a whole but also the individual that was being sterilized. "A justified means for the good of all," Popenoe wrote. The Nuremberg book mentioning Kesseling said the defense used the Popenoe's study to support the Third Reich's sterilization policies, especially since their racial purification laws were enacted with the purpose of creating a more fit society.

The thing that struck me was Popenoe's big, broad smile on the inside page of his book. Under the photo it said he was an extremely respected marriage counselor in California. I just kept staring at his face and thinking how this dapper, friendly-looking man thought it was perfectly fine to sterilize people against their will. I was wondering what he thought about his opinions being used to defend someone like Kesseling when I heard the clickety-click of the librarian's shoes approaching.

"I wasn't sure you'd still be up here," she said, handing me a newspaper folded over to one page. "But I found something else that might interest you."

It was an article about a local physician who had given a two hour speech to the Denver Conservative Sociological Association. The speech, given in November 1940, was focused on a need for heightened concern that defectives were having a negative effect on social progress. Defectives being the mentally retarded or handicapped. They, the physician said, would divert resources, siphon wealth and drag all of society down. This, he insisted, would lower the overall purity of the genius class and the country's ability to advance in a challenging world. He proposed these inferiors should be left on their own to sink or swim, with criminals and deviants being eliminated from society as a whole. That physician was Dr. William Loftesness.

CHAPTER 38

The office phone rang and rang but I let it go, rolled over onto my side, and went back to sleep. Sometime later it started again. That time I forced myself off the couch. It was Johnny.

The Italian restaurant where he told me to meet was no more than four blocks from the office so I walked. Ugo was on guard at the end of the bar. He had just begun to maul me up and down when Johnny called from the back for him to let me go. I flashed the monster one of his own signature snarls and went on by.

Johnny was alone in a booth with a bowl of soup and bottle of red wine wrapped in wicker. He wore a brown suit with robin's egg blue pinstripes as thick as a pencil.

"Bring a glass for Mr. Thorpe, Sal," Johnny said to a little man hiding behind an apron that touched the floor.

"Just water," I said.

Waving his hand he told Sal to bring the wine glass. To me he said, "Wine's good for you."

"I like wine alright."

"You look like shit," he said shaking his head. "What horse kicked you in the head?"

"I slipped in the tub."

"Have some soup. It'll fix you right up. Best minestrone in the city."

"Thanks. I'll keep that in mind."

The waiter returned with my glass. Johnny poured the wine himself, the waiter scooting away backwards. I took a sip while he watched and smacked my lips for effect. "There," I said, making sure he was satisfied.

"It's from Umbria. In central Italy. Where I come from. Do you know wine?" he asked, swirling his glass and putting on a big show looking at it against the little shaded lamp on the table. "Wine is like a person," he blathered on, "each with its own personality and traits. Each with its goodness and with its flaws. Wine is a whole lesson in history and culture. Just from the one sip you can taste an entire generation of labor and ambition. It tells you a lot about the people who tended the grapes and worked the soil. You should pay attention to such things, Thorpe. There's a lot of subtleties in life that can teach you things."

I drank my entire glass in one sloppy gulp. I was hoping I could muster up a belch to punctuate my show, but instead said, "Get on with it, Johnny. I don't need a lesson in everything you think is important."

His silly face transformed into one that was cold and hard. "Do you have my money?"

I put the envelope on the table. Johnny held it up and Ugo swung by to take it.

"You're lucky I was told to deal with you," he said.

I shrugged.

"My guy says it's a tall German. Blonde hair and a thick accent. And he's got a dame with him."

"That's not exactly a newsflash."

"It's a skinny dame. With a taste for the hard candy."

I knew he meant Loren and for a second I could see myself knocking his teeth out. Instead I said, "Who feeds you this shit?"

"I told you. I get it from my man. Did that strike a nerve or something? You jumped like someone touched a conduit to your asshole."

"What man? Is he one of your guys? Or are you dealing with someone else?"

"I got a guy. And he's dealing with the German. Haven't we been over this? Do you actually make a living as a detective?"

"Fuck you," I said just as the waiter came up with a basket of bread and bowl of soup for me. This time he didn't scoot away, he practically ran back to the kitchen.

"Don't provoke me, Mick. I don't want to do something I might regret later."

"Like what, Johnny?"

"Like teach you some goddamned manners."

"Teach me manners! What do you know about manners? A taste for wine and a $500 diamond stickpin doesn't mean you actually know anything about manners. It might mean you're a poof. But it doesn't mean you have class."

"You need to watch your lip. I've used a vice grip on a man's balls for less than what you're saying. So keep your big fucking Mick mouth shut and do what you're told. The end is near. If there's something you want to settle, we can do it after. But right now, you need to do what I tell you and finish this up."

"First–I'm not a fucking Mick. And second–what do you know about the end being near? What the fuck does that mean?"

Johnny dropped his napkin and leaned forward with his hands on the table. "The exchange is scheduled. All you got to do it go get the German and his skinny junky whore. My man said the German even asked if he could buy some smack for her when they did the exchange. But my guy don't sell shit like that. That's too bad, huh? I bet that German is going to love fucking that skinny bitch real good while she has her junky jitters, right on top of that big pile of freshly washed, dead baby money. Ever fucked a junky, Thorpe? Their pussy clamps on your cock tighter than hell when they're jittering. It's like nothing else. Then you give them their candy and fuck them all over again and if they pass out you can do whatever you want to them if you know what I mean. It's something worth trying. Unless you've already dabbled in junky pussy. Then you know what I'm talking about."

I stared into his eyes. The whites were bright and the pupils steady. For a split second I think even he thought I might make a move and that's just what he wanted with his big grin and hands splayed casually on the table. It was all the usual stuff to egg a guy on, to make you lose your cool and do something stupid. And quick as a flash he'd have the drop and you might not even know what happened until you woke up in the hospital or they were lowering your dumb ass into the ground.

"Where's the meeting?" I asked.

Johnny sat back and took a drink of his wine. "It doesn't matter," he said. "The German's got all the dough with him right now. At his house. Call the little kike and send in the cavalry. Everything is waiting there for you."

"And if he doesn't have the money?"

"I'll give you a refund."

"You're sure about this?" I said, getting to my feet.

His kissed two fingertips and raised them in the air. I started out of the restaurant. Johnny called after me, something about me not even trying my soup. But I continued out and almost ran back to the office. I called the detective bureau at the State Patrol. A sergeant told me Greenberg was off duty. I explained it was urgent and involved the Marquand case. He said he'd call Greenberg at home and have him contact me. Five minutes later the phone rang. "This better be good, Thorpe. It's shabbos and I'm with my family," Greenberg said.

I told him I knew who had the money and gave him the address and as many details as I could without actually mentioning the mob and Johnny.

"Call you back," he said, the phone going dead. Not five minutes later he did. "We're never going to get a warrant this fast on some bullshit tip. I'm going over there and we'll figure out a way to get inside. You better be right with this. Who's got the list of serial numbers?" he asked.

"I have a copy in my safe."

"Bring it. But stay the fuck out of the way."

I took the list from the safe, ran down the stairs and drove like a madman the three miles to Loitzel's dirty meringue bungalow. I was the first to arrive. After switching off the headlights I swung around, coasted up and stopped a half dozen yards or so from Loitzel's Ford. The lights were on in the house but I didn't see any movement. It looked nice and quiet. Even the horrible meringue stucco looked okay in the glow of a streetlight.

About five minutes later a marked State Patrol car slid down the next block, headlights off, and stopped at the corner. Two uniforms got out and trotted Indian-style across 11th Avenue. They both ducked behind an untamed hedge bordering Loitzel's property. A minute later Greenberg came up the street like a torpedo. He somehow parked just in front of me without taking the bumper off my car. As he started across the street he motioned for me to stay where I was. Together he and the uniforms went through Loitzel's little gate and up the walk. One of the uniforms disappeared around the side of the house while Greenberg and the other, guns drawn, proceeded up onto the porch. I couldn't tell who, but one of them banged on the door. I could hear Greenberg yelling they were the police. When there was no response they banged more. The uniform moved off the porch and stood on his tiptoes to look in the front window. He said something and Greenberg jumped off the porch and pulled himself up on the window ledge with both hands. Then he ran back up and threw open the screen so the other could use his shoulder against the door. I got out of the Dodge just as they were going in. A minute later one of them came out and jogged down to the marked car. He lit the gumball on the roof and pulled up to park right in front of the house. I could see him speaking into the radio receiver but I couldn't make out any words. Then Greenberg came out onto the porch and waved me up.

"Lots of fun in here," he said, stepping aside so I could go in.

There was Loitzel, on the couch with his head back, eyes closed and mouth hanging open in that unmistakable way that dead people's mouths inevitably do. He had a single bullet hole right through the center of his forehead, a big splatter of blood, bone and bits of brain decorating the wall behind him. It didn't look like there had been a struggle. Whoever popped the hole through him was either a welcomed visitor or it was the biggest surprise of Loitzel's life.

On the floor near the body was the suitcase Marquand had purchased for the ransom drop and a scattering of about five hundred dollars' worth of bills in different denominations.

"Looks like whoever knocked this guy off took most of the money. You got that list?" Greenberg asked me.

I gave it to him.

"And for the sake of procedure, let me hold your weapon," he said, holding out his hand.

I gave him the .45. "Are you making me a suspect?"

"That doesn't look like a .45 hole to me. But the whole world is going to be here in about five minutes. I just want to cover the bases." He tucked my gun into his coat pocket. I knew he was referring to Loitzel's head, but there was my .45 hole in the wall from my previous visit and I made sure not to look at it. "You got anything else I should be concerned with?" he asked. "I don't want to pat you down."

"No, just the one. I left my machine gun at home."

"Okay. You can stay. For a while. Just sit over there. We're going to have to give you the third degree at some point."

I sat in the dining room as he told me and lit a cigarette. From that angle I could clearly see the chunk that was missing at the back of Loitzel's head. It wasn't anything I wanted to keep staring at but I had to drag my eyes away. His hands lay peacefully next to his thighs and his stockinged feet were flat on the floor. Other than the missing chunk, and the grotesquely hanging mouth, he could have been a guy who'd settled in for a nap.

I turned in the chair so I wasn't facing him. On the table next to me was a map. It was unfolded and had marks drawn on it as if Loitzel had just finished planning a big getaway. I was about to tell Greenberg but I decided to let them find it on their own.

Obviously I'd been set up by Johnny to find this little staged scene. But who was behind it? For argument's sake it could be Johnny and the mob. They could easily wash Marquand's money and it wouldn't be any big deal to knock off Loitzel to get hold of it. But I wasn't so sure they'd be stupid enough to get fully embroiled in the Marquand kidnapping. The logical answer, therefore, would seem to be Loftesness. He inserted himself into the kidnapping out of the blue, and talked Marquand into letting him be the intermediary for all the communications. He could have easily clobbered me in the cemetery to cover up the fact that no one was actually going to meet him there. On top of all that, he was probably crazy enough to go through all those lengths to protect Marquand's legacy from a retarded baby. That was percolating in my head when an army of Denver cops arrived. Right after that some of the fellows I recognized now from the State Patrol joined the party, including the same fingerprint guy who had worked the Marquand house. He opened his case and began to pull out the jars of dust as a photographer started snapping shots of Loitzel. A few minutes later, Dmytryk showed up and Greenberg gave him the official rundown. He eyed me up and down when Greenberg explained I was the one who called with the tip. It looked like they were about to come over and start working on me when a detective rushed in saying baby socks had been found in Loitzel's Ford. With that news they were all sucked out of the room. Only the fingerprint man and another DPD detective remained in the house with me. The print man was working the coffee table and everything on it. The detective was intent on making a scene diagram in a notebook.

"Who're you?" he asked, when he finally looked up.

"Private dick. I work for Marquand." I took out the license and let him study it. He wrote down my name.

"And why're you here?"

"I got a tip this guy had the Marquand money," I said. "I passed it on to Lieutenant Greenberg, State Patrol. He's the little guy in the tan windbreaker. He told me to meet him here."

"Okay. Did you know this guy?" he asked, jerking his head at Loitzel.

"We met once."

He nodded and went on with his notes. The print man had moved to the suitcase, twirling his brush and the black dust over every inch. Then Greenberg and some of the others returned. They were all worked up over the baby socks and sounded convinced that Loitzel had been one of the kidnappers.

Since I was apparently forgotten and might end up sitting there for two hours I eventually got Greenberg's attention and asked him if he needed me to stick around. He said I could take off, but he wouldn't give my gun back. He said I could pick it up the next day when they called me in for questioning. I told him I couldn't wait and left.

Outside was a circus with all the cars and red flashing lights. The entire neighborhood had turned out to take in the excitement. Adding to the revelry was the coroner's wagon, just pulling up as I weaved my way over to the Dodge. A woman standing near my car with her two kids asked me what was going on. I told her there was a dead guy splattered all over the place. She gave a harrumph and feigned putting hands over one of her little angel's ears but they were still standing there when I drove off.

I hadn't liked looking at Loitzel's brains on the wall. Nothing good ever comes from seeing shit like that. I began to wonder if he had any family and if they'd survived the war. Would they ever know what happened to Andreas Loitzel? I doubted it. It wouldn't be a whole lot different if something happened to me. Would anyone even know who to notify, and if they did, would anyone from back east even show up to claim my body? Probably not. They never gave a shit about me before. So, it would have to be someone like Marquand or Greenberg that would make the formal I.D. Then they'd toss me in a hole and it would all be over, like I'd never existed. Except for all those things I did in the war. There was no taking any of that back. Once you push the button and those bombs are free falling, you can never do anything to stop them or change their fate. It was just something you lived with. It was like the vision of that dead baby or the boy in the box. Or Loitzel's brains. You never get those things out of your head. And you never forgive yourself.

CHAPTER 39

Greenberg called the next morning and I went in for questioning. He wanted to play hard ball with me for some reason so I played along. It didn't matter, and even with everything he fired at me I only revealed the basics that I knew he would already know. I admitted I got a tip from a confidential informer and that the same person told me Loitzel was looking to launder a lot of money. I didn't give any specifics about Johnny or a skinny dame or heroin. And I never mentioned the Howdy Partner and Sonja Hoff. That's when he dropped an evidence bag on the table. Inside was a slug.

"Know where that came from?" he asked.

"Loitzel's head."

"Nope. From the wall next to his head."

I dug out my cigarettes and he pushed the tin ashtray into the middle of the table. I gave him one and we puffed in silence.

"Okay," I said. "And what's that got to do with anything?"

"Guess what caliber it is?"

I picked up the plastic envelope and gave it a look, then dropped it on the metal table. "Looks like a .45 to me."

"Now, who do you suppose carries a Colt 1911? Hmmmm," he said, his hand to his chin pensively.

"What was the caliber that killed him?"

"Three eighty. Lucky for you."

"Oh yeah? Am I the only guy in the city that carries a .45?"

"No. But you're the only guy with a .45 that's been shooting holes in Loitzel's wall."

I flicked an ash and gave him a look. "Think you can make that stick?"

"Brother, I can make anything stick." He flipped a chair around and straddled it, his arms resting on the back. "Look–I couldn't care less about Loitzel. One less German is what I'm thinking. I know I shouldn't hold them all responsible for what happened over there." He flicked his ash on the floor. "But, I guess I do."

"I suppose that's natural," I said. "Considering."

"Considering what? That I'm a Jew."

"I meant your burns. That was a tough break." I tapped my cigarette on the rim of the ashtray. "But I'm sure being a Jew figures in somehow."

"Is it yours?" he asked, pointing at the evidence bag with his cigarette.

"Yeah, it's mine. I stopped over and had a chat with him awhile back. He wasn't as talkative as I like, so I let one fly."

"What'd he tell you?"

"Nothing. His place was clean and he seemed clean. He said he and Hoff had nothing to do with it."

"Well, he had the money. The baby socks were in his car. The lab guys think the wood for the ladder came from his attic. And he was the perfect height and stature to climb it and go in and out of the window. Plus he had a getaway map and packed suitcases. What's not to like about all that?" He dropped his butt to the floor and ground it out with his toe. "After you left last night we found some lipstick on a broken glass in the trash. On some cigarette butts too. So now we look for the match, which I'm betting will on Hoff's lips. I'm also willing to bet she's got a dirty heater and the rest of the money. Looks like a greedy accomplice to me. Case closed."

"So the money's a match?"

"Serial numbers are exactly what we wanted them to be. And, Marquand and what's-his-name Loftesness came in last night. They said that's the suitcase they bought for the drop."

"Loftesness came in with Marquand?"

"He did. Weird fucker, huh?"

I put my cigarette out and said, "Well, let's hope they're actually the kidnappers before you fire Hoff up in the electric chair."

"Loitzel had the goods. What more could we want? It's like Santa Claus slid down my chimney." He gave me a look. "*Unless* you know some shit you're not telling me that will shake this up."

"What if it's a frameup? How convenient is it for everything to be dumped on Loitzel? The goods were scattered around him like a movie set."

"Just tell me what you know, Thorpe."

"I don't know anything, Greenberg. Loitzel wouldn't cop to anything with me. Other than the fact that he and Hoff were lovebirds. I'm just saying I think it's all too convenient."

"I can't give a fuck about that. And sometimes convenience is a good thing. Maybe you should go home and read another *True Detective*," he said, standing and scooping the evidence bag up in his hand. "Let me get your cap gun and you can get out of here." After a minute he came back into the room and held out my .45, tagged with an evidence card that had my name along with his on it. "Sorry, we're keeping the bullets."

"As evidence?" I said, looking into the empty butt before slipping it into my shoulder holster.

"No. But I can't let you out into the squadroom with a loaded gun. Not today, anyway. What if *you're* Loitzel's accomplice? You'd put holes in us all."

He held the door for me.

"Yeah, that's exactly what I'd do," I said.

Down on the first floor I found a phone booth and banged the door shut. When the operator came on I asked her to connect me to Dr. William Loftesness in Aurora. I let it ring until she came back on the line to see if I'd like to try again later. I told her that was fine and asked for the address.

It took about half an hour to get out to Loftesness' place. I drove up and down a couple times before parking a block away and walking back up the street with the brim of my hat turned up as if I were a salesman. Most of the houses in the area were pre-fab, post-war models with driveways and attached garages and trees not much taller than me. Loftesness' was a two-story brick on a double lot with a massive oak. No one answered the bell so I went around back and banged several times on the door. After a minute or two I went ahead and let myself in, jimmying the door with the stiff plastic card from my wallet.

A narrow back porch opened onto a large square kitchen where bacon grease hung so thick in the air the walls seemed fuzzy with it. A single chair and table were pushed against one wall, on it was a large stack of newspapers and a percolator pot and coffee cup, both cold to the touch. The next room was a formal dining room bathed in chintz. After that was a small foyer with stairs going up and French doors open to a long room that was probably used as a visiting parlor in the past. Loftesness had it set up as a study, one wall lined with bookcases while the other was splattered with photographs, awards and diplomas. At the far end, a massive desk sat like a sleeping beast curled up before a green brick fireplace. The desk was loaded down with articles pertaining to everything from bird-watching to optometry to local politics. One of the stacks was solely devoted to the Marquand kidnapping. Next to it was a thick leather-bound album containing stories Loftesness had cut from various newspapers and glued in related groupings. One of the sections was devoted to news stories covering the Nuremberg trials. There were at least a dozen clippings on the Doctor's trial alone. I went through them, turning crinkly page after crinkly page while scanning headlines until I came across a story that mentioned Kesseling. Accompanying it was a photograph. He looked frail with sunken eyes and an ill-fitting suit, wearing an interpreter's headset. If I had to guess I would say he was in his early fifties. On the very next page was a large glossy photograph of a handsome young man in an elaborate Nazi uniform. His full hair was swept up and back and his eyes were alive from the camera flash. That was Kesseling too, only it was two years before the Nuremberg photo. The next page had a snapshot of Kesseling amongst a group of people surrounding Hitler. It looked like someone had just told a joke. They were all laughing.

I pulled open drawers looking for anything that may have been used to create the odd shapes that served as the signature on the kidnapper's notes. There was nothing. Even a tin box I found in a bottom drawer was nothing more than loose buttons, paperclips and an old watch. I closed all the drawers and made sure the piles on top were just as I had found them.

Mixed in with the framed diplomas and typical egocentric trash on the wall were pictures of Loftesness at various ceremonies or posing with people. I glanced at each, looking for faces I might recognize. One had Loftesness with former Denver mayor, Ben Stapleton. Another showed Governor Carr with his arm draped over Loftesness' shoulder. Next to them stood Marquand.

I took a final couple minutes to look over his book collection. There was a copy of Popenoe's book about the California sterilizations and another called *Heredity in Relation to Eugenics* by Charles Davenport. The name and title was familiar from the library visit. Davenport was a bigwig with the American Eugenics Society. There was another of his books titled *Race Crossing in Jamaica*. I pulled it from the shelf and scanned the premise on the dust jacket. It was all about interbreeding between whites and coloreds in Jamaica and how that had resulted in genetic degradations. I flipped it over to the back cover. There was a photograph of Davenport, a thin man with a mustache and goatee topped by heavy eyebrows, all of which seemed suddenly familiar. I went back to the Nuremberg album and turned to the photograph of Kesseling and the group with Hitler. There, standing two people away from Hitler was Davenport. Still holding the open album, I moved along the wall of photographs again. There I found Davenport with Loftesness and several others. Standing at the back of that group was Marquand.

I put the album in its place on the desk and went back through the house. I made sure the lock on the back door would engage before pulling it closed. At the garage in the rear of the yard I tried peeking in a window but it was too dark inside to make anything out. I tried the door. It was locked, and thinking I'd already been there too long, I left through a gate on the alley and walked to the Dodge.

I flipped a u-turn so I wouldn't have to go by the house again and drove straight to the office. The first thing I did was ring up Marquand.

He came on the line just seconds after Victor asked me to wait. "Well, Thorpe," he said, with almost cheer in his voice, "it looks like things are coming together. This Loitzel character is taken care of. Now we just need to find Sonja."

I wasn't sure I liked how he phrased that about Loitzel. "I have to tell you," I said, "I'm not so sure about the Loitzel-Hoff connection with this, Colonel."

"What do you mean? Loitzel had the money. He had Christian's socks!"

"Yeah, but it all seems so staged."

"You got the tip from Capra's men, right?" he said, the cheery tone in his voice all but gone.

"Yeah, but I think I've come on to something else. You never told me you knew Loftesness from before. How well do you really know him?"

I thought the line had gone dead.

"Colonel? Are you there?"

"What do you mean?"

"I came across a couple photos of you together."

"I've never met the man before in my life."

"One was with you and Governor Carr with Loftesness."

"That doesn't mean anything. Do you know how many people have their pictures taken with me? I don't know ninety percent of them."

"Do you know a man named Charles Davenport?"

"No. Who is he?"

"Well, it might be a coincidence. Or it could be that Loftesness has been shadowing you. I'm not sure we can trust him. He's got some questionable connections."

"What sort of connections?"

"You know those people who believe in all that racial purity stuff? Those eugenicists? He's involved with them. It's a long shot, maybe, but it raises a lot of questions. And you know I've always been suspicious how he showed up in the first place."

"And that has something to do with Loitzel?"

"No. I think Loitzel might be a patsy. And Hoff too."

"Really, Thorpe. What the hell are you talking about?" Marquand said, his voice now filled with the usual annoyance.

I was about to explain my thoughts on Loftesness when it occurred to me that I might sound completely irrational. How could I possibly tell this man that I thought Loftesness had murdered his child because he had been trying to clean up Marquand's genetic mistake? When you stacked it like that, it not only seemed offensive, it also sounded like a preposterous motive for a preposterous crime.

"Thorpe?"

"I'm here."

"Well?"

I looked at my fingers on the desk blotter and said, "I'm not sure, Colonel."

"You're not making sense, son," he said, his tone softening. "How could Loftesness frame Loitzel? And how in hell would he

209

be able to take Christian, by himself, when there are so many clues pointing to an insider with an accomplice?"

"What if Loftesness *is* the accomplice?" I said, knowing there wasn't any conviction left in my voice.

"Are you listening to yourself? Loftesness?" After a long pause Marquand continued, "I talked to Dmytryk this morning. They're positive the insider was a woman. And who would that be except for Sonja? Hold on," he said, his voice changing to a soft conspiratorial tone. I could hear a door closing and a second later he came back on the line. "I have a theory too. Think about this. We know it had to be someone who knew the intimate details of the family, and the house, but who was not present that night. Right? So it's either Sonja. Or Loren. Those are the only two that fit. Capra's men told you it was Loitzel trying to exchange the money. Did they mention a woman with him?"

"They did," I said.

"And? Did they give any clues it was either one of them?"

"No," I said, even though I could hear Johnny's voice in my head saying all that shit about the skinny junky whore.

"Are you sure, son? Think!"

"No. There wasn't anything, Colonel."

"Don't you think it would be important for us to know for sure," Marquand said.

"Would it really make a difference?"

"Of course! We nearly have these bastards, Thorpe. We're so close now. There's no doubt it was Loitzel. We just need to get the goddamned accomplice to set this right. For little Christian. Okay? Are you wavering on this all of a sudden?"

"No...I just..."

"C'mon, man. Keep your head about you. It's just like flying. Right? Don't let the flak get to you. Straight and narrow. Steady as you go, right over the target. Do you remember that?"

"Yes, sir."

"Good. Don't forget. We're doing this for little Christian."

Before I could say anything else the line went dead.   I sat on the couch for a long time with my head in my hands. An hour or so later I put on my coat and locked up.

CHAPTER 40

The house was lit up like I'd invited the whole neighborhood to cocktails with yellow light streaming out across the darkened lawn. I coasted past looking for movement inside but I didn't see anyone. Around the corner I jammed the wheels into the curb and killed the engine. Before jumping out I pulled the slide back on the .45 to make sure a round was in the chamber. Nothing! I flipped it over and saw the empty butt. I'd completely forgot Greenberg kept my clip. I rummaged around for a spare clip in the glove box, but found none so I grabbed the sap instead.

I made my way down the block, tree by tree, then dashing across open spaces just as they'd taught us in OCS. Suddenly the lights went off. I bolted through the neighbor's yard, hopped the porch rail and flattened myself against the bricks. It was quiet inside so I crawled practically on my belly under the wide front window and positioned myself next to the front door. Something made a rustling sound in the flowerbed and I nearly jumped out of my skin before remembering the little brown mouse I'd seen a hundred times before. Just then a car roared to life in the alley. The engine raced as the driver excitedly stomped the pedal to the floor, tires squealing when he shifted into gear. I used that as an opportunity to pull the screen open and kick at the front door, making it swing wide. The streetlamp rained a sliver of light into the dark interior. I couldn't make out much but I was able to see the end of the couch and one leg of the coffee table. Charging the door I dove in low next to the couch. The only sound I could hear was my own breath and the thudding of my heart in my ears. After a second I reached up and flicked the switch for the overhead light. On and off. Like a strobe. I could tell, even in that split second, the place had been ransacked. But I didn't see anyone and nothing happened. I flicked the light again, then switched it on and left it on. Everything was tossed. Books littered the floor, ripped and shredded. The dining room table lay wounded on its side, its chairs splintered into kindling. Gutted cushions from the couch bled stuffing.

I sprinted across the jumble of books to the kitchen and positioned myself just outside the doorway. The room was dimly lit by the open refrigerator. Everything from it, and my cupboards, was on the floor, smashed and broken. I called out but no one answered so I went on in, closed the back door and bolted it. When I was sure the house was empty I locked the front door, pulled the blinds and dropped the sap on the floor. The bedroom was the same. Mattress and pillows were slashed and my clothes ripped and cut into nearly unidentifiable shreds. Glass crunched underfoot in the kitchen where everything had been smashed, crushed and broken. Oscar wasn't far from his shattered bowl, but he only floated on his side when I filled the sink for him.

After a while I came across the tin flask I used on stakeouts. It was covered in egg yolks, with a new dent, but still had bourbon inside. I rinsed it clean and plopped down on the ruined couch. It was pretty clear that whoever had done this wasn't really looking for anything. I'd obviously crossed an invisible line and someone thought I needed a nice clear message to back off. After a minute I got the sap and switched off the light. Then I settled in with the dented flask. In the morning I stood up and left. There wasn't anything to salvage so I walked back down the street to the Dodge and drove away.

A couple blocks later I noticed a blue Chevy with a driver and passenger hanging back but staying with me in traffic. At first I thought I might just be paranoid, so I sped up and switched lanes to see what would happen. They changed lanes too, keeping the same distance but staying one car back. I moved into the far right lane. So did the Chevy.

At the next intersection I smashed the gas pedal to the floor and used the hand brake to make a squealing left turn across a wall of oncoming cars. Horns blared and drivers slammed on brakes as two of the cars almost skidded into each other. I continued flooring it while checking the rear view mirror and rocketed down a residential street. For a moment it seemed I'd lost the Chevy but then I saw it coming fast. Luckily, I was almost a full block ahead. I made two hard lefts, the second taking me down a narrow dirt alley and heading in the exact opposite direction of them. But my tires were kicking up a huge cloud of dust as I bounced and swerved my way between fences and garages, dodging trash cans and ashpits. Knowing all the dust was a dead giveaway I swerved left at the end of the alley, taking out two trash cans, their contents exploding in the air, then turned hard right. I skidded sideways out onto the street and power-shifted the clutch and column shifter. Two more turns and I was back on the boulevard where I had first noticed the Chevy following me. I zigged and zagged through traffic while checking the rearview mirror but I didn't see them.

Instead of parking in the usual lot I parked two streets over and put a nickel in the meter. When I got to the building I waited across the street to see if the Chevy would come by, but it never did. Upstairs, the outer office was fine. But the inner office had been ransacked just like the house. Everything was scattered about the floor and all my papers had been ripped and torn. The couch was completely ruined, the cushions and back sliced and shredded. The phone cord was yanked from the wall. Desk drawers were emptied and broken. It was as if someone had tossed a grenade in there and pulled the door closed behind them. The only things left in a pristine condition were a bottle of Old Grand-dad and a glass from my shelf above the sink, sitting on a window ledge. A little gift to me I suppose, from whoever had tossed the place.

I hurled the glass from the window ledge against the wall. Then I flipped the desk onto its side and threw the chairs into the outer office. When I'd had my fill of that, I flopped panting onto what was left of the couch. After a while I went down to the pay phone in the lobby and asked the operator to ring a locksmith. An answering service picked up. I told the girl I needed someone fast and I was willing to pay double. She took the address and said she would pass the information on. Once I had the operator back on the line I asked her to connect me to the Howdy Partner Mo-tel in Golden. Two rings and the front desk lady picked up. I told her I wanted number eleven. After a minute the line in the room finally picked up.

"Hello," I said. "Hello? Miss Hoff?"

Still nothing from the other end.

"Miss Hoff, it's Harry Thorpe. Please! We need to talk. Right away. Things are getting dangerous for me...and you."

"I can not, Mr. Thorpe. I can not talk anymore," she said. "I have to go now."

"Wait! I know you and Loitzel didn't do it. Do you hear me? But I need to talk to you. I need to know who you've talked to and what you've told them." I could hear her breath on the other end but she didn't say anything. "Meet me. Tonight. Can you do that? Please."

"You will be there this time?"

"Yes. I promise. There's a bar near your Mo-tel. What's it called? The Roadhouse?"

"Rail House," she said.

"Okay, meet me there. At nine o'clock."

"Can I trust you, Mr. Thorpe?"

"You most definitely can." I told her and hung up.

I dug the last nickel out of my pocket and dialed the Marquand house. Victor answered after a couple rings. I put a snobby air in my voice, made up a nonsense name and asked for Loren.

"This is Loren Chambers," she said when she came on the line.

"Loren, it's Harry."

"Harry?"

"Shhh! Look, I need to speak to you. Right away. Can you come down to my office? I can't tell you why over the phone. But I need to talk to you."

"I can get Richard to drop me at the library and walk over."

"Are you alright?" I asked.

"Yes. Are you alright?"

"No," I said. "But I'll tell you about it when you get here."

After we hung up I went back up to the office. It was a shock all over again. I thought about having a couple swigs from the bourbon bottle but couldn't be sure that it hadn't been spiked with something. Even after sniffing it and swirling the contents in the light I felt I couldn't trust it. I put it back on the window ledge.

I took a little time trying to clean up. Or at least make piles. It really didn't do a whole lot of good. The place still looked ransacked. At a minimum I put the desk upright and brought the chairs back into the office.

The locksmith arrived first. I told him I wanted whatever he could install that could keep an army out. He said he had some new locks that were nearly impossible to pick. They were expensive, but worth it. I told him to do it and as promised, I would pay double. He went back down to his truck to get them after sizing up both doors. He had just returned and started on the outer door when Loren arrived.

"Oh my God! What happened?" she said, putting a gloved hand to her face when she saw the couch.

"Got tossed," I said, pulling her into the inner office and closing the door.

"Your couch is ruined!"

"You should see the house."

"It's like this too?"

"Worse. And they killed Oscar."

"Oh no!" she said, touching my arm. "Poor Oscar! What about your bass?"

"Thankfully, it was in the car."

"Do you know who did this?"

"I have an idea."

I took her coat and draped it over one of the chairs. She looked fantastic in a bright green, long-sleeved sweater and black skirt that hugged her slim figure. My eyes traveled all the way down to the ankle straps on her shoes. "Don't you look fetching," I said.

"Seriously, Harry. What's going on?"

"I don't know. Lots of shit, I guess. Apparently someone kicked a hornet's nest, and I think it was me." I shook two cigarettes out of my pack, lit them both and handed one to Loren. "What's going on at the house? Anything different?"

"No."

"Look, Loren, there's a lot of buzz out there about you. I need to know the deal. No bullshit. I need to know if I can trust you."

"I thought we'd already gone over all this."

"Did you know Andreas Loitzel?"

Without flinching, blinking or breathing she said, "The kidnapper? No!"

"You're sure?"

"I've never heard that name before yesterday."

"From Marquand?"

"Harry! The news. Everyone is talking about him."

"And you weren't seen with him two nights ago trying to buy heroin?"

Her eyes widened and her lips closed together.

"Were you?" I asked.

"No!" she said. Then she looked down at the cigarette and flicked an ash at the squashed trash can I'd set next to the desk. When her eyes came back up to my face she said, "I did get some dope. It was a few pills," she whispered. "But I swear, I've never seen Andreas Loitzel before."

"But you got dope. Two nights ago. Where?"

"Casper's."

"From Seth Crane. Do you pay him?"

"What is that supposed to mean? Or what? Do I sleep with him?" She threw the cigarette at the trash can and turned to pick up her coat, but before she could I grabbed her shoulders in my hands. "Let go of me!" she said.

"Hold on!" I said, forcing her to face me. "Just listen to me. People are saying shit about you."

"So what. Let them talk."

"Stop!" I said, pulling her back again. "Listen a minute. They're saying you're an accomplice. Do you understand what I am saying? They're trying to pin these murders on you." She slowly stopped fighting me as the words sunk in so I let go of her. "They're saying you were with Loitzel the other night. When he was exchanging the ransom for clean money. They described you to a T and said you were looking to score some heroin."

"That's not true. First off, I didn't get any heroin. Secondly, I don't know Andreas Loitzel. I've never heard of him before in my life."

"Okay. I believe you," I said, moving to step on her cigarette that had missed the trash.

"Then why are you telling me this?"

"Because you have to start being really careful. Someone has it in for you, just like they have it in for me now. Look, I need to ask you something and I don't want you to go crazy on me. Okay?"

She said nothing.

"Just tell me the truth," I said going on. "Do you really sleep with Seth Crane? I don't care. I just need to know. Alright? I think you're getting pulled into all this because you're sleeping with a negro."

"I told you all that already. What exactly more do you want me to say?"

"Okay, okay. I'm only asking for the sake of the investigation."

We stood in silence for a minutes, her gaze boring a hole through my soul. I pulled the cigarettes out of my pocket and offered her another but she didn't move.

"How long?" I asked finally.

"Does it matter?"

"No. Not really. Not to me. But it's got someone worked up over you," I said even though I knew I was lying. Right then I was sure that I knew her dreams, her pain, her suffering. I wanted to tell her I cared so much that it was destroying me to know, but I needed to know. Instead I said, "They think Loitzel was murdered by his accomplice. A woman. Some people think that's Sonja Hoff. And other people are saying it's you. Personally, I don't think it's either one of you. I don't even think Loitzel had anything to do with the kidnapping. I think he and Hoff were set up to throw the investigation off the real reason the baby was taken. There's no real evidence that points to them that doesn't look planted. You, on the other hand, I think you're getting pulled into the whole thing because of your relationship with Seth Crane."

The locksmith knocked and said he was ready to work on the inner door. I asked him to give us a minute.

"I need to get something to eat," I said to Loren.

She pulled her coat on by herself. The locksmith gave me the new keys and said he'd leave a bill on the desk when he was finished. I told him I needed the same thing done at the house, new locks, barricades, whatever he thought would be best. He said he could come by the next day so I jotted the address down for him.

Loren and I walked a block to the Ship Tavern in the Brown Palace Hotel, neither saying a word. We slipped into one of the high-backed, red leather booths. A tuxedoed waiter with a penciled mustache took my order. Two double bourbons and a prime rib sandwich. When he was gone I stood up and got in the same side of the booth as her.

"Loitzel took the fall. I don't think he had a single thing to do with it. And I'm beginning to think the money doesn't have anything to do with it either. I think it all has to do with eugenics. You've heard of that, right? The idea that selective breeding in people can lead to a super race where people are genetically superior and all that shit. Did you know that the Nazis sterilized people and performed euthanasia to weed out what they thought were the unfit or undesirables? It was all about killing people they felt were inferior. They shot them. Gassed them. Poisoned them. The whole death camp thing, right? Well, they also did all kinds of horrific medical studies on people, on children, all in the name of eugenics or genetic studies. I bet you didn't know that we've sterilized people in this country. Retards and deformed people. All under the guise that it would be good for society. So they wouldn't affect society with their fucked up genes."

I saw the waiter coming and paused while he set our drinks down.

"Anyway," I said when he'd left, "Marquand has people around him who are involved in all that eugenics shit. And I've been thinking maybe they killed little Christian because he was...well, you know. Not right. These crazy people worship Marquand. He's not just their hero, but like their God or whatever. And I think they might have done it to save him from a legacy of a retarded child because they want him to run for president. It's that Homeland First shit. He's their poster boy for pure perfect Aryan genes and yet he has this deformed and probably retarded kid. Basically, they were doing him a favor. And pinning it on some nobodies like Loitzel and Hoff is just plain easy."

"That's just crazy," she said, her hand came up from below the table and taking her glass. She raised it to her lips and paused. "But, what's all that got to do with me?" she asked, turning to look into my face. Her eyes were beautiful in the light.

"You're a target of opportunity," I said, reaching out to take her left hand in mine. "These eugenicists are nothing but a bunch of racists. I think they're trying to get at you too. Because, you know, the whole..." I let go of her hand, which had not moved or responded to my touch, and took out my cigarettes. I offered her one but she shook her head so slightly than I would have missed it had I been mid-blink. I lit mine and slid the ashtray closer, across the white linen tablecloth.

"It's not that I don't care," I said. "Of course I care. I told you I think I've fallen in love with you. It hurts me to think you're sleeping with another man. But I tell myself it's just the dope. And, if it is, I suppose I can try to understand and hope that maybe you'll want only me at some point."

She said something but the words were too soft for me to hear.

"What?"

"I do care..." she said.

I put the cigarette down and took her hand again. This time her fingers intertwined with mine.

"Okay. Let's not worry about any of that right now. We just need to make sure you're safe. And we need to find out who it is that's trying to drag you into all of this. I've got an idea, but I need to do some checking first. And you need to be really careful right now, Loren. Things could get dangerous. It's not only those goddamned nutjobs, the mob is involved too. So, I don't want you going anywhere alone. Okay? And you need to stay away from Casper's. Shit," I said, looking at my watch. "I need to get back to the office and get a phone repairman. And you should probably get back to the library."

I waved to the waiter and asked him to pack my sandwich to go.

"We can't trust anyone right now," I said to Loren. "Someone's obviously putting the heat on both of us. But to be honest, that's a good thing. It means we're on the right track."

"I'm so...I don't even know what to think," she said. "I mean, it's hard to imagine people like that exist. That they would go to these lengths to..." She paused, looking up at me, her lips parted enough that I could see her wonderful teeth. I leaned in and kissed her, and to my relief she kissed me back.

"We'll get through all this fine. Just stay aware at the house and see if anything is weird. Try to keep an eye on who comes and goes. Especially Loftesness. You know who he is, right?"

"The guy with the big mustache," she said.

"Exactly. I'm meeting with Sonja Hoff tonight. I've got to try and get her to either come in or we need to figure out a way to hide her better. She's in more danger than we are."

"You know where she is?"

"Yeah. I've been talking to her."

CHAPTER 41

The entire lot was full at the Rail House so I put the Dodge on a side street and walked back. Inside it was loud and smoky with workmen standing two deep and yelling over each other. Sonja Hoff couldn't have stood out more at the far end of the bar if they'd lit her with a spotlight. For someone who had their face plastered all over the news I couldn't believe her choice of a bright beige suit and sky blue scarf. If the whole damn place wasn't so busy thinking of ways to hit on her they'd be calling the cops and making arrangements to collect on her $10,000 reward. She gave me a wave as if I wouldn't have noticed her.

I skipped the scolding about the attire and said, "What're you drinking?"

"Just this," she said pointing at a Coca-Cola.

I ordered a double bourbon and made sure the bartender knew we were moving to a booth. He nodded without really looking at me, his eyes moving up and down her. I took the Coke and had her sit with her back to the room. I wanted to keep an eye on the door even though I was sure I hadn't been tailed.

"You don't have a hat?" I said.

"Not with me."

"Can you maybe put that scarf over your hair," I said. "Someone's going to recognize you." She did as I asked but it was no better so I had her take it off.

"Look, I'm really sorry about Loitzel," I said. "I know now that he was totally set up. And I'm going to do everything I can to find out who killed him. But right now we've got to think about you. It's not safe for you out here anymore. First thing's first though– you've got to stop lying to me. I can't help you if you aren't telling me everything."

"I have not lied to you," she said, rolling the scarf and putting it into her purse.

"Come on!"

"I do not tell lies."

The bartender came up and banged my glass down, sloshing bourbon onto the table. Without raising his eyes from Sonja Hoff's cleavage he asked if we wanted to run a tab.

"I'm over here, chum" I said.

His head came around. "And do you want to run a tab?"

"What do I owe you?"

"Forty five cents, *chum.*"

I took a dollar out of my pocket and tossed it onto the table. "Got fifty cents?" I said.

He dug into his pocket, held up two quarters for me to see, and dropped them on the table. Then he scooped up the dollar and went away. I tasted my drink, it was watered down shit.

"You're going to sit there and tell me you haven't been lying?"

She pulled off her gloves and put them with the scarf. "What?" she said, picking up her Coke. "What would I be lying about?"

"They hung Kesseling for war crimes. Did that just slip your mind?"

Eventually she took a little drink from her bottle.

"Okay," I said. "Obviously you knew that. So, what's the connection to Marquand? And why did you run off on the very night the baby went missing?"

"I tell you already all of this."

"Tell it again."

She let out a sigh and said, "I worked for *Herr* Kesseling. He was an associate of Colonel Marquand. That is how we met."

"Worked for him as what?"

"A nanny."

"Try again." I leaned back and stared at her.

"I was an assistant," she mumbled.

"Why didn't you just tell me that in the first place?"

"I was afraid."

I pushed the cigarettes towards her but she shook her head.

"Are you running from an indictment?"

"I do not know," she said, her fingers tracing the raised edges of the Coca-Cola bottle.

"You were involved in the medical experiments?"

"No, no, no. I was in Berlin. I keep records and make information, um, compile. And when *Herr* Kesseling was in Berlin, I entertain important people with him. I help him build influence. In the party."

"And you were his lover," I said.

The thought of her stripping naked and letting that monster make love to her made me want to slap that sad little look off her face.

"Kesseling liked to show you off, didn't he? Is that how you met Marquand?"

"You do not know what you are speaking. *Herr* Kesseling was an important man. He had meetings with many important people. Not just Christian. He was a very respected man and he, um," she thought for a second and finally said, "he relied on me."

"How did it work? Did you parade around nude for them? Is that it? The perfect German specimen they could all fuck."

"Why do you say such things?"

"Do I have that wrong? You told me yourself you were fucking Marquand even though you wanted to run away with Loitzel." I said blowing smoke over her head and stamping the butt out in the ashtray.

"Stop saying that!"

"What? That you fucked them all? You're going to tell me it wasn't like that? Isn't that what you do?"

"It *was not* like that."

"What was it like then?"

She put the Coke bottle on the table, leaned forward and spoke in a level voice, "I will tell you how it is…Christian looked for *me*. He was not looking for anyone else. He wanted me. And he offer to pay me $5,000 to come to America and have his baby. Yes, that is right. And so I come. Sure, I do it to get away from Germany and I do it also for the money. So Andreas and me could start over. You want to make me into a whore. Well, I guess I am just that. I *fuck* your Colonel Marquand, as you say. But it was the only choice we have. I am sure you can never understand something like that."

When she finished she settled back against the booth and pulled her eyes off me as if she would never look at me again.

"And then what? You saw the opportunity to get some more money out of him so you kidnapped his kid? Then you let Loitzel do all the dirty work so you could knock him off in the end and take it all."

"I did not kill anyone!"

"No? Good for you then. Tell that to God. If there is one." I finished my drink and slammed the glass on the table.

"You said you wanted to help. You do not want to help me," she said, gathering her things as if she were going to leave. "You really think I killed Andreas for that money? I would never have done anything like that. There is no amount of money in the world that would have made me kill Andreas. He was the only man in this whole world who I truly loved. Andreas was my husband, Mr. Thorpe. Yes. So now you know. We came together and were supposed to get away from all this and finally have a life…" She began to cry and struggled to get out of the booth.

I took her arm. "Wait, wait, wait!" I said, scanning the room to see who might be watching. The bartender was looking our direction. So were some of the others. I got her to settle back down and gave her my handkerchief.

"Please," I said, "Let's not make a scene."

She dabbed at her eyes. "You ask me here to…to…to do this to me. Why? Why don't you just call police? Go now. Get them. I have nothing to fear. I did not kill anyone."

I let her cry for a minute while all of that rolled around in my head. Once she'd regained her composure she took a compact from her purse and began to fix herself.

"So you accepted Marquand's offer so you and Andreas could get to America," I said. "Did Marquand even know about Andreas?"

"No. Of course not."

"But why did you run off the night the baby disappeared?"

"It was stupid mistake," she said raising her eyes to mine. "We didn't realize we would be blamed for everything. We just thought it was a perfect chance to get away. We had been planning for months to leave, and with all the distraction, Andreas said it was our chance to be gone without being noticed." She put the compact away and snapped her purse shut. "We didn't know the baby had been taken by someone. Everyone was saying he wandered off in the night. We thought he would be found in a couple days and by then we would be far away."

"Yeah, that wasn't the best timing."

"But we couldn't wait much longer. I am pregnant now. We had to go soon anyway."

"And Marquand knows?"

"It does not matter. This is not his baby."

"You know that for sure?"

"You are going to ask such a thing?"

"I'm sorry. Did Andreas know?"

"Yes, of course. That is why we had to leave. Christian would take my baby. He would say it was his," she said. "There. Now you know everything. Now, are you going to help me or not, Mr. Thorpe?"

I thought about Greenberg's remarks about blaming all the Germans for what happened. I got it. There was a lot of blame to go around for some really horrific shit. And it wasn't like Sonja was an angel. But I found it hard to believe she was keeping any of Kesseling's records or even knew what he was actually doing at the camps. She probably started out as a nanny and ended up being a whore for that sick fuck. It made sense, considering the whole Loitzel thing, that she would rather be labelled a Nazi co-conspirator than be thought of as a whore. Either way, it's what I wanted to believe, so I said, "Yes. I'll help you. But first we need to get you moved somewhere safer. There's a hotel downtown that will be much better. I know the desk man and there's only one way in and one way out. Let me see if I can get you a room there and we can move you tomorrow. We just need to keep you under wraps until this all blows over and the real murderers are caught. Okay?"

She nodded, a look of relief smoothing out her face.

"Do you know a guy named Loftesness? Dr. William Loftesness."

"No. Should I?"

"You're sure? He's an older guy with a huge mustache. He's probably been in to see Marquand over the last year or so."

"No. I do not recall anyone like that."

"Okay. Well, don't talk to anyone. Don't answer the door or the phone or anything. I'll come for you tomorrow at two o'clock sharp, so be waiting for me. And if anything happens between now and then, call me. But if the cops get you, which I don't think they will, don't say anything. Definitely do not say anything about Kesseling. Especially to the cops. Do you understand? Ask for a lawyer. Those should be the only words out of your mouth."

"Of course," she said, handing me back my handkerchief.

The bartender came over then. "There a problem here?" he asked.

"We're on our way out," I said.

"Why's she crying like that?"

I got up out of the booth and told him again that we were leaving. I put a hand out for Sonja Hoff, she took it and scooted out.

"Are you okay, lady?" the bartender asked her.

"Yeah, she's fine," I said.

"I was talking to her."

I took her arm and guided her past. Then I squared off with him. He was my size and it would have been a good match but he didn't want to dance after all. I followed behind Sonja and we went across the bar and outside.

"I'm out on the street," I said, pointing to where I'd left the Dodge.

"No, no. It is okay. I have walked."

I gave her arm a little squeeze. "You can't be walking."

She nodded.

I was about to say something else when a big truck went by on Colfax. I turned to look and saw a car parked on the other side of the boulevard. It was the Chevy that had tailed me. A streetlight lit just enough for me to see someone behind the wheel.

"Shit! Wait right here," I said, pushing her back into a shadow. I slipped the .45 out and held it tight against my leg.

"What is going on?" she said when she saw the gun.

I trotted across the parking lot staying low behind the cars. When a break came in the westbound traffic I started out into the roadway. Whoever it was must have seen me at that point. The headlights came on and the engine roared to life. I made it to the middle of the four lanes but there wasn't a big enough break in eastbound traffic for me to get all the way across. A driver laid on a horn, nearly clipping me as he went by. The Chevy was lunging forward, trying to pull out into the flow. Then its wheels began churning the dirt on the shoulder and it fishtailed out in front of another car whose tires screeched as it skidded and slid sideways into the next lane. I had to jump to keep from getting clipped and when I swung around the Chevy was passing. In a single second I was able to see it was Ugo at the wheel.

When I got back to Sonja she was breathing harder than I was.

"No worries," I said, taking her by the arm. "He's a friend of a friend."

"But your gun…"

"With some friends you need a gun."

I drove around for a long time, making sure the Chevy was nowhere to be seen before dropping her at the mo-tel. As she moved to get out of the car she leaned over and kissed me. Her lips were warm against my cheek and I could smell her perfume and a hint of powder.

"Thank you, Mr. Thorpe."

"You're welcome."

"Maybe…maybe you want to come in with me?" she said.

"No, I better not."

"We could just talk," she said.

"You'll be okay."

When she moved away I looked into her blue eyes and I did feel sorry for her. She looked like she might cry again.

"I am sorry," she said. "I am just afraid. And alone now."

"You're not alone. And everything will be fine," I said. "No one knows you're staying here. Tomorrow we'll get you moved to that other place."

She swallowed and nodded and pulled the door lever with a gloved hand.

I drove on over to Billy's Inn and ordered two shots, a beer and a cheeseburger. When I'd finished the shots I ordered two more. It wasn't long before the pain in my shoulder seem to slip away and that pleasant wooziness came on like a warm blanket. My mind kept filling with images and ideas that bounced off each other like rubber arcade balls. There was Ugo's profile, lit by headlights as he surged past me. There was Loftesness and his giant mustache, standing next to Marquand in those photos. And Marquand with Sonja. And with Loren. Then there was Loitzel with his brains all over the wall. And the dead baby looking more and more like the boy in the box.

I waved Billy over.

"You're going at this with a vengeance tonight, Harry," he said, putting two more shots and another beer in front of me. "You should eat some of that burger or you're not going to be able to drive home."

"It's all good, Billy," I said, waving him away.

I was deep in my thoughts, following every lead to get at the Loftesness connection. After all, he was the guy with the notes. He arranged the money drop. He was the one that recorded the serial numbers. He delivered the money to the kidnappers. He was an outspoken eugenicist and *adored* Marquand. It *had* to be Loftesness. Hell, he was the one that said we should contact the mob for help. It only made sense that Loftesness was behind the whole thing. Who else had that much control or that much influence on Marquand? It had been Loftesness and the Homeland First fanatics that pushed him to run for president.

I ordered two more shots, drank one quick and took the other with me into the phone booth by the restrooms. It took about a hundred rings before Victor came on the line. I told him it was me and that I needed to speak to the Colonel right away. After what seemed like twenty minutes and two mauled hangnails Marquand came on the line.

"Thorpe! What's going on?"

"Sir, I really think I might be onto something…"

"It's almost one o'clock in the morning…"

"I know, I'm sorry, Colonel. But I wanted to let you know that I think I might be onto something that could close this thing. Wrap it up, like a neat little Christmas package. Bow and all, sir."

"You're drunk."

"I only had a couple, sir. But wait, you've got to hear me out. This time I've solved the whole thing. I know who took Christian."

"Go on."

"Whose idea was it to contact the mob?" I asked.

"What?"

"No, go on, Colonel. Whose idea? Think. It's an easy one," I said before slamming back the other shot and quietly putting the glass down on the little shelf. "Was it your idea? Or was it Loftesnessesses' idea to involve the mob?" I said, butchering the name.

"Really, Thorpe. You're not making any sense."

"Did you know Loftesnessness–Lofty–I'm gonna call him

Lofty, okay? Did you know Lofty has a scrapbook with clippings? It's filled with stuff about that Nazi Kesseling. You knew him, right? Well, I think he's the one that did all this. Lofty, I mean. Not Kesseling. Think about it. I'll tell you why. Okay? It was Lofty that suggested we go to Tony Capra. It was Lofty that had the ransom note and made the deal for the money drop. It was Lofty that delivered the money. Lofty, Lofty, Lofty. It comes back to him every time. Every single time. No matter how you shake it up or order the pieces. Lofty! Do you see what I'm saying, Colonel? Colonel? Are you there?"

"I'm here, Thorpe."

"It's all Lofty, Colonel. He's a eugenicist. Do you see what I mean? Remember when he said he idolized you? Like god-like worship kind of shit, right? Five thousand dollars! Who is going to put up their own five thousand dollars like that? I think he wanted you to be rid of little Christian because of the whole retarded thing. He was protecting you, or your legacy, or whatever from that. Are you following all this, Colonel? It's because those Homeland First assholes want you to run for president. That's what I think. I was in Lofty's house and I saw his books and pictures and coffee cup and all of it. He lives like some nutjob out there in Aurora." Peering suspiciously out the phone booth window I whispered, "We need to be watching him, Colonel. And see what he's up to, who he meets with, who he talks to. I'm serious. I just got done meeting with Sonja and there's no goddamned way she's involved. Pardon my French. She's just scared of you because of the whole baby thing. That's why she took off like she did."

"You talked to Sonja?"

"Oh yeah. She told me about Kesseling and how you met. She told me…did you know she and Loitzel were married? Yep! Married and everything. I know! I was surprised too. So there's no way she'd shoot Lofty—I mean Loitzel. She's going to have his baby. They were just trying to get away from you so you wouldn't take it. She told me all about all of that. But, there's no way, Colonel. There's no way she's involved with the kidnapping. I'm getting her tomorrow. Gotta get her out of that mo-tel and somewhere safe, especially since I've seen them following me. That fucking Ugo was right there tonight. I saw him. I would have shot the…"

"Where is she?"

I had been rocking back and forth in the tiny space and completely lost my balance almost falling. I lowered myself to the little triangular seat. The shot glass fell to the floor. When I reached for it I nearly fell off the seat.

"She don't have the money," I said carefully, trying not to stumble on my words. "I bet Johnny got it all. I'm sure of it. Most definitely."

"Well, it certainly sounds like you've stumbled onto something, son. Where is Sonja staying now?"

"She's in some shithole on Colfax. Should I start tailing Lofty? That's probably the next thing. Follow him around. See who he meets?"

"Why don't you get some sleep. I'll make some calls in the morning."

"I could catch him meeting with that dirtbag Johnny!"

"Not just yet. Let me make a few calls and I'll let you know. Okay? Go get some sleep."

He clicked off and I put the receiver back in the cradle. I fumbled with a cigarette for a while before finally getting it lit. Then when I got up I knocked the tip off on the door and had to spend another minute or two getting it lit again. I went back to the bar and pulled myself onto my stool. The conversation with Marquand was like a blur in my head but I felt like we'd really connected and he understood what I was thinking. I was feeling pretty damn good about things. *I've busted it wide open this time,* I thought, waving Billy over.

CHAPTER 42

Knock, knock, knock...like the kick of a Corsair engine turning over. I peeled my eyes a fraction and a firebomb ignited causing me to slam them shut again. When I went to move I nearly feel off a cliff and had to scramble for a handhold. Someone with a sick sense of humor had drilled a hole in the top of my head and filled it with cement and the weight of this massive new head made it impossible to keep any balance.

Knock, knock, knock!

Straining I forced one eye open to a slit. I was spread out on the front seat of the Dodge. It took a minute but my hand found my face. I covered my eyes and tried with little success to move something else, a leg maybe. My spine felt folded in two. I must have laid all night on my bad shoulder as red hot pain was radiating down my neck, side and lower back. I pulled my hips up. Tried to straighten my body. Then I gave up.

Knock, knock, knock!

"What the fuck!" I sat upright, my cement head throwing me off balance. Someone was at the passenger side window. I shielded my eyes and blinked hard. He looked familiar. It took me forever to get the window rolled down an inch.

"Mr. Thorpe. It's me. George Alvarado. The locksmith. You told me to come this morning and change the locks at your home."

I blinked at him. And when all of that news had been processed I opened the door and did my best at getting out.

The locksmith was saying something but I was too busy

concentrating on the porch steps and then the front door, all with him trailing, almost helping. Inside he let out a whistle when he saw what had been done to the place. And to be honest I was surprised at how bad it was too. I left him to do whatever he was doing and stumbled to the bathroom. I tortured myself with a cold shower then dug around in the shredded clothes, which was a challenge considering the new cement head seemed to want to topple me over at every turn. I ended up putting on the clothes I'd been wearing. In the kitchen I made a pot of coffee and drank down three cups while the locksmith worked on the back door.

"I think your fish is dead," he said, motioning toward the sink.

"Yeah. He is," I said.

I left him to close up, another shiny new key on my chain, and drove down to the office. I figured I should keep an eye out for Ugo and the blue Chevy, but the cement head didn't care. At the office I was just working the new lock when I heard the phone start to ring in the inner office.

"Do you ever answer that phone?" It was Greenberg, and he sounded chipper compared to his usual self. "Sonja Hoff killed herself last night."

"What?"

"Yep, shot herself in the head at the Howdy Partner mo-tel on West Colfax, almost to Golden. I'm heading out there now. Looks like case closed. Come and join the party."

Before I could even respond Greenberg had already clicked off.

CHAPTER 43

She was wearing the dress I'd seen her in the night before, the sky blue scarf discarded on the bed near her feet, which seemed so exposed in worn and tattered stockings. It was easier to look at her neglected toenails than the offensive splatter of blood and brains on the wall, but I couldn't keep my eyes from drifting back to her face. The way her mouth hung open it was as if she were trying to say something, if only Greenberg would shut up and let her into the conversation. He was almost giddy in the stench of the moment. Thankfully, once I confirmed it was Sonja Hoff, he practically sprinted from the room to make a call and my gaze settled on the smudged lipstick on her lower lip. I put a hand to my cheek, remembering her kiss, in the car when I dropped her off. And her eyes, rimmed with tears, which were now dry in the photographer's flash. Everything else seemed bathed in a thick haze. As if it happened to someone else and I was only conjuring visions from a story relayed to me. The photographer snapped another picture and the bulb popped out onto the floor. I moved to stay out of his way, to stay out of his shots and the fingerprint man's black dust. I almost reached out to touch her foot. I had an urge to fix her stocking. Then I saw the Rail Yard matchbook with the splayed contents of her purse. I snapped it up as I made my way out, not wanting anything from the previous evening to come to light. I needed to pursue this turn of events for myself.

I drove directly from the Howdy Partner to the Cavalcade Club. The bartender returned with Friar Tuck, who gave me a quick pat down and told me to wait. No one offered a beverage and I wasn't about to beg. About an hour later Johnny showed up with Ugo in tow. Johnny settled in to a booth while Ugo stood me up and fondled me thoroughly.

"What do you want, Thorpe? Haven't you heard? Case closed on the kidnapping. It's in the afternoon *Post.*"

"I want to know who paid you to feed me all the horseshit."

"Who paid me? You paid me."

"Don't fuck with me, Johnny. I know you guys have been tailing me. I saw Ugo last night. Outside the Rail House. And for that matter, it's all but completely obvious that you killed Loitzel and Hoff."

"Hey! Keep your voice down," Johnny said, sitting forward. "Do we have to go back to our discussion about manners?"

The bartended sidled up with two scotch and rocks while Johnny and I stared at each other. Finally Johnny sat back and said, "It's over, Thorpe. Just be done with it. Let it go now."

"What's over?"

"Don't be stupid. The Germans did it. Everything stacked up just right, and you made some money along the way." He picked up the glass and held it for a toast.

"Three innocent people are dead," I said. "And one of them is a baby. I'm not walking away from that."

Johnny put his glass back on the table and sat forward. "Don't be so dense. This isn't a goddamned game. Look—it's all finished now. Just let it go and everyone will be good. Even us."

"What's that supposed to mean?"

"Let's just say I been told to leave you alone. So long as you play nice. Go home and stay out of everyone's business," he said.

"You've been told to leave me alone? By whom?"

"If you're a good boy, everything will be–as your Jew cop friend would say–*kosher*. So don't be *deficiente*. Do you know what that means, Mick? Don't be a goddamned moron. People don't want you to get hurt. And that could easily change if you don't let it all go. Everybody's real happy. The Jew is happy. Marquand's happy. Tony Capra's happy. Even I'm happy. Join the party. Get happy. And forget about being a hero and all that shit. The war is long over. No one is going to give you a medal for anything these days. Be smart. Take care of yourself. You got some money in your bank account…buy a couple new couches. Get those fancy leather ones.

Get some new suits. Hell, Thorpe, get a real fucking pet. Get a poodle. Just *walk away*."

"Nothing's over for me."

"You're making a big mistake," Johnny said.

"Like I fucking care," I said, standing. "See you in hell, Johnny."

"That's not smart, Thorpe," he said, calling after me. "You're gonna get yourself hurt."

"Fuck you," I said, walking out.

There weren't a whole lot of reasons for going home so I went by a liquor store and then to the office. I lay on the shredded couch and drank from the bottle. I didn't really want to think about it, but I knew at that point I had truly been played. And then I knew for certain Marquand was somehow involved. Otherwise Johnny wouldn't have said that stuff about not touching me. Loftesness didn't give a shit about me. If it were up to him, I'm sure I would be dead like the others. Marquand had to figure into it some way, but it was hard for me to imagine him being involved from the very beginning. Sure, he was ruthless. He'd sent a whole lot of men plunging to their deaths and was one of the coldest human beings I had ever met. But could he really murder his own kid? I didn't want to think about that. Not even for a minute. I took a long drink from the bottle. No, I thought, if that was the case then I was complicit from the very start. I definitely played a part in getting both Sonja and Loitzel killed. And I was as responsible for that baby's death as anyone.

The next morning I got up and drove home. It was dark and cool inside, just as I'd left it, with the drapes pulled tight. I took the bourbon bottle I'd brought from work and climbed into the shredded bed. It was actually nice that Johnny or Ugo or whoever had done me a big favor by ripping the phone off the wall. I was able to sit and drink all day without a single interruption. The following day I buried Oscar in the flowerbed before going out to buy bread, bologna, cigarettes and a bag of liquor. I also stopped off at a little shop a couple doors down from Dina's Diner to buy a drinking glass. I knew from experience, the more drunk you get, the harder it is to drink straight from the bottle without wearing most of it. I needed to shut off every thought, every feeling. I couldn't allow myself to think about that baby or Sonja and Loitzel or the boy in the box or all those dead Japs. I had to keep all that away. Far away, if I was going to find a way to live with myself. A couple days later someone rang the bell. I heard them open the screen and knock on the door but after a while they went away. Over the next week or so I left the house only to restock. Mostly I went out for booze and cigarettes. Occasionally I bought a couple dozen cans of food. I began to lose track of time and days. One hour slipped into the another, days bled into more days. Most times it was difficult to know if it were morning or night unless I pulled the drapes. And when I did, and it was daylight, I would yank them shut. If it was night I sometimes left them open so the streetlight could throw gloomy shadows on the wall. Shadows that matched my mood. Dark and lonely and seemingly filled with doom. They were comforting somehow, those shadows. Maybe I thought I deserved the creeping gloom of nothingness that climbed my walls and crawled across my ceiling. Maybe I hoped those shadows would overtake me. Swallow me up.

One night I thought I heard Loren's voice on the porch. At first I lay perfectly still, not sure I could see her in my condition. But then I struggled to my feet and flung the door open. If she had even been there at all she was gone. I thought about Loren a lot after that. I thought about her wonderful teeth and her dark eyes and of her naked in my bed. I thought of the way she wrapped her heels around my ankles and how her skin felt against mine. I wondered about all the things we could be together, if only we weren't who we were. And sometimes I cried. If I wasn't quietly sitting, or crying, I talked to myself. Sometimes for hours on end. Rambling sentences that made no sense. Phrases and words bubbling up in my mind. *Deficiente.* I pissed myself. I woke up soaking in it. I filled the tub with water and climbed in. Had the .45 not been locked in the trunk of the Dodge I might have shot myself. I thought about it. Wrapping it all up with a bow. Neat and pretty. But when I went out to get food or booze or cigarettes I always left it locked in the trunk. One night I stumbled onto some of the broken glass I had pushed aside in the kitchen and cut my foot. I left a trail of blood all through the house. It took a day for it to stop bleeding. Once in a while after that it would open up again. I threw my last good suit away. It didn't fit anymore anyway, so I bundled it up with the shredded shirts and suits and put them out in the alley. I kept my hat and wore it with a khaki shirt and wool trousers I pulled out of my seabag in the basement. I began to wear my flight boots when I went out. One day I drove on down to the office. There was a huge pile of mail on the floor inside the outer door. Most of it was trash, except for one envelope with the Marquand Country Club return address. I let it sit on the desk for a long time before finally opening it. Inside was a check for ten thousand dollars. I put it back in the envelope and went down to the freight dock to pick out some boxes. Everything went into the boxes. Files. Papers. Pencils. A crushed tin of coffee. When I was finished I sat at the desk and smoked, thinking about the day Marquand had first come in. I tapped the envelope on the blotter. I ran an edge under a thumbnail. The bottle of bourbon that Johnny or Ugo or whoever had left unbroken for me was still on the windowsill. It tasted fine. Even if it was poisoned. When it was empty, I added it to one of the boxes. Then I took them one by one down the freight elevator to the trash behind the building. On the last trip I stopped by the office to cancel my lease. I had to pay a penalty for breaking early. I borrowed a pen from the girl to write the check, then I printed *Return To Sender* on Marquand's letter. The girl taped it shut and dropped it in the outgoing mail box.

A few days later I got a job washing dishes at a pizzeria about five blocks from the house. Close enough to walk. The dishwashing station was a little room off a hall that divided the rear of the kitchen. A window, not much larger than a phone book, looked out over the parking lot and alley. The window came in handy for allowing the steam from the dishwasher to dissipate. Sometimes I would lean against the wall and peek out while puffing on a cigarette. Most of my time was spent at a deep sink, scrubbing pizza pans and pots crusted with burned tomato sauce. On especially hot days I used the spray nozzle to douse my head. Carmine, the owner, was a funny man, shaped like a globe, belt as an equator, with a head like a little orbiting moon. He would venture into the tiny room to talk to me for long stretches of time about the Red Sox and the Dimaggio-Williams trade that never happened. I didn't want to spoil his fun by telling him I was actually a Yankees fan. He let me use a cart for the full bus tubs when delivering the stacks of plates back to the kitchen on account of my shoulder. At night, when I had scrubbed all the pots and cleaned all the dishes, Carmine had a pizza or some spaghetti with a fat meatball for me to take home. Sometimes I'd find garlic bread or a piece of cheesecake in the bag. A couple times, it was fried shrimp. Then I came in late one day. Drunk too. Carmine took me out back by the trash cans. I figured he was going to kick my ass but it was worse. If it happened again, he said, he'd let me go. I believed him. And it never did. I got good at scraping plates and loading dishwasher racks. The pots became a personal speed challenge. The pans were easy. I liked how hot the plates and glasses were coming out of the machine, steam billowing when you opened the door. Forks and knives so hot they'd leave welts on your skin. When it was busy I would get lost in the work: scrape, load, start, scrub, rinse, cool, dry, deliver. My days went by cleanly. Over time I drank less. I was occupied enough during the day to be distracted from my thoughts. At night I immersed myself with reading or playing the bass which I'd finally brought in from the car. Playing made me think about Lew Pettigrew and the boys. I missed the camaraderie. But I wasn't ready to go back. Not to them or to anything. One day I came in and Carmine had a transistor radio hanging from a new nail in the wall. He let me listen to ball games and music when no game was scheduled. Pretty soon I had enough of the dishwashing money saved up to have a new mattress delivered. Then a couch. Not leather though. Then one day, on a whim, I stopped off at Dina's Diner. I had just finished ordering from another girl when Dina came out of the kitchen and saw me sitting at the counter.

"Harry Thorpe!" Dina said. "Well, I never in a million years..."

"Hi Dina."

"And look at that beard!"

"Yeah, I know," I said running a hand over my face.

"Wow. What's it been? Three, four months?"

"Something like that," I said softly.

"Not a phone call or even a single visit."

I could feel the man to my right looking at me over his coffee cup.

"Yeah, I know. I'm sorry about that," I said. "It's been...um...you know, sort of crazy."

"Oh, I'm sure it has."

"I never really thanked you for that night. I had a nice time."

The man on my left lowered his paper.

"Good for you," Dina said, grabbing a coffee pot and filling my cup right to the brim.

I ate my eggs and toast while she did everything she could to ignore me. I caught her looking at one point but she quickly averted her eyes. The girl that took my order picked up my plate. The man on my right got up to leave. When I gave him a nod he said, *Good luck, bud.*

After a while, when things were slower and I was one of two people left at the counter, Dina came over. "You've lost weight," she said.

"I've changed jobs."

"You're no longer a detective?"

I shook my head and pushed my cup around just so I wouldn't have to wither under her gaze. She thought I wanted more coffee and grabbed the pot.

"I'm good. Thanks," I said, holding my hand over the cup. "I guess I needed a change."

"I saw your picture in the paper. With Christian Marquand."

"Yeah. I worked on that for a while."

"I'm sorry," she said. "I'm sure that wasn't easy. At least they found out who did it. And they got what was coming to them. You must have helped with that, right?"

"Yeah, I guess I did," I said, seeing Sonja and Loitzel with those holes in their heads.

"I'm sorry I acted like a jerk earlier."

"It's okay. I totally get it. I was an absolute shit for not calling you or coming by. I guess that's why I'm here today. I wanted to tell you I'm sorry."

"Harry," she said, touching my sleeve. "You don't have to apologize for anything. I figured it was the whole Marquand thing." Dina took my hand. "Look," she said, "if you need a friend, I'm here for you. Okay? If you need someone to talk to."

"Thanks, Dina. I really appreciate that. I can't even begin to tell you how touched I am by your offer. Really, I..."

She squeezed my hand. "Hey—don't worry about it. You're a good guy, Harry. I just don't want to see you in a bad place. You can always count on me if you need a friend."

CHAPTER 44

A couple days after I saw Dina I was smoking by the little window in the dishwashing room when I thought I heard Johnny's voice. Standing on tiptoes I peeked out. Sure enough, it was Johnny, with that goddamned ape Ugo by his side. They were having a little chat with Carmine in the parking lot. I couldn't really make out what was being said but it didn't look like Carmine was all that thrilled with the direction of the conversation. I figured it was a shakedown. After all, if they'd been there for me, I would be dead already.

I spent the rest of the afternoon working my way through stacks of dishes and pans while thinking back through the previous months. There was Sonja and Loitzel and the baby and all the useless shit Johnny fed me that I was supposed to be leaking to Greenberg. And Marquand's voice, saying Sonja or Loren's names over and over anytime there was a question of who was involved. It was as if everything that happened served the single purpose of diverting me away from the truth, and in turn, lead Greenberg further and further away from Marquand. But just how involved was Marquand? Was it from the first day he showed up at my office? Was it after Loftesness showed up or when Johnny ended up in the mix? Either way, Marquand was obviously calling enough of the shots that he could spare me in the end. But the thought that tormented me most was how I walked away when it became clear I had been used all along. I'd given up. I'd done exactly what Johnny told me to do. But, it wasn't a new thing. I'd walked away before.

Like the day I wrote down sandwich orders for my law school study group and never returned from picking them up. On the way to the deli I passed a Marine Corps recruiting office. The idea of joining the Marines never entered my mind. Not even after Pearl Harbor. I figured I would ride out some time in law school and eventually end up in my own practice. But a half block later I turned around, went back and joined. The next day I was on the train at Penn Station for Officer Candidate School, the list of names and sandwiches still in my pocket. When I took it out, I realized I'd never really known those people. I'd never actually fit in, not after the countless hours we'd studied together or all the times we'd gone for drinks. Walking away was definitely easier than staying. Once that realization sunk in, I felt like shit. And no matter how many pots or pans I scrubbed I wasn't able to shed the total disgust I had for myself. My hands were red and ragged from the steel wool, burned from the detergent and hot water. I stood staring at them and for a moment and I thought about taking off the apron and going out the back door, more to escape myself than anything else. I might have even took hold of the string tied behind my back. And right about then, Louis, one of the cooks showed up with a large pot crusted with burned sauce. I dropped it into the sink and went to work on it. When that was clean I turned to a stack of pizza pans. Then a load of dishes in the bus tub. Two days later I used the pay phone by the bathrooms to call Greenberg.

"Where the hell have you been?" he asked.

"I needed to get away," I said.

"I guess you heard, huh? Captain Greenberg!"

"Yeah. Captain Greenberg. Good for you."

"Nice little bump in pay with that too." He lowered his voice and said, "And I'm sure you've seen. That fuck Dmytryk is planning a run for governor."

"Yeah," I lied again, "I saw that."

"Jesus. Can you imagine that dipshit as governor? We'd all be fucked. Anyway," he said, returning to a normal tone. "Things turned out really good in the long run. I wasn't sure we were ever going to solve that thing. But everything fell into place."

"Yeah, it sure did," I said. "But you know, I've been thinking. I got some ideas I'd like to run by you."

"You looking for *Captain* Greenberg to pull some strings and get you into the academy?" I could hear his grin over the phone.

"Yeah, that's exactly it. No, I been thinking. About the case."

"The Marquand case? Don't tell me you're going to start again with the Loitzel and Hoff shit again."

"I just don't think they did it," I said.

"Jesus Fucking Christ, Thorpe. Please don't start this."

"I think Marquand was involved."

"Oh God no!" Greenberg moaned. "You have got to be kidding me."

"No, really. I think he arranged the mob hit on Loitzel. And Hoff. And had the mob plant everything. Just hear me out on this. You know he was paying Tony Capra all along. He paid for all that shit I fed to you. And he let them launder ransom money that didn't need laundering."

"What the fuck, Thorpe?"

"The baby was deformed. You know that. The coroner said it was retarded. Marquand was never going to be able to run for president with that around his neck. If it wasn't him directly, then it was those Homeland First assholes who killed the kid to keep Marquand pure. Capra was just a way to make sure everything got cleaned up. And I was the unwitting fool of a middleman."

"Sounds like I should just arrest you…for being fucking crazy."

"Open a new investigation. Look into Marquand and the mob connection," I said.

"Oh Sure. That's a wonderful idea! I'm going to start investigating the greatest American hero we've ever had for killing his kid when we just closed the whole goddamned thing and pinned it all on some fucking Germans. What evidence do you want me to use? Some rummy's ramblings about the mob and Marquand working together? Seriously, Thorpe. You need to get off the bottle."

"You don't care that Marquand is going to walk for this? He either killed his own kid or had someone else do it."

"Hold on," Greenberg said. I heard a door close and he came back on the line. "Think it through, blockhead. Even if this nonsense was true, we'd never get anything to stick on Marquand. Not in court. And never in the eyes of the people. It'll never happen. The fucking guy is untouchable."

"So, what about justice?" I said.

"Fuck justice. There's no such thing anyway. Or, maybe there is, in some twisted way. Did you know that piece of shit Hoff worked for some madman that tortured people in the camps? That's right. She worked for a fucker that did experiments on people, and not just Jews I might add since you're going to throw that on me. All sorts of people. And when they were finished they'd shoot them so they could do an autopsy and see what effects the experiments had on them. I'm not talking about giving them too much aspirin, Thorpe. I'm talking about burning these people, exposing them to mustard gas, freezing them. They performed experiments on twins. They injected shit into their eyes to try and change their fucking eye colors. And your girl Hoff, that piece of shit you think is so innocent, she kept the records on all that. Do you really think I'm going to get weepy-eyed that someone popped a cap in her? Fuck that. Not happening."

"What about little Christian? You're telling me there's no justice for him?"

Greenberg paused a moment. "Here's the way I see it. I like to think there was some kind of accident. Maybe he suffocated in his cot. Maybe someone dropped him. And if I play on this little hunch of yours, I can see that Marquand might have set everything in motion to protect himself and his family. As anyone like him would do, especially if you're scared and you're a maniacal control freak. So he started with the kid just disappearing and then shifted that to a kidnapping once the body was found, which I am sure he never imagined would happen. Then we got too close to the truth and he needed someone to put it off on. So, I'll give you that...Loitzel and Hoff probably were framed. But I truly doubt Marquand shot them. So it was Capra. Not surprising in the least. But to be perfectly honest, whoever shot those two scumbags deserves a medal. They got what they had coming to them. In the long run, nothing is going to be any better than what we have right now. There's no point digging shit up. It's all in the past."

I didn't say anything.

"Did I get through that fog of booze, Thorpe?"

"Marquand said it was a kidnapping on that first night. When the baby first went missing."

"Oh brother."

"And he actually hired me before that..."

"Let it go. Thorpe," Greenberg interrupted. "Okay? Can you do that? Now stay in touch, buddy. Unless of course, you're going to bring this shit up again." The line went dead.

I went back to the dishwashing room and worked on a big pile of pizza pans leftover from the lunch rush. Greenberg had a point. It might have been an accident and Marquand might have been trying to protect himself or someone else in the house. Neither of the examinations on the body were conclusive for the cause of death. So I could see where Greenberg was going with that. But what about the letters? If it was an accident, why was Marquand making a big deal out of threatening letters before the baby went missing? Letters he never actually showed me. Did they even exist? And why would Marquand start accusing Loren at the start and then change that to Sonja? I suddenly felt an impulse to hear Marquand's voice and see what he said about how things wrapped up. So as soon as I finished all the pizza pans I went back to the pay phone. After nine or ten rings Loren answered breathlessly, as if she'd ran the stairs to pick it up.

"Loren. It's Harry."

Cold silence came from the other end. For a second I thought about slipping the receiver back in the cradle.

"Look, I'm sorry," I said. "I should have called. Or sent a note or something. I just needed time to think and sort things out. I bet you're really mad at me."

"What do you think?" she said.

"Please know that it wasn't about you."

"I was actually worried about you."

"I know," I said. "It's hard to explain."

"I went by the house. The office. Cyril's. It's like you disappeared. I didn't know what happened."

"I'm okay. Really, I am. I'm sorry."

There was another long silence and to fill it I said, "I was actually calling to speak to the Colonel."

"Oh!" It was as if she'd been slapped. "He's not here. Call back another time."

"Wait! I didn't mean it like that."

"How did you mean it then?"

"I don't know. Can I see you? I've thought about you a million times."

"Why?"

"I just want to see you is all," I said. "Meet me for a drink."

There wasn't any sound on the other end and I wasn't sure if she hung up or not.

"Loren?"

"What?"

"Will you at least meet me for a drink?"

"I don't see the point," she said.

"Meet me Friday at the Zebra Room. I've got some things I've got to do before then, but I promise I'll be there. Okay? Two o'clock."

"I'll think about it," she said before clicking off.

I found Carmine in the storeroom, a pencil perched over one ear. He was disappointed but said he never expected me to stay forever. I offered to work through the dinner shift but he said he had a nephew who needed a job anyway. We shook hands and he told me to take care of myself. I was going to say something about Johnny, but what could I do about it anyway. So I left him standing at the back door and headed down the alley. Before I could make the turn to the street he called after me. I met him halfway. He held out the transistor radio.

I drove downtown and bought two new suits, four shirts and a handful of ties. Then I picked out a new brown hat and went for a haircut and shave. At the last minute I told the barber to just trim the beard. Loren would get the scruff she wanted after all. That night I listened to Carmine's radio while I buffed my shoes to a high gloss. After I put the brush and polish away I spent an hour cleaning and lubricating the .45. The next day I would call Marquand..

CHAPTER 45

Victor didn't recognize my voice. When he asked who was calling I said I was Dr. Loftesness. We both knew I didn't sound anything like Loftesness so he asked again and I responded the same. I could hear him setting the receiver down and his footsteps receding on tile. After a minute Marquand came on the line. "Who's calling?" he asked.

"Colonel! It's Thorpe. How are you?"

"Thorpe?"

"Yes, sir. Captain Harry Thorpe. We flew together in New Guinea."

"I have it Victor. You can hang up the extension." After the click Marquand said, "What are you doing, Thorpe?"

"Sorry, sir. I thought maybe you didn't remember me."

"Don't be an ass."

"It's been a little while. I thought I should check in and see how you were doing."

"Get to the point. I have a very busy day." Marquand said.

"Okay, no problem. We can skip the chit-chat. I called because I've been thinking a lot about those letters, Colonel. The ones that started back in February with all the threats." I said with a lilt in my voice that I knew would annoy him. "I'm a little was worried they might start up again."

"Case closed, Thorpe. You know that. Have you been drinking again?"

"Oh yeah. Wrapped up. With a big bow, just like a pretty

245

package at Christmas," I said. "But I do think we might have some business to discuss."

"What exactly are you getting at?"

"You hired me to protect you and your family, right?. I just feel an obligation to follow through on that. It's the least I can do, Colonel. Your safety is paramount, especially if you decide to start campaigning. So I've been thinking. We should probably have a plan in case those letters start up again. Wouldn't you agree?"

"I sent you some money," he said, lowering his voice. "But it was returned in the mail. I can make sure that gets to you."

"Do you really think ten thousand is adequate? I was thinking my continued service would warrant a bit more. After all, look at everything I know that would be absolutely crucial to guaranteeing your safety. You always said money was no object when it came to protecting your family. What was it you paid Capra? Fifty thousand? A hundred thousand?"

After a long moment of silence Marquand said, "I think I see what you mean." he said, his words dragging, which I knew was an indication his mind was racing. "Maybe we should meet to discuss this in greater detail. I could bring a much more adequate retainer of sorts."

"That would be great, Colonel. I can meet you somewhere today, if it's convenient."

"Let me see." I heard paper rustling, then he said, "I have appointments all week. Can you meet on Saturday?"

"Absolutely."

"I'll have my secretary call you with a time and place."

"I've changed my number. Have her leave a message for me at the front desk at the Oxford Hotel. I'll pick it up there."

"Fine," he said and clicked off.

I hung up and slid the phone booth door open. The lobby at the Wellborn Hotel was long and narrow, not so much a lobby as it was a hallway with the front desk tucked into the wall under the stairs. The thing I liked about the set up was the inability to go in or out without going by whoever was on duty, and in most cases that meant getting past Butch. An ominous looking man, Butch had a neck as thick as most men's thighs and ragged red scars connecting his nose to his mouth as if someone had once tried to give him a triangular smile. I couldn't remember a single time I'd been to the Wellborn when Butch wasn't on guard. And for that fact alone, the Wellborn was the perfect place to hole up if you needed to be hiding from someone. I'd put a number of clients up at the Wellborn, mostly abused wives, and could always trust Butch to give me a ring if something strange was going down. It's where I was going to put Sonja Hoff. Now I'd have a room for myself.

I lit a cigarette, the click and spark of the lighter made Butch look up. Without saying a word he lowered his gaze back to his crossword puzzle. Taking the stairs, I went up to the fourth floor and used the key on 413. It was small with not much more than a twin bed and side chair but it was clean. I took off my shoes and lay on top of the chenille bedspread and did my best not to think about how bad I wanted a drink.

CHAPTER 46

I waited across the street from the Zebra Room until Loren arrived. She got out of the cab wearing a black, belted dress with a high collar and a wide-brimmed hat. As I approached I could see the dress and the ribbon on the hat were of the same taffeta material. It looked like she'd had some sun, little freckles dotted the bridge of her nose.

When she saw me she said, "Have you been shipwrecked?"

I touched the hair on my chin and said, "You said I'd look good with some scruff."

"It's so thick. It overpowers your face."

"Okay. The beard will go." Touching her arm, I said, "I'm glad you came."

"You're lucky I came," she said, pulling away and opening the door herself.

The Zebra Room was just finishing their lunch rush. Only a few leftovers who either had nowhere to go or preferred to forgo a monotonous afternoon back at the office were scattered around the room. I held up two fingers and we followed the maitre'd to a zebra-striped booth adorned with African scenes carved into ebony head panels.

"Did you want something to drink?" I asked.

"Aren't you going to decide for me?"

I thought about getting a coffee or a Coke but when the waiter materialized I ordered dry martinis with olives.

"Martini. That's different for you," she said.

"You look like a woman who should be drinking a martini in the afternoon."

"And what does that mean?"

"Just what it sounds like. You look fantastic," I said. "You've lost weight."

She took a cigarette from a silver case I'd never seen before. I brought out the Zippo to light her. I couldn't tell if she noticed it was the one she'd given me that first night at my house so I held it up. "I still have it," I said. "I've thought about you a lot, Loren."

"That's nice," she said, pointing at the ashtray.

I slid it towards her. "I've missed you."

"I bet you have," she said.

I reached across the table to take her hand but she pulled it away.

"I really did. I'm sorry I hurt you."

She put the cigarette in the ashtray and pulled off her gloves. Her nails were blood red and she wore a thin silver ring on a middle finger.

The waiter buzzed up, placed the martinis on bar napkins and launched into a soliloquy of daily specials.

Loren interrupted him to say we were just drinking and he drifted away.

"I can't expect you to fully understand. But I needed some time. Oh hell, I don't know what I needed. I needed to blow my brains out," I said, fingering the cool stem of my glass. "I just had to get away from it all. To get some distance. It really didn't have anything to do with you. I was just trying to find myself again."

"I don't know why I'm here," she said.

"What do you mean?"

"You just said it had nothing to do with me. How's that supposed to make me feel?"

"I meant I wasn't running away from you," I said looking into her eyes. "I was hoping you of all people could understand what I was going through."

"Oh my God! Isn't that presumptuous. What do you think I was going through? Can you even imagine what it was like in that house? And then right when I needed you the most, you disappear without even a goodbye. You know what you are, Harry Thorpe? An asshole. You're really no better than Christian."

She picked up her glass and took a long drink without taking her eyes off my face. A lipstick mark remained on the rim when she returned it to the table. "I may not seem like the type," she said, "but I'm actually a woman who wants a man in her life. A man who will care for her and want her and need her as bad as she needs him. You're probably shocked to hear me say that. But that's who I really am inside. And I thought maybe…"

"I want to be that someone."

"Really? Didn't you just disappear for almost two months? How could I ever trust you?"

I stirred the martini with the olive skewered toothpick. Two olives, which is not only cheap, but bad luck. Eventually I said, "I don't know. Maybe you can't. Maybe I'm not that guy."

It took a second then tears welled up in her eyes. I offered my handkerchief but she dug in her purse and brought out her own. I jumped up and moved to her side of the booth. I wanted to hold her, to take her in my arms. I wanted to say something, but all the words in my head seemed stupid and contrived. So I sat quietly next to her and waited until it seemed like the right moment to say I was sorry.

Loren finished dabbing at her eyes and began examining her face in a compact. She put on fresh lipstick and powder then packed everything back into her purse. She took several quick drinks from her glass and when it was finished she dropped her olives into my glass, which made it slop over on the table. "I have somewhere I need to be," she said.

"Please. Don't go."

"Excuse me," she said, nudging me.

"Why did you cry?"

"Are you going to let me out? Or do I have to make a scene."

"Wait. Please," I said. "Just tell me why you cried."

She sighed and looked away. When she turned back she said, "I cried because I can't believe you wouldn't do everything you could to keep me. You gave up. Without even trying. Now may I *please* go?"

"I didn't think you wanted me."

She let her eyelids sink and exhaled audibly. Then she pinched the bridge of her nose and breathed again. When she opened her beautiful, dark eyes she said, "I did."

I took the purse from her and put it on the table. Holding her hands in mine I said, "I want you too, Loren. I need you in my life.

I've never felt this way about anyone. Ever. You're the first person who has ever made me feel I'm not truly alone in this world. And I'm thinking you might feel the exact same." I moved closer to her, our bodies touching. Then I moved to kiss her. For a second I thought it was a mistake, expecting her to give me one of those slaps. But she kissed me back.

"You can't disappear like that again..."

"I won't. I promise."

"Because I won't allow it..."

"I'm not going anywhere."

"If you're going to be in my life..."

"I'm right here, Loren."

She looked at me. "I'm frail and crazy, you know," she said finally.

"I know," I said, kissing her again. "I love that about you."

Her hand snaked into mine and our fingers intertwined. We ended up sitting like that for nearly two hours talking and laughing and telling stories from our lives in a way like we had never done before. I ordered more martinis and we drank them down, giddy with everything and all the possibilities. We sneaked kisses not caring who might be watching. Eventually I tossed money on the table and we practically floated out of the Zebra Room on a cloud.

"Where are we going?" she asked, as we pulled away from the curb.

"I don't know. Where do you want to go?"

"I want you to make love to me!"

She sat close while I drove and we held hands between shifts. The sun was bright and warm so I pushed the top down. She took off the hat and let the wind blow her hair. I was so caught up in the moment, I completely forgot about the room I'd rented at the Wellborn and drove to the house. Inside, we raced through the living room, bumping into each other. I threw myself on the bed and she dove on top. She was giggling so hard we could hardly kiss. I let my hands enjoy the contours of her slim figure. I found the zipper in the back of her dress and inched it down. She unsnapped the belt. In a single swift motion she pulled the dress over her head, tossing it to the floor. Teasingly she covered her breasts with an arm while pulling at my tie and pushing me out of my clothes.

Darkness was settling into the room by the time we finished. Loren tucked into the crook of my arm, her arm draped across my stomach. I had gotten up and opened the window so every once in a while a little breeze would rattle the blinds and pass over us. I fell asleep for a while and when I opened my eyes I could tell by her breathing that she was sleeping too. I wanted to stay like that forever but my shoulder was screaming and my fingertips had gone numb. I moved a little and she said, "Am I making you uncomfortable?"

"No. It's just my shoulder."

"Oh! I'm sorry!," she said, sitting up Indian style.

I stretched and moved my arm in circles, my shoulder popping and creaking. The movement was only intensifying the pain so I stopped and massaged it instead.

"That sounds horrible," Loren said, taking over the massage. "Isn't there anything they can do about it?"

"Not really."

She traced her fingers lightly over the scars. One foot was against my leg, the polished red nails on her tiny toes looked like Red Hot candies. "Were you shot?"

"Shot down. I think it was part of the instrument panel that got me or something like that. I had to bail out over Bougainville. Sorry it's so ugly."

She kissed me. "It's not ugly. It's you." She massaged it a bit longer before turning her head toward the window and saying, "You really can hear Elitch's from here."

"We could go, if you want."

"Really?"

"Sure, why not? It's a perfect night."

"I'd love to!"

I made a drink we shared while I shaved off the beard. She sat on the toilet lid watching the process. First it was scissors. Then a thick lather of shaving cream followed by slow short swipes with the razor considering how long it had been since my last shave. When I was finished Loren kept touching my face and that led to another tryst that started in the bathroom and ended in the bedroom.

Even though the park was just a few blocks we took the Dodge. As soon as I paid our nickels and we stepped onto the grounds Loren grabbed my arm and began to drag me, only playfully resisting, to the roller coaster. With a little maneuvering I was able to get us into the very front car. Loren was like a child, throwing her hands in the air and shrieking as we went over the first huge drop and with each drop after. When the car slid to a stop at the end of the ride she was breathless.

"Oh my God!" she exclaimed. "Can we do it again?"

"What about your heart?" I said.

"As you can see, it's just fine. Perfect, as a matter of fact."

I knew just what she meant, so we rode it three more times before she was satiated. Since none of the other rides appealed to her we strolled hand in hand while looking at people; teenagers on dates giggling at every little thing, families and children hopping with excitement for all the animals in the zoo, couples dressed for a night at the theatre or dancing. Loren and I played Skee-Ball until we had enough tickets for me to get her a little stuffed monkey. I tried to impress her at the shooting gallery but I wasn't so good with the air rifle after all. Eventually I bought her a big pink cotton candy and we climbed aboard the Ferris wheel.

"Are you having fun?" she asked.

"Absolutely! I'm just happy you're here with me."

She tore off a piece of the cotton candy and crammed it into my mouth. "What do you want to do next?"

"Hmmmm," I mused. "We could go to the Trocadero. It's Freddy Martin tonight."

"Sure, I'm game."

"Okay. But I have to warn you, I'm not a very good dancer."

"Have a couple beers before we go in. That'll loosen you up."

"You know," I said around another mouthful of cotton candy. "I've been thinking about quitting. Drinking, I mean. I know that's weird to say when we've been drinking all day. But, I feel like it's time."

She didn't say anything and watched me while feeding herself bits of the fluffy candy.

"That was part of it. For a while," I said. "When I disappeared. I drank a lot. Too much."

"Maybe you got it out of your system. Or maybe you can learn when to and when not to drink," she said. "Like today. We're having fun, so what's it hurt to have a couple drinks? Maybe you should try not to drink when you're alone. That's probably a good start. That way you have boundaries for it."

"Yeah, you're right." We went a full loop without saying anything before I asked, "What about you?"

"Sometimes. But not as much now," she said, turning to look out across the park. "It's different though. It's not something you share socially."

"I get that."

"I know you do," she said, looking me in the eye. We rode a little longer in silence and she said, "We both need to work on it."

"Yeah."

A big smile came over her face. "So we can go dancing?"

"Sure, kiddo. I'll give it a whirl."

"Watch out, Troc! Fred and Ginger are on their way," she yelled, cramming a huge chunk of cotton candy into my mouth.

I stopped at the beer garden along the way so I could drink down two pints of beer all in the name of loosening up for some dancing. I could see Loren smoking a cigarette and waiting for me by one of the potted palms near the Trocadero entrance. Inside she was ready to hit the floor but I talked her into finding a place to sit while I warmed up to the idea. Anyway, the vibe was a bit understated as Freddy and the orchestra made their way through the rather somber *To Each His Own*. I nudged Loren so she wouldn't miss a floorwalker admonishing a couple for dancing too close. A few minutes later she squeezed my hand and moved her arms in a way to say I should be ready to dance soon. I nodded my head and pointed to my other hand which was holding an invisible drink. She shook her head, but I knew it wasn't anything but an affirmation.

"Give me five minutes," I said into her ear. I made my way back to the beer garden, guzzled two more beers, stopped at the pisser and was back just as Freddy was launching into *Managua, Nicaragua*. I gave her a nod and we scooted onto the dance floor.

She was an effortless dancer. Her hips swayed sensuously and she pulled me around with her until I finally gave in and did my best. After a minute or two she stopped and leaned in to say, "You're good!" I laughed and made a face like she was crazy, then took one of her hands and spun her around into my arms. We danced five or six songs before I fanned myself, tongue hanging out and feigned a heart attack. She smiled and led me back to where we had been sitting.

"Do you play piano at all anymore?" I asked her.

"Not so much anymore," she said.

"You could play for me sometime. I'd love to hear you."

"Sure. You just need to buy a piano. Oh, I love this one," she said jumping up as *Hamp's Walkin' Boogie* started up. She knew all the right moves and while I felt foolish she seemed to be thoroughly enjoying herself. We danced a couple more after that, the beer giving me all the confidence I needed to keep up with her. Then the beat slowed and I held her close, but not too close, while we drifted across the floor. At one point she looked up. Making sure there weren't any floorwalkers watching I sneaked a quick kiss.

By the time we were ready to leave I was having trouble getting two cigarettes lit for us, so she took the Zippo and let me sway into the flame.

"Oh boy, you're tight," she said laughing. "Don't let a cop see you, they'll throw us out."

"Wow! I don't know how that happened," I said dumbly.

"No? You don't think it was beer on top of martinis and bourbon? Maybe you should sit down before you fall on someone—like me!" She led me over to a patch of grass and I playfully acted like I was going to trip and fall, and then I did. She sat next to me and took off her shoes. Wiggling her toes she said, "I wish I didn't have hose on."

"Me too."

"Naughty man! I meant so I could feel the grass on my toes."

"Yeah, that's what I meant too."

"You might be the happiest drunk I've ever known," she said.

"I have no reason not to be happy. It's a gorgeous night and I'm with the most beautiful woman on the planet. Life seems pretty good to me," I said, tickling her and making her scream and slap at my hands.

"Plus," I said. "I think you really do like me."

"I do like you," she smiled.

I was about to attack her again, only this time with kisses, when a cop came up and asked us to get off the grass. He wasn't entirely unfriendly about it. But once he saw what I was like on my feet he suggested we go home and followed along at a decent distance until we exited the park.

"Are you going to stay with me tonight," I asked as we made our way through the parking lot.

"Do you mind?"

"God no! I want you to," I said, nearly falling over a cement parking barrier.

"Maybe I should drive, wild man," she said grabbing my arm.

"Sure, sweets, you're piloting tonight. I'll copilot this one. But let it be known, you're the first dame ever to drive old Harry Thorpe's Dodge."

"Oh, a virgin! I'll be gentle with him."

"She's a she, actually."

"Good thing I'm a partially recovered Bryn Mawr lesbian then."

"This I can't wait to see," I said, clapping my hands and almost tripping again.

Loren wasn't able to see over the steering wheel with the sag in the seat on the driver's side. I got the blanket I use on stakeouts out of the trunk and we folded it up for her to sit on. Once she was situated I pulled off her hat and replaced it with mine.

"You got to be dressed for the job, lady. It's like a flight cap and goggles for a pilot," I explained.

She adjusted my hat cockily to one side and said, "Pilot to bombed one, here we go." She hit the starter, cranked the wheel and began to back out of our spot. When she'd turned out onto the street, she gave it more gas and said, "Away we go!"

She looked cute behind the wheel, concentrating so hard.

"I told you, I'm a terrible driver!" she said glancing at me. "I don't think I've driven a car in a year."

"Well, you're the prettiest driver this Dodge has ever had."

"Ha! You said I was the first woman to drive it."

"See what I mean. I don't lie." I slumped down against the door, nearly lying flat across the seat. "Wow! Someone slipped me a Mickey Finn!"

"Where do I turn?"

"Left on Tennyson." I closed one eye to get rid of the double vision and watched her turn the wheel. "Maybe we should get a drink at Billy's. Billy would love you. And you him. Prince of a guy. On top of all that I'm buying," I said.

"Maybe tomorrow, co-pilot. You seem pretty high flying as it is already. It's right on 42nd?"

"Yes, then left on Stuart."

I closed my eyes and let her make the turns on her own.

"We're home. Are you alive over there?" she asked.

"This isn't Billy's?" I said, opening my eyes.

"I wish you weren't so drunk. One thing I definitely can't do is parallel park," she said, struggling with the wheel and looking over her shoulder.

"Just get it close. I can fix it in the morning."

Headlights from behind lit the interior and Loren's face like a spotlight from the rearview mirror.

"Jeepers, this guy's coming fast..." she was saying right as the screech of tires overtook us. For a second I was sure we'd been hit as a deafening flash and bang erupted on Loren's side of the car and glass flew everywhere. Another blinding flash-bang made me instinctively throw my arms up to protect myself just as the car was launched forward with a massive roar. A huge crash threw me off the seat and onto the floorboards.

For a minute I was unsure where I was, only aware of a hissing and the sticky stench of engine fluids. I had to untangle from wires and twisted metal before I could begin to pull myself up. My shoulder screamed and my head might have been bleeding from the impact with the dashboard, which was bent from the collision and pinning me to the floor. Making it even more difficult to get a grip on the seat was the fact that everything seemed covered with a slippery substance. I called out to Loren and tugged at her dress, but it wasn't until I was able to get my upper body onto the seat that I saw she was covered in blood and twisted in a bad way. I clamored up, pulling her to me. When she came into my arms I saw the entire side of her head and face was a mass of jagged wounded flesh.

CHAPTER 47

My tongue hurt. I tried to swallow but there was nothing to swallow, and the effort threw me into a seizure of dry coughing. I rolled over onto a my good side but even it was so tender I gasped out loud. I eased onto my back again. The ceiling was a splotchy gray and riddled with chipped paint. I studied it for a minute while trying to gather my thoughts and eventually, upon seeing the bars, I realized I was in a jail cell. I sat up after some time and puked on the floor. When I finished I laid back down.

I tried to remember. I worked hard in my head to bring it up. Then I saw the image of Loren, lying in the street with so much of her head missing and I began to sob. I turned on the tender side, toward the wall and cried until I couldn't possibly produce another tear. Then I closed my eyes and focused on breathing.

After a while I heard Greenberg talking to someone followed by footsteps coming my direction. The cell door opened and someone sat on the edge of the bunk next to me.

"Thorpe." It was Greenberg. "Thorpe," he said again touching my arm.

"What?"

"Are you okay?"

"No."

"You can go if you want."

"Why am I here?"

"Do you remember what happened last night?"

"Yes."

"Okay, well, you can go now."

"Why am I here?" I said again.

"You were hysterical. I had to give you a bottle and let you put yourself out. I figured this would be the safest place for you." He waited for me to respond and when I didn't he said, "It looks like you've emptied your guts, so you might as well go."

"What about Loren?"

"She's dead, Harry."

"She was hurt in the accident," I murmured.

"She was shot. Do you remember that?"

I let that sink in. "Yeah. I remember," I said, after a minute. "It was supposed to be me."

"Yeah. I'm sure it was." He patted me. "Come on. Why don't you go home."

I rolled over to face him. "Who?"

He shook his head. "There's not a lot to go on."

"Tell me what you do know."

"An old guy walking his dog heard the shots and wreck. He saw a Chevy or Olds come from that direction in a big hurry. Probably two men but he couldn't be sure. They went south on Tennyson. That's it. No plate number and it was too dark to get a good look at them." Greenberg lit a cigarette. I waved him back away from me. He switched it to his other hand and blew his smoke out through the bars. "See, you got me smoking again," he said. "Anyway, Denver P.D. is expecting you to come by later today to answer questions. You need to see a Detective Wheeler."

"Didn't I answer questions last night?"

"As much as you could."

"Anything else about Loren?"

"You remember her last night?"

"Yes."

"Okay. Then you know all there is to know. You don't want me to go into details do you?"

"What about my car?"

"It's totaled. Loren probably hit the gas when she was…when it happened…and took out the parked car in front of you. DPD will have it in evidence anyway."

"DPD's got it all. So nothing upsets your perfect little apple cart?"

"This is Denver's case. It's their jurisdiction. Besides, at this point, there's no connection to the Marquand case."

"Isn't that convenient."

"It's not convenience. It's the way things are. I can't get involved if there's no legitimate connection."

"Fuck you," I said pushing him off the bunk with my legs and swinging my feet to the floor.

"Hey, I'm doing what I can. Give me a little time…"

"Fuck off!"

Greenberg took a couple steps back and said, "Fine. Don't listen to me. And as far as last night, you were hysterical. What was I supposed to do? You're lucky I pulled you in here instead of letting DPD take you."

"You think I give a shit that I'm in here? Jesus, Greenberg. Lock me up forever for all I give a fuck. But how in hell is this not connected to Marquand? I called him the night Sonja Hoff was killed. He knew where she was hiding. He knew how to get to her. Don't you see? There's more to this. But you just won't listen."

"He knew she was at the Howdy Partner?" he said, leaning against the bars.

"Whatever, man. Can I just go?"

"He told you that?"

"Oh fuck off. You don't have to act like you suddenly give a shit," I said, pushing past him.

"Jesus, Thorpe!" he called out to me. "What do you want from me?"

At the front desk they gave me back my tie, shoes, wallet and .45 which had been in the trunk of the car. Outside the sun had a late afternoon intensity that was like a flamethrower on my eyeballs. I had to shield my face with my hand when passing between buildings since Loren had my hat.

I wandered a block or two in the direction of the Wellborn and fell into the first bar I came across. I told the bartender to pour four shots.

"Jesus, Mac! What happened to you?" he said.

I threw a twenty on the bar and he got busy.

I slammed each back, one after the other. The bartender had enough sense to leave me alone. After a while I slid off the stool and went into the men's room to wash my hands. I saw a large part of my shirt and suit were splattered with Loren's blood as well. So was the side of my face. My hair was matted with it. Blinking hard I tried not to picture Loren lying in the street with her mouth hanging open and eyes staring blankly but I couldn't keep the vision away. I lowered my head and let the tears come. When I was able to finally control myself I washed up as best as I could in the little sink. I used the roll towel on my face, hair and hands. I tugged until all the bloodied cloth disappeared up inside the dispenser. I walked a few blocks until I found a men's store. I bought a new white shirt, tie and a black hat. The blood didn't really show on the black suit so I didn't worry much about that even though the salesman seemed horrified. I flashed him the P.I. license and said I'd been in a car accident. It didn't seem to make him feel much better about the whole thing, especially since I left the old shirt and tie with him. Then I waved down a cab and told the driver to take me to the Egyptian Theatre in North Denver. A couple blocks away I had him pull over and got out.

It was hard to know what time it was. My watch had apparently stopped that morning while I was sleeping it off in lockup. Based on the position of the sun I figured there was maybe an hour until dusk. And since it would be far too risky to do anything in daylight, I wandered up and down streets going nowhere and wasting time. A few blocks later I came upon a grocery and bought an apple and Milky Way bar. The clerk told me it was seven fifty-four. I set my watch and wound it several times. The second hand jerked to life. Tick, tick, tick. After a little while I came upon a liquor store, but after walking the aisles I ended up getting a 7Up.

Across from the Cavalcade I found a spot between a garage and fence that had once been an ashpit but was now just a pile of rubble. I sat on the chunks of brick and cement, sipping from the bottle and eating my dinner. I had no idea if Johnny would show up or not, and if he did it would be careless for him not to be on guard unless he thought I was dead. For nearly two hours there was a predictable stream of dopers and players marching in and out, all wearing cloudy expressions of regret. I began to think Johnny wasn't going to show at all and then he arrived in a brand new Lincoln with Ugo at the wheel. They both got out and Ugo was laughing at whatever Johnny had been saying. I made my way unnoticed to the rear of the car, the .45 in my hand in the small of my back.

"Hey, Johnny," I called out.

"Thorpe!" he said when he saw me, the grin deflating fast.

Ugo stopped dead in his tracks as he came around the front of the car. "Come over here, blockhead," I told him. "And try not to do anything stupid."

"What's going on, Thorpe?" Johnny asked.

"I thought maybe we could chat," I said.

"Sure, sure. Come on, I'll buy you a drink."

"No, let's stay out here. These summer nights are so nice, aren't they? How about last night? Wasn't that a beauty?"

"Ugo, why don't you leave me and Thorpe alone a minute," Johnny said, his voice raising an octave as if to send a message to the big idiot.

"No. I'd like Ugo to stay right there. As a matter of fact, why don't we all move over here a little," I said, waving them out from under the streetlight. Both hesitated a second, then Johnny began to move where I pointed.

"Slowly," I said, "on the side of the building."

"What you got there, Thorpe?"

"I brought something for you, Johnny," I said, letting them see the gun. I knew it wouldn't be much of a surprise but I enjoyed their expressions nonetheless. "Keep your hands out where I can see them, Ugo. Thank you."

He raised his arms a couple inches and splayed his sausage fingers.

"Hell," Johnny said, "I thought this was a friendly visit. Why you got to give us the treatment?"

"Oh it's a friendly visit, alright. I wanted to see if you guys heard about the action last night."

Neither said a word but their eyes were speaking a million words.

"No? You didn't hear what happened in front of my house? Apparently someone tried to take me out. But, as you can see," I said, with a move like a magician, "they missed! I thought maybe you'd know who it was?"

"I hadn't heard," Johnny said. "Did anyone get hurt?"

"Nope. Whoever it was, they must have been complete amateurs."

"Well, you can't say I didn't warn you, Thorpe. You remember what I said about letting things go? Maybe you should rethink that. Next time you might not be so lucky. They could come back."

"Are you so fucking cavalier as to stand here and say all that while I've got this pointed at you?"

"I'm just trying to help. It's bigger than you, Thorpe. You should know that."

"Nothing's bigger than me, Johnny. Not right this second, anyway."

Ugo's eyes were darting around in his face as if he was getting ready to do something. I pointed the .45 at him and said, "Go ahead and try something and it'll be the last thing you do."

"Come on," Johnny said. "Shooting us isn't going to solve anything."

"No. You're right. It won't. So why don't you just tell me who put the hit on me so I can shoot them instead?"

"How the hell would I know?" Johnny said.

"It wasn't Marquand?"

Johnny raised his eyebrows and shrugged his shoulders.

"Where's your blue Chevy, Ugo? I know you got one. I saw you clear as day that night Sonja Hoff got whacked. And there was a witness last night that saw a blue Chevy. So I know it was you."

Ugo stared at me with narrowing pig eyes.

"Just tell me it was Marquand and I'll be on my way."

"Right after you kill us," Ugo blurted.

"I don't plan on killing anyone here," I said. "Just tell me who's at the bottom of it, and I'll be on my way."

"*Posso prenderlo*," Ugo said.

"*Stai zitto!*" Johnny snapped.

Headlights swept across us as a car rounded the corner from the next street. I turned to look and caught Ugo moving in the corner of my eye. He was digging for something in his coat and his arm was just coming out as my first shot caught him in the throat. I wasn't sure exactly where the second one went, but by the way he jerked I knew it had been on target too. He went down as if he'd fallen into a hole. When I turned back on Johnny he lunged. I had just enough reach on him to smash my left hand in his face while keeping my gun out of his grasp. The impact knocked me off balance and we fell backwards, Johnny on top. It was just one shot but after we landed on the sidewalk he wasn't moving anymore. I pushed him off and got to my feet. The car was nowhere to be seen and everything was quiet. Johnny lay on his back with a leg kicked up under him, almost how Loren had been in the street before I fixed her. His eyes and mouth were closed in such a peaceful way that if it were another time or place I might have felt bad. The blue pinstriped coat was flung open and blood was politely spreading under his pink tie as if to purposely bring attention to the fingertip-sized diamond stickpin. Ugo, on the other hand, was a giant pile of laundry oozing a river headed for the gutter. Next to him lay a Colt with pearl grips. I grabbed up my brass and ran.

Two blocks away I stepped onto a bus headed towards downtown. My hands were a bit shaky and my shoulder ached from the tussle. I took off the new hat and wiped the sweat from my face with the sleeve of my coat. I'm not going to lie, I didn't feel all that bad. As a matter of fact, I was surprised at how cool I did feel. I never intended to shoot them, but in the long run I was glad it had been me. It made me feel Loren's death hadn't gone completely unanswered. But as my thoughts drifted towards Loren I began to picture her lying in the street, her head a mass of blood and matter. A hollow feeling the size of the Pacific opened up around me. I looked down at my coat still splattered with her dried blood and ran my fingers over the hardened spots. Little flecks of her clung to my fingertips. I suddenly had the urge to put the .45 to my head and even took it out of the holster and clicked the thumb safety off. I didn't want to create a scene so I pressed the muzzle against my side. I pushed it hard up under my ribcage making sure not to engage the slide safety. At that angle I was sure I couldn't miss my heart. I was thinking about pulling the trigger when a heavy-set colored woman with a grocery sack came down the aisle. I slid the gun under my coat and gave her a little nod as she went by. She reminded me of Bertie, the colored cook that worked in the Marquand house. I clicked the thumb safety on. In all the excitement I had stupidly forgotten about Marquand.

I got off the bus and walked several blocks to the Oxford Hotel. The front desk clerk had Marquand's message for me. It said, *Arabian Brewery 2pm*. That was an interesting choice. The Arabian had been shut down since the start of prohibition was completely abandoned. I suppose that made it a good location for a payoff. Or a murder. I thought about both of those possibilities all the way to the Wellborn. Almost as if reading my thoughts, Butch gave a reassuring little nod when I passed.

It was stifling in the tiny room so I striped off all my clothes and lay naked on the bed with the windows open. I tried not to dwell on Loren but there wasn't any way I could stop my mind from doing exactly that. If only I hadn't drank so much. If only I had been driving. I tormented myself with all those thoughts for a long while and no matter how tightly I kept my eyes clamped the tears seemed to work their way out and down the sides of my face. I thought about putting Loren in my horrible little box, where I stored all my hurt and pain and regret. God knows, I'd done that with so many other things. It's one thing to rationalize all life's horrible deeds as a duty to one's country or a necessity for a greater good, like dropping bombs on people you don't know. They're just the enemy, you're told, people with unhinged political ideologies and screwy cultural traditions, and they're supposedly filled with an unquenchable desire to kill. If you believe all that and you're witless or naive or a bit of a sociopath you'll never be bothered to think about those people again. But if you give even a little thought to life's actions, you'll agonize over those bombs and the people who received them like a fiery rain. And that begins to eat you. Bite after bite. It's like one ant finding a scrap of food on the sidewalk. Pretty soon there are three, then fifty and in no time you can't see the bit of bread or whatever the scrap was because it's engulfed by a mass of ants, chewing and ripping. So in order to live with yourself, you take those thoughts and lock them up in the horrible little box, and you never ever allow that box to be opened again. Johnny and Ugo would need to go into that box. Locked in so any thoughts about Johnny being a father or a son to a loving mother can't rip and chew. Because no matter how despicable he might have been, there's always those thoughts. And I suppose I could do the same for Loren. I could put her in the little box and essentially act like she'd never existed. That would allow freedom from the abyss of pain and loss. But no matter how deep the hurt, I knew I could never put Loren in that box. Not with all those bad things. Putting Loren in there meant nothing at all would remain of me outside the box.

I rolled over on my side and worked at clearing my mind. I used the same technique I'd used before a mission, when I needed sleep but the endless worries burrowed through my soul. I pictured total dark, complete blackness, and then a single ray of light in the distance. I concentrated on the light and gently pushed all the other thoughts that tried to intrude away only focusing on the light. It took a lot of effort at first but soon the brightness would grow and overtake everything else and I was able to slip away. When I woke my watch said it was a little past two in the morning. I lie in my sweat for a long time listening to the traffic outside the window, wishing for one of those delightful breezes that caressed Loren and me the night before. It never came so I pulled on my trousers and made my way to the bathroom at the end of the hall. I filled the tub with cold water and inched in. The chill was refreshing and I settled in to soak with my eyes closed. After a while I opened them to see the water had taken on a pinkish hue. I knew that would be Loren. And probably Johnny too.

CHAPTER 48

I made my way across the Arabian's broad expanse of property, which at one time must have been a wide lush lawn and impressive drive. It was now home to ten thousand gopher holes, knee-high weeds and at least a ton of scattered trash. At a distance, the building almost resembled a giant grinning face with its three-story upper arched windows and rows of lower block windows. Having been constructed as a series of symmetrical squares stacked upon rectangles, in the vein of the Second Empire style of architecture, it included plenty of elaborate brickwork and even had a rectangular tower that reached six stories into the sky that was capped with a bright green mansard roof and dormer windows. Across the junction where the tower connected to the lower building were sun-faded letters that I guessed to be at least six feet tall. They spelled out Arabian minus the I, which I came upon in the drive below, bent and broken from its fall.

Marquand's Cadillac was nowhere in sight and looking through the chain link I could see the doors across the front were either locked or boarded. I went on around the side, lined with a row of steel carriage doors, each featuring a weathered logo of a particular lager or ale. The tallest door was decorated with a fifteen foot high painting of the namesake Arabian; a dark-skinned man in a beard and turban holding a frothy mug of beer.

The area behind the building was pure factory with grimy windowless walls, a long dock and a remote outbuilding topped by a giant blackened smokestack. The tired fence across the back was

267

centered with a double-wide gate, pushed against a chain to create an opening wide enough to accommodate a man. Even though the puddle-pocked road leading up had fresh tire tracks both coming and going, as if someone had just been dropped off, Marquand wasn't anywhere in sight. I slipped through the space in the gate and went on up to a forced door on the dock. It didn't appear to be recently pried, it was more like that had happened sometime in the previous decade. I called out. There wasn't any response so I stepped over fragments of the splintered door frame and went in only to be accosted by a retched smell. Not quite the shitty-rotten-egg-stench of decomposition, but more like a million beer-soaked rags had been tossed into a pile and left to molder for a generation. All the same, it reminded me of the worst parts of the New Guinea jungle, filled with unknown layers of musty rot and mildewy dead. I covered my mouth and nose with a handkerchief and quickly went down a long dark hallway, passing several pitch black rooms. Thankfully, the horrible smell dissipated as I moved deeper into the building and the hallway eventually opened onto what must have been the main brewing room, lined with the immense arched windows I'd seen across the front. In the center of the space were two copper vats sunk into the floor, their covered rims about waist high. One must have been at least fifteen feet across while the other was maybe half the size. The smaller vat still had a tangle of tubing and pipe work stretching from the lid up towards the ceiling. At the back of the room a staircase led to a balcony decorated with an ornate railing. It was an impressive space, almost cathedral-like with the huge windows, gothic metalwork and white walls dotted with motifs of chipped paint. Somehow all the graffiti and the congregation of discarded bottles only added to the effect. I wandered over to an open hatch in the cover of the larger vat. It revealed only absolute blackness. I was thinking how it probably extended two or more stories into the depths of the building when movement caught the corner of my eye. I spun and there was Marquand in a blue summer suit and tan hat.

"Colonel," I said.

"All these windows," he said, looking up. "Rather reminds me of the first time I climbed into the cockpit of a B-29. You probably never got to fly one of those."

"You're alone?" I asked.

"Are you?"

"Who the hell would come with me?" I stated.

"Maybe your little Jew cop friend."

"He's happier than you at how things turned out." I said, scanning his waistline and pockets for the bulge that only a gun makes.

"That figures. He got a nice promotion out of it. I brought your money." He pulled open his coat. There it was, a revolver in a shoulder holster. He made sure I knew he was going for an envelope. "Thirty thousand," he said holding it out to me.

I didn't take it. Instead I dug out my cigarettes and lit one. He moved to hand it to me again. "Suddenly you don't want it? I thought we were meeting about money."

"Before I start taking a payoff I'd like to get a few things straight."

"Is that what this is? A Payoff?" he said, lowering his outstretched arm.

"Isn't it?"

"I thought we discussed a retainer."

"And how long before I end up dead like the others? Although I guess you'll need a new hit man. The one you had didn't make it."

"I never expected you to start shooting people in the street, Thorpe. Very impressive."

"I never expected that you'd try to have me killed, Colonel. But, then again, I'm an idiot to underestimate you. Especially, considering your proficiency at killing."

"Maybe we just had to come to a new understanding. Take the money," he said, holding the envelope out again. "There's more where this came from. Tell me your price. We can strike a deal."

"It doesn't feel good to be used. It makes me think I might be on a string right now." I spat a piece of tobacco off my tongue. "Besides, how do you know I can accept that and just walk away?"

"I think I know what kind of man you are. We flew together. I can understand you're playing up the hurt feelings, to up your payout. But really, Thorpe, I've always known you're a man of loyalties."

"That's why you tried to kill me? Because I'm loyal."

"Let's just say I see we're now on an even playing field."

"That's an interesting perspective considering your wife's sister is laying on a slab at the morgue and you're responsible for that."

"You're risking a lot. I could just as easily walk out of here and take the money with me."

"I could just as easily take out my gun and put a hole through you. Before I take anything, I need to know why you did it? Tell me that and I'll take the money and go. You'll never see me again."

"What do you want to know?"

"How the hell could you kill your own son."

He blinked as if I'd splashed water in his face. "You don't really think that's what happened. Do you?"

"It didn't?"

"God no!"

"You're going to tell me he accidentally ended up in that ditch?"

"It *was* an accident. I thought you'd see that."

"Go on," I said.

He raised his eyes to the ceiling then wandered over towards the windows. "I'm not sure what it is you want to know."

"All of it. Who took Christian and killed him. And Hoff and Loitzel? Why were they murdered when you paid Sonja to come here and have your child in the first place."

Marquand sighed and said, "She told you that?"

I motioned with my hand for him to continue.

"That is where it started," he said. "Louise and I wanted another child but she's unable. We agreed a surrogate was an acceptable option. So I contacted Sonja and, well, she agreed."

"I thought you said your wife was pregnant?"

"That was all part of the plan. Louise would say she was expecting at the same time Sonja was pregnant. Then Sonja would go away to have it and we would take the child as our own."

"She agreed to that?"

"Louise? I wouldn't say she loved the idea, but she desperately wanted another child. It was the option I gave her."

"The option you gave her...ah, so generous of you," I said, flicking my cigarette away. "So, what happened?"

"Really, Thorpe. Just take the money." He raised the envelope again.

"Go on," I ordered. "What happened to Christian?"

He shuffled his feet and finally said, "Sonja was going to take him. That was the plan. She'd give us her baby and then she would take Christian. In return, I'd make sure she would be comfortable for the rest of her life."

"There's no way your wife was ever going to agree to that."

"She never knew about that part. It was always supposed to look like a kidnapping. And Christian would just disappear. I thought it best if it happened right before Sonja would go away to have her child. That way Louise could be in mourning for a period of time and then we'd come out of it with a new baby. It would help to give her focus. Distract her."

"But what? The timing wasn't so good? Everyone thought Sonja took him?"

"No. Sonja backed out," he said slowly.

"Because she thought the baby was Loitzel's."

"That, I didn't know, until you told me. She'd just told me she didn't want to give up the baby anymore. And that she wasn't going to take Christian. Up until you told me the part about Loitzel, I figured she was trying to finagle more money."

"So you had her killed."

"You make it sound so…"

"Sound like what? Murder?"

"She was never going to forgive me for what happened to Loitzel. And she did know everything."

"Like the fact you killed Christian."

"I told you, that was an accident."

"What happened? You dropped him climbing on the ladder?"

"Something like that."

"Banged his head against the wall?"

"What difference does it make?"

"Or Hoff left you no choice so you smothered him?"

"I said it was an accident."

"Because he was a retard."

"Stop!"

"A retarded child was too inconvenient for the *Mighty* Marquand. So you smothered him in his bed and tossed him in the woods."

His face hardened into a mask, his jaw set.

"I know it must have been a huge embarrassment with your Homeland First buddies, only being able to produce a miserable, defective retard. Just think what they would do. Of course you'd get tossed off the presidential ticket, and you'd be hard-pressed to get another invite to their little fascist rallies. But of course, you knew all that. Good thing you had a rube like me to get you out of that indelicate retard problem."

"Stop saying that word."

"If only you knew," I said, watching his eyes. "If only you knew it really had nothing to do with genetics. How sad," I said, staring into his cool gray eyes.

"What are you talking about?"

"Remember the XA-13 flight? And what happened with Louise? Don't you remember how she got really sick and almost lost the baby? You did know she almost lost the baby, right? Well, that's what turned your perfect little son into a retard, Colonel. You made Louise fly that day. You subjected your unborn son to limited oxygen and high stress. You actually *made* him a retard."

"You're crazy."

"I spoke with Christian's pediatrician. He told me all about it. He also told me that Louise knew too. See, Colonel, that's why she agreed to the whole Sonja Hoff thing. Not because you gave her a fucking option. But because your little stunt fucked her up too. I wondered about that when you told me she was pregnant. The pediatrician said he didn't think it would be possible for her to carry another baby. At first, I thought maybe you'd got lucky. But now I get it. She'd do anything for you. She'd even let you father a child with Sonja Hoff and pretend it was hers. That's how much she loved you. And to thank her, you smother her perfectly fine child that you made into a retard. Damn, Colonel, I'm sure glad I was able to help you with all that."

"You need to shut your mouth." Marquand said, his face flushed.

"Or what? You won't give me my thirty grand?"

"Take it," he ordered, holding out the envelope again.

"Just one more question."

"No more!"

I slapped the envelope out of his hand, it hit the floor with a thud. "Why the back and forth on Loren?" I asked.

"You are a rude, despicable man," he said.

"Did you ever love her?"

His eyes narrowed. "What do you care?"

"But her heart problem got in the way? Is that it? Lord knows, you didn't want to get your perfect genes mixed up with that."

Slowly he took a step forward. I could see a vein in his neck throbbing. He opened his mouth, his teeth coming apart as if they had been welded together. "You're mighty smart, huh, boy," he almost whispered. "You've got it all figured out. Do you even know why I picked you? Does the boy in the box ring a bell? You don't think I chose you because I actually thought you'd be able to do anything. Do you?" He moved another step closer, a toothy grin coming across his face. "I guess you don't have it all figured out after all. I planned your role completely, from the very start. I knew a drunk like you wouldn't be able to get over something like the boy in the box. It's pure science. A weak piece of shit becomes paralyzed by their own fear and remorse. It's no different from all those men I defeated in the sky. I had no doubt that you'd sabotage yourself with your pitiful self-doubt and drunken ways. I must congratulate you, Thorpe. You acted the role perfectly."

The grin turned cold.

"And, as far as Loren is concerned," he said, lowering his voice even more. "I don't mix with nigger-loving tramps. You don't realize it, smart ass, but in that regard, I actually did you a favor. She never would have loved you. Not like she loved nigger cock and those ghetto drugs."

I hit him with everything I had. I reached back as far as I could and swung for his belly with all the intention in the world of splitting him in two. He slammed into the wall and doubled over clutching his stomach. I was just about to hit him again when someone yelled from the balcony. I spun around and there was Loftesness with a gun pointed down at me.

"Don't move!" he yelled. "Hands in the air."

I did as he said.

"I'm serious Thorpe. Not a single muscle or I'll shoot," Loftesness screamed even louder. Even at that distance I could tell he was so worked up he was shaking like a leaf.

"Are you fucking serious?" I said, looking at Marquand. "You brought Loftesness."

Marquand was bent over, spittle hanging from his mouth. He spat a couple times and wiped it away with the back of his hand. "You sonofabitch," he panted.

"So you planned to kill me all along?"

"Plan B," he huffed, slowly straightening up. "Which is now obviously in play." Clinging to the wall he fumbled to get his own gun out. "I thought maybe there was a chance you'd take the money and go," he croaked. "But of course you're too obstinate for anything that easy."

"No problem," I said, nodding toward the envelope on the floor. "I'm happy to take it."

"It's too late for that, asshole." He pointed his revolver at my chest.

I glanced up at Loftesness. If I was going to overtake Marquand I'd have to gamble that the nervous ophthalmologist wouldn't be able to accurately shoot from that distance.

"Don't even try it," Marquand said.

"So you're going to shoot me now?"

"Live by the sword, die by the sword."

"That seems harsh. After all we've been through."

"And you didn't come here today thinking you might kill me?" he said.

"I came for the money."

"You think I'm giving you a goddamned dime after what you said to me?" his voicing rising in anger. "After you called my boy a retard? After you insulted me? After you HIT ME?" he said, spitting all over me.

"I wanted to get at some truth," my hands in the air. "So I could live with myself."

"Oh my God. You're so pathetic." Marquand called up to Loftesness, "Doctor, come on down here."

Loftesness scooted almost sideways along the balcony. It looked like he was afraid to take his eyes off me for even a split second. At the point he reached the top of the staircase he stumbled, as if his rubber-soled shoes had stuck to the floor, and right then it became the luckiest day of my life as he tumbled head first down the entire flight. And what a fall it was with the metal stairs and steep incline. It was pretty obvious from the way he fell and the pile he'd become at the bottom that he'd broken his neck at the very least. I swung on Marquand, chopping at his gun hand while landing a cross to the left side of his face. He pitched back, went off the wall and onto the floor, his revolver skidding away.

"Well, that sure turned out to my advantage," I said, taking out the .45 and pointing it at him. "As you can probably tell, I'm a bit sensitive when it comes to Loren. I can take all the shit you want to dish on me. I know who I am. But when it comes to Loren you might even say I'm downright upset. As a matter of fact, I'm not sure I'll ever get over it," I said, clicking the thumb safety off.

"Thorpe..." he sputtered. "Wait!"

I hit him with the barrel of the gun. It not only made a satisfying sound against his skull but opened a nice wound above his eye that began to bleed profusely. I moved to lean against the rim of the copper vat and watched as he tried to stem the flow of blood that was ruining the pretty blue suit.

"That's for killing Loren, you piece of shit," I said, digging out a cigarette and lighting it with the lighter she'd given me. "And I'm just getting started."

"That was an accident..." Marquand moaned.

"Everything's a goddamned accident with you."

"It was."

"Fuck you."

Marquand scooted back against the wall. His revolver about ten feet away. I saw him glance at it as he moved.

"A hundred thousand?"

"Is that what your life is worth? One hundred thousand dollars?"

"Name your price then," he said, using his canary yellow pocket square on the cut.

I laughed. "You can't afford me. Not anymore, you sonofabitch. Your days of buying your way out of shit are over."

"Isn't it funny how you went along until things got inconvenient for you."

"Is that what Loren was? An inconvenience?"

Marquand shook his head to show disgust. "Who would have thought you'd fall in love with that tramp. There was a time when I thought you had class. But look how far you've fallen."

"You're living on borrowed time, asshole, which I was going to let you have until I finished this cigarette. But if you start that shit about Loren again we can end this now."

"You don't have the balls," Marquand said.

"No?"

"All of a sudden you're some kind of avenger?"

I made sure he saw me take a long drag on the cigarette. "Keep talking. Time's running out."

"A hundred thousand can buy you all the Lorens your heart desires."

I charged him, flicking the cigarette into his face and pressing the tip of the .45 to his forehead. "Say goodbye, mother fucker," I said.

Marquand closed the eye below the muzzle and said nothing. It was a long moment. I wanted to pull the trigger. I wanted with everything inside my soul to shoot him. To avenge everything. Not just Loren, but little Christian and all the others. For Sonja and Loitzel. For all those men he shot down and then gloated over. For my own demise into hell. I wanted to end him right there, but I couldn't do it. It was like being frozen in place, like in the dream where I can't move to save myself from the cockpit fire. I pressed the muzzle harder into his skull, his head pushed back against the cement wall. I wanted to push the muzzle right through him. It was then I realized I was screaming.

I lowered the gun and took a couple steps back.

Marquand's one closed eye slowly opened. It was the only move he made.

I bent over panting, my heart racing. The sound of my own screams still echoing in my head. It took a minute or more for me to get my shit together and when I did, I turned back to Marquand. He was sitting just the same on the filthy floor, the front of his suit covered with blood.

"Cash or check?" he said.

I shot him in the face. The wall behind him lit up with his blood and brains and he slumped over to one side. It seemed almost anti-climatic, especially for Marquand. After a while I slid to the floor across from him to lean against the vat and smoke cigarettes. My mind really didn't go anywhere in particular, instead my thoughts bounced around images of the *Mighty Marquand* in all his glory. When I eventually began to feel the creeping blackness of remorse, I thought about Loren on the labyrinth that day I met her. The snow swirling around her and how she took my cigarette with a gloved hand.

I was pulled from all that by the sound of someone moving down the hall. I scrambled behind the vat and got low to the grimy floor. The footsteps stopped when they came into the room.

"Holy shit!" a voice said, upon apparently seeing the crumpled Loftesness. Then he yelled, and that's when I recognized who it was, "Police! Come out with your hands up."

"Come out with your hands up? Does anyone really do that?" I called out.

"Thorpe? Is that you?" Greenberg said.

"Who were you expecting? A waitress with a frosty Arabian?"

I could hear his feet shuffling as he moved for cover. "Where are you, Thorpe?"

I tapped the vat with the muzzle of the gun. "Over here."

"Okay. Don't do anything stupid. I don't feel like shooting you. Alright?"

"Oh? Now you're going to shoot me?" I said.

"Did you kill Loftesness?"

"I sort of wish I did. But he fell down the stairs on his own accord. What are you doing here?"

"Where's Marquand?"

I looked at the heap that used to be Marquand. "He's over here with me," I said. "What are you doing here, Greenberg?" I repeated.

"How about you toss that .45 out where I can see it and we can talk about it."

"Don't tell me you're working for Marquand."

"What? Fuck no! I just don't want you putting holes through me."

"I promise you, I will indeed shoot you dead if you're working for Marquand."

"Fuckhead! Do you think I'd be working for that piece of shit?" After a few moments of silence, Greenberg said, "Where's Marquand, Thorpe? What have you done?"

"Why are you here?"

"I came to see what Marquand and Loftesness were up to."

"You missed all the excitement," I said.

"Okay," he said slowly, as if he was thinking that through. "How about you toss the gun out here so you and I don't end up killing each other."

I weighed my options and finally slid the gun across the floor into the opening. Greenberg came slowly. I was smoking a cigarette as he rounded the vat. Marquand was bathed in his bloody nap.

"Holy shit, Thorpe!" Greenberg said, not really pointing his gun entirely at me.

"He had it coming," I said.

"No one is questioning that. But do you really think that was a good idea?"

"It just kinda happened." I flicked an ash and brushed it off my pants. "How did you know to come here?"

"You remember Richard Carmasino, the chauffeur? Denver

P.D. pinched him on a drug bust. So we flipped him. He called to say he'd just dropped Tweedle Dee and Tweedle Dumb off at the Arabian. I wanted to see if they were cleaning something up."

"Nope. They just came to meet with me. Or, kill me to be more precise." I said, making a move as if I were going to stand up. Greenberg motioned me up with the tip of his revolver. "I didn't think you gave a shit anymore about Marquand."

"I tried to tell you I wasn't finished with all that. But you wouldn't listen."

"Oh well. For the record, he did confess everything. But, that doesn't really matter anymore," I said, dusting off my suit and holding out my wrists for the bracelets. "I guess this is it for me,"

"Don't be a drama queen," Greenberg said.

"What? No electric chair?"

"There's no doubt you fucked up royally. But, as you said, the piece of shit had it coming."

"What's that supposed to mean?"

"It means I didn't see a goddamned thing," he said, slowly lowering the gun, eyes still on Marquand. Then he looked straight at me. "It also means I'm not saving your ass either. If you get collared for this, it's all you. Do you understand? I wasn't here and I'm not your friend. I don't even know you. You'll have to answer for what you did like a man. All on your own."

"You can't be serious. You're not going to arrest me? You know I shot those other two assholes outside the Cavalcade."

"Like anyone gives a shit about them. That's just another mob hit," Greenberg said. "Those slugs could easily get lost and that shit will go cold. No one's going to lose sleep over that."

"Don't play with me."

"I'm not playing with anyone," he said. "Marquand was nothing but a racist, anti-semite who killed his own kid. Do you really think I give a shit about him? My only regret is not having the chance to perp walk the fucker. Granted, nobody's going to give you a medal for this, but you did the world a favor. Imagine that cocksucker as president. But, I didn't say that because I didn't see anything. Now I suggest you clean up your mess before someone else comes across this shit. Like a goddamned bum or something. Then you'll have an even bigger mess on your hands. I'm not telling you what to do because I was what…?"

"You were never here," I said.

"Exactly. I was never here. But, if I had been here, I'd tell you to empty their pockets and pull their teeth. Take Marquand's fucking $30 shoes too. Then toss the bodies into one of those vats. Get some lime. And lots of it. And that heater," he said, motioning to my .45, "strip it down and toss the pieces into a couple different lakes. Not the river. Some idiot panning for gold or whatever will come up with a piece. The teeth too. And Marquand's rod. Into the lake. Got it?"

"Jesus," I said. "Maybe I should just let you take me in."

"You made your bed."

"Fucking hell," I said, looking at Marquand. "If once a man indulges."

"Whatever that means," he said, holstering his revolver. "I got a pliers in the car. Get to work on those teeth. But not before I get the hell out of here."

"I got it. Because you were never here."

THE END

279

ACKNOWLEGEMENTS

I'd like to thank all those who not only encouraged me in this endeavor but who diligently helped with edits, contributed ideas and read the manuscript over and over when it was a huge pile of printed sheets. Without my wife Julie, who gave me the impetus to write the novel by literally saying, "Stop talking about it, and write," it would never have made it to the page. She not only read the giant mess countless times, but she did a fantastic job editing out all the superfluous nonsense.

To my friends Steve Jonsen, Tammy Walden and David Newcomer, I was always buoyed by your enthusiasm for the project. You pushed me onward when I often imagined it would never see print. I wish Michael Bonamer, Larry Crane and Nick Kelsey were still with us to see this published.

And finally, to my mom, who supported and indulged me when I fashioned myself a novelist, even at the age of twelve, as I sat before an IBM Selectric wearing a fedora with a pipe dangling from my lips. She has always been an inspiration and guiding force in my love for the printed word. (The pipe did not actually have tobacco in it.)

T.K.

ABOUT THE AUTHOR

Tony Kelsey is Vice President of Marketing for a premier cycling apparel brand headquartered in Denver, Colorado. He's the recipient of several awards for UI design and was VP of Global Creative for an international, $1B IT consultancy where he oversaw web and brand strategy. Prior to that, Tony served 12-years in the US Marine Corps as a combat air controller, attending the prestigious Navy Fighter Weapons School (aka TOP GUN). He is a *summa cum laude* graduate in political science and history from the University of Colorado. In addition to his love for cycling and traveling the world with his wife Julie, he is currently working on his next novel.

MORE INFORMATION

Visit the author's site at www.tonykelsey.com

Join the email list and receive updates about upcoming books,
including excerpts, cover reveals and more.
www.tonykelsey.com/newsletter

AND PLEASE...

If you enjoyed this novel, I'd really appreciate a review on Amazon.
The number of reviews a book accumulates has a direct impact on
how it is positioned on the website, and subsequently its potential
for sales. So, when you write a review, no matter how short, it
helps make it possible for others to find and enjoy my work.

Thank you,
T.K.

COMING SOON FROM THIS AUTHOR

THE BOTTOMLESS PIT
A Harry Thorpe sequel to *Once a Man Indulges*

While hiding out in a small Colorado mountain town from mobsters and a past littered with unspeakable acts, private detective Harry Thorpe reluctantly agrees to take on a simple probate case. He quickly discovers that Mabel Dennison, the powerful attorney who hired him, has questionable motives and links to the very entanglements he is trying to escape. As Harry grapples with the predicament and his own intentions, he uncovers a host of mysterious undercurrents that unexpectedly throw him into a mix of greed and murder. Can he trust the kinship he feels with fellow veteran Del O'Sullivan, who could be the source to unraveling the town's secrets, but can't shake the horror of the dead German in his trench? Or, does Harry ally himself with Sheriff Joe Charboneau, who doesn't always play by the rule of law? When Leah, a beguiling bartender at the town's only watering hole appears to be at the center of everything, Harry must steel himself to her allure in order to get at the truth and get away unscathed.

THE MOST DANGEROUS PLAYTHING
A Harry Thorpe prequel to *Once a Man Indulges*

It's 1944, and while recovering from injuries sustained from being shot down in the Pacific, Marine Corps Captain Harry Thorpe finds himself attached to the Los Angeles JAG office. Despite having no experience other than two years of law school, he's been made a criminal investigator. What was supposed to be a routine assignment in the waning days of the war, is turned upside down by a seemingly random murder. As he digs deeper and deeper, Harry finds himself lost in a sinister Hollywood underworld and propelled down a trail of monstrous crimes involving young women.

Made in United States
Orlando, FL
19 February 2022

14974017R00159